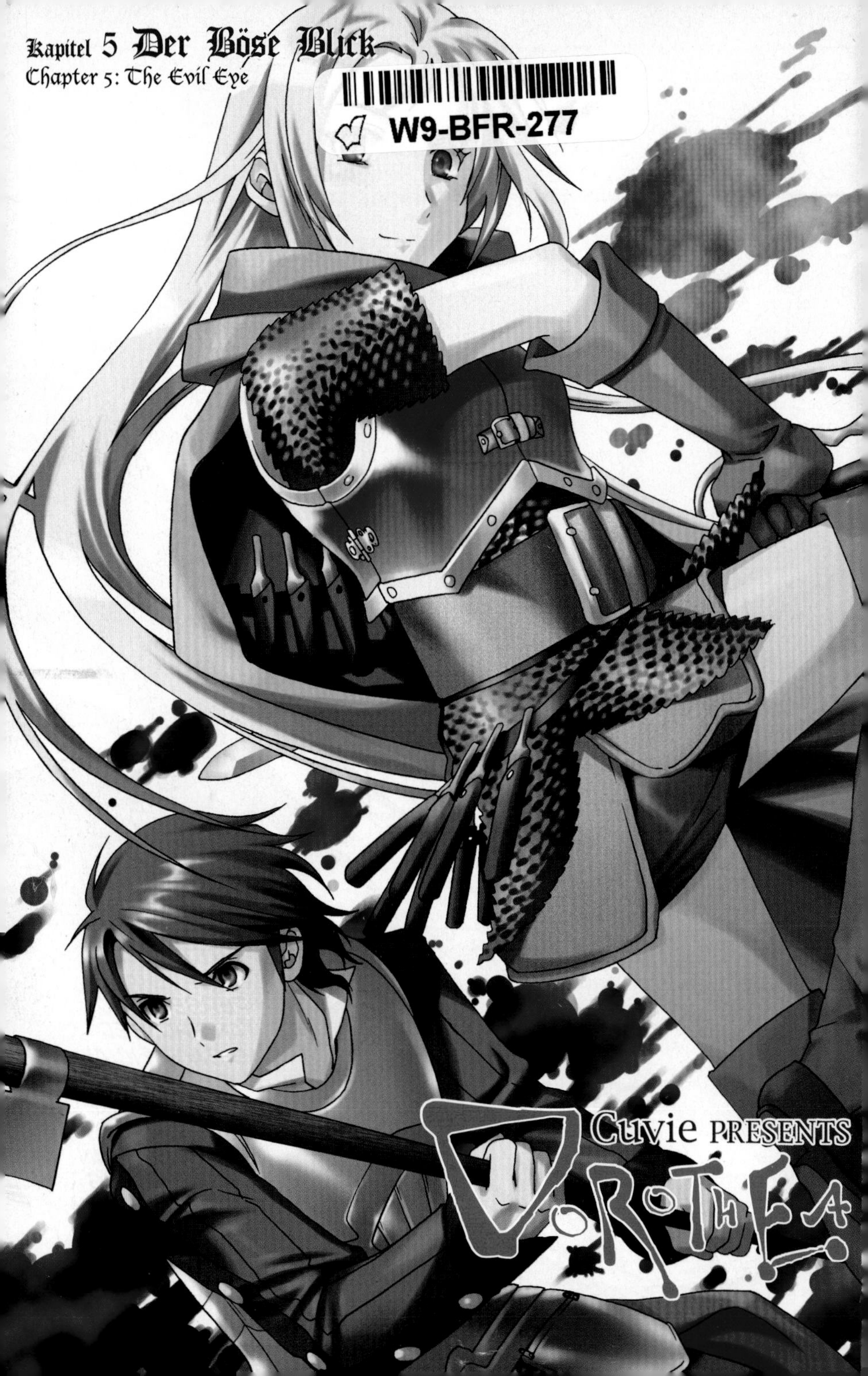
Kapitel 5 Der Böse Blick
Chapter 5: The Evil Eye
Cuvie PRESENTS
DOROTHEA

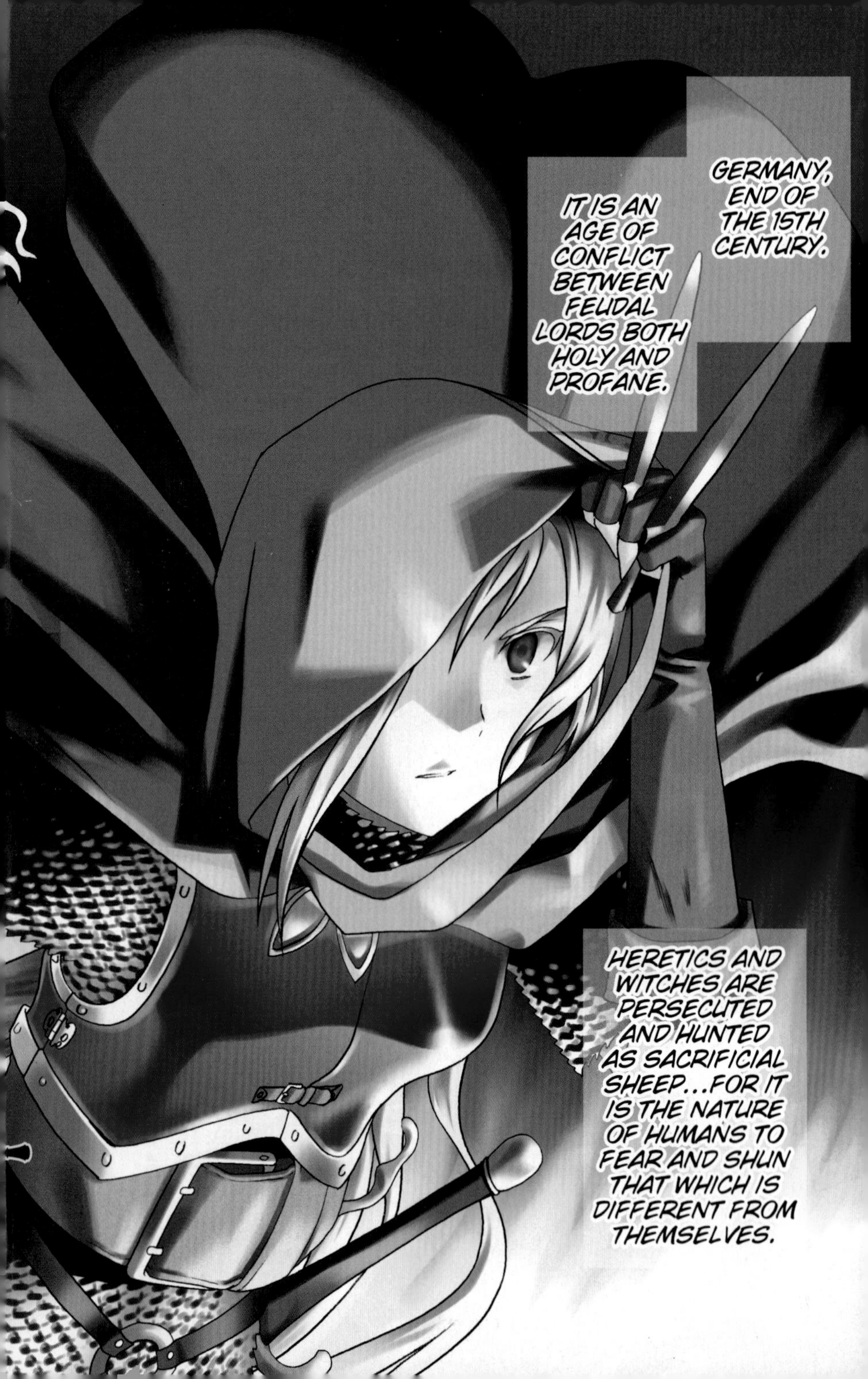
GERMANY, END OF THE 15TH CENTURY.
IT IS AN AGE OF CONFLICT BETWEEN FEUDAL LORDS BOTH HOLY AND PROFANE.
HERETICS AND WITCHES ARE PERSECUTED AND HUNTED AS SACRIFICIAL SHEEP...FOR IT IS THE NATURE OF HUMANS TO FEAR AND SHUN THAT WHICH IS DIFFERENT FROM THEMSELVES.

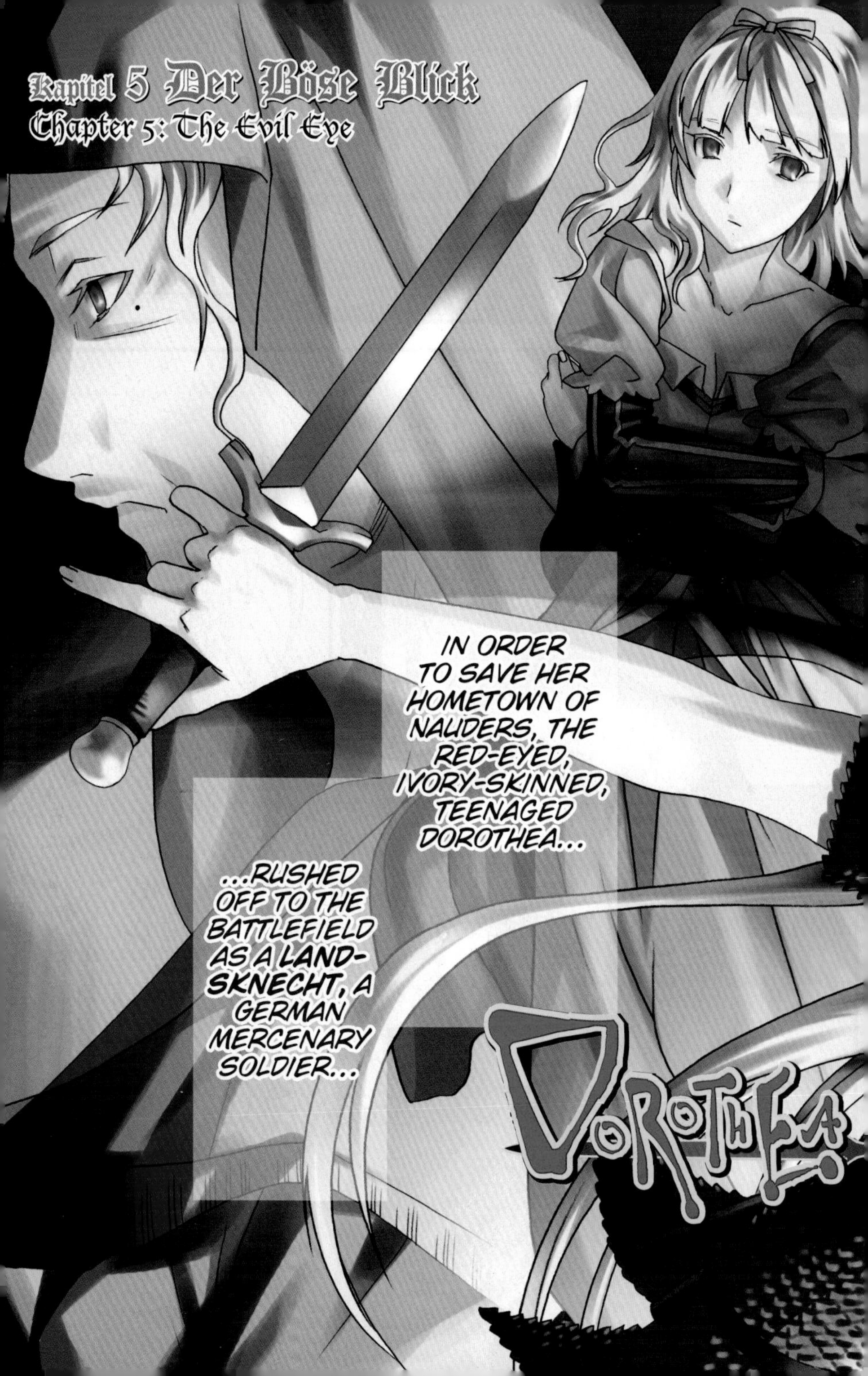
Kapitel 5 Der Böse Blick
Chapter 5: The Evil Eye
IN ORDER TO SAVE HER HOMETOWN OF NAUDERS, THE RED-EYED, IVORY-SKINNED, TEENAGED DOROTHEA...
...RUSHED OFF TO THE BATTLEFIELD AS A **LANDSKNECHT**, A GERMAN MERCENARY SOLDIER...
DOROTHEA

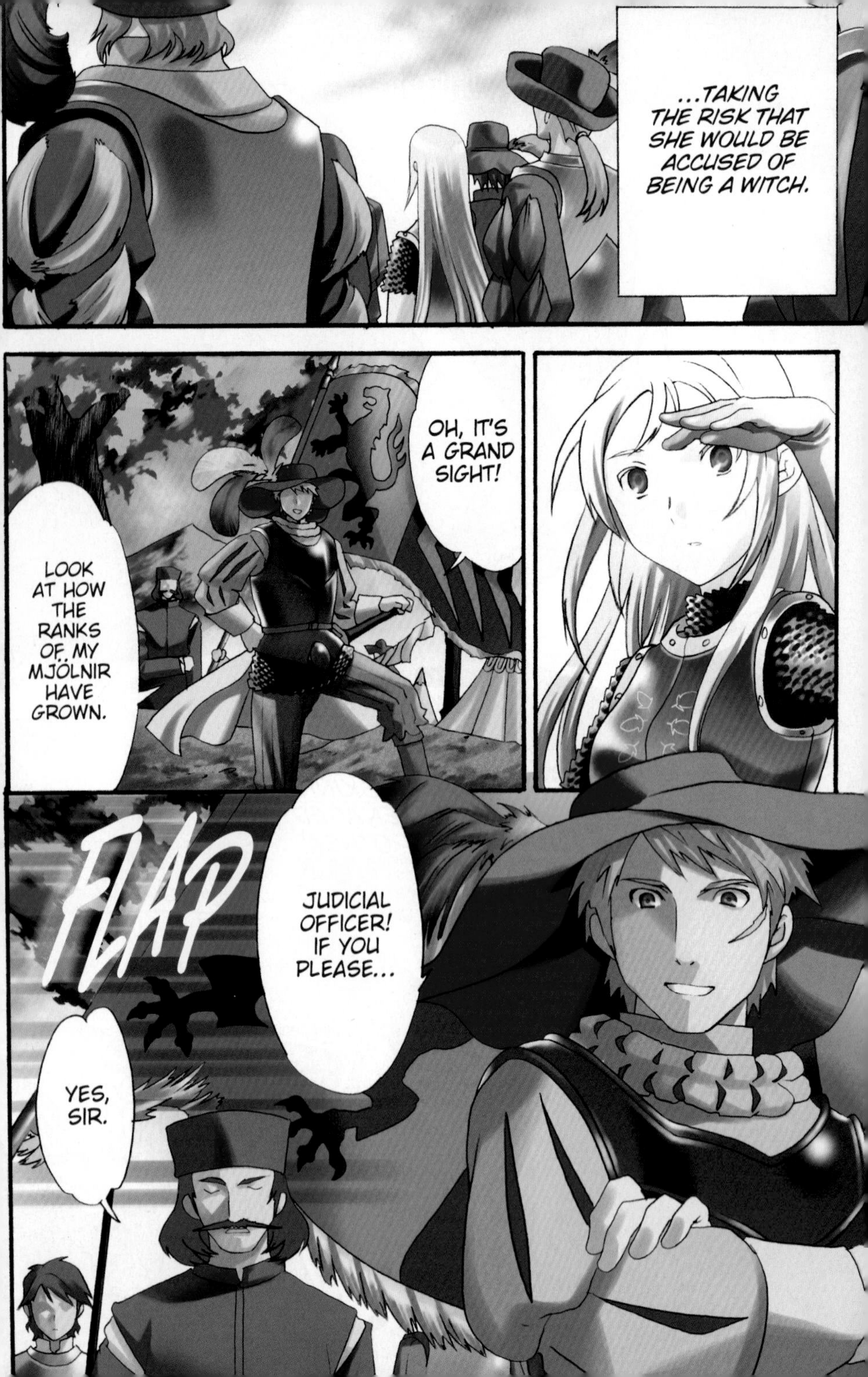
...TAKING THE RISK THAT SHE WOULD BE ACCUSED OF BEING A WITCH.
OH, IT'S A GRAND SIGHT!
LOOK AT HOW THE RANKS OF MY MJÖLNIR HAVE GROWN.
JUDICIAL OFFICER! IF YOU PLEASE...
FLAP
YES, SIR.

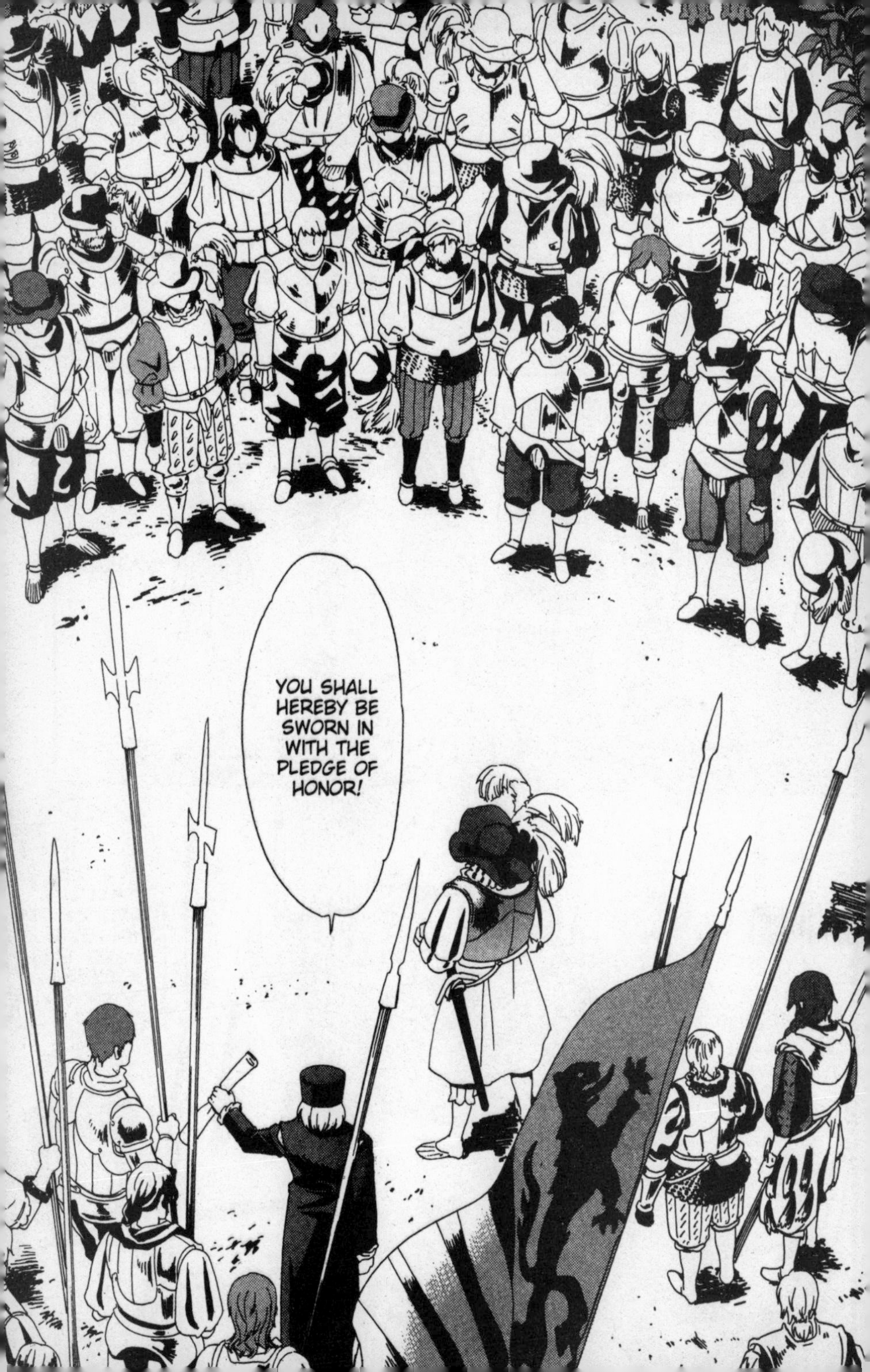
YOU SHALL HEREBY BE SWORN IN WITH THE PLEDGE OF HONOR!

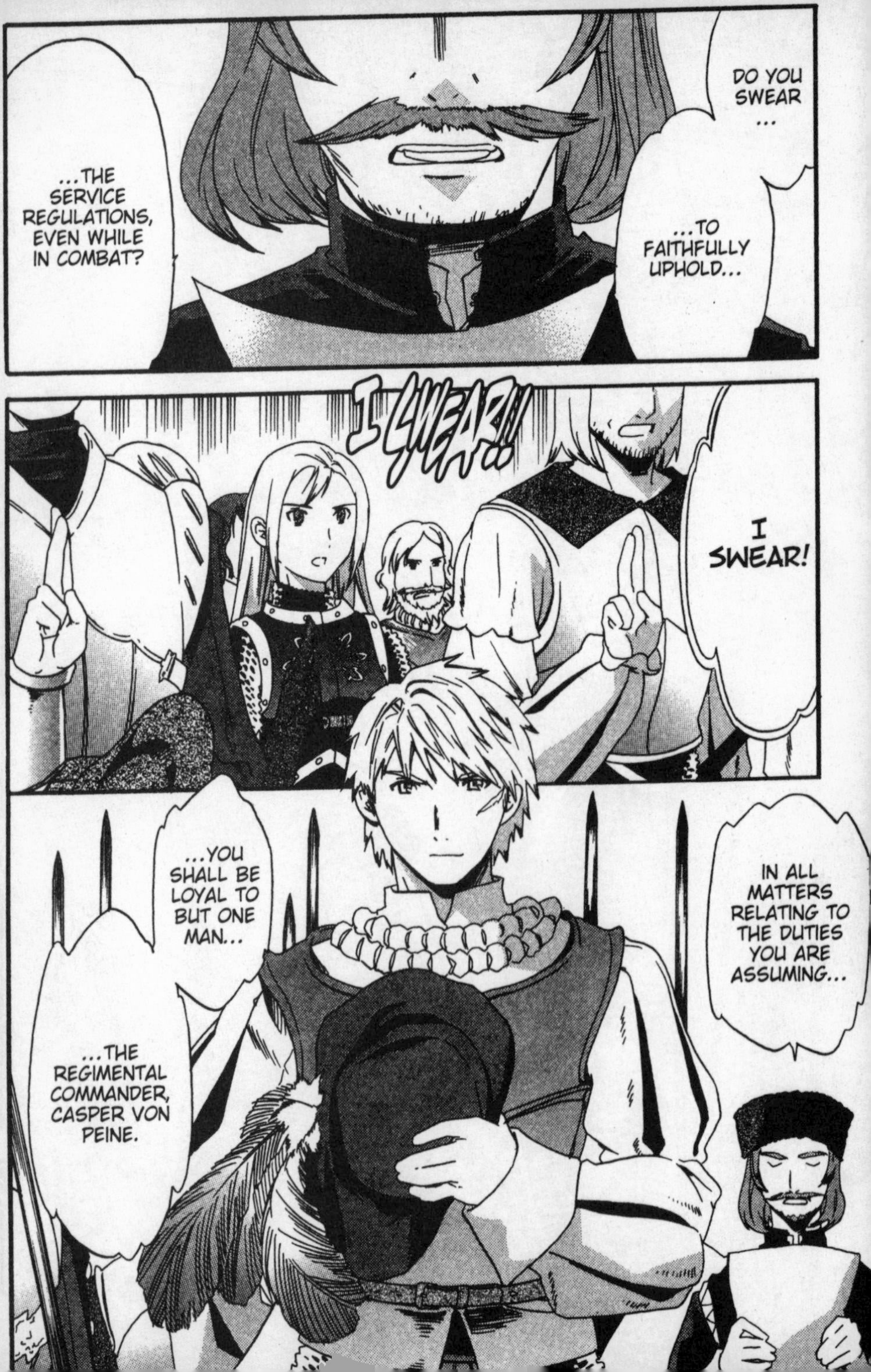
DO YOU SWEAR ...
...TO FAITHFULLY UPHOLD...
...THE SERVICE REGULATIONS, EVEN WHILE IN COMBAT?
I SWEAR!
I SWEAR!!
IN ALL MATTERS RELATING TO THE DUTIES YOU ARE ASSUMING...
...YOU SHALL BE LOYAL TO BUT ONE MAN...
...THE REGIMENTAL COMMANDER, CASPER VON PEINE.

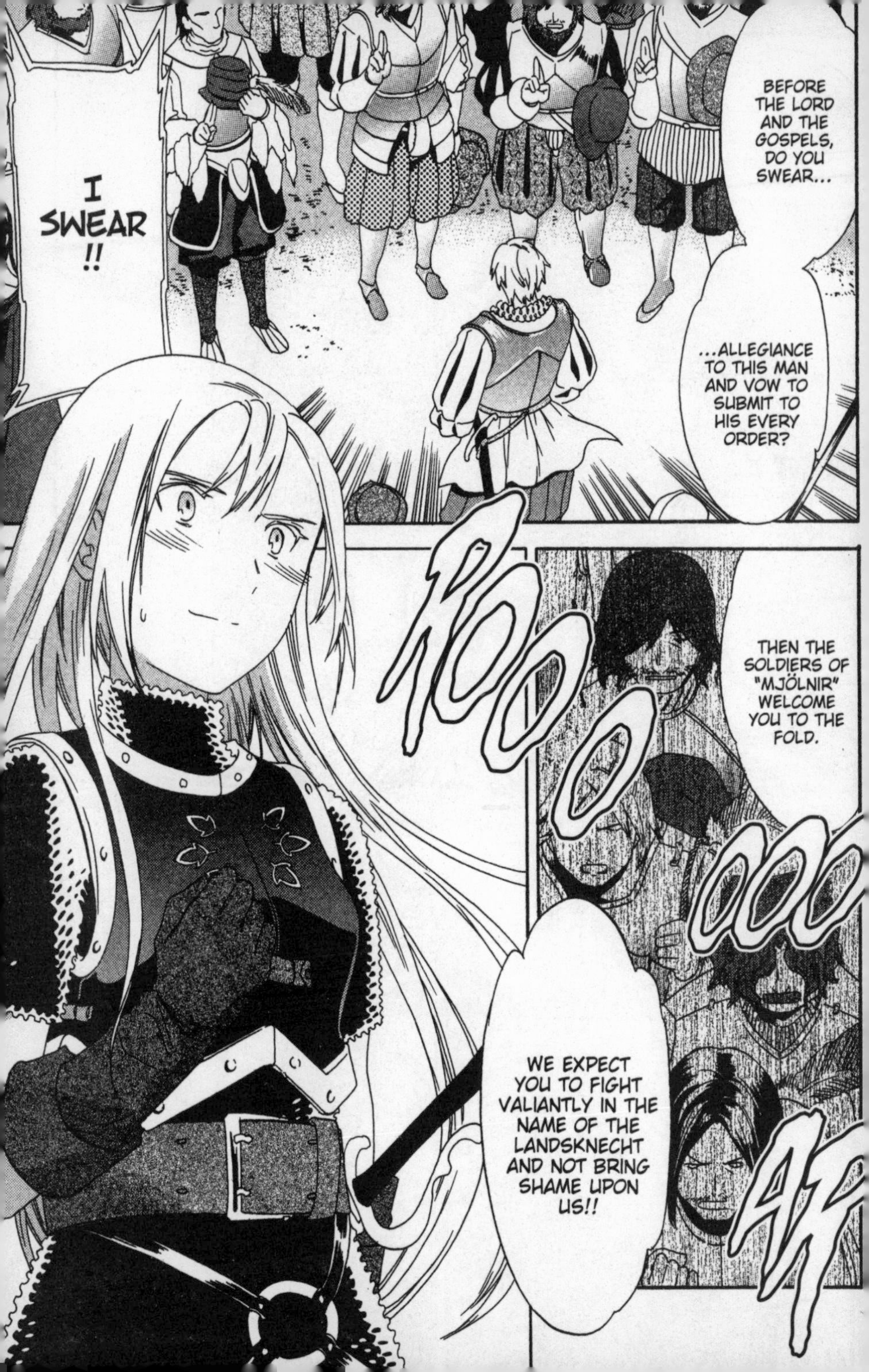
BEFORE THE LORD AND THE GOSPELS, DO YOU SWEAR...
...ALLEGIANCE TO THIS MAN AND VOW TO SUBMIT TO HIS EVERY ORDER?
I SWEAR!!
THEN THE SOLDIERS OF "MJÖLNIR" WELCOME YOU TO THE FOLD.
WE EXPECT YOU TO FIGHT VALIANTLY IN THE NAME OF THE LANDSKNECHT AND NOT BRING SHAME UPON US!!

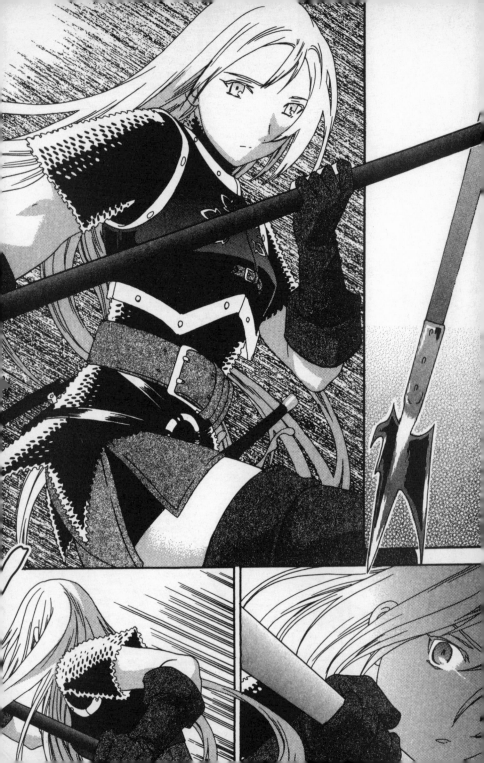

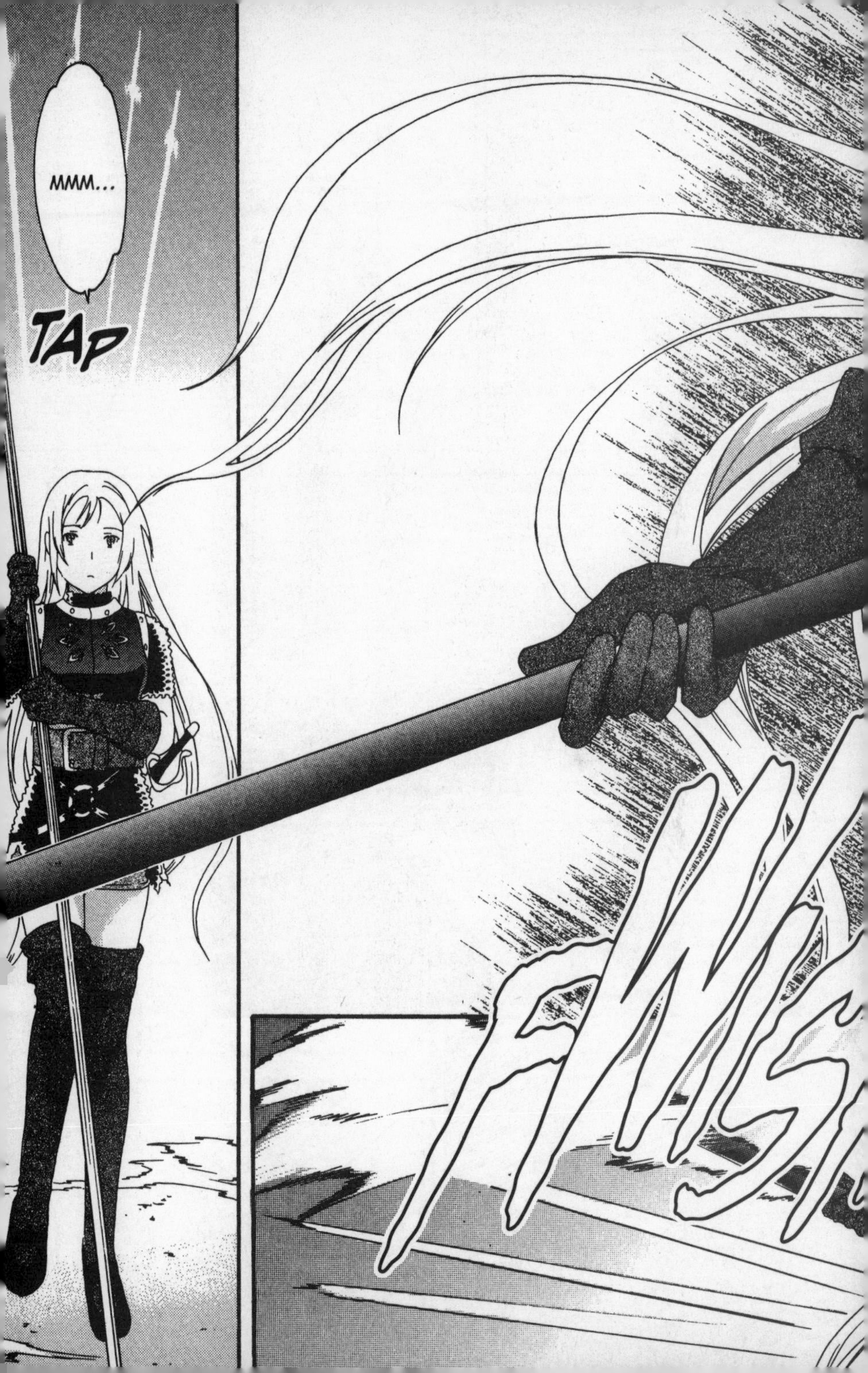
MMM...
TAP

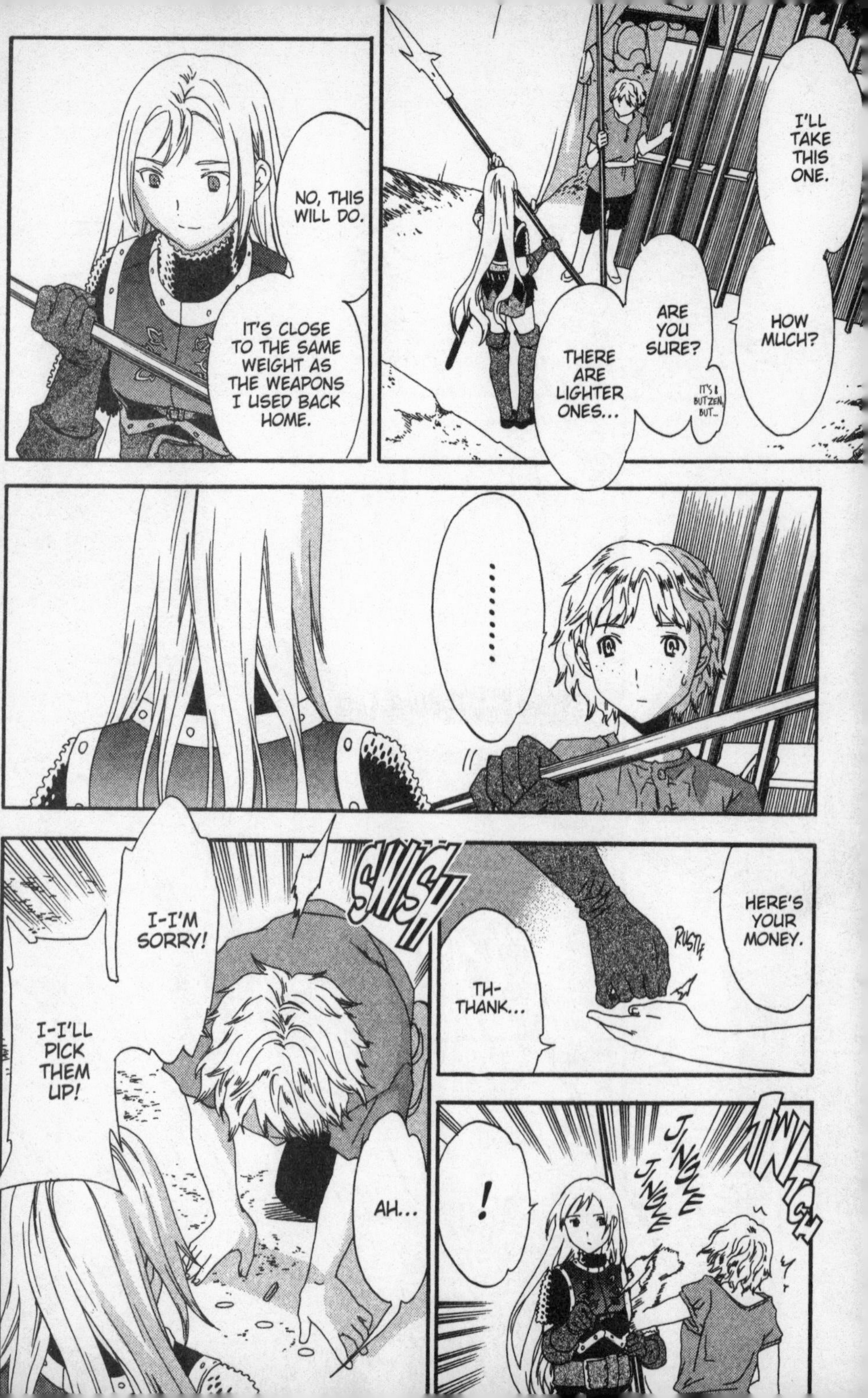
I'LL TAKE THIS ONE.
HOW MUCH?
ARE YOU SURE?
IT'S 8 BUTZEN, BUT...
THERE ARE LIGHTER ONES...
NO, THIS WILL DO.
IT'S CLOSE TO THE SAME WEIGHT AS THE WEAPONS I USED BACK HOME.
......
HERE'S YOUR MONEY.
RUSTLE
TH-THANK...
JINGLE
JINGLE
!
I-I'M SORRY!
I-I'LL PICK THEM UP!
AH...

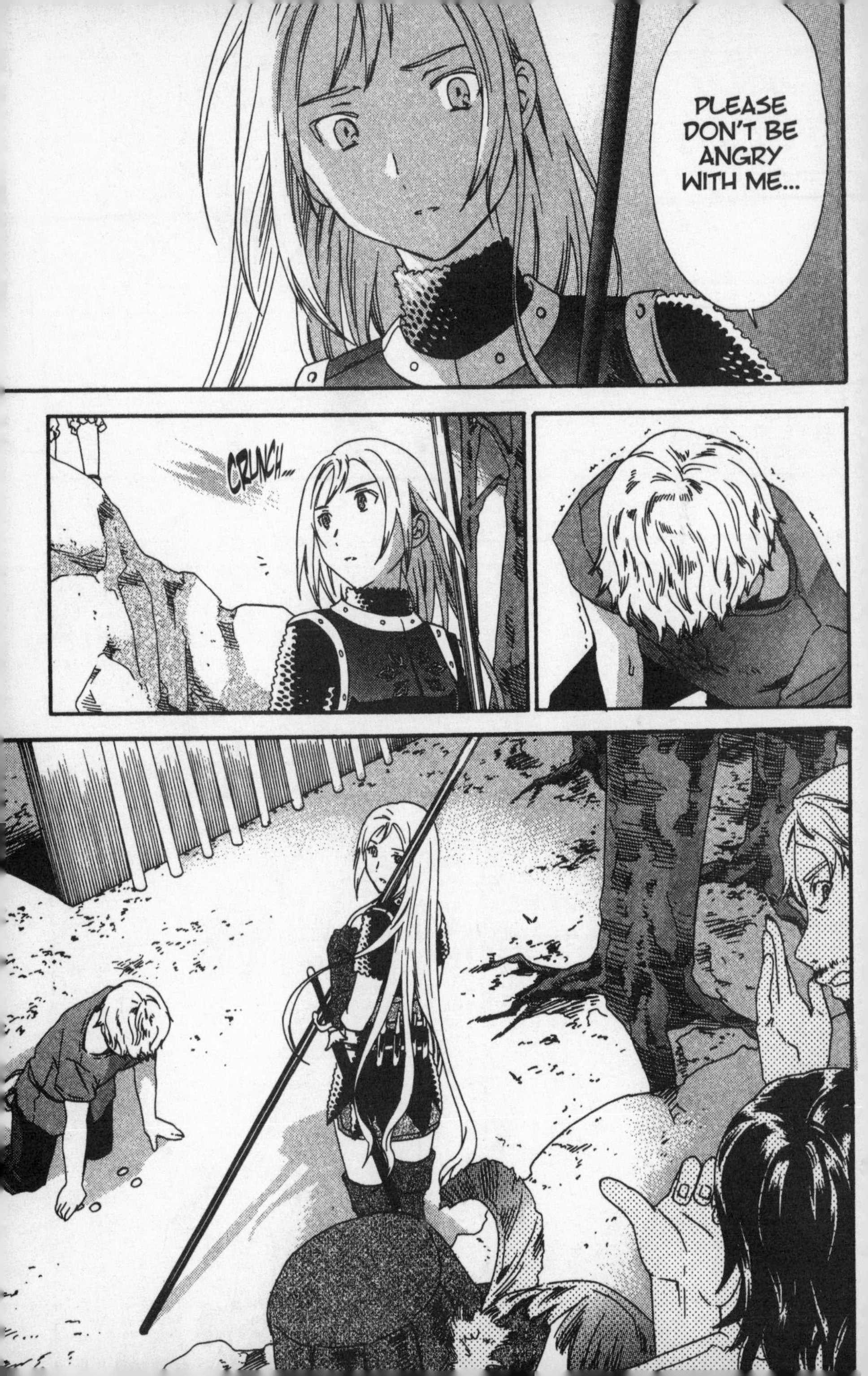
PLEASE DON'T BE ANGRY WITH ME...
CRUNCH...

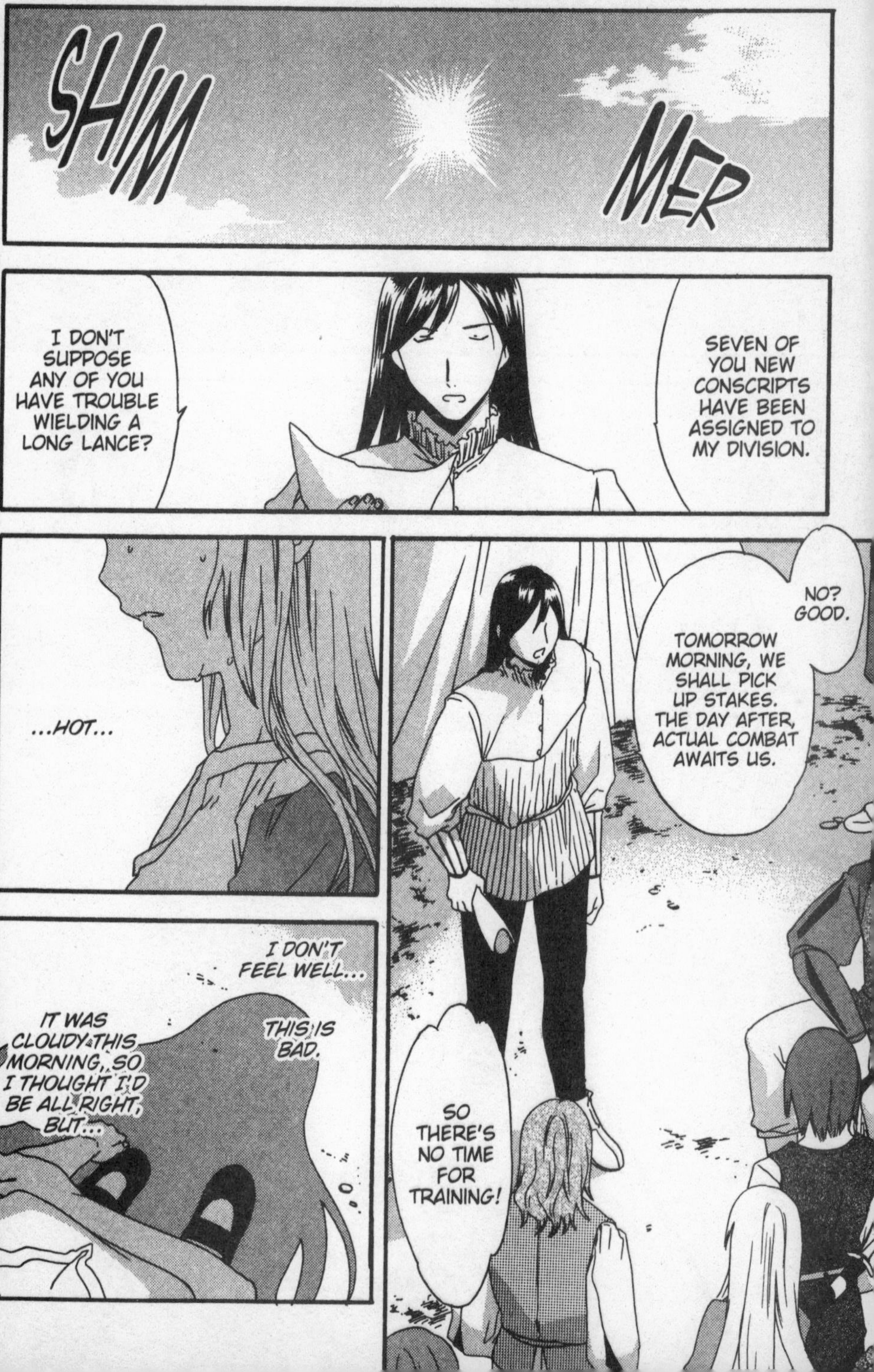
SHIM MER
SEVEN OF YOU NEW CONSCRIPTS HAVE BEEN ASSIGNED TO MY DIVISION.
I DON'T SUPPOSE ANY OF YOU HAVE TROUBLE WIELDING A LONG LANCE?
NO? GOOD.
TOMORROW MORNING, WE SHALL PICK UP STAKES. THE DAY AFTER, ACTUAL COMBAT AWAITS US.
SO THERE'S NO TIME FOR TRAINING!
...HOT...
I DON'T FEEL WELL...
THIS IS BAD.
IT WAS CLOUDY THIS MORNING, SO I THOUGHT I'D BE ALL RIGHT, BUT...

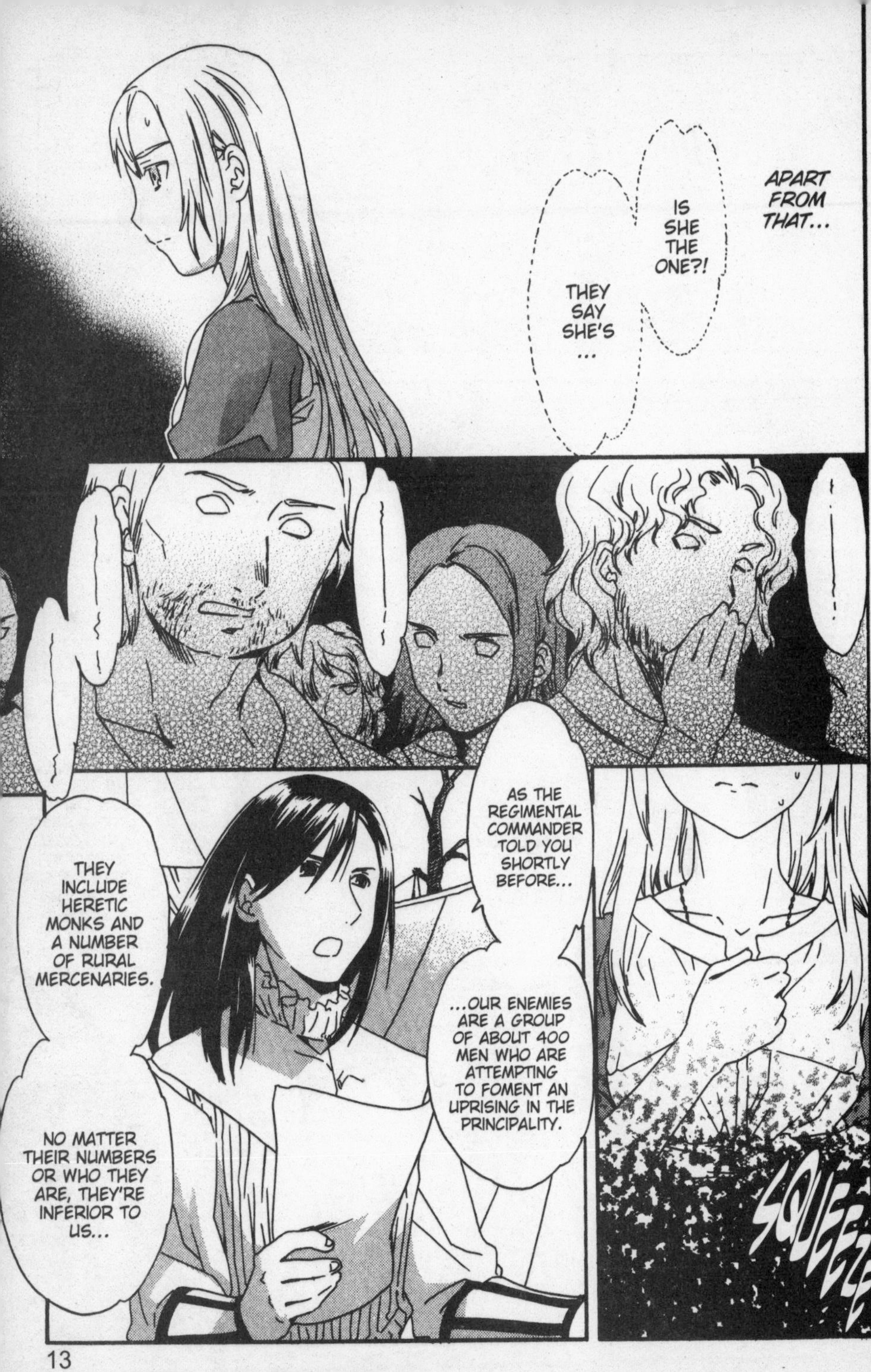
APART FROM THAT...
IS SHE THE ONE?!
THEY SAY SHE'S ...
SQUEEZE
AS THE REGIMENTAL COMMANDER TOLD YOU SHORTLY BEFORE...
...OUR ENEMIES ARE A GROUP OF ABOUT 400 MEN WHO ARE ATTEMPTING TO FOMENT AN UPRISING IN THE PRINCIPALITY.
THEY INCLUDE HERETIC MONKS AND A NUMBER OF RURAL MERCENARIES.
NO MATTER THEIR NUMBERS OR WHO THEY ARE, THEY'RE INFERIOR TO US...

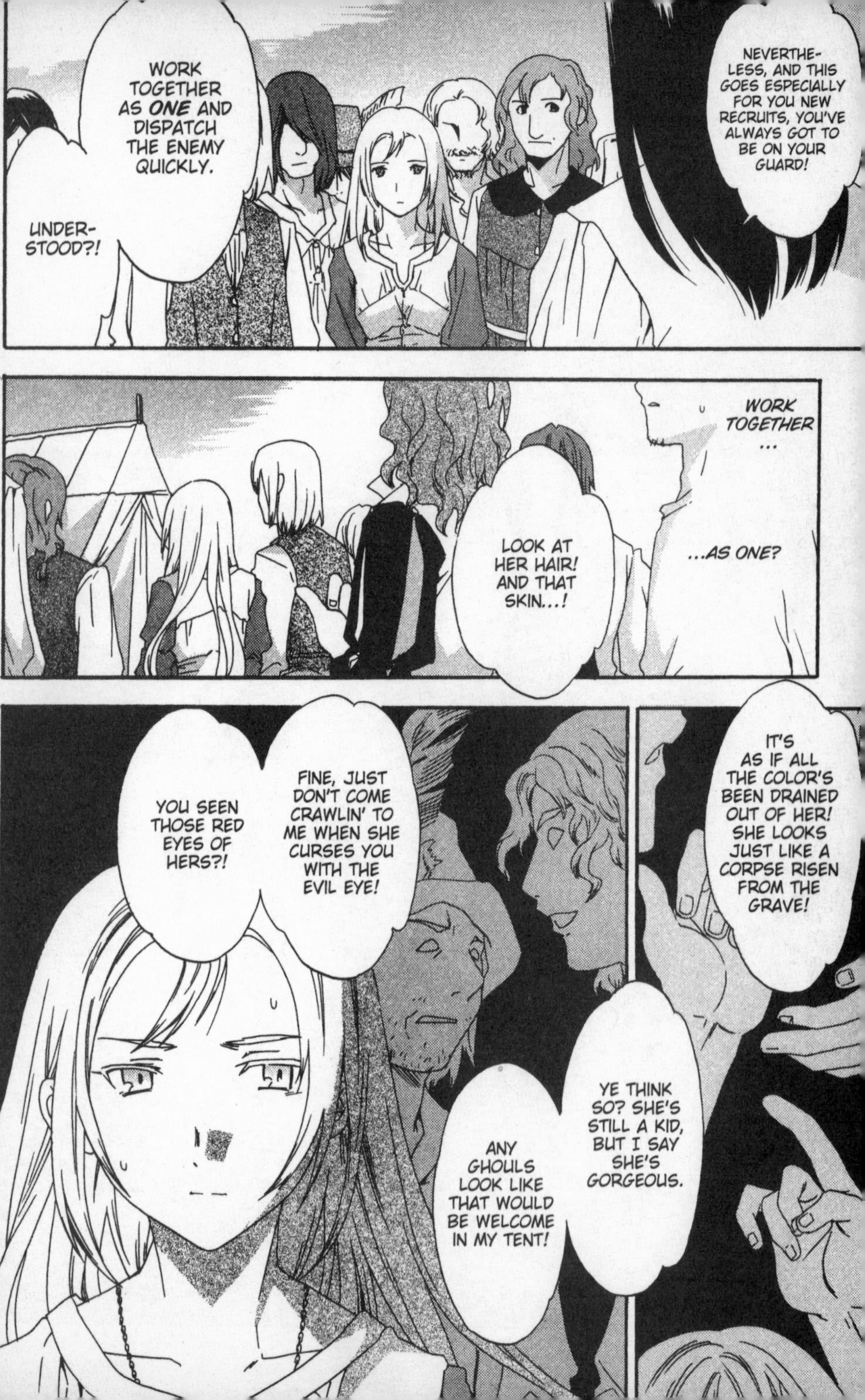
NEVERTHE-LESS, AND THIS GOES ESPECIALLY FOR YOU NEW RECRUITS, YOU'VE ALWAYS GOT TO BE ON YOUR GUARD!
WORK TOGETHER AS *ONE* AND DISPATCH THE ENEMY QUICKLY.
UNDER-STOOD?!
WORK TOGETHER ...
...AS ONE?
LOOK AT HER HAIR! AND THAT SKIN...!
IT'S AS IF ALL THE COLOR'S BEEN DRAINED OUT OF HER! SHE LOOKS JUST LIKE A CORPSE RISEN FROM THE GRAVE!
YE THINK SO? SHE'S STILL A KID, BUT I SAY SHE'S GORGEOUS.
ANY GHOULS LOOK LIKE THAT WOULD BE WELCOME IN MY TENT!
FINE, JUST DON'T COME CRAWLIN' TO ME WHEN SHE CURSES YOU WITH THE EVIL EYE!
YOU SEEN THOSE RED EYES OF HERS?!
--

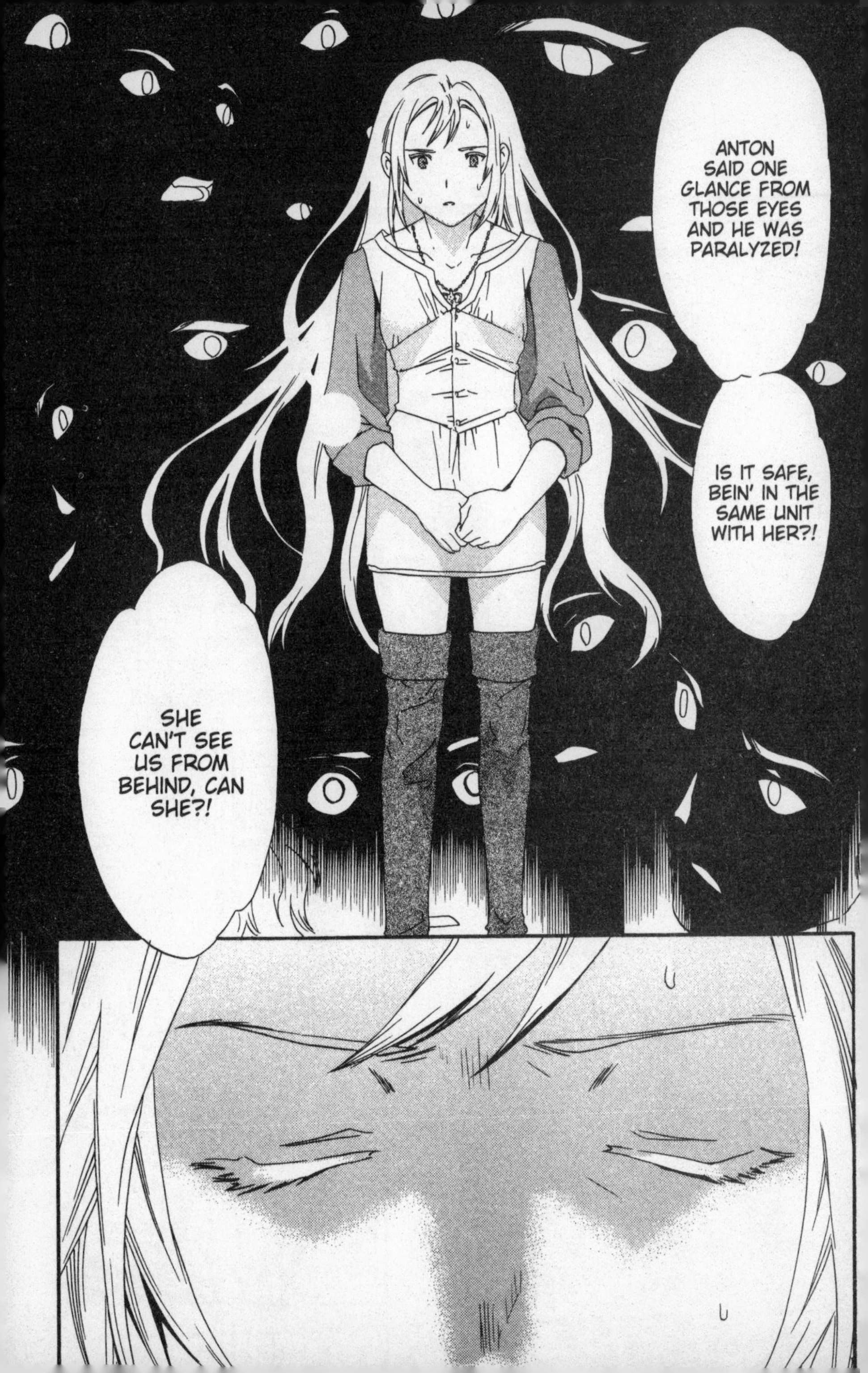
ANTON SAID ONE GLANCE FROM THOSE EYES AND HE WAS PARALYZED!
IS IT SAFE, BEIN' IN THE SAME UNIT WITH HER?!
SHE CAN'T SEE US FROM BEHIND, CAN SHE?!

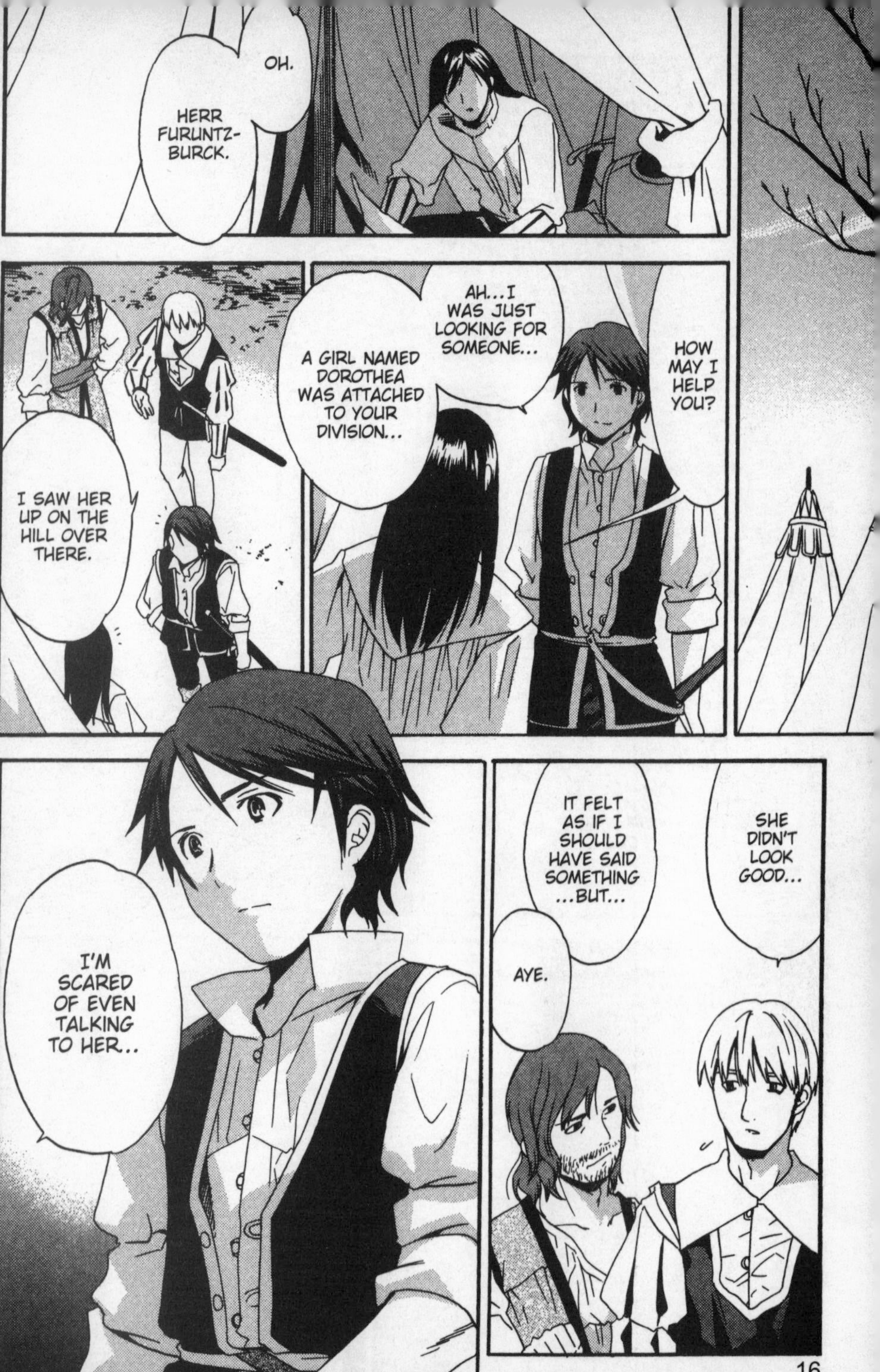
OH.
HERR FURUNTZ-BURCK.
HOW MAY I HELP YOU?
AH...I WAS JUST LOOKING FOR SOMEONE...
A GIRL NAMED DOROTHEA WAS ATTACHED TO YOUR DIVISION...
I SAW HER UP ON THE HILL OVER THERE.
SHE DIDN'T LOOK GOOD...
IT FELT AS IF I SHOULD HAVE SAID SOMETHING ...BUT...
AYE.
I'M SCARED OF EVEN TALKING TO HER...

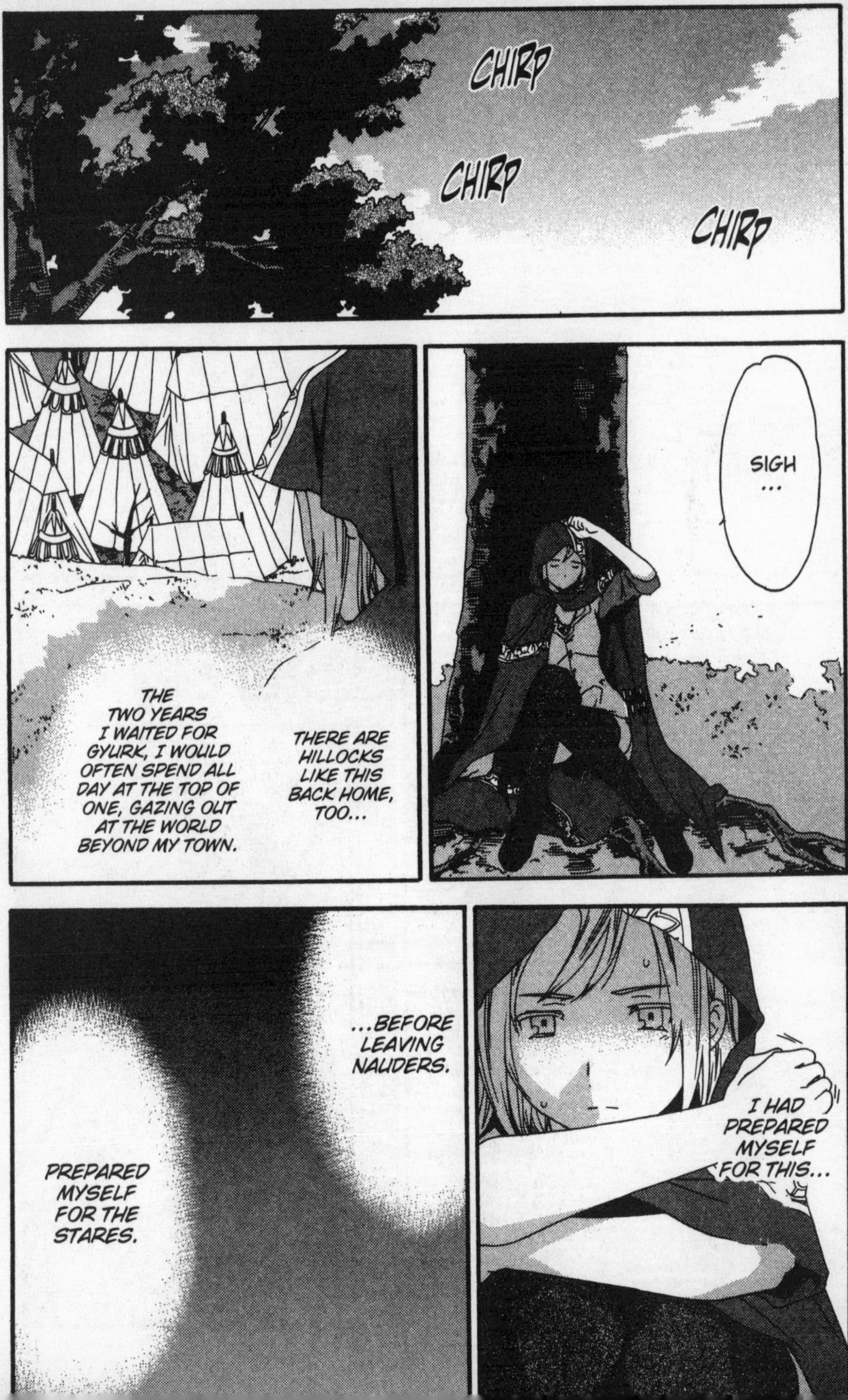
CHIRP
CHIRP
CHIRP
SIGH...
THERE ARE HILLOCKS LIKE THIS BACK HOME, TOO...
THE TWO YEARS I WAITED FOR GYURK, I WOULD OFTEN SPEND ALL DAY AT THE TOP OF ONE, GAZING OUT AT THE WORLD BEYOND MY TOWN.
I HAD PREPARED MYSELF FOR THIS...
...BEFORE LEAVING NAUDERS.
PREPARED MYSELF FOR THE STARES.

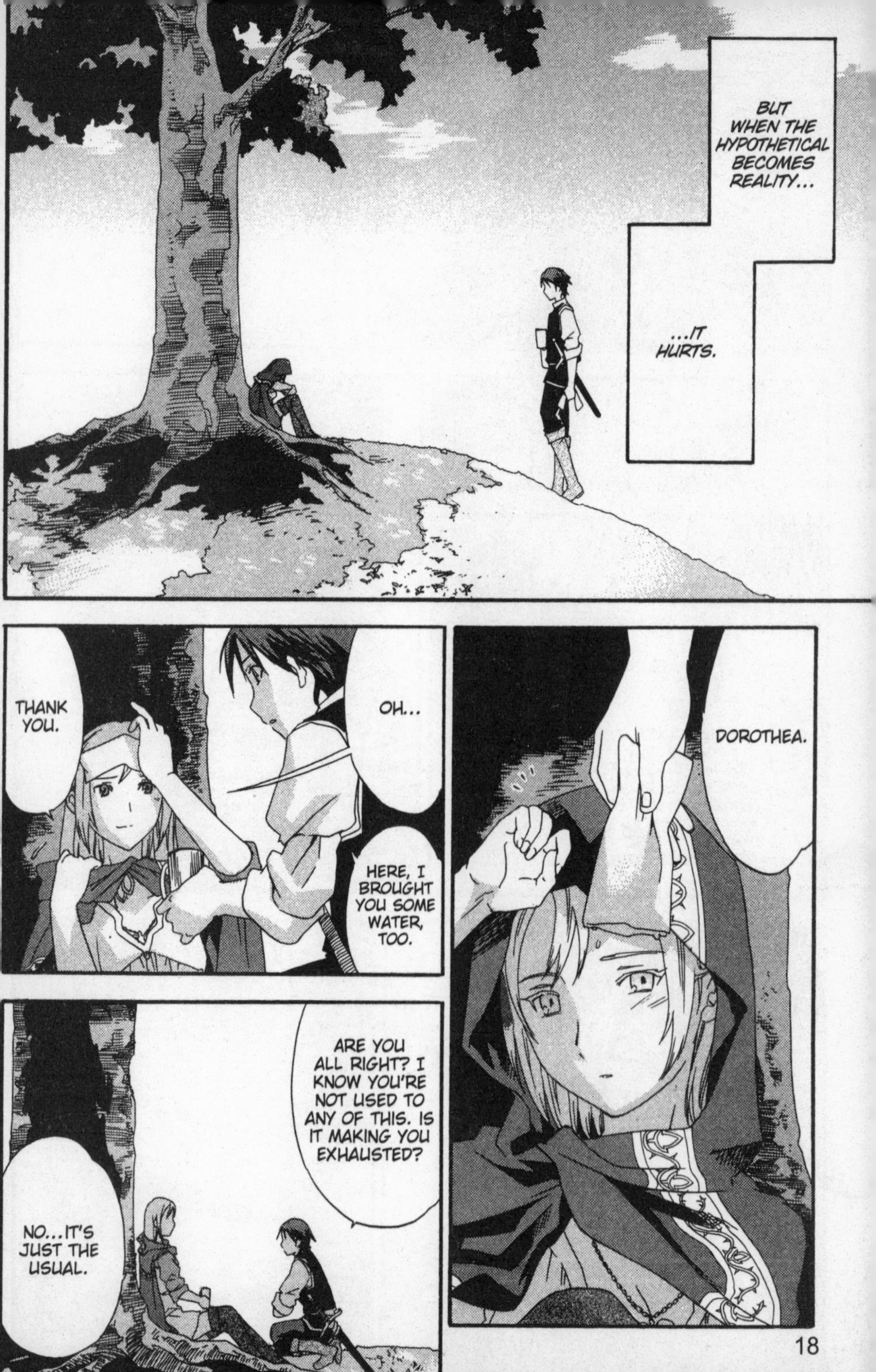
BUT WHEN THE HYPOTHETICAL BECOMES REALITY...
...IT HURTS.
DOROTHEA.
OH...
HERE, I BROUGHT YOU SOME WATER, TOO.
THANK YOU.
ARE YOU ALL RIGHT? I KNOW YOU'RE NOT USED TO ANY OF THIS. IS IT MAKING YOU EXHAUSTED?
NO...IT'S JUST THE USUAL.

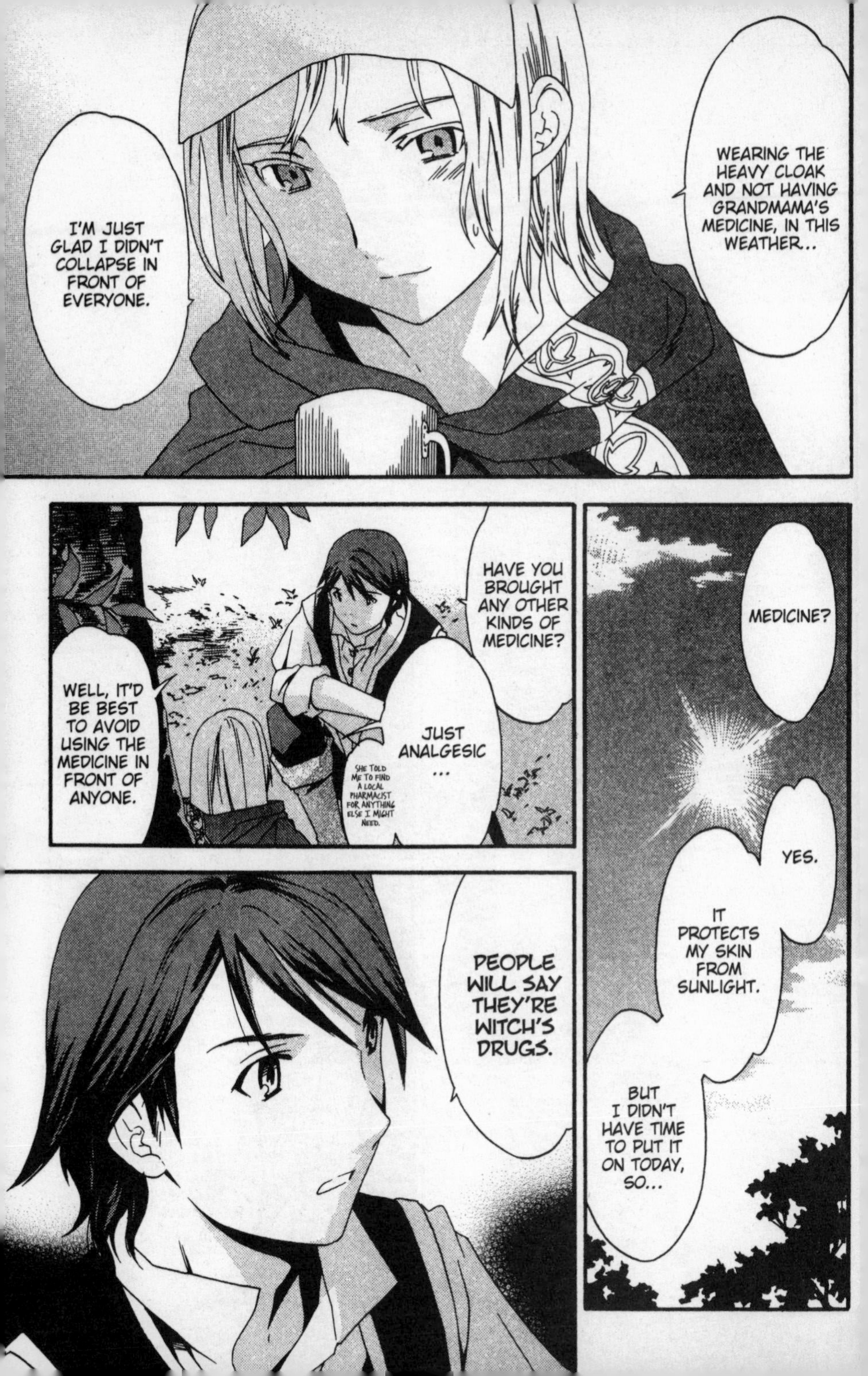
WEARING THE HEAVY CLOAK AND NOT HAVING GRANDMAMA'S MEDICINE, IN THIS WEATHER...
I'M JUST GLAD I DIDN'T COLLAPSE IN FRONT OF EVERYONE.
MEDICINE?
YES.
IT PROTECTS MY SKIN FROM SUNLIGHT.
BUT I DIDN'T HAVE TIME TO PUT IT ON TODAY, SO...
HAVE YOU BROUGHT ANY OTHER KINDS OF MEDICINE?
JUST ANALGESIC...
SHE TOLD ME TO FIND A LOCAL PHARMACIST FOR ANYTHING ELSE I MIGHT NEED.
WELL, IT'D BE BEST TO AVOID USING THE MEDICINE IN FRONT OF ANYONE.
PEOPLE WILL SAY THEY'RE WITCH'S DRUGS.

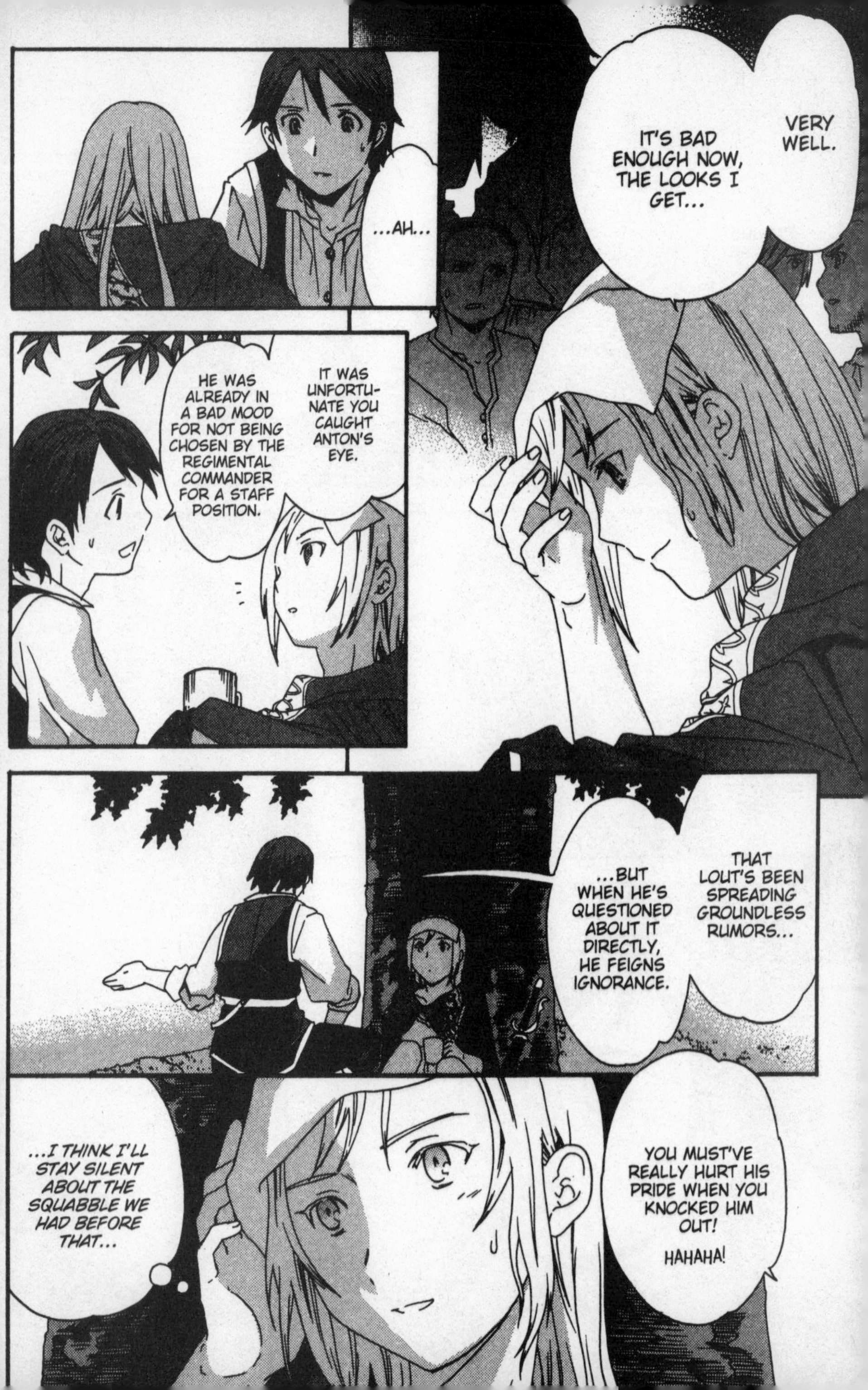
VERY WELL.
IT'S BAD ENOUGH NOW, THE LOOKS I GET...
...AH...
IT WAS UNFORTUNATE YOU CAUGHT ANTON'S EYE.
HE WAS ALREADY IN A BAD MOOD FOR NOT BEING CHOSEN BY THE REGIMENTAL COMMANDER FOR A STAFF POSITION.
THAT LOUT'S BEEN SPREADING GROUNDLESS RUMORS...
...BUT WHEN HE'S QUESTIONED ABOUT IT DIRECTLY, HE FEIGNS IGNORANCE.
YOU MUST'VE REALLY HURT HIS PRIDE WHEN YOU KNOCKED HIM OUT!
HAHAHA!
...I THINK I'LL STAY SILENT ABOUT THE SQUABBLE WE HAD BEFORE THAT...

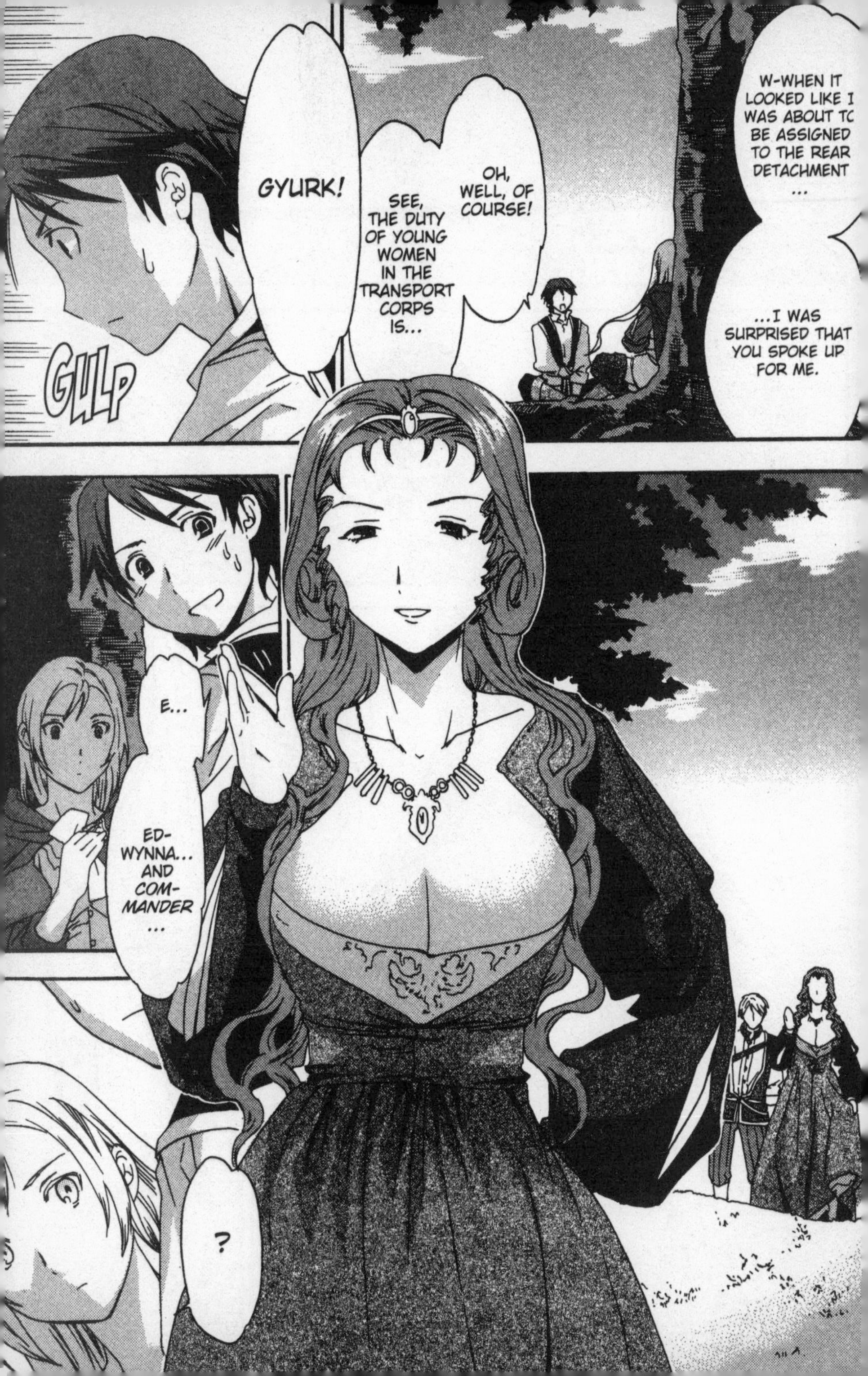
W-WHEN IT LOOKED LIKE I WAS ABOUT TO BE ASSIGNED TO THE REAR DETACHMENT...
...I WAS SURPRISED THAT YOU SPOKE UP FOR ME.
OH, WELL, OF COURSE!
SEE, THE DUTY OF YOUNG WOMEN IN THE TRANSPORT CORPS IS...
GYURK!
GULP
E...
ED-WYNNA... AND COM-MANDER...
?

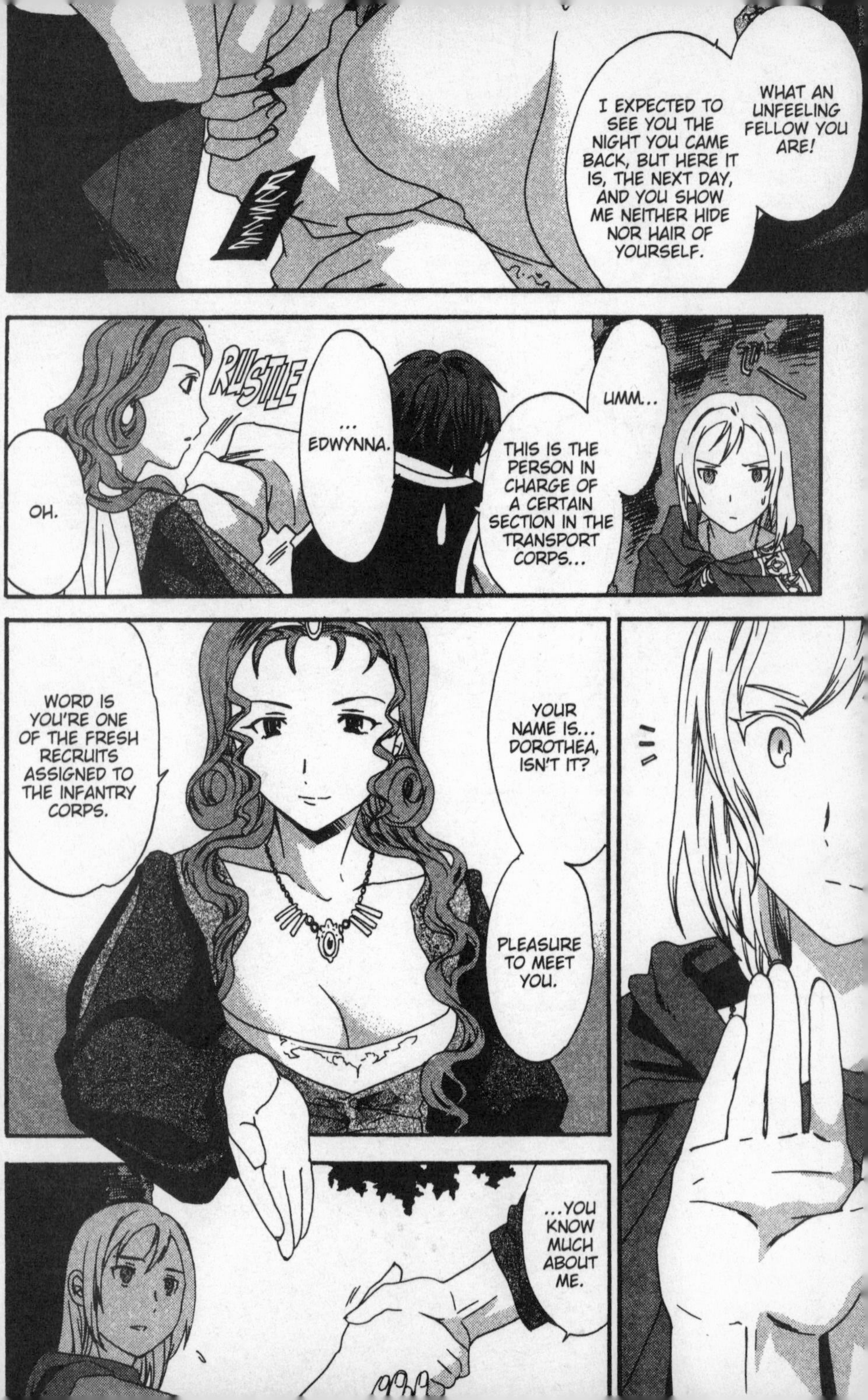
WHAT AN UNFEELING FELLOW YOU ARE!
I EXPECTED TO SEE YOU THE NIGHT YOU CAME BACK, BUT HERE IT IS, THE NEXT DAY, AND YOU SHOW ME NEITHER HIDE NOR HAIR OF YOURSELF.
UMM...
THIS IS THE PERSON IN CHARGE OF A CERTAIN SECTION IN THE TRANSPORT CORPS...
... EDWYNNA.
RUSTLE
OH.
YOUR NAME IS... DOROTHEA, ISN'T IT?
WORD IS YOU'RE ONE OF THE FRESH RECRUITS ASSIGNED TO THE INFANTRY CORPS.
PLEASURE TO MEET YOU.
...YOU KNOW MUCH ABOUT ME.

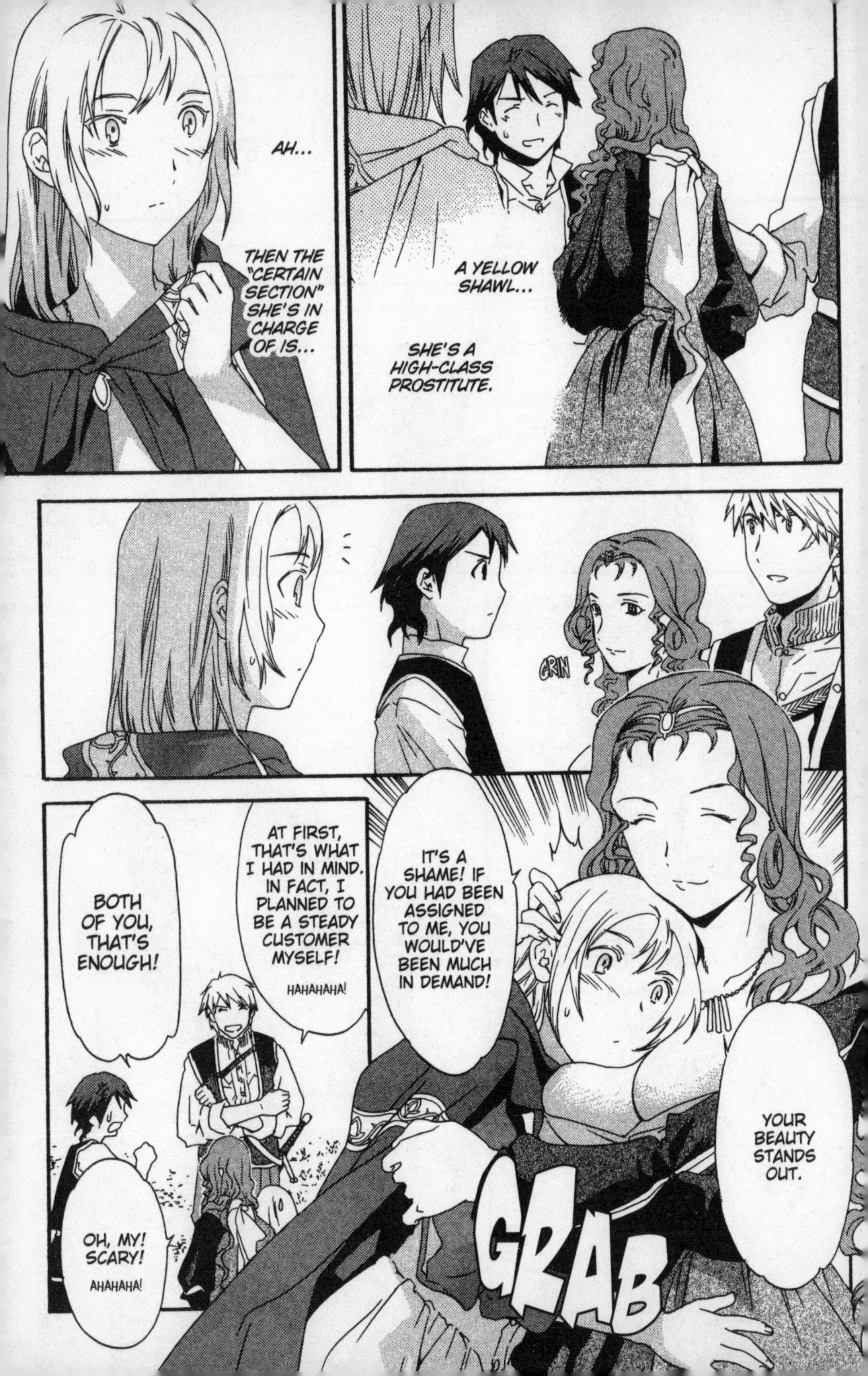
A YELLOW SHAWL...
SHE'S A HIGH-CLASS PROSTITUTE.
AH...
THEN THE "CERTAIN SECTION" SHE'S IN CHARGE OF IS...
GRIN
IT'S A SHAME! IF YOU HAD BEEN ASSIGNED TO ME, YOU WOULD'VE BEEN MUCH IN DEMAND!
YOUR BEAUTY STANDS OUT.
GRAB
AT FIRST, THAT'S WHAT I HAD IN MIND. IN FACT, I PLANNED TO BE A STEADY CUSTOMER MYSELF!
HAHAHAHA!
BOTH OF YOU, THAT'S ENOUGH!
OH, MY! SCARY!
AHAHAHA!

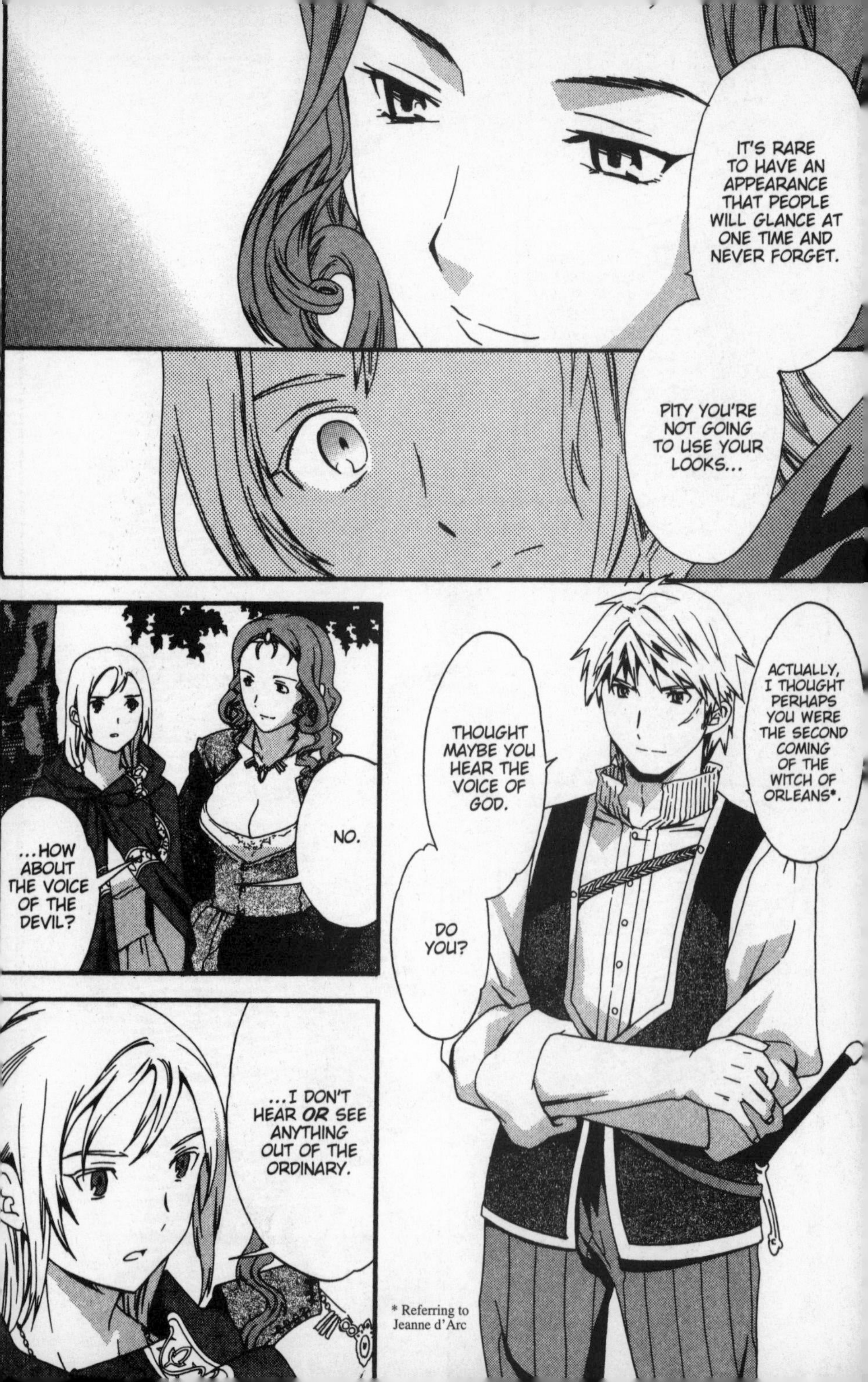
IT'S RARE TO HAVE AN APPEARANCE THAT PEOPLE WILL GLANCE AT ONE TIME AND NEVER FORGET.
PITY YOU'RE NOT GOING TO USE YOUR LOOKS...
ACTUALLY, I THOUGHT PERHAPS YOU WERE THE SECOND COMING OF THE WITCH OF ORLEANS*.
THOUGHT MAYBE YOU HEAR THE VOICE OF GOD.
DO YOU?
NO.
...HOW ABOUT THE VOICE OF THE DEVIL?
...I DON'T HEAR *OR* SEE ANYTHING OUT OF THE ORDINARY.

* Referring to Jeanne d'Arc

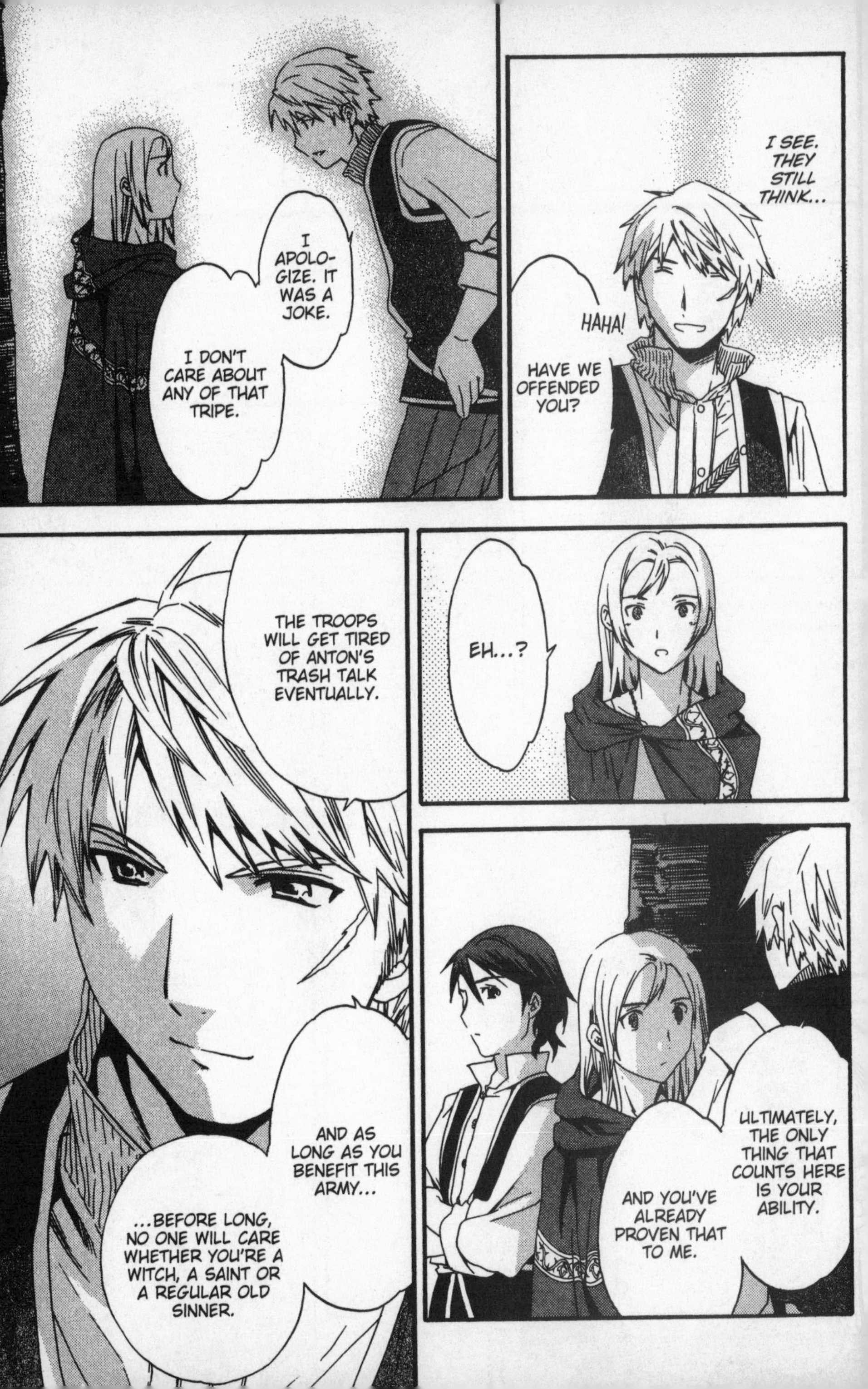
I SEE. THEY STILL THINK...
HAHA!
HAVE WE OFFENDED YOU?
I APOLOGIZE. IT WAS A JOKE.
I DON'T CARE ABOUT ANY OF THAT TRIPE.
EH...?
ULTIMATELY, THE ONLY THING THAT COUNTS HERE IS YOUR ABILITY.
AND YOU'VE ALREADY PROVEN THAT TO ME.
THE TROOPS WILL GET TIRED OF ANTON'S TRASH TALK EVENTUALLY.
AND AS LONG AS YOU BENEFIT THIS ARMY...
...BEFORE LONG, NO ONE WILL CARE WHETHER YOU'RE A WITCH, A SAINT OR A REGULAR OLD SINNER.

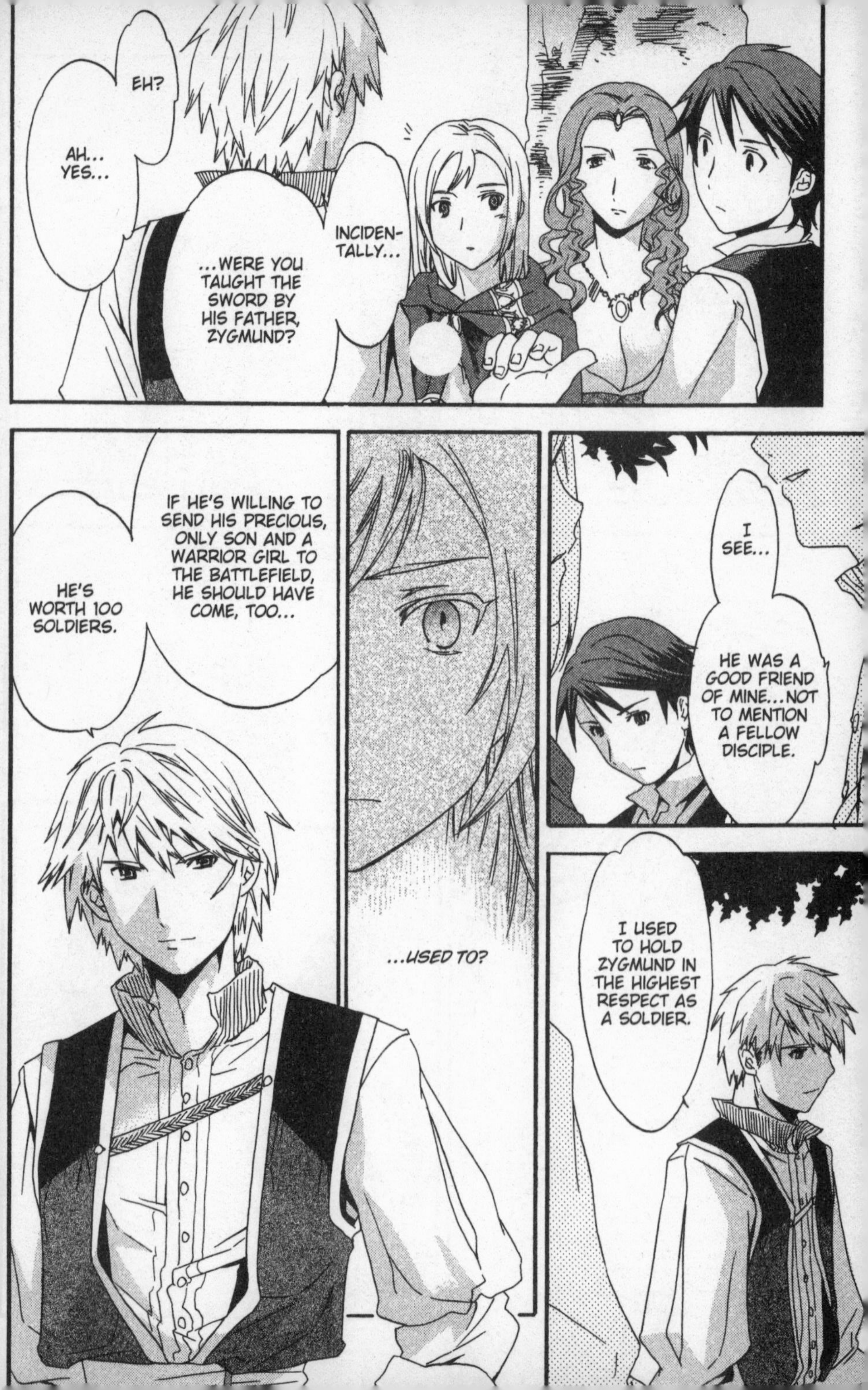
INCIDENTALLY...
...WERE YOU TAUGHT THE SWORD BY HIS FATHER, ZYGMUND?
EH?
AH... YES...
I SEE...
HE WAS A GOOD FRIEND OF MINE...NOT TO MENTION A FELLOW DISCIPLE.
I USED TO HOLD ZYGMUND IN THE HIGHEST RESPECT AS A SOLDIER.
...USED TO?
IF HE'S WILLING TO SEND HIS PRECIOUS, ONLY SON AND A WARRIOR GIRL TO THE BATTLEFIELD, HE SHOULD HAVE COME, TOO...
HE'S WORTH 100 SOLDIERS.

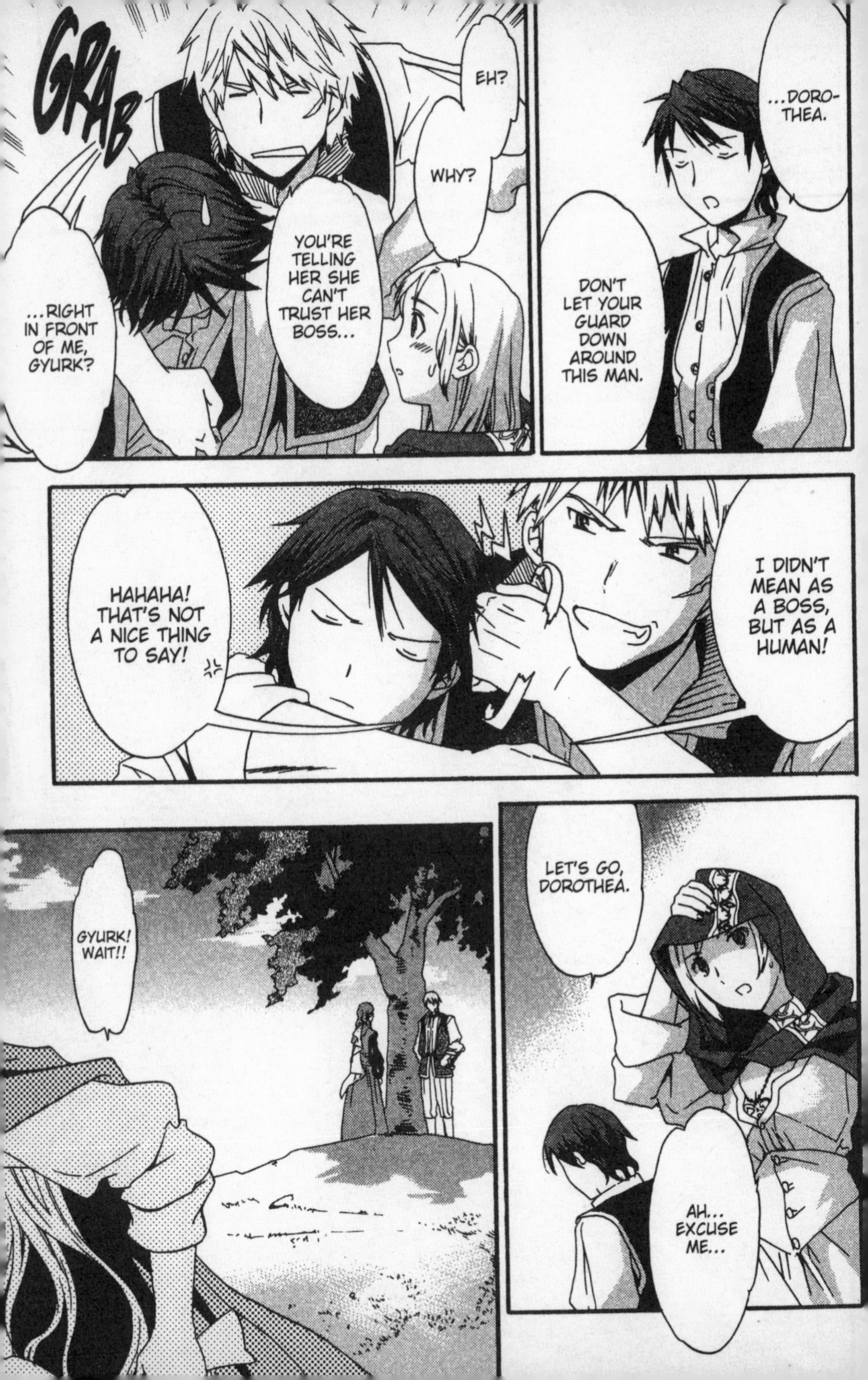
...DORO-THEA.
DON'T LET YOUR GUARD DOWN AROUND THIS MAN.
EH?
WHY?
YOU'RE TELLING HER SHE CAN'T TRUST HER BOSS...
GRAB
...RIGHT IN FRONT OF ME, GYURK?
I DIDN'T MEAN AS A BOSS, BUT AS A HUMAN!
HAHAHA! THAT'S NOT A NICE THING TO SAY!
LET'S GO, DOROTHEA.
AH... EXCUSE ME...
GYURK! WAIT!!

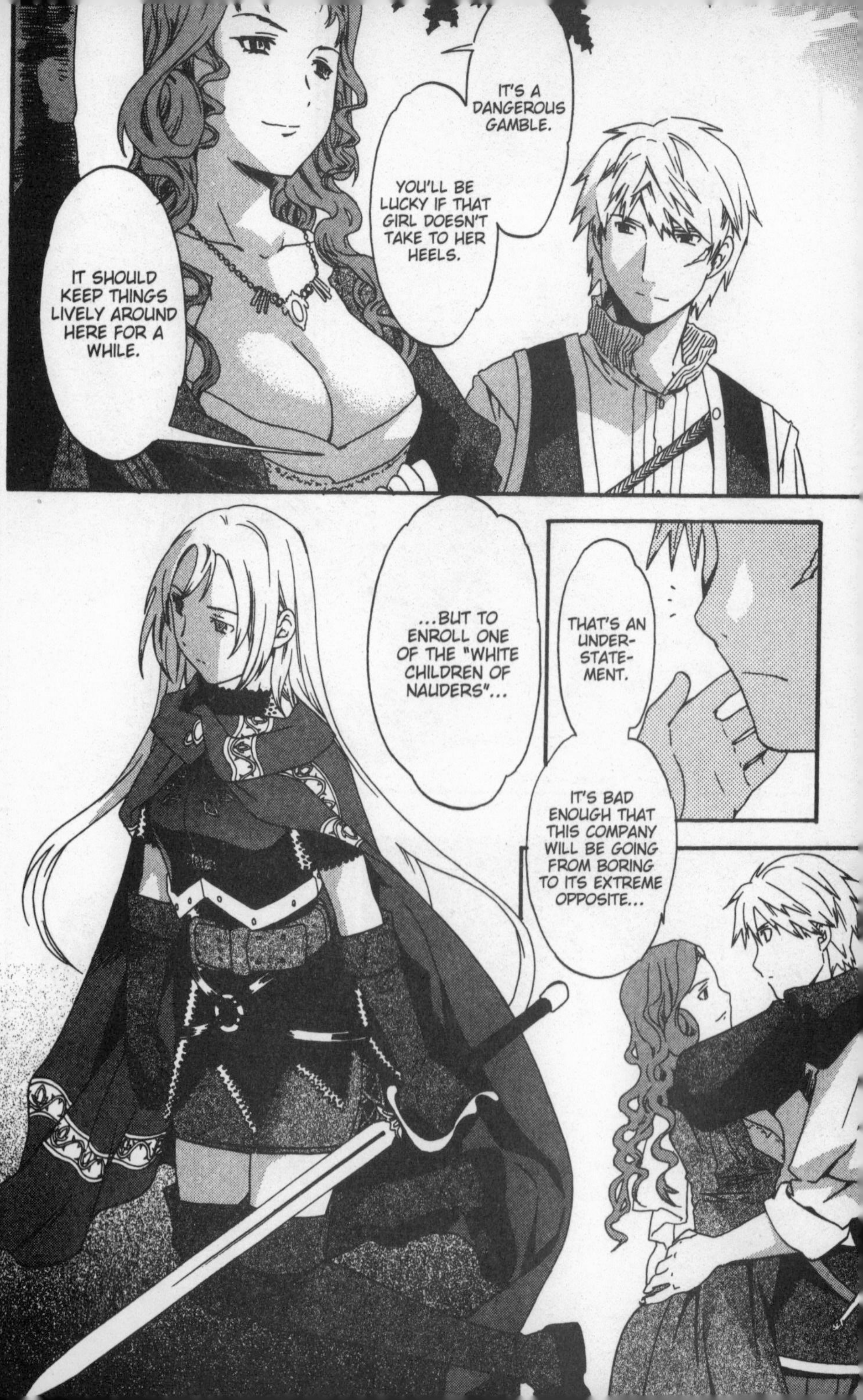
IT'S A DANGEROUS GAMBLE.
YOU'LL BE LUCKY IF THAT GIRL DOESN'T TAKE TO HER HEELS.
IT SHOULD KEEP THINGS LIVELY AROUND HERE FOR A WHILE.
...
THAT'S AN UNDER-STATE-MENT.
IT'S BAD ENOUGH THAT THIS COMPANY WILL BE GOING FROM BORING TO ITS EXTREME OPPOSITE...
...BUT TO ENROLL ONE OF THE "WHITE CHILDREN OF NAUDERS"...

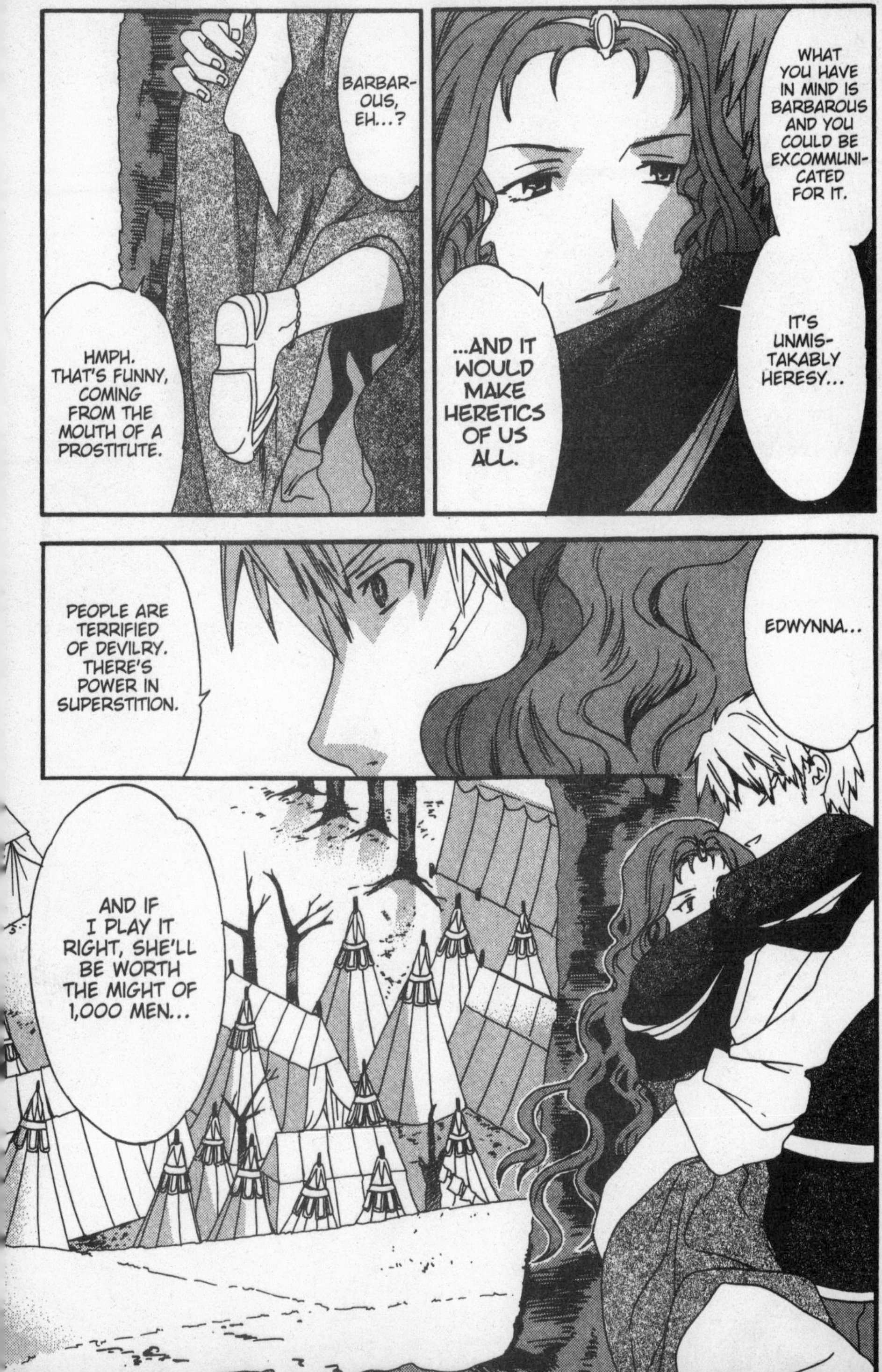
WHAT YOU HAVE IN MIND IS BARBAROUS AND YOU COULD BE EXCOMMUNICATED FOR IT.
IT'S UNMISTAKABLY HERESY...
...AND IT WOULD MAKE HERETICS OF US ALL.
BARBAROUS, EH...?
HMPH. THAT'S FUNNY, COMING FROM THE MOUTH OF A PROSTITUTE.
EDWYNNA...
PEOPLE ARE TERRIFIED OF DEVILRY. THERE'S POWER IN SUPERSTITION.
AND IF I PLAY IT RIGHT, SHE'LL BE WORTH THE MIGHT OF 1,000 MEN...

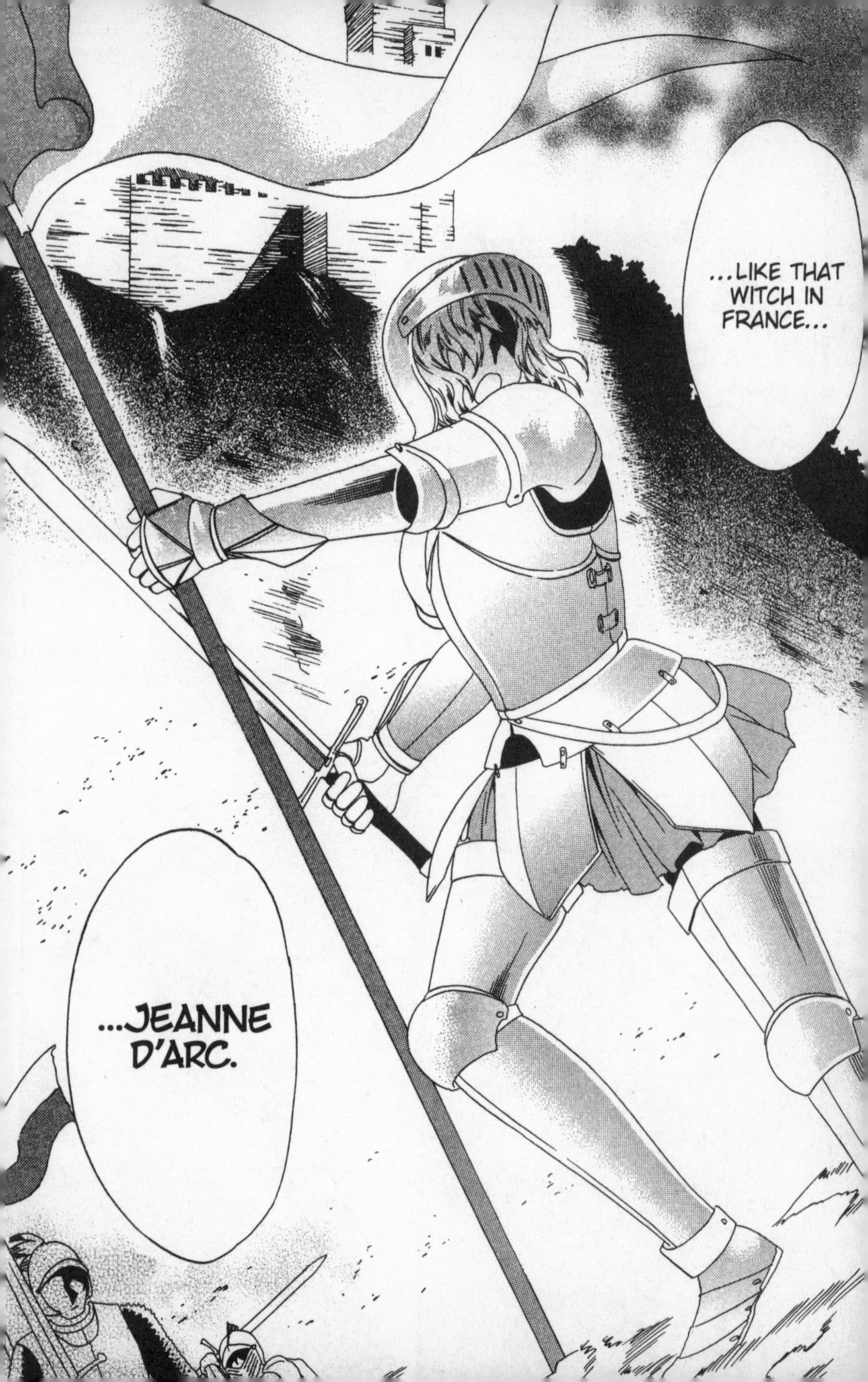
...LIKE THAT WITCH IN FRANCE...
...JEANNE D'ARC.

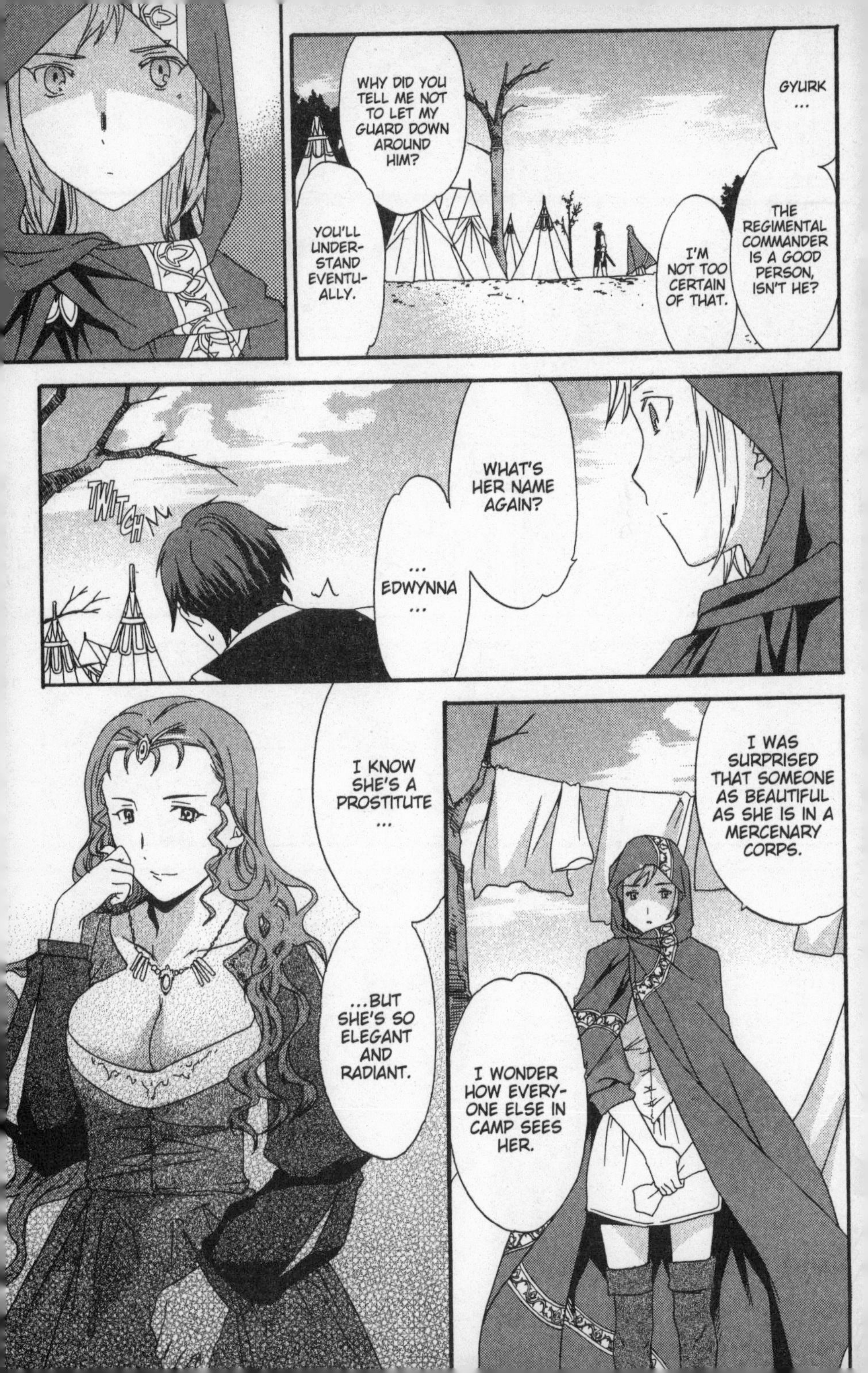
GYURK ...
THE REGIMENTAL COMMANDER IS A GOOD PERSON, ISN'T HE?
I'M NOT TOO CERTAIN OF THAT.
WHY DID YOU TELL ME NOT TO LET MY GUARD DOWN AROUND HIM?
YOU'LL UNDER-STAND EVENTU-ALLY.
WHAT'S HER NAME AGAIN?
... EDWYNNA ...
TWITCH
I WAS SURPRISED THAT SOMEONE AS BEAUTIFUL AS SHE IS IN A MERCENARY CORPS.
I WONDER HOW EVERY-ONE ELSE IN CAMP SEES HER.
I KNOW SHE'S A PROSTITUTE ...
...BUT SHE'S SO ELEGANT AND RADIANT.

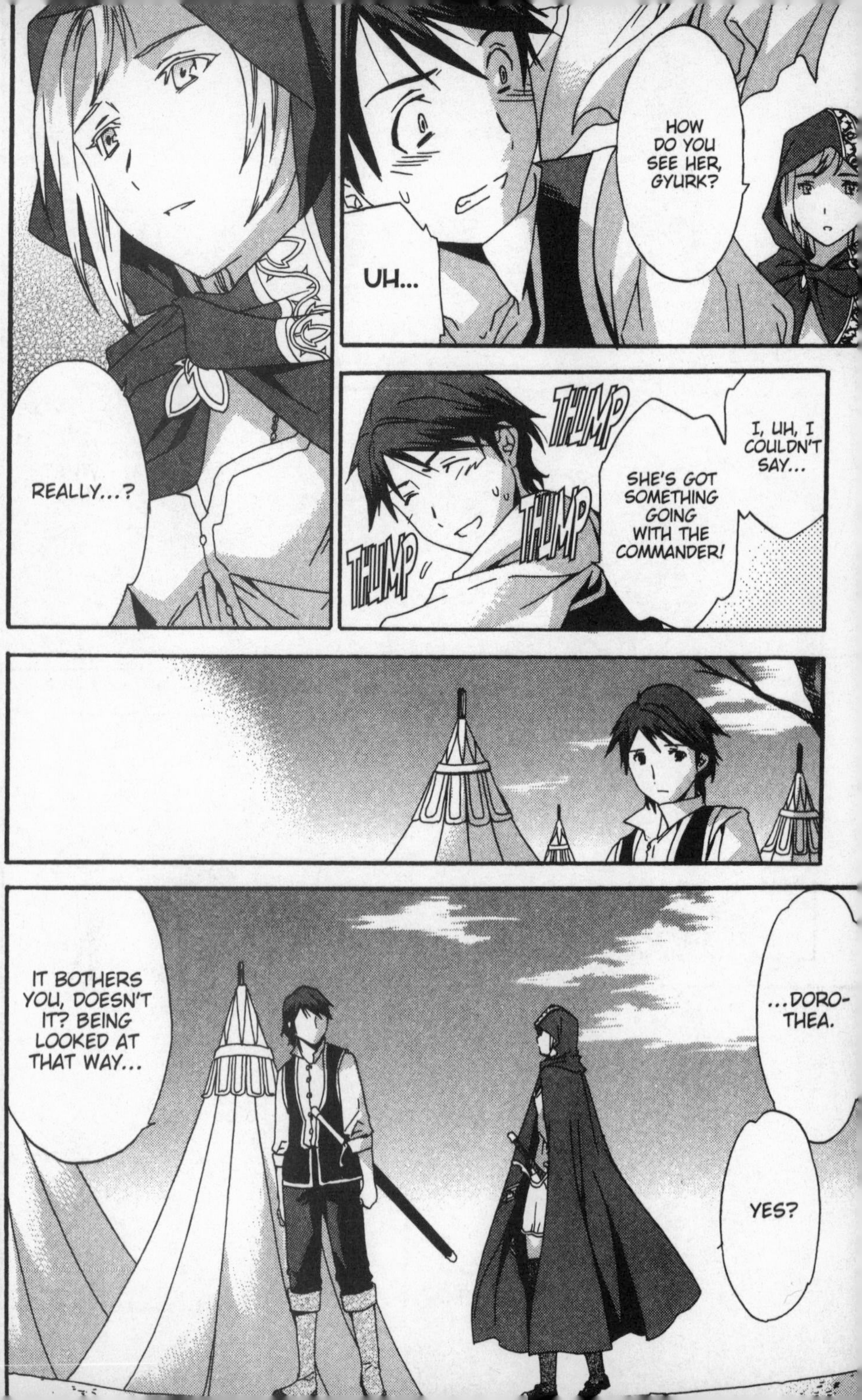
HOW DO YOU SEE HER, GYURK?
UH...
I, UH, I COULDN'T SAY...
SHE'S GOT SOMETHING GOING WITH THE COMMANDER!
THUMP
THUMP
THUMP
REALLY...?
...DORO-THEA.
YES?
IT BOTHERS YOU, DOESN'T IT? BEING LOOKED AT THAT WAY...

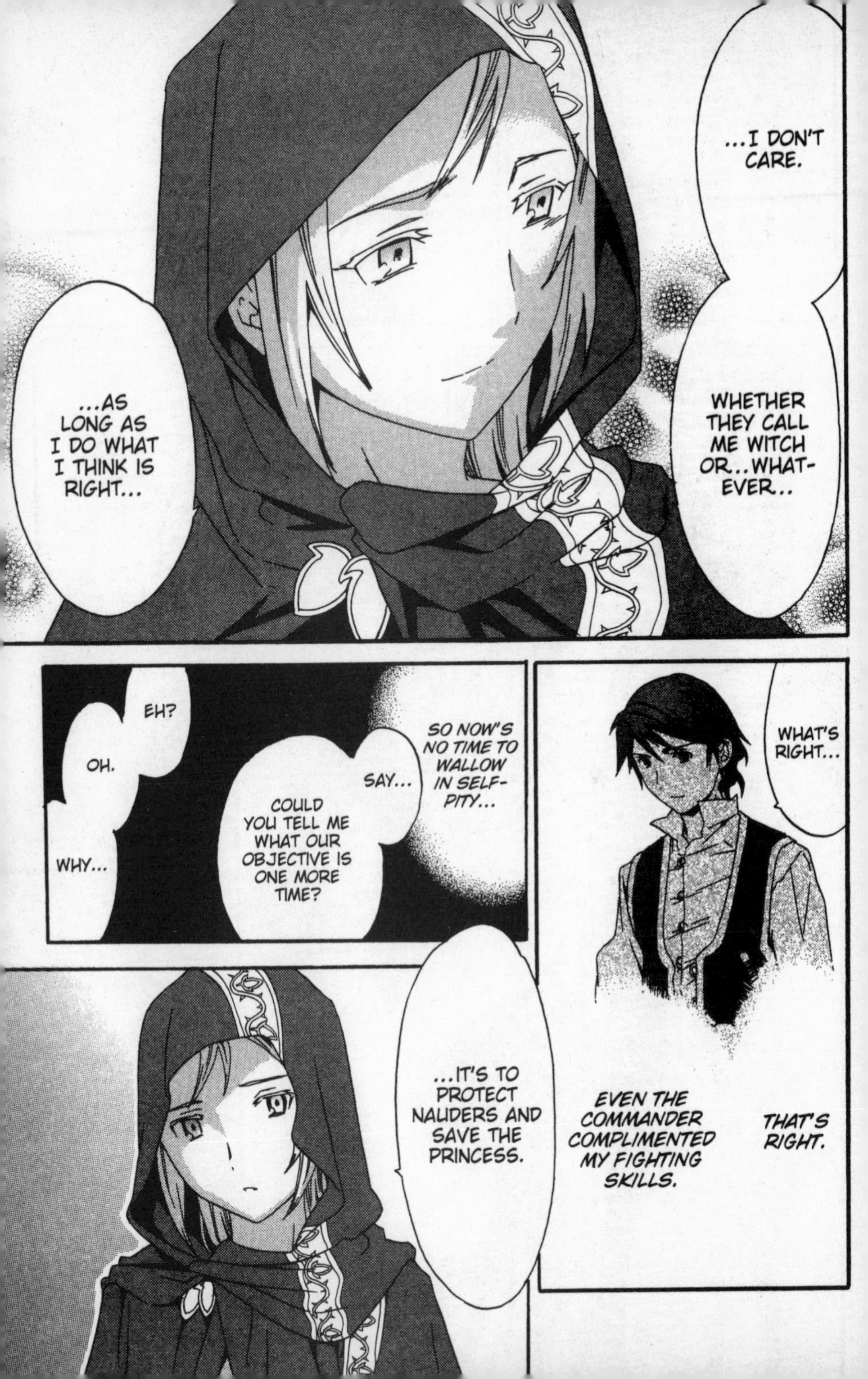
...I DON'T CARE.
WHETHER THEY CALL ME WITCH OR...WHAT-EVER...
...AS LONG AS I DO WHAT I THINK IS RIGHT...
WHAT'S RIGHT...
THAT'S RIGHT.
EVEN THE COMMANDER COMPLIMENTED MY FIGHTING SKILLS.
SO NOW'S NO TIME TO WALLOW IN SELF-PITY...
SAY...
COULD YOU TELL ME WHAT OUR OBJECTIVE IS ONE MORE TIME?
EH?
OH.
WHY...
...IT'S TO PROTECT NAUDERS AND SAVE THE PRINCESS.

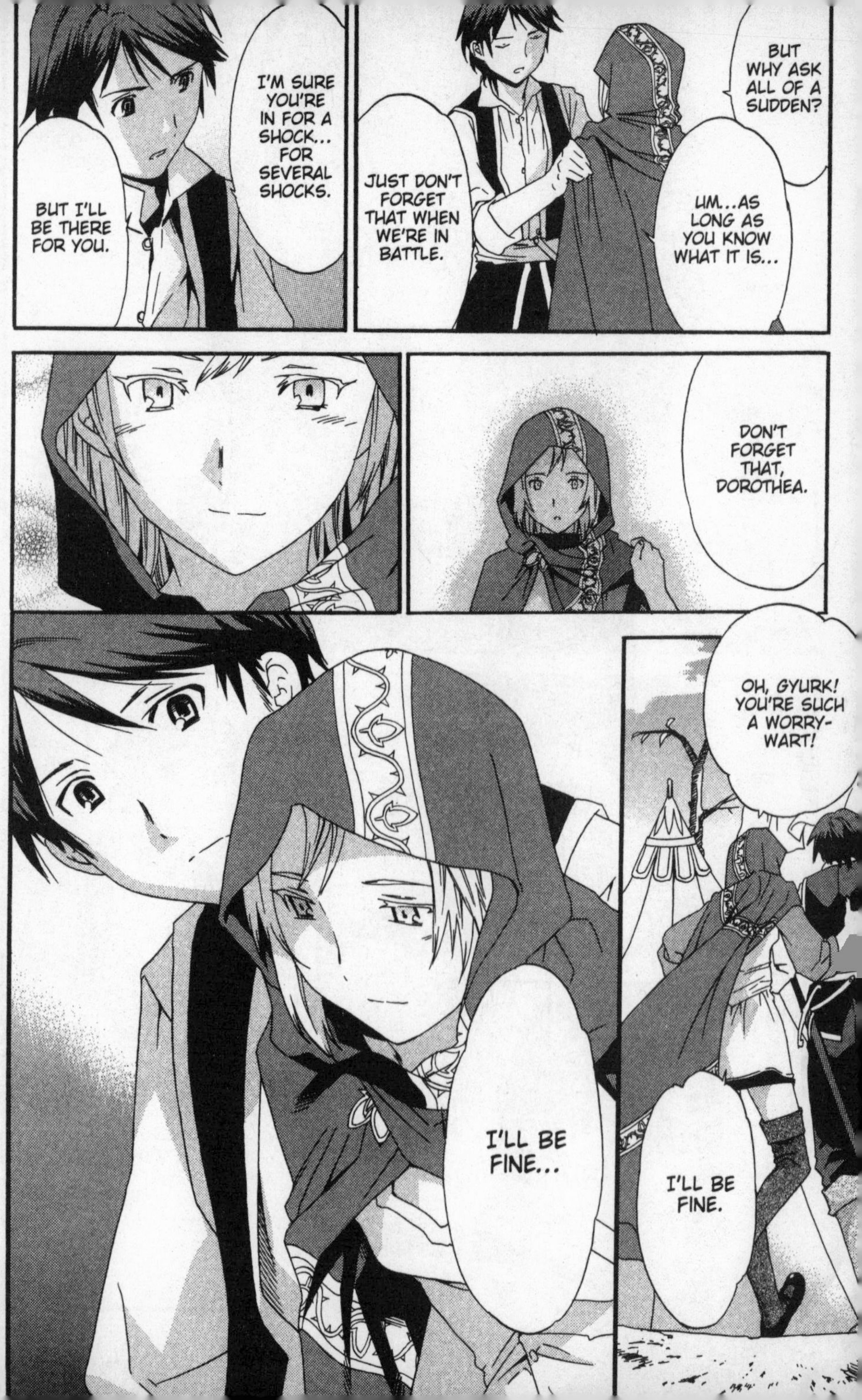
BUT WHY ASK ALL OF A SUDDEN?
UM...AS LONG AS YOU KNOW WHAT IT IS...
JUST DON'T FORGET THAT WHEN WE'RE IN BATTLE.
I'M SURE YOU'RE IN FOR A SHOCK... FOR SEVERAL SHOCKS.
BUT I'LL BE THERE FOR YOU.
DON'T FORGET THAT, DOROTHEA.
OH, GYURK! YOU'RE SUCH A WORRY-WART!
I'LL BE FINE.
I'LL BE FINE...

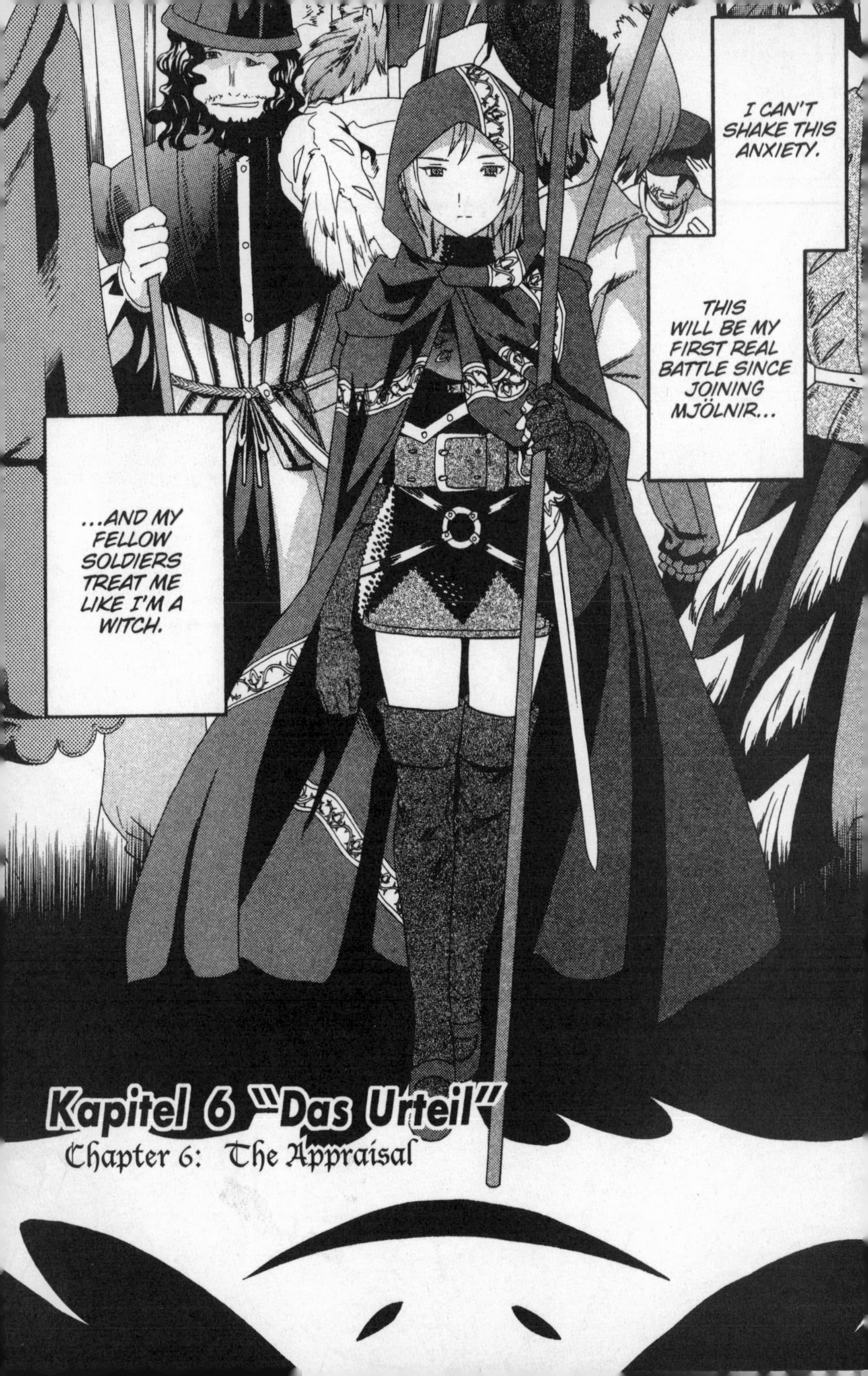
I CAN'T SHAKE THIS ANXIETY.
THIS WILL BE MY FIRST REAL BATTLE SINCE JOINING MJÖLNIR...
...AND MY FELLOW SOLDIERS TREAT ME LIKE I'M A WITCH.
Kapitel 6 "Das Urteil"
Chapter 6: The Appraisal

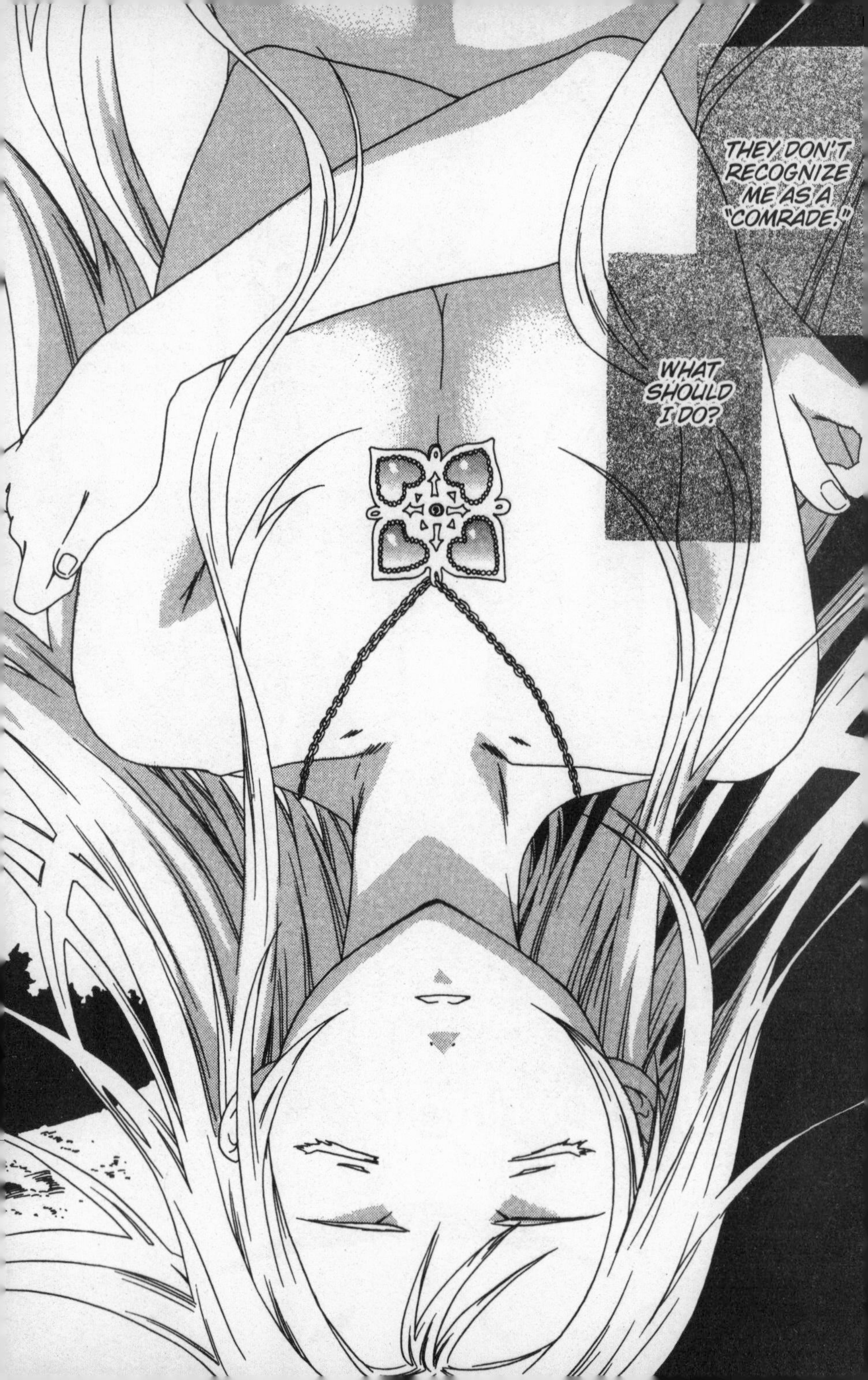
THEY DON'T RECOGNIZE ME AS A "COMRADE."
WHAT SHOULD I DO?

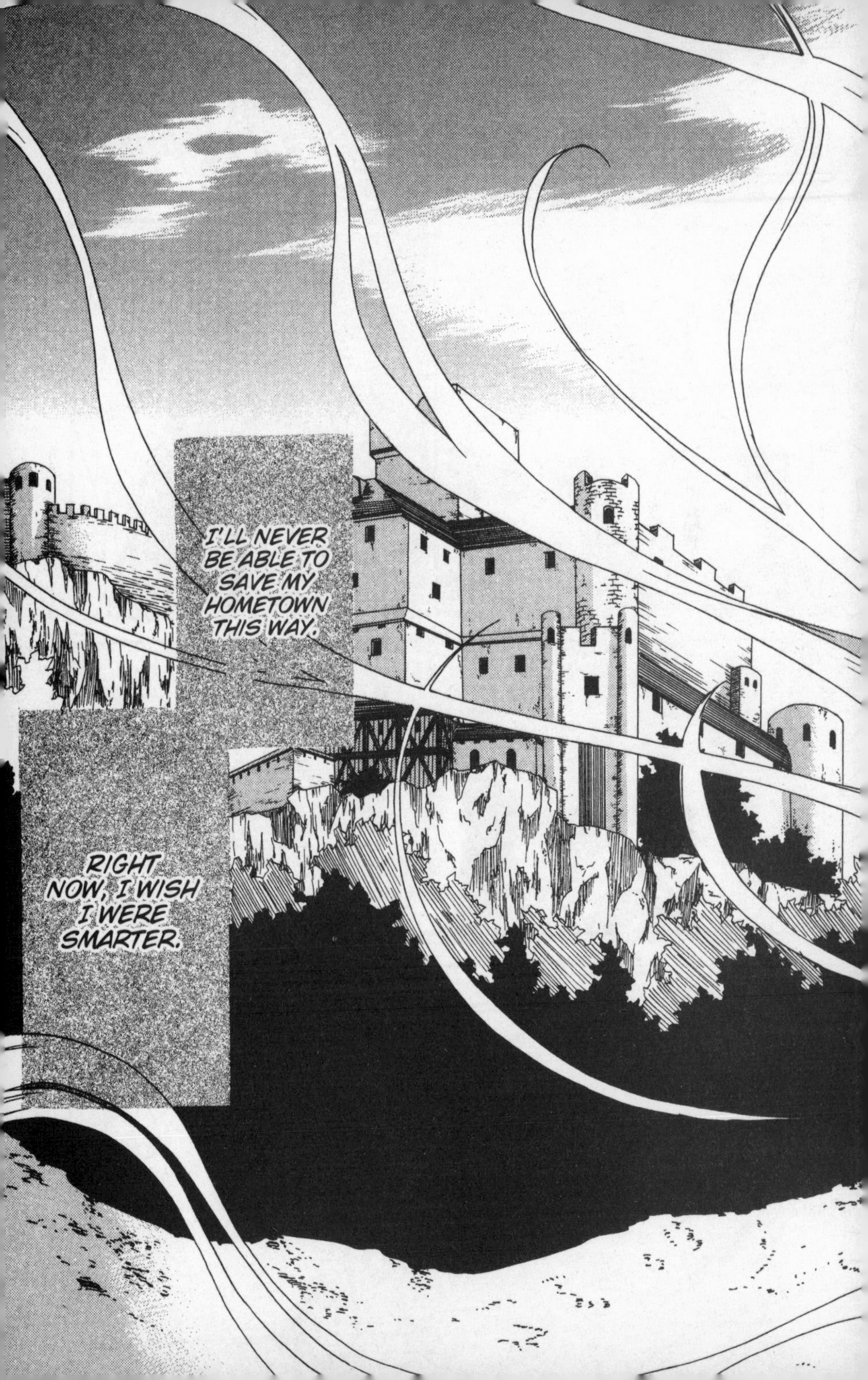
I'LL NEVER BE ABLE TO SAVE MY HOMETOWN THIS WAY.
RIGHT NOW, I WISH I WERE SMARTER.

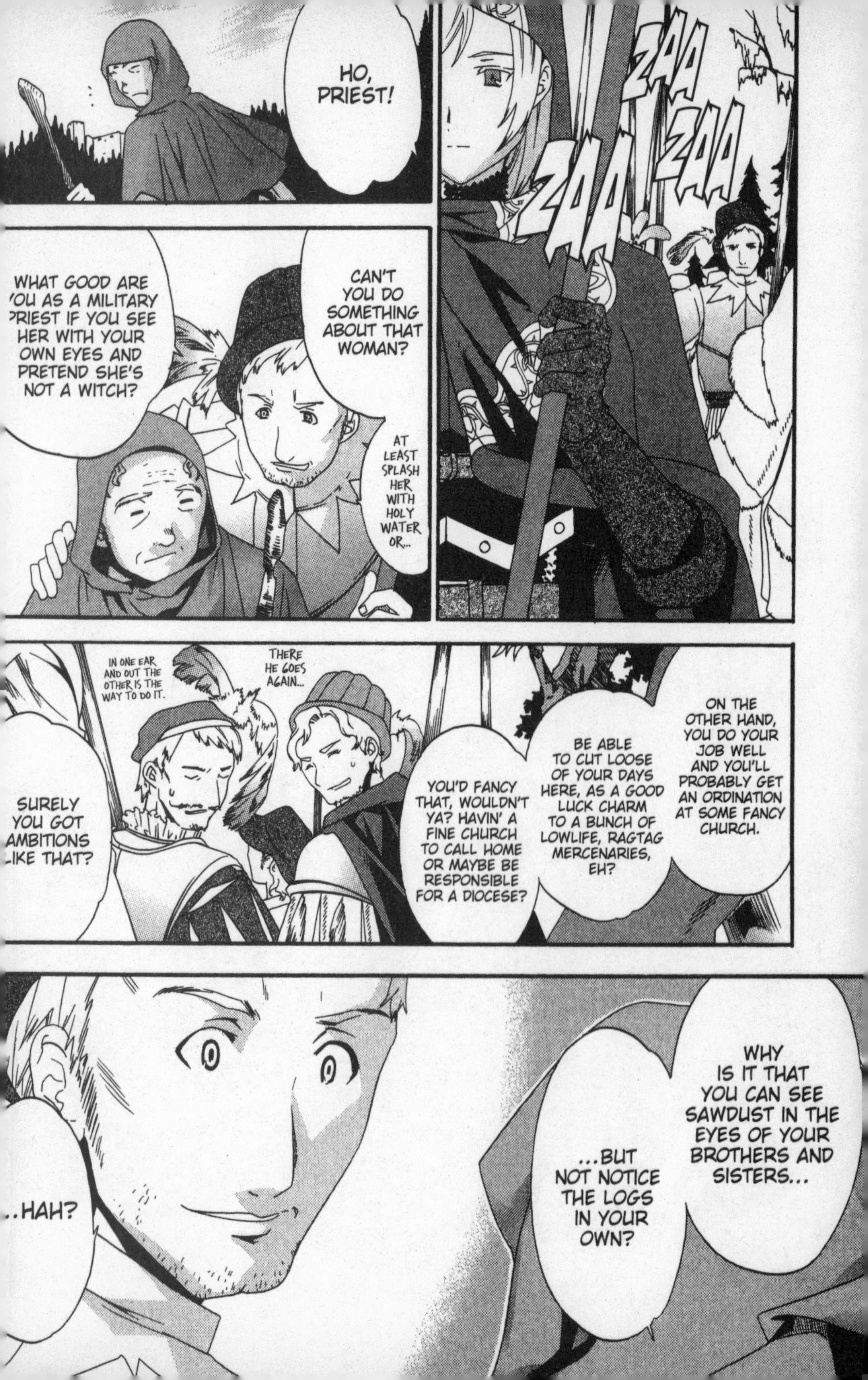
ZAA ZAA ZAA ZAA
HO, PRIEST!
CAN'T YOU DO SOMETHING ABOUT THAT WOMAN?
WHAT GOOD ARE OU AS A MILITARY RIEST IF YOU SEE HER WITH YOUR OWN EYES AND PRETEND SHE'S NOT A WITCH?
AT LEAST SPLASH HER WITH HOLY WATER OR...
ON THE OTHER HAND, YOU DO YOUR JOB WELL AND YOU'LL PROBABLY GET AN ORDINATION AT SOME FANCY CHURCH.
BE ABLE TO CUT LOOSE OF YOUR DAYS HERE, AS A GOOD LUCK CHARM TO A BUNCH OF LOWLIFE, RAGTAG MERCENARIES, EH?
YOU'D FANCY THAT, WOULDN'T YA? HAVIN' A FINE CHURCH TO CALL HOME OR MAYBE BE RESPONSIBLE FOR A DIOCESE?
THERE HE GOES AGAIN...
IN ONE EAR AND OUT THE OTHER IS THE WAY TO DO IT.
SURELY YOU GOT AMBITIONS LIKE THAT?
WHY IS IT THAT YOU CAN SEE SAWDUST IN THE EYES OF YOUR BROTHERS AND SISTERS...
...BUT NOT NOTICE THE LOGS IN YOUR OWN?
..HAH?

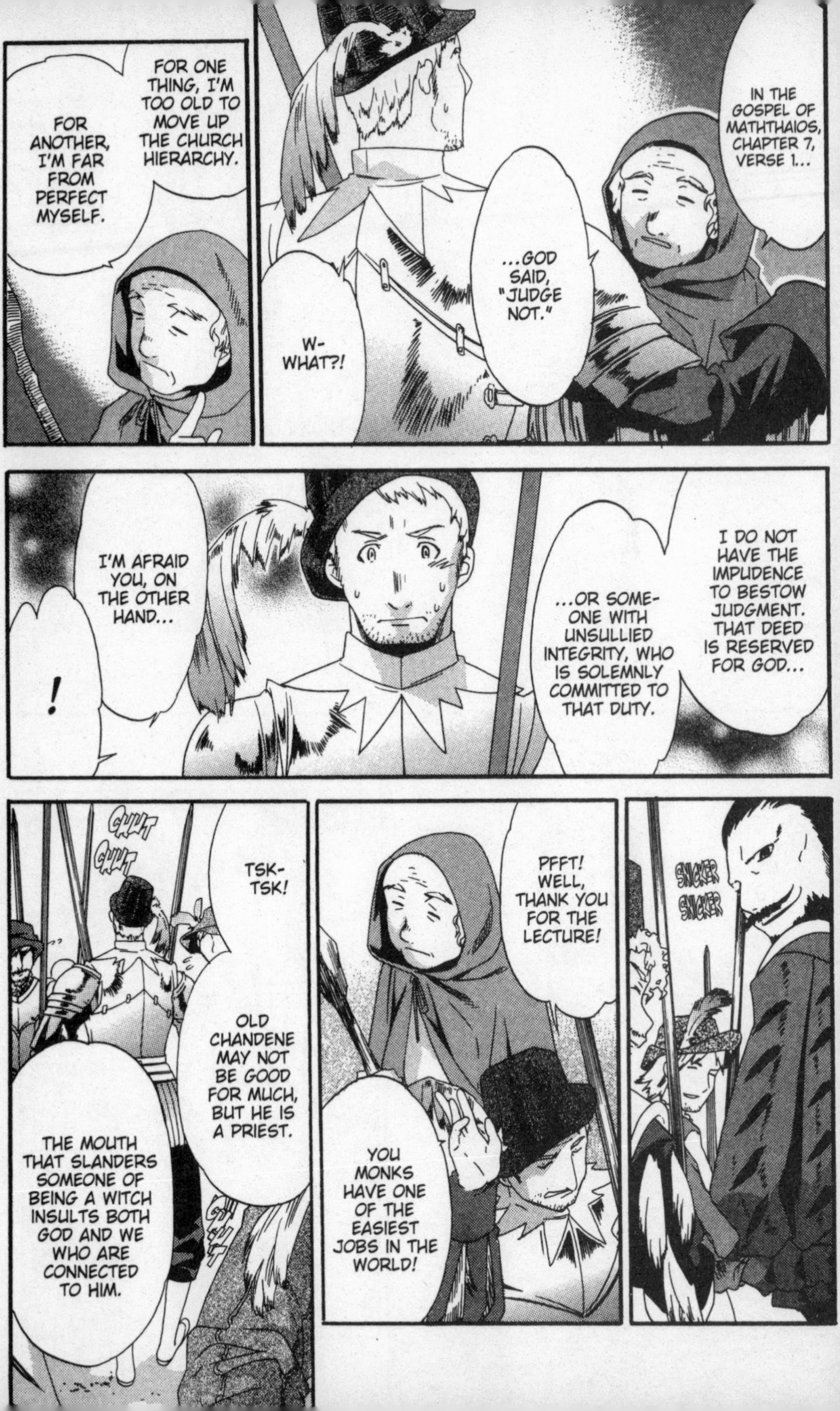
IN THE GOSPEL OF MATHTHAIOS, CHAPTER 7, VERSE 1...
...GOD SAID, "JUDGE NOT."
W-WHAT?!
FOR ONE THING, I'M TOO OLD TO MOVE UP THE CHURCH HIERARCHY.
FOR ANOTHER, I'M FAR FROM PERFECT MYSELF.
I DO NOT HAVE THE IMPUDENCE TO BESTOW JUDGMENT. THAT DEED IS RESERVED FOR GOD...
...OR SOME-ONE WITH UNSULLIED INTEGRITY, WHO IS SOLEMNLY COMMITTED TO THAT DUTY.
I'M AFRAID YOU, ON THE OTHER HAND...
!
SNICKER
SNICKER
PFFT! WELL, THANK YOU FOR THE LECTURE!
YOU MONKS HAVE ONE OF THE EASIEST JOBS IN THE WORLD!
CHUT
CHUT
TSK-TSK!
OLD CHANDENE MAY NOT BE GOOD FOR MUCH, BUT HE IS A PRIEST.
THE MOUTH THAT SLANDERS SOMEONE OF BEING A WITCH INSULTS BOTH GOD AND WE WHO ARE CONNECTED TO HIM.

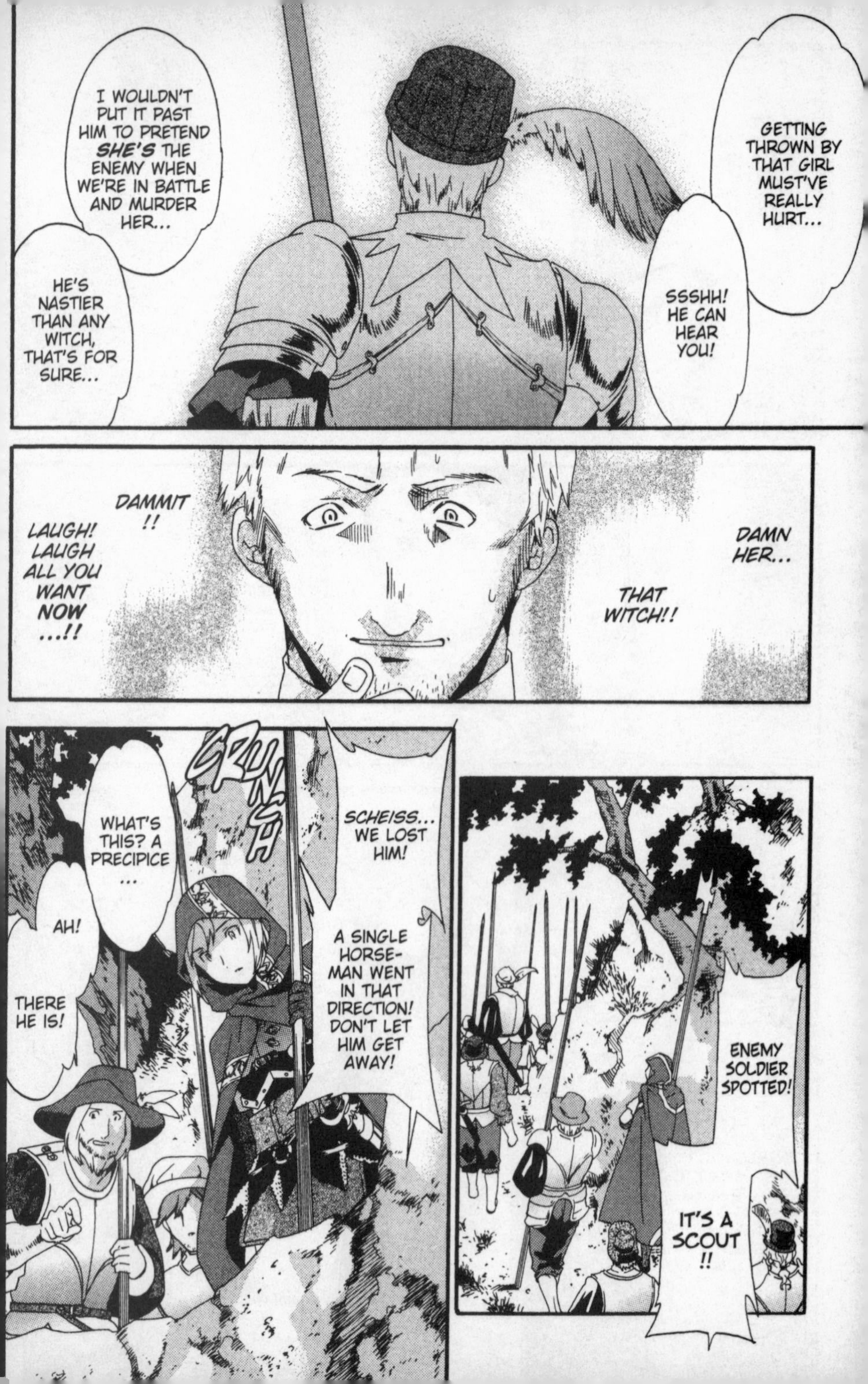

GETTING THROWN BY THAT GIRL MUST'VE REALLY HURT...
I WOULDN'T PUT IT PAST HIM TO PRETEND *SHE'S* THE ENEMY WHEN WE'RE IN BATTLE AND MURDER HER...
HE'S NASTIER THAN ANY WITCH, THAT'S FOR SURE...
SSSHH! HE CAN HEAR YOU!
DAMN HER...
THAT WITCH!!
DAMMIT!!
LAUGH! LAUGH ALL YOU WANT NOW...!!
ENEMY SOLDIER SPOTTED!
IT'S A SCOUT!!
SCHEISS... WE LOST HIM!
A SINGLE HORSEMAN WENT IN THAT DIRECTION! DON'T LET HIM GET AWAY!
CRUNCH
WHAT'S THIS? A PRECIPICE...
AH!
THERE HE IS!

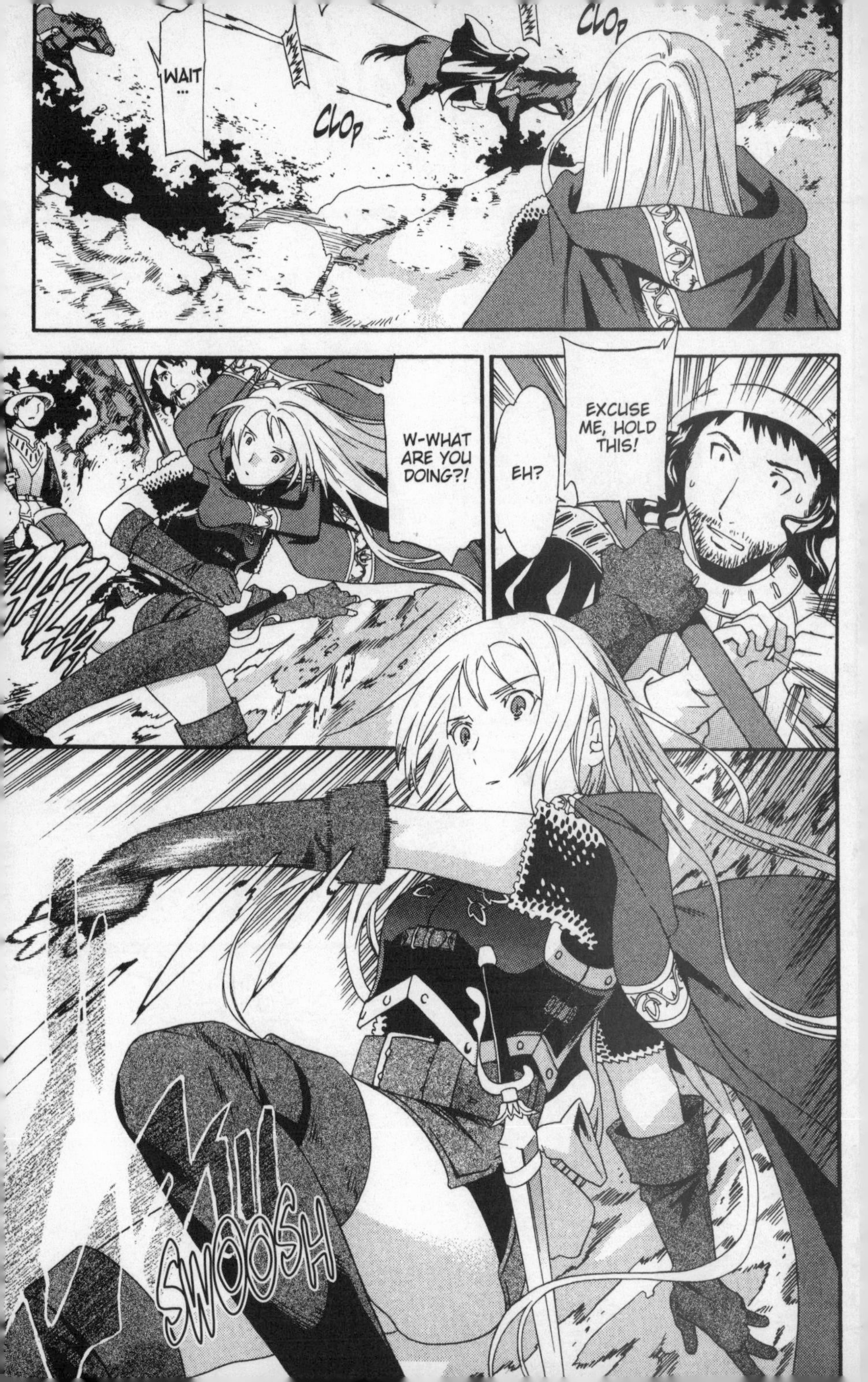
CLOP
WAIT ...
CLOP
EXCUSE ME, HOLD THIS!
EH?
W-WHAT ARE YOU DOING?!
SWOOSH

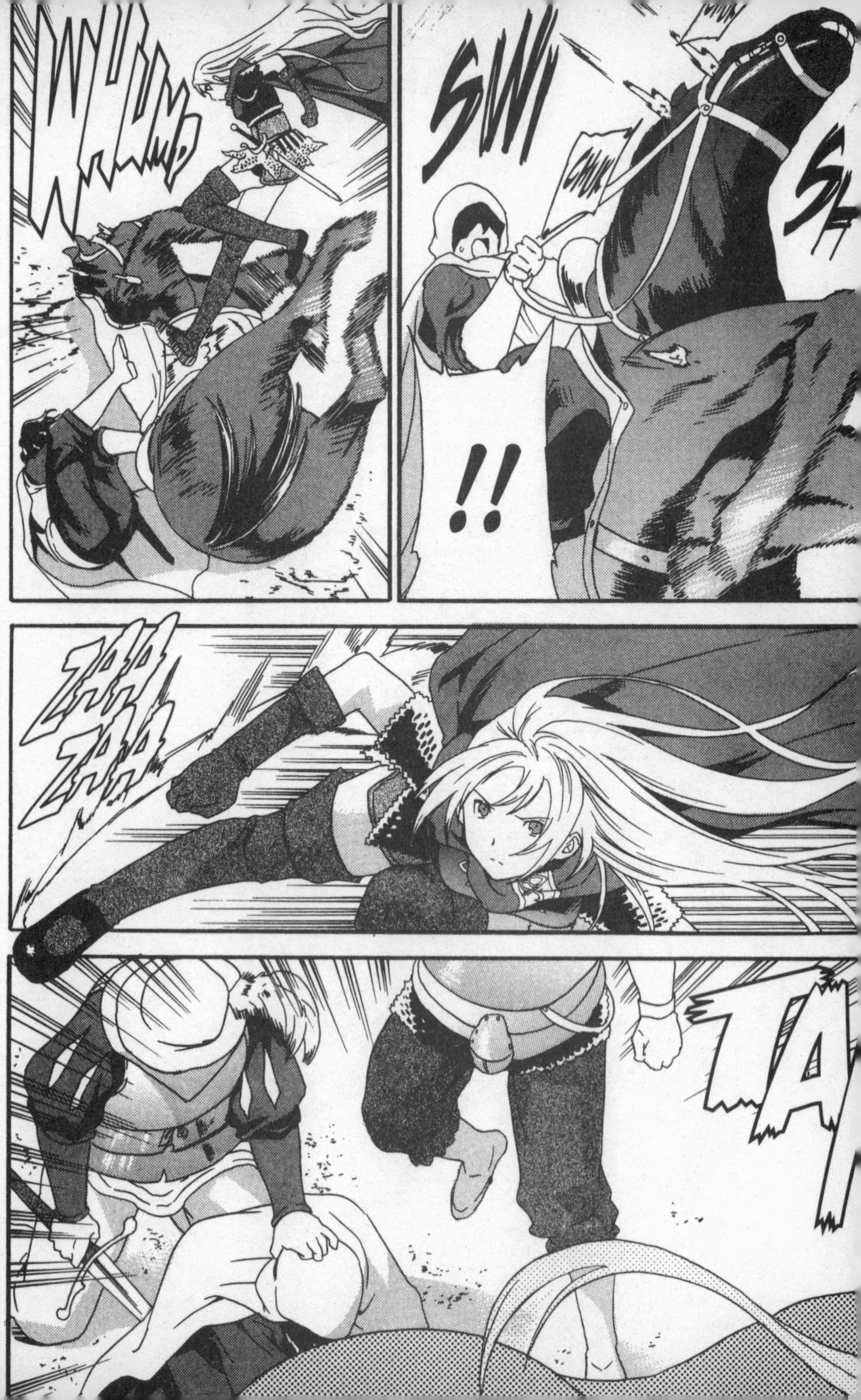
SWI
!!
WHUMP
TA

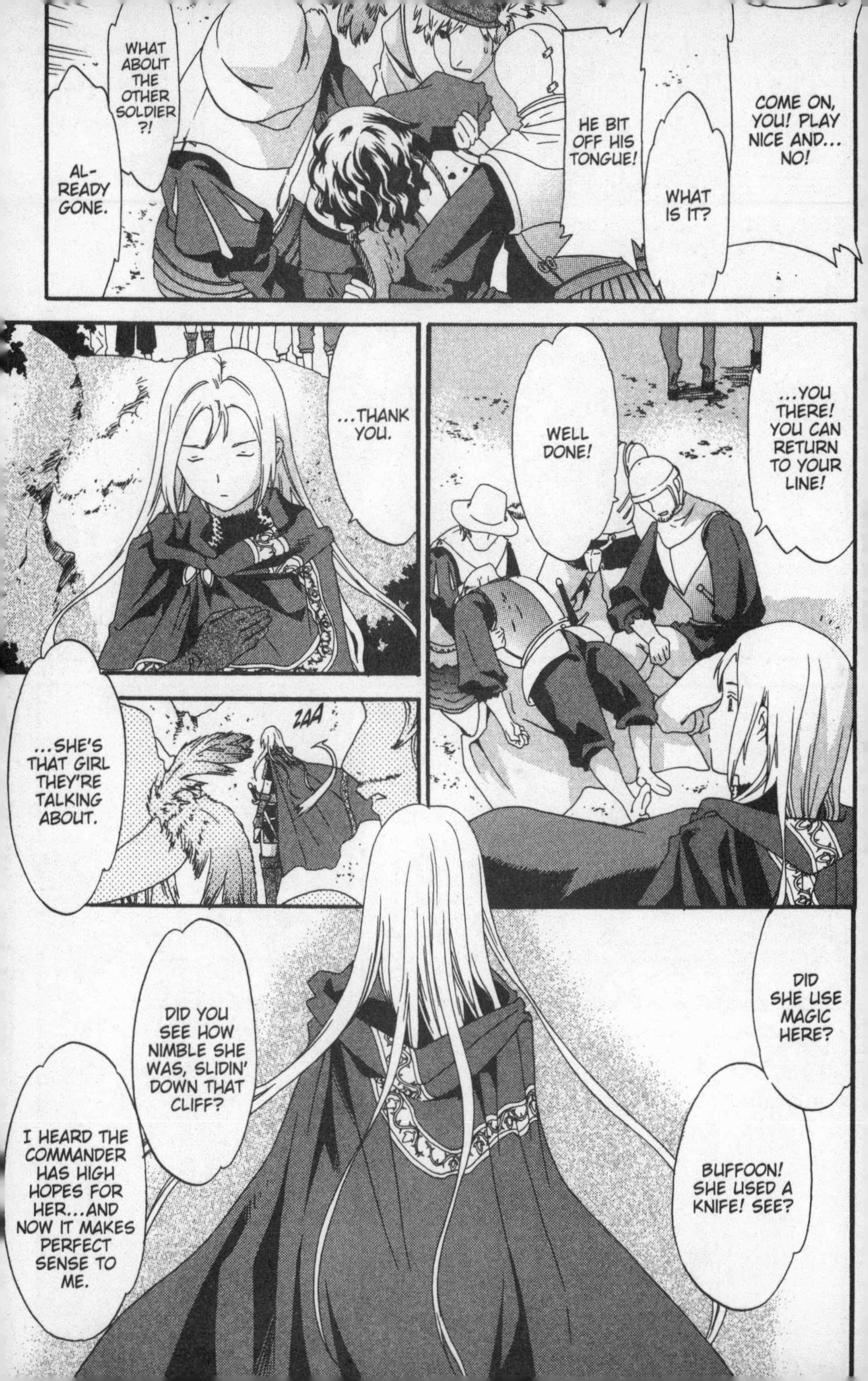
COME ON, YOU! PLAY NICE AND... NO!
WHAT IS IT?
HE BIT OFF HIS TONGUE!
WHAT ABOUT THE OTHER SOLDIER?!
AL-READY GONE.
...YOU THERE! YOU CAN RETURN TO YOUR LINE!
WELL DONE!
...THANK YOU.
ZAA
...SHE'S THAT GIRL THEY'RE TALKING ABOUT.
DID SHE USE MAGIC HERE?
BUFFOON! SHE USED A KNIFE! SEE?
DID YOU SEE HOW NIMBLE SHE WAS, SLIDIN' DOWN THAT CLIFF?
I HEARD THE COMMANDER HAS HIGH HOPES FOR HER...AND NOW IT MAKES PERFECT SENSE TO ME.

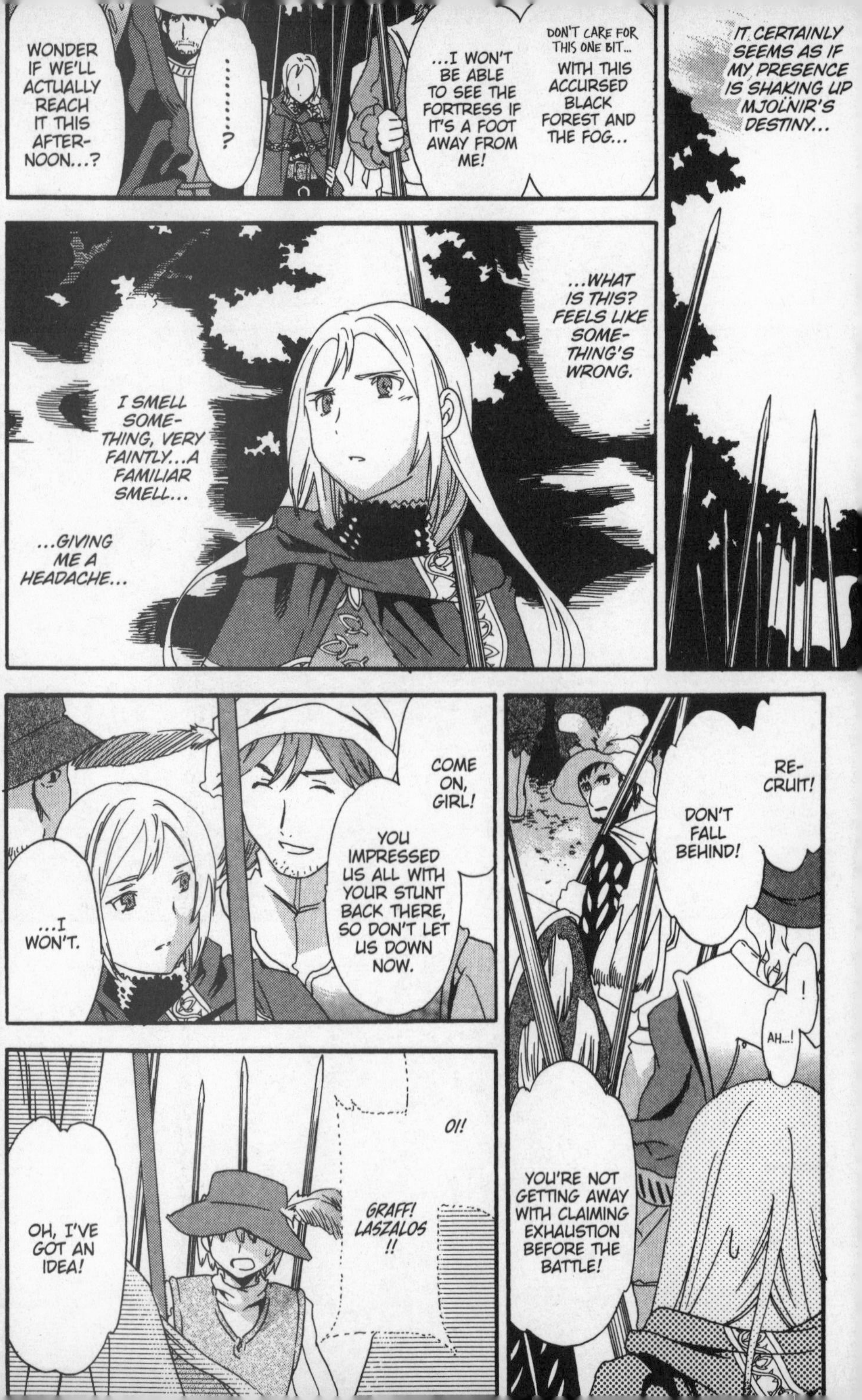
IT CERTAINLY SEEMS AS IF MY PRESENCE IS SHAKING UP MJOLNIR'S DESTINY...
DON'T CARE FOR THIS ONE BIT... WITH THIS ACCURSED BLACK FOREST AND THE FOG...
...I WON'T BE ABLE TO SEE THE FORTRESS IF IT'S A FOOT AWAY FROM ME!
......?
WONDER IF WE'LL ACTUALLY REACH IT THIS AFTER-NOON...?
...WHAT IS THIS? FEELS LIKE SOME-THING'S WRONG.
I SMELL SOME-THING, VERY FAINTLY...A FAMILIAR SMELL...
...GIVING ME A HEADACHE...
RE-CRUIT!
DON'T FALL BEHIND!
!
AH...!
YOU'RE NOT GETTING AWAY WITH CLAIMING EXHAUSTION BEFORE THE BATTLE!
COME ON, GIRL!
YOU IMPRESSED US ALL WITH YOUR STUNT BACK THERE, SO DON'T LET US DOWN NOW.
...I WON'T.
OI!
GRAFF! LASZALOS!!
OH, I'VE GOT AN IDEA!

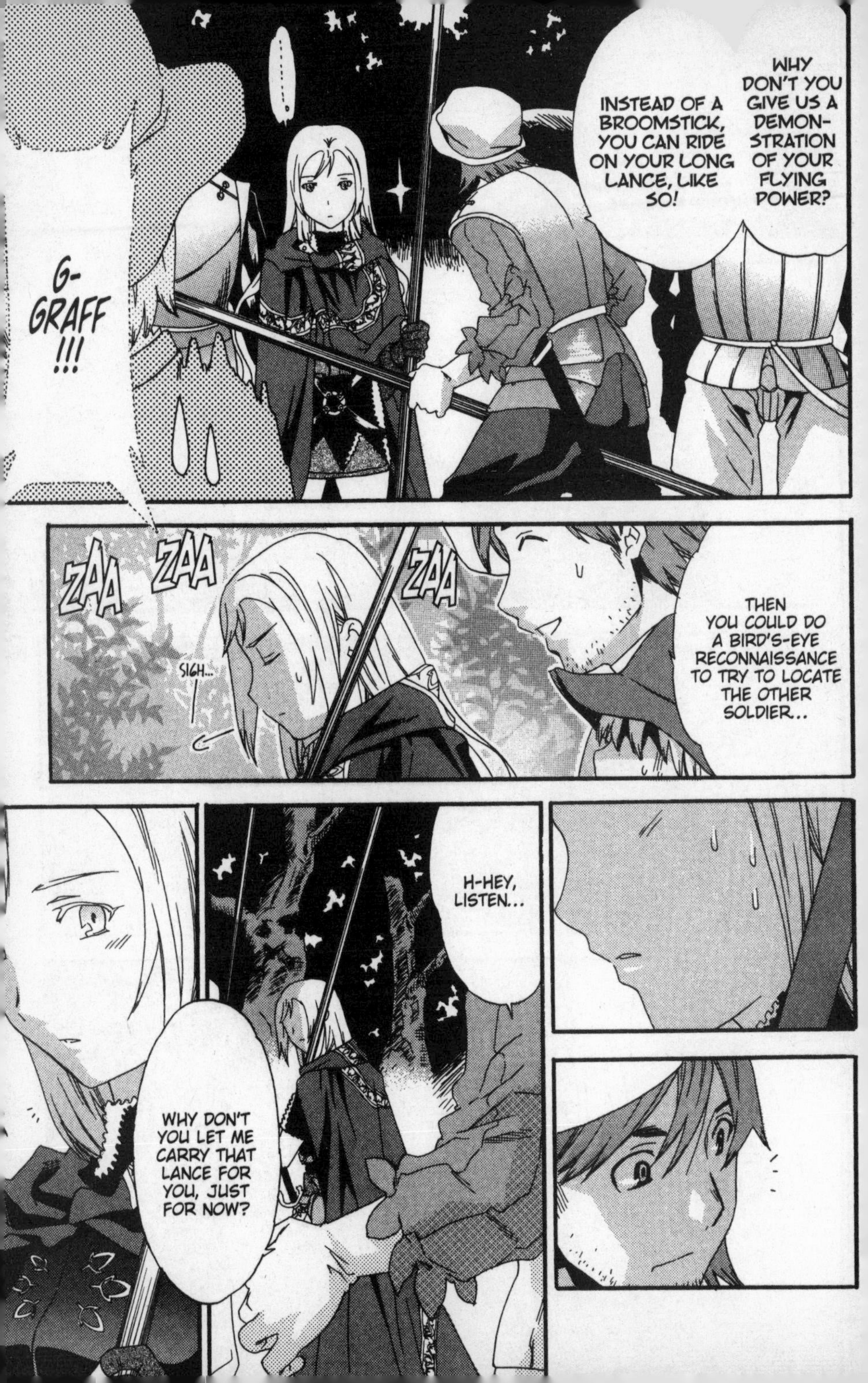
WHY DON'T YOU GIVE US A DEMON-STRATION OF YOUR FLYING POWER?
INSTEAD OF A BROOMSTICK, YOU CAN RIDE ON YOUR LONG LANCE, LIKE SO!
......
G-GRAFF!!!
THEN YOU COULD DO A BIRD'S-EYE RECONNAISSANCE TO TRY TO LOCATE THE OTHER SOLDIER...
ZAA
ZAA
ZAA
SIGH...
H-HEY, LISTEN...
WHY DON'T YOU LET ME CARRY THAT LANCE FOR YOU, JUST FOR NOW?

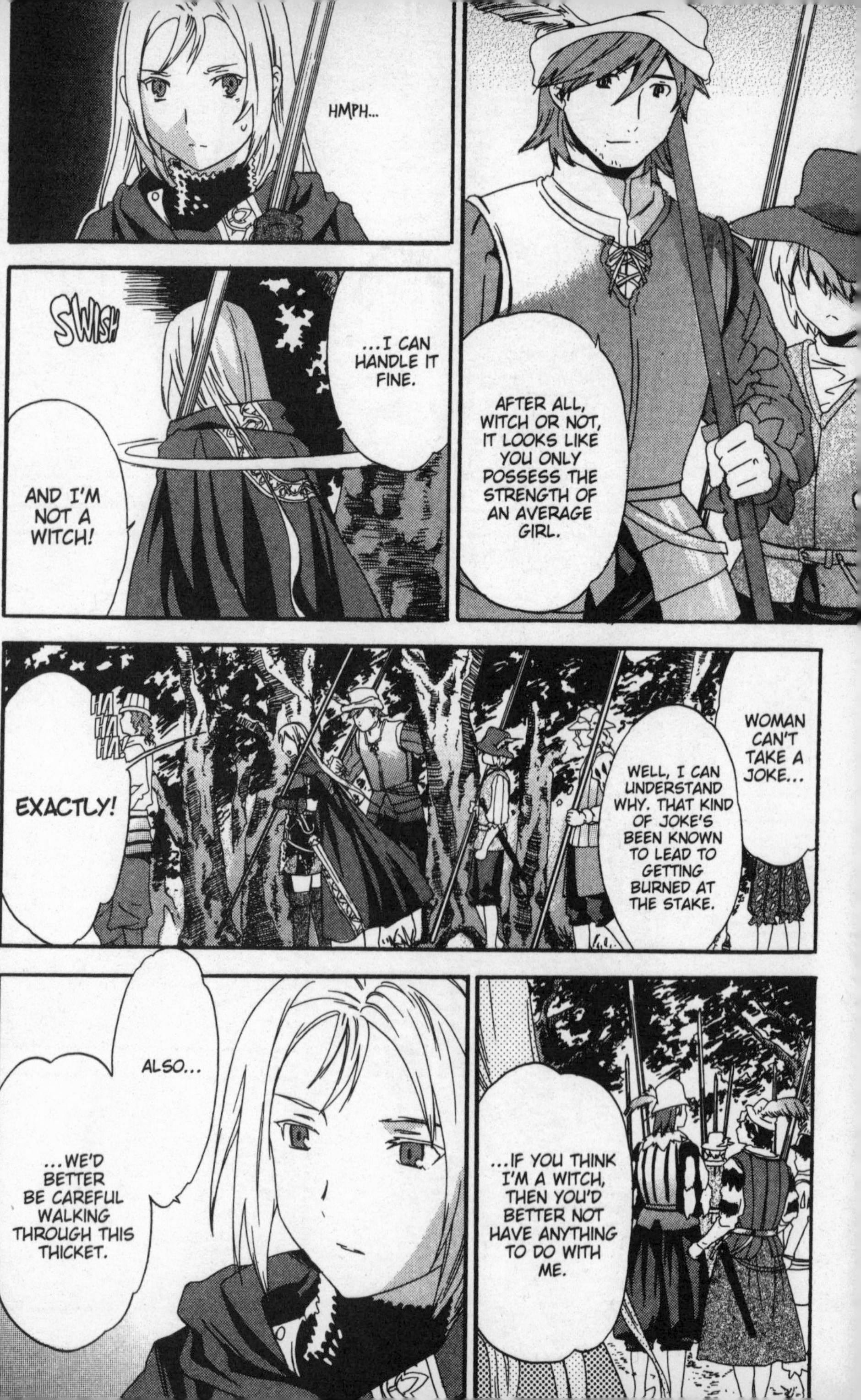
AFTER ALL, WITCH OR NOT, IT LOOKS LIKE YOU ONLY POSSESS THE STRENGTH OF AN AVERAGE GIRL.
HMPH...
SWISH
...I CAN HANDLE IT FINE.
AND I'M NOT A WITCH!
WOMAN CAN'T TAKE A JOKE...
WELL, I CAN UNDERSTAND WHY. THAT KIND OF JOKE'S BEEN KNOWN TO LEAD TO GETTING BURNED AT THE STAKE.
HA HA HA HA
EXACTLY!
...IF YOU THINK I'M A WITCH, THEN YOU'D BETTER NOT HAVE ANYTHING TO DO WITH ME.
ALSO...
...WE'D BETTER BE CAREFUL WALKING THROUGH THIS THICKET.

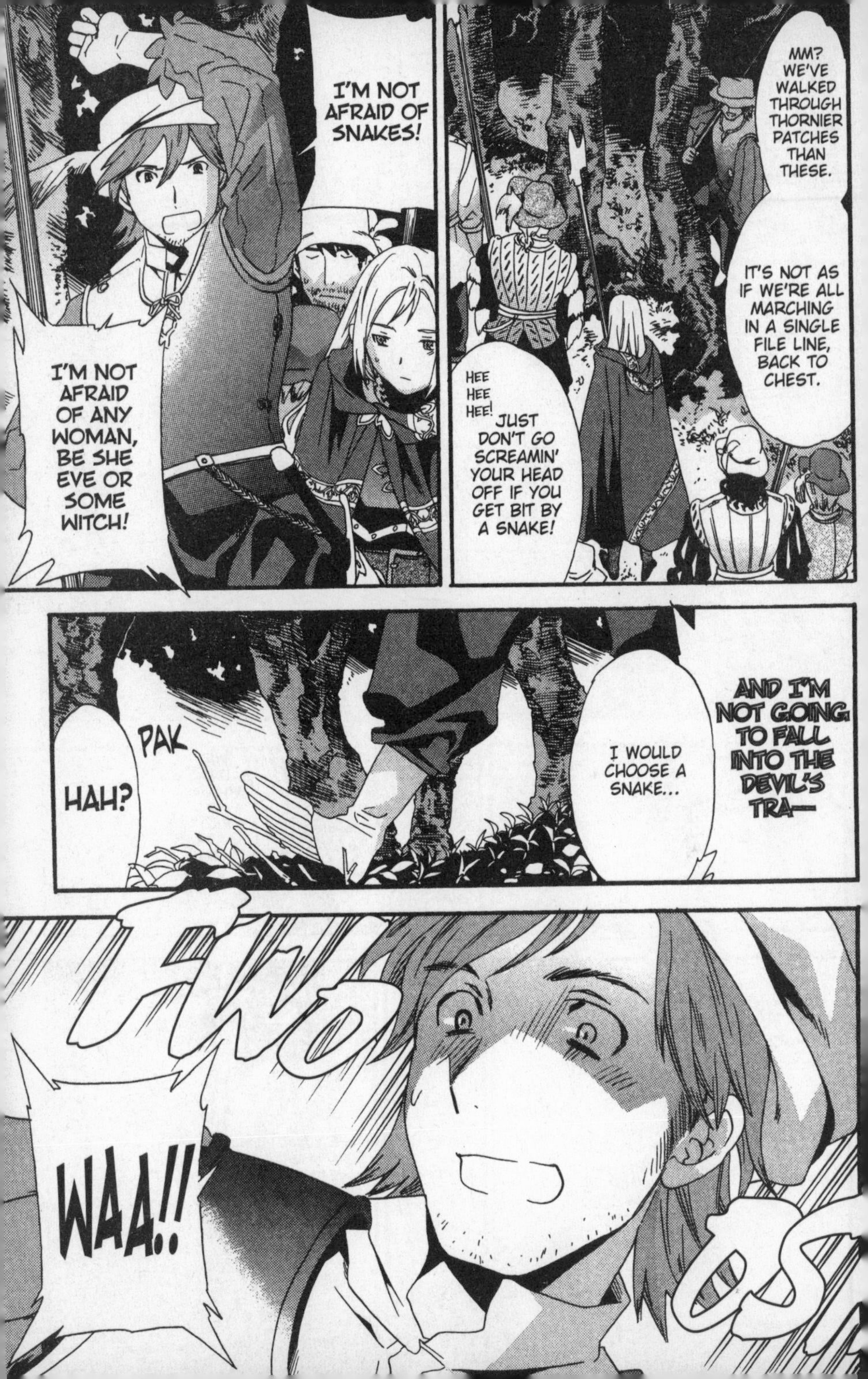
MM? WE'VE WALKED THROUGH THORNIER PATCHES THAN THESE.
IT'S NOT AS IF WE'RE ALL MARCHING IN A SINGLE FILE LINE, BACK TO CHEST.
HEE HEE HEE!
JUST DON'T GO SCREAMIN' YOUR HEAD OFF IF YOU GET BIT BY A SNAKE!
I'M NOT AFRAID OF SNAKES!
I'M NOT AFRAID OF ANY WOMAN, BE SHE EVE OR SOME WITCH!
AND I'M NOT GOING TO FALL INTO THE DEVIL'S TRA—
I WOULD CHOOSE A SNAKE...
PAK
HAH?
WAA!!

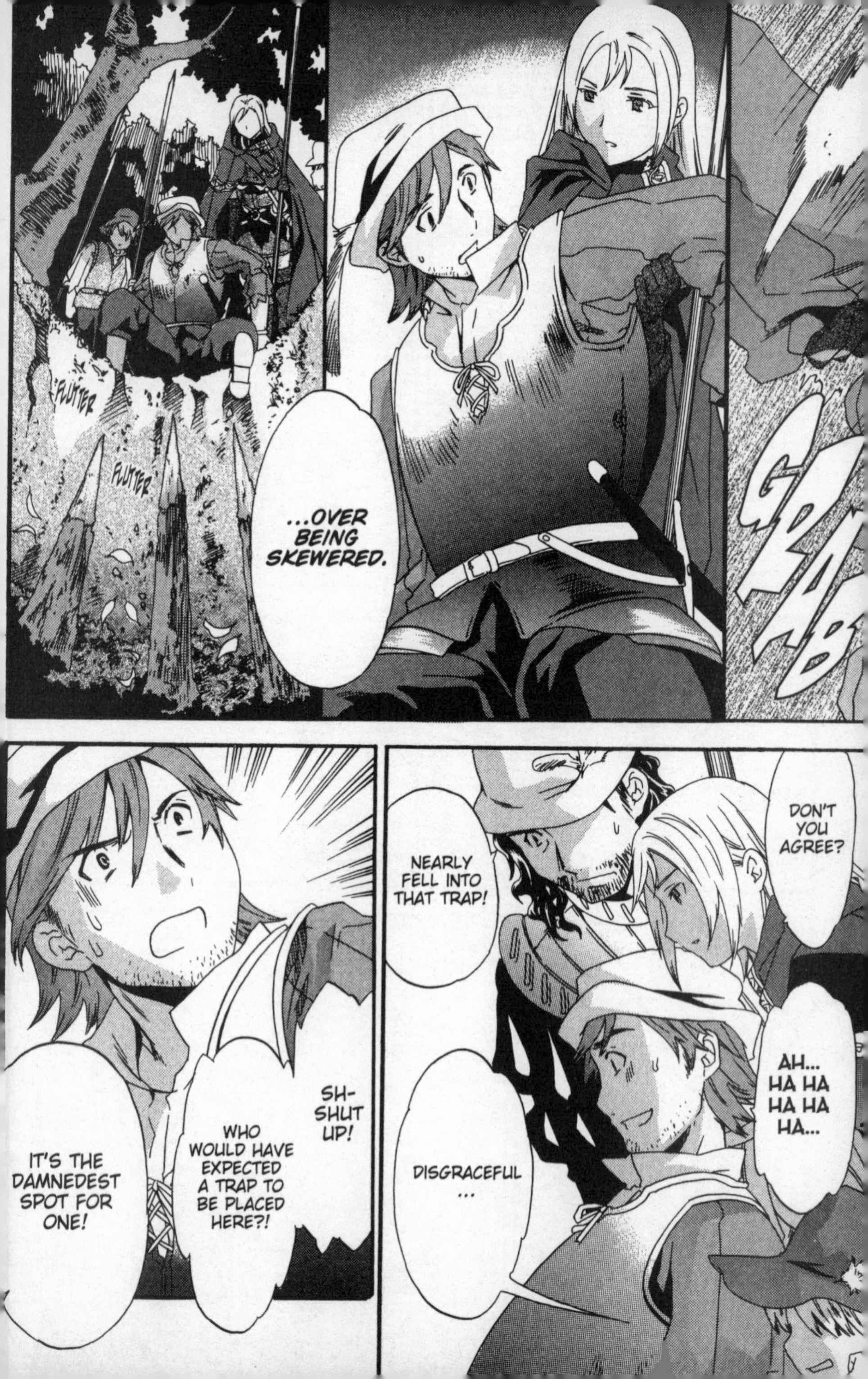
GRAB
...OVER BEING SKEWERED.
FLUTTER
FLUTTER
DON'T YOU AGREE?
NEARLY FELL INTO THAT TRAP!
AH... HA HA HA HA HA...
DISGRACEFUL...
SH-SHUT UP!
WHO WOULD HAVE EXPECTED A TRAP TO BE PLACED HERE?!
IT'S THE DAMNEDEST SPOT FOR ONE!

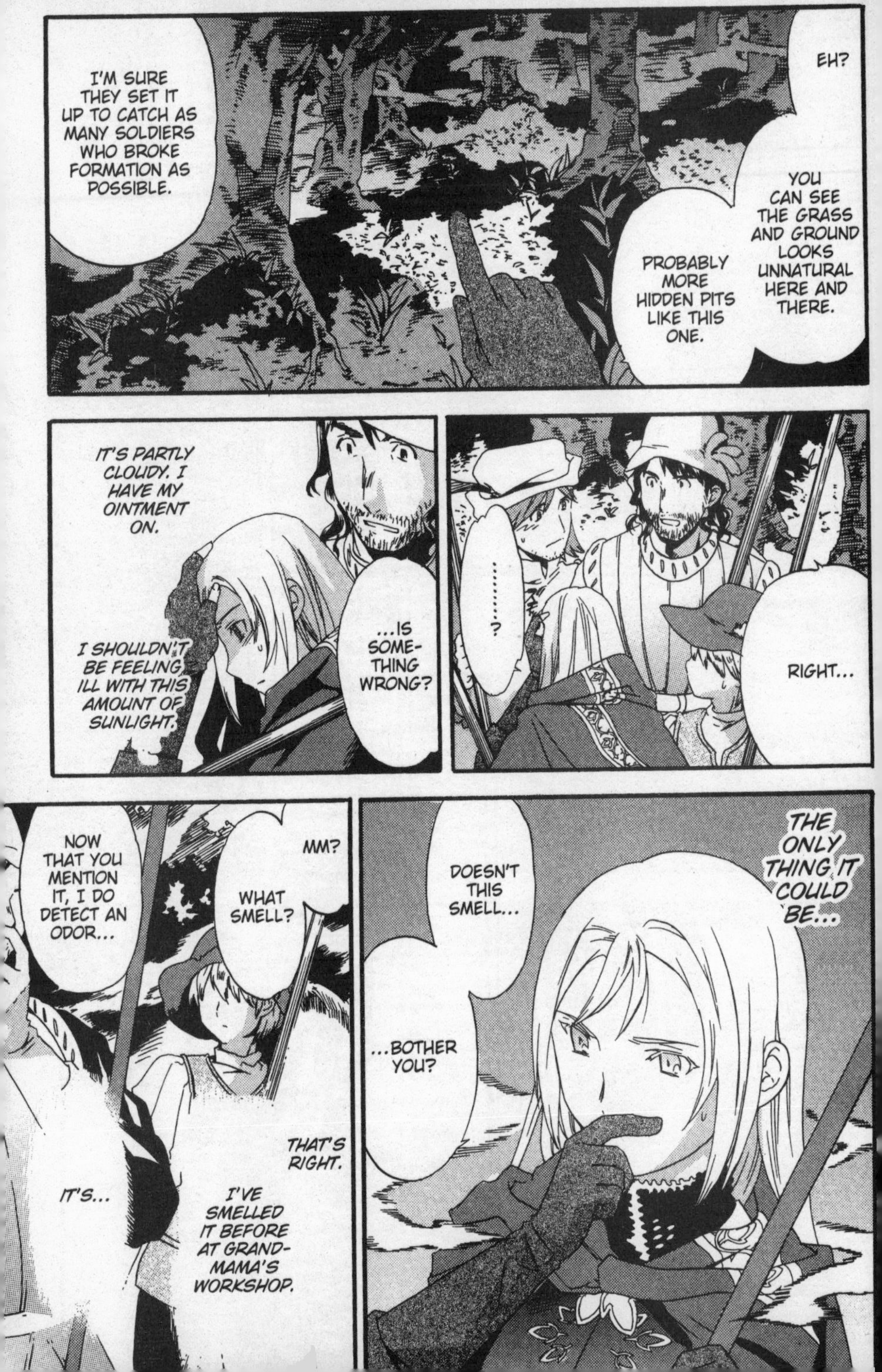
EH?
YOU CAN SEE THE GRASS AND GROUND LOOKS UNNATURAL HERE AND THERE.
PROBABLY MORE HIDDEN PITS LIKE THIS ONE.
I'M SURE THEY SET IT UP TO CATCH AS MANY SOLDIERS WHO BROKE FORMATION AS POSSIBLE.
RIGHT...
........?
...IS SOMETHING WRONG?
IT'S PARTLY CLOUDY. I HAVE MY OINTMENT ON.
I SHOULDN'T BE FEELING ILL WITH THIS AMOUNT OF SUNLIGHT.
THE ONLY THING IT COULD BE...
DOESN'T THIS SMELL...
...BOTHER YOU?
MM?
WHAT SMELL?
NOW THAT YOU MENTION IT, I DO DETECT AN ODOR...
THAT'S RIGHT.
I'VE SMELLED IT BEFORE AT GRAND-MAMA'S WORKSHOP.
IT'S...

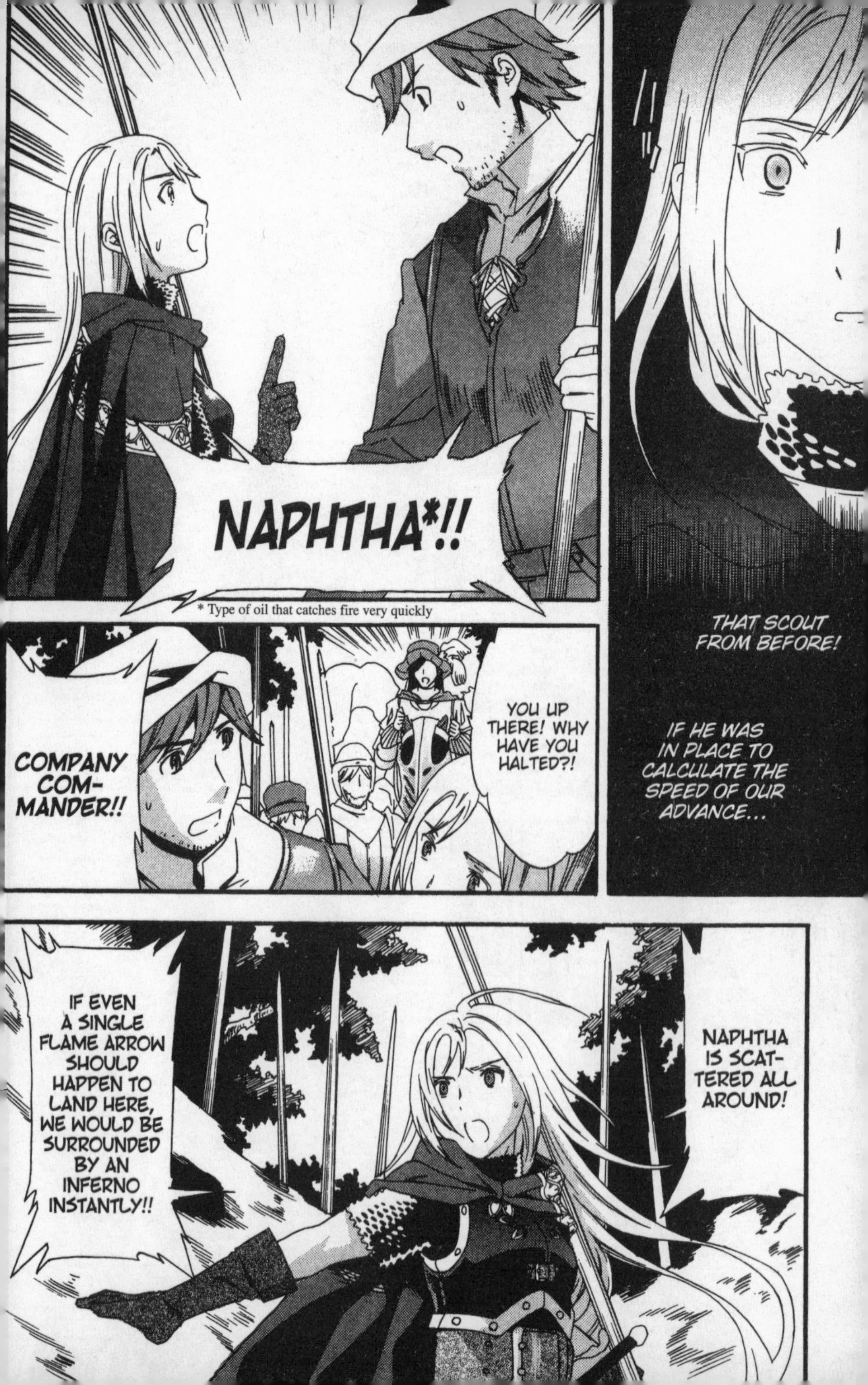
THAT SCOUT FROM BEFORE!
IF HE WAS IN PLACE TO CALCULATE THE SPEED OF OUR ADVANCE...
NAPHTHA*!!
* Type of oil that catches fire very quickly
YOU UP THERE! WHY HAVE YOU HALTED?!
COMPANY COMMANDER!!
NAPHTHA IS SCATTERED ALL AROUND!
IF EVEN A SINGLE FLAME ARROW SHOULD HAPPEN TO LAND HERE, WE WOULD BE SURROUNDED BY AN INFERNO INSTANTLY!!

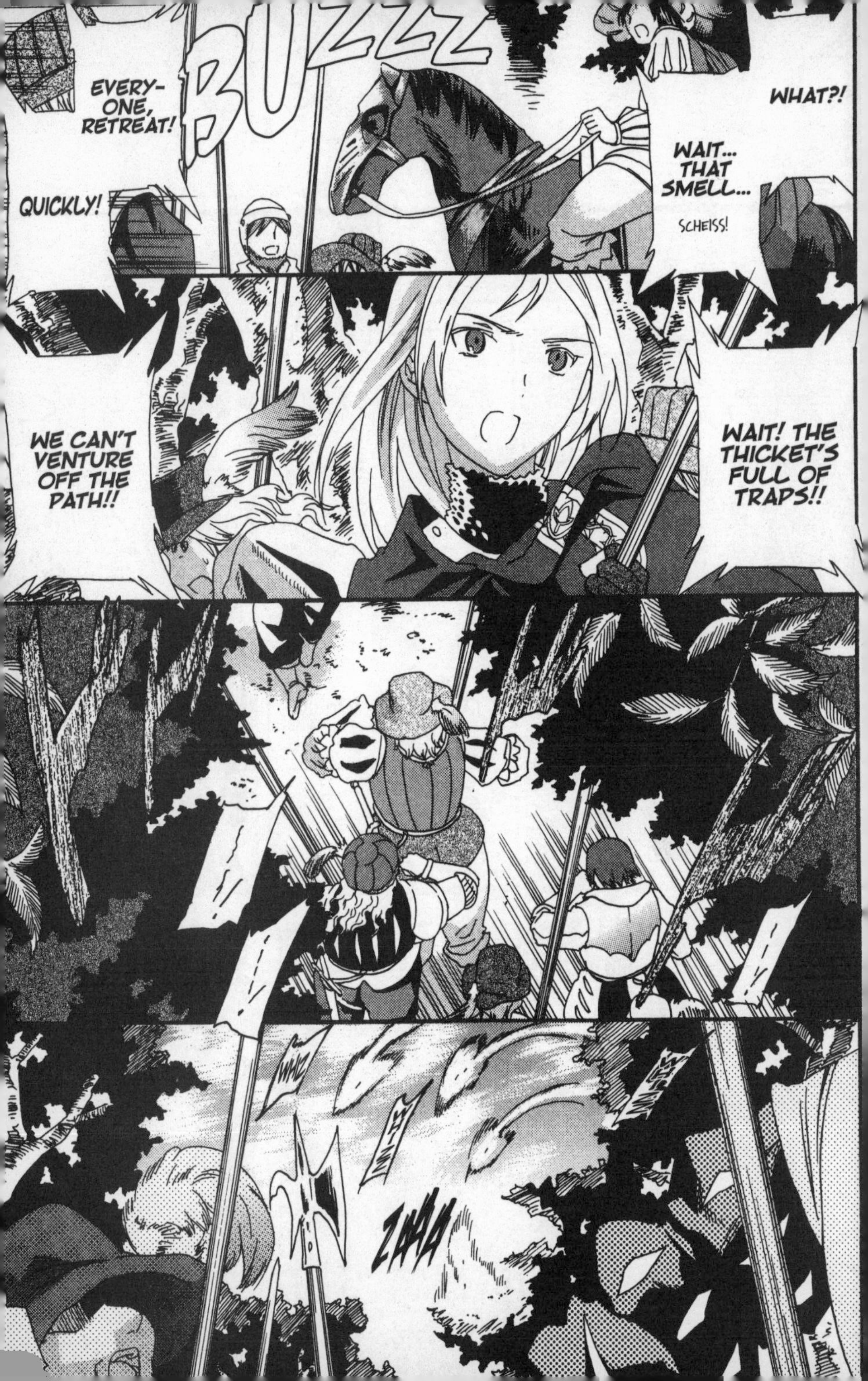
WHAT?!
WAIT... THAT SMELL...
SCHEISS!
BUZZZZ
EVERY-ONE, RETREAT!
QUICKLY!
WAIT! THE THICKET'S FULL OF TRAPS!!
WE CAN'T VENTURE OFF THE PATH!!

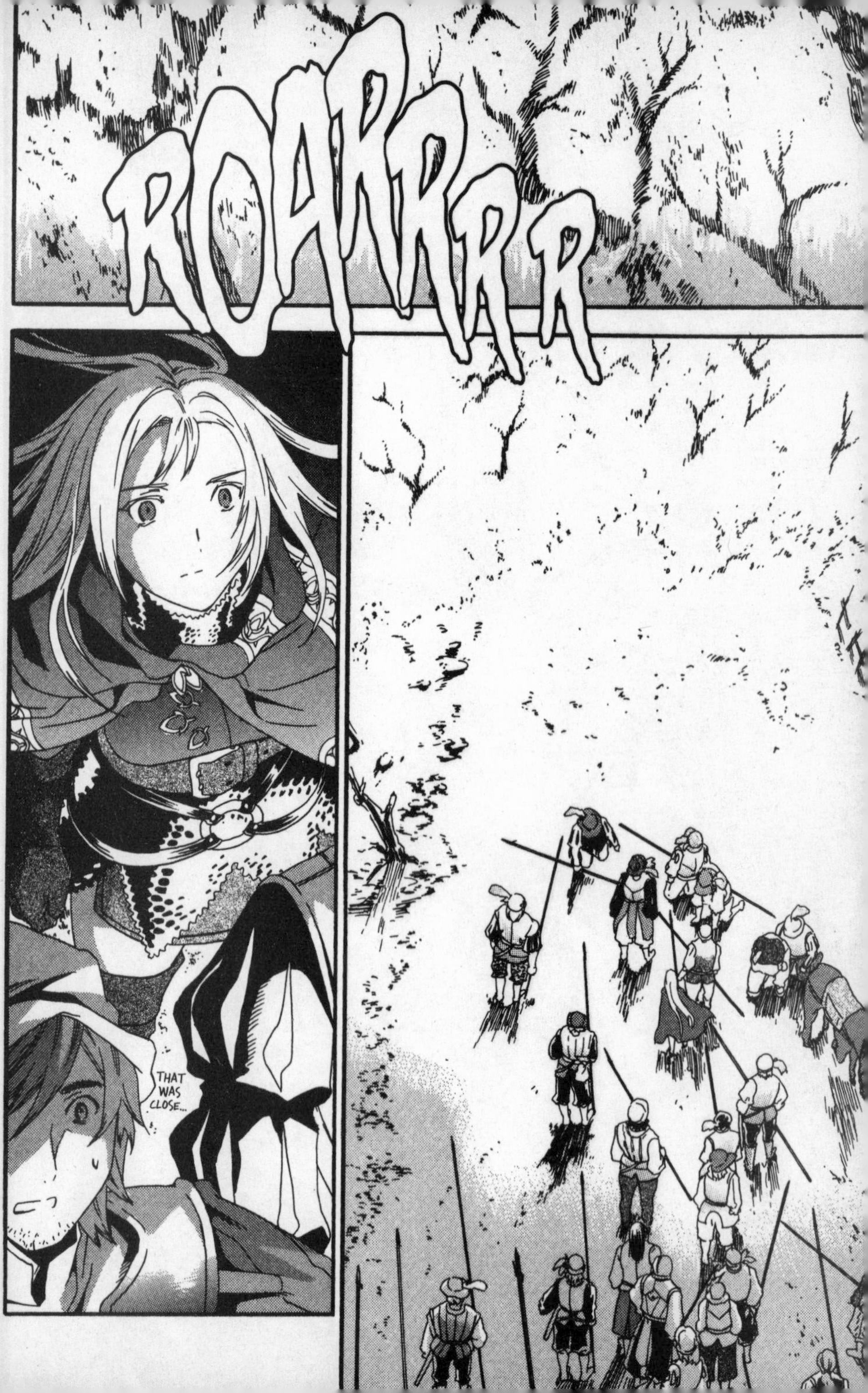
ROARRRR
THAT WAS CLOSE...

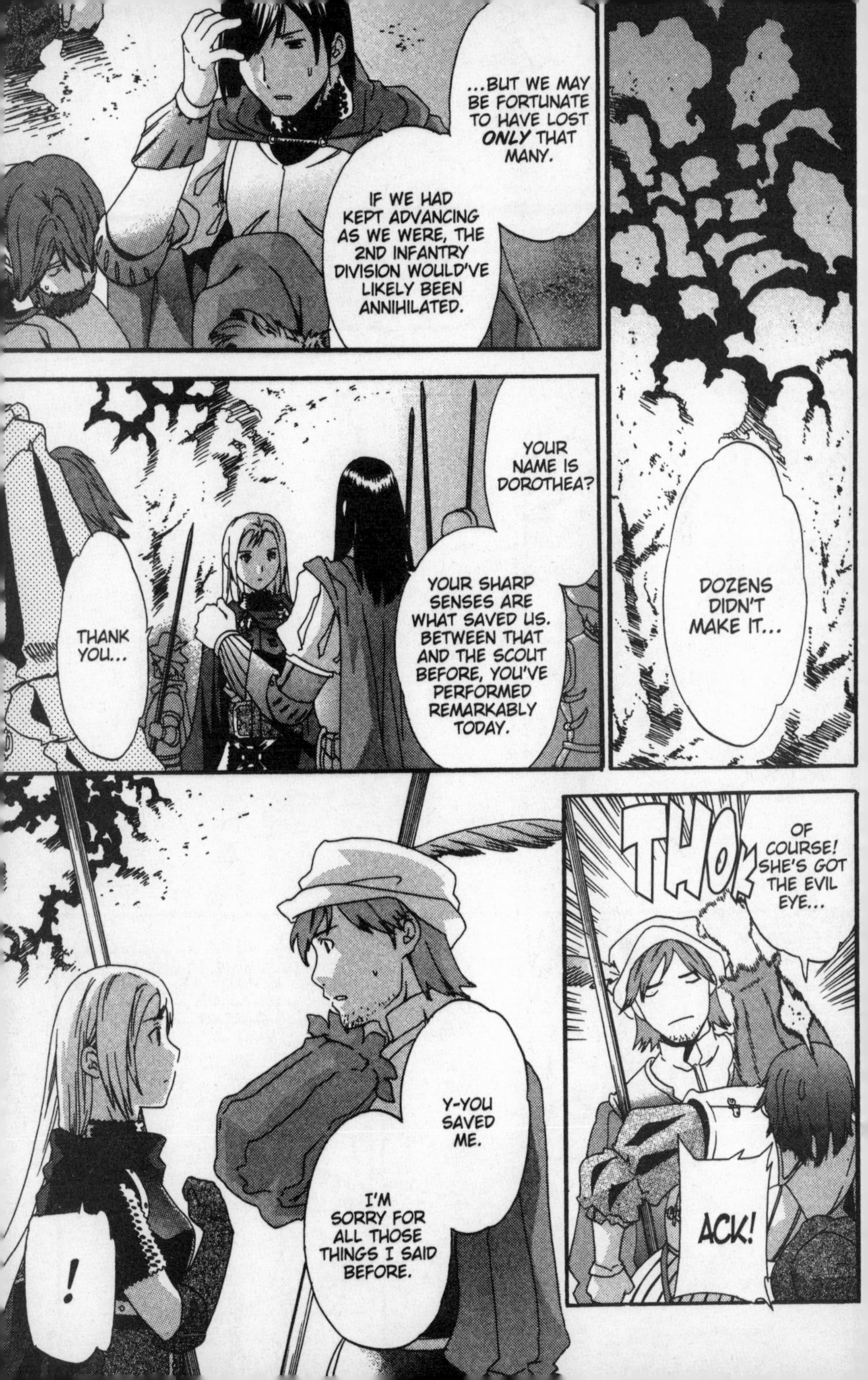
DOZENS DIDN'T MAKE IT...
...BUT WE MAY BE FORTUNATE TO HAVE LOST *ONLY* THAT MANY.
IF WE HAD KEPT ADVANCING AS WE WERE, THE 2ND INFANTRY DIVISION WOULD'VE LIKELY BEEN ANNIHILATED.
YOUR NAME IS DOROTHEA?
YOUR SHARP SENSES ARE WHAT SAVED US. BETWEEN THAT AND THE SCOUT BEFORE, YOU'VE PERFORMED REMARKABLY TODAY.
THANK YOU...
THOK
OF COURSE! SHE'S GOT THE EVIL EYE...
ACK!
Y-YOU SAVED ME.
I'M SORRY FOR ALL THOSE THINGS I SAID BEFORE.
!

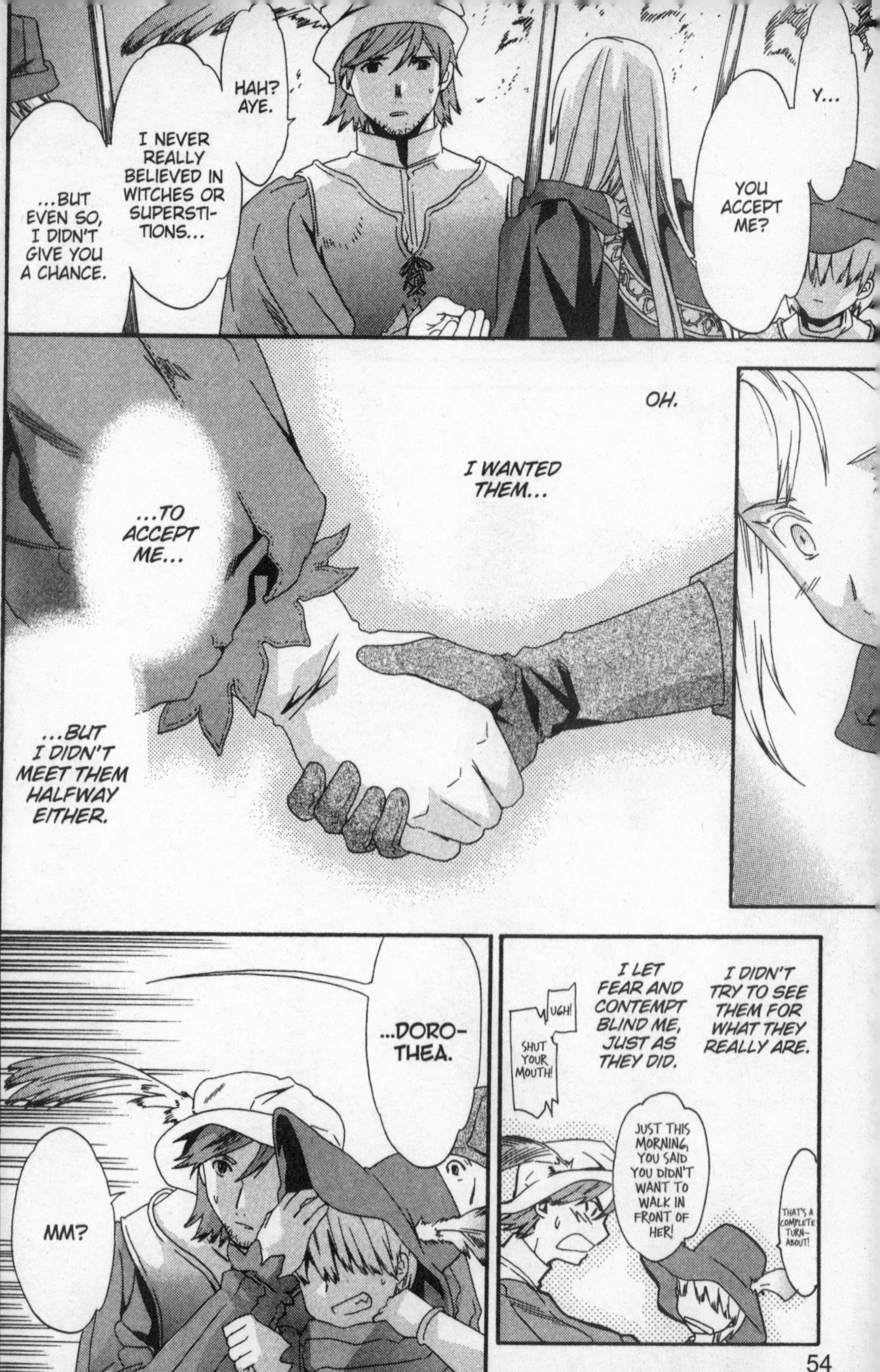
Y...
YOU ACCEPT ME?
HAH? AYE.
I NEVER REALLY BELIEVED IN WITCHES OR SUPERSTI-TIONS...
...BUT EVEN SO, I DIDN'T GIVE YOU A CHANCE.
OH.
I WANTED THEM...
...TO ACCEPT ME...
...BUT I DIDN'T MEET THEM HALFWAY EITHER.
I DIDN'T TRY TO SEE THEM FOR WHAT THEY REALLY ARE.
I LET FEAR AND CONTEMPT BLIND ME, JUST AS THEY DID.
JUST THIS MORNING, YOU SAID YOU DIDN'T WANT TO WALK IN FRONT OF HER!
THAT'S A COMPLETE TURN-ABOUT!
UGH!
SHUT YOUR MOUTH!
...DORO-THEA.
MM?

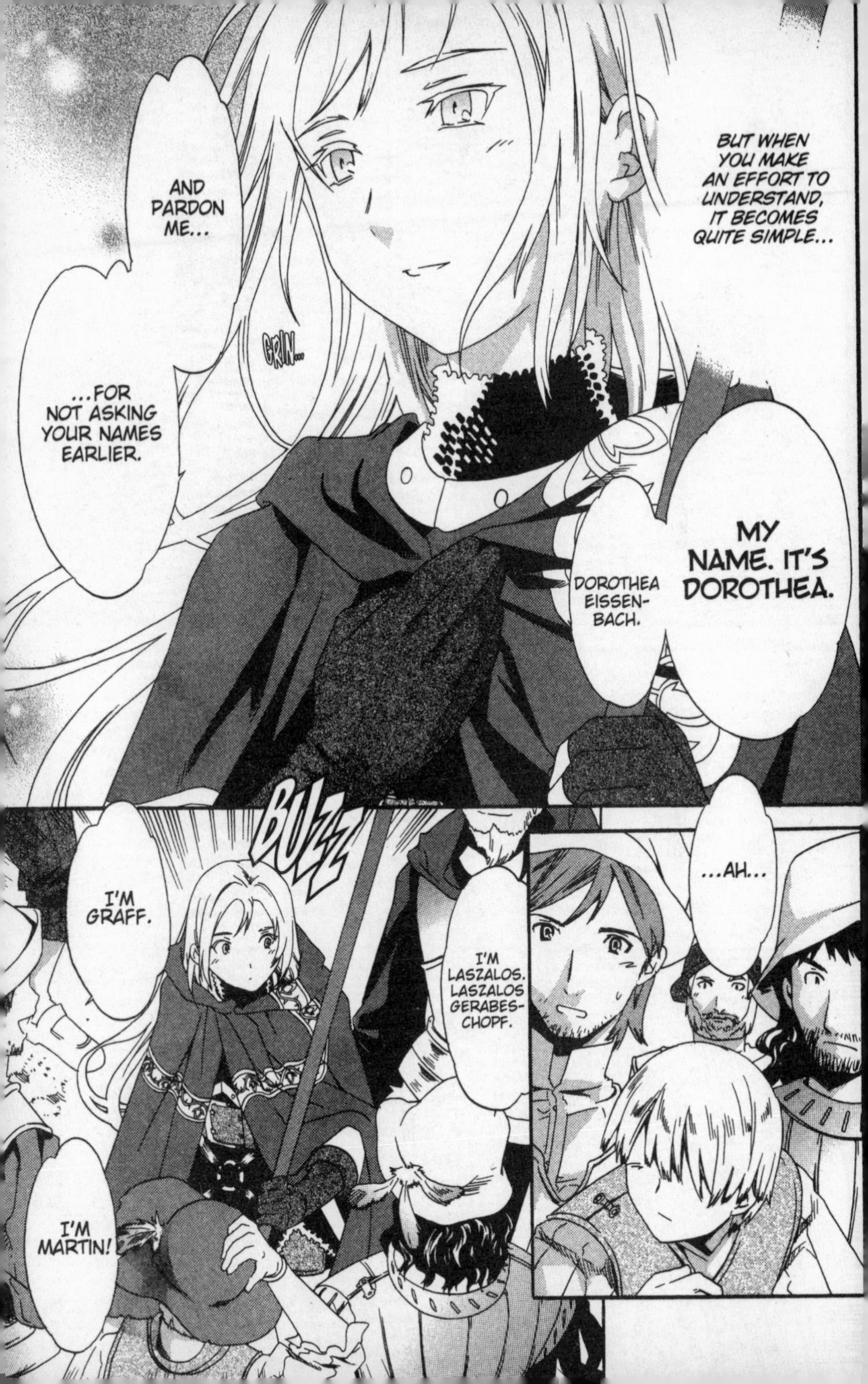
BUT WHEN YOU MAKE AN EFFORT TO UNDERSTAND, IT BECOMES QUITE SIMPLE...
AND PARDON ME...
GRIN...
...FOR NOT ASKING YOUR NAMES EARLIER.
MY NAME. IT'S DOROTHEA.
DOROTHEA EISSEN-BACH.
...AH...
I'M LASZALOS. LASZALOS GERABES-CHOPF.
BUZZ
I'M GRAFF.
I'M MARTIN!

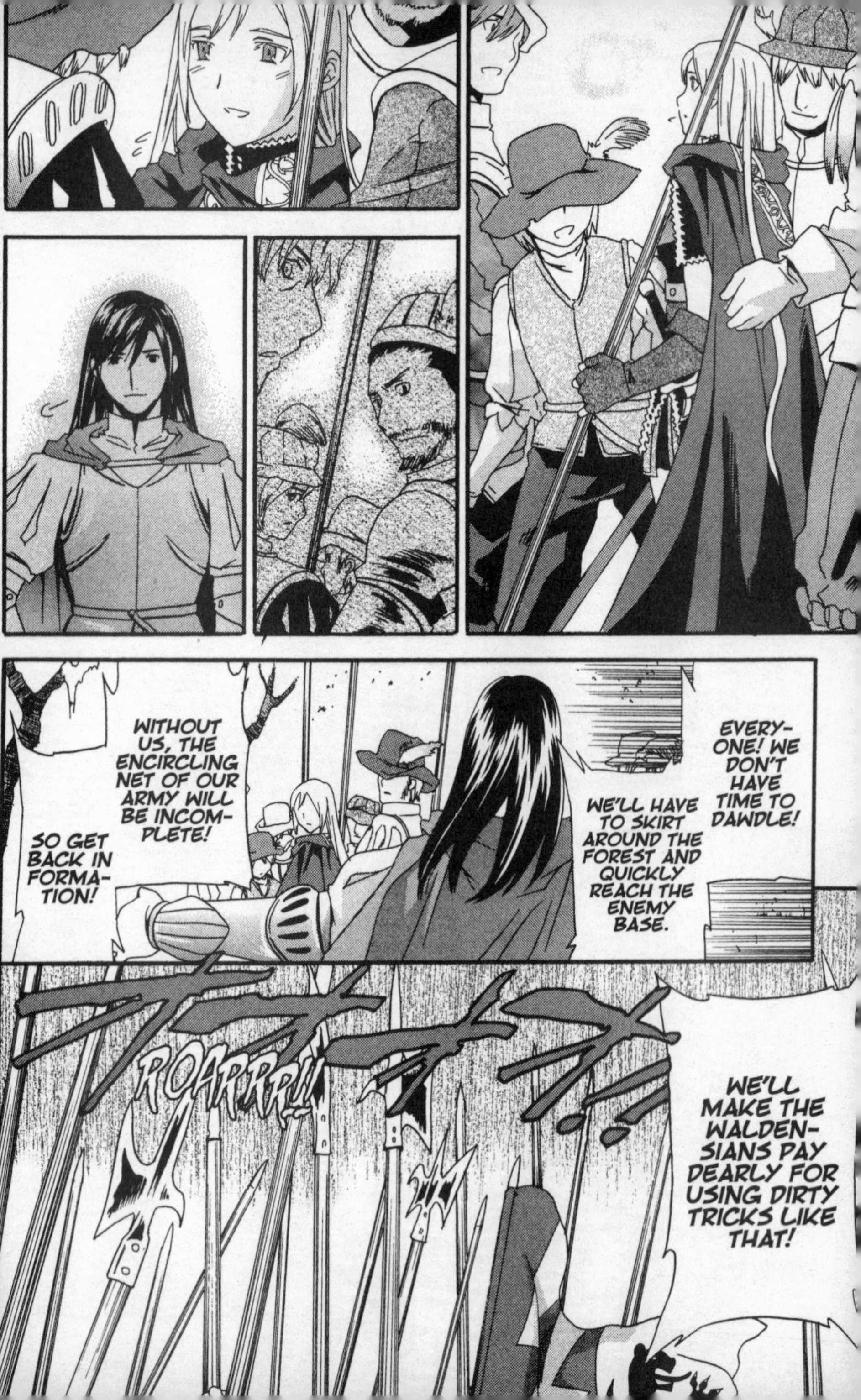
EVERY-ONE! WE DON'T HAVE TIME TO DAWDLE!
WE'LL HAVE TO SKIRT AROUND THE FOREST AND QUICKLY REACH THE ENEMY BASE.
WITHOUT US, THE ENCIRCLING NET OF OUR ARMY WILL BE INCOM-PLETE!
SO GET BACK IN FORMA-TION!
WE'LL MAKE THE WALDEN-SIANS PAY DEARLY FOR USING DIRTY TRICKS LIKE THAT!
ROARRR!!

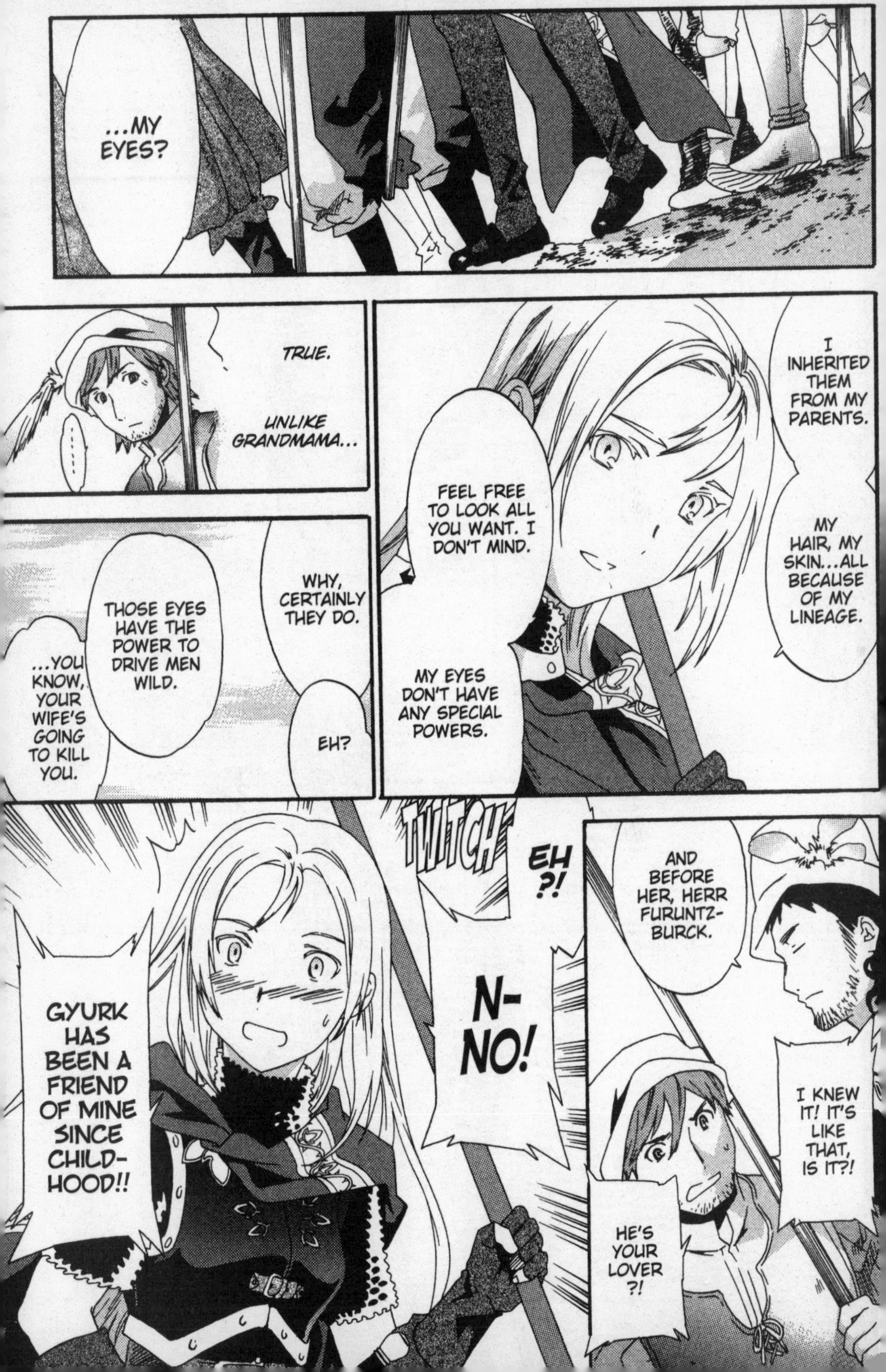
...MY EYES?
I INHERITED THEM FROM MY PARENTS.
MY HAIR, MY SKIN...ALL BECAUSE OF MY LINEAGE.
FEEL FREE TO LOOK ALL YOU WANT. I DON'T MIND.
MY EYES DON'T HAVE ANY SPECIAL POWERS.
TRUE.
UNLIKE GRANDMAMA...
......
WHY, CERTAINLY THEY DO.
THOSE EYES HAVE THE POWER TO DRIVE MEN WILD.
EH?
...YOU KNOW, YOUR WIFE'S GOING TO KILL YOU.
AND BEFORE HER, HERR FURUNTZ-BURCK.
I KNEW IT! IT'S LIKE THAT, IS IT?!
HE'S YOUR LOVER?!
TWITCH
EH?!
N-NO!
GYURK HAS BEEN A FRIEND OF MINE SINCE CHILDHOOD!!

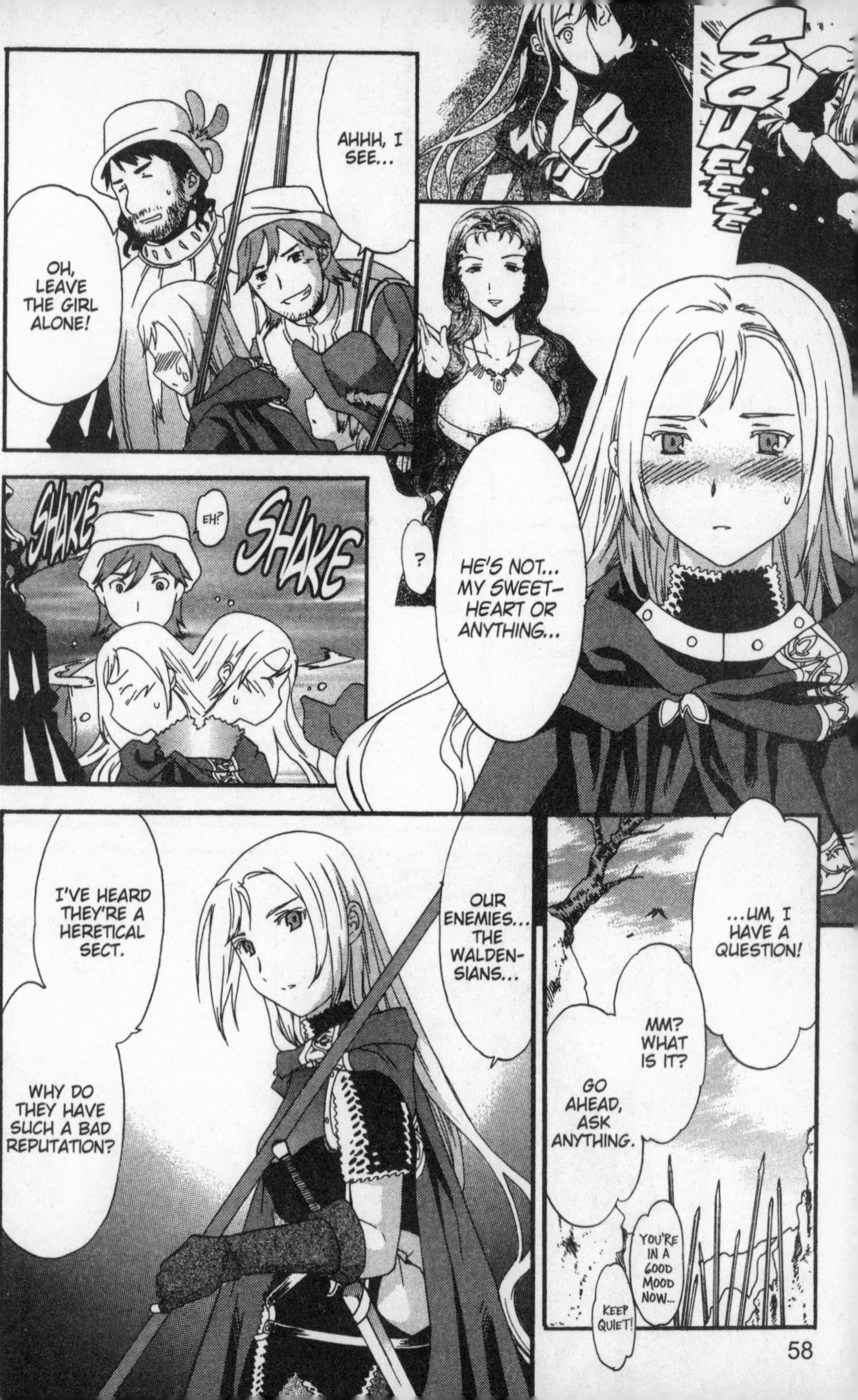
SQUEEZE
AHHH, I SEE...
OH, LEAVE THE GIRL ALONE!
?
HE'S NOT... MY SWEET-HEART OR ANYTHING...
SHAKE
EH?
SHAKE
...UM, I HAVE A QUESTION!
MM? WHAT IS IT?
GO AHEAD, ASK ANYTHING.
YOU'RE IN A GOOD MOOD NOW...
KEEP QUIET!
OUR ENEMIES... THE WALDEN-SIANS...
I'VE HEARD THEY'RE A HERETICAL SECT.
WHY DO THEY HAVE SUCH A BAD REPUTATION?

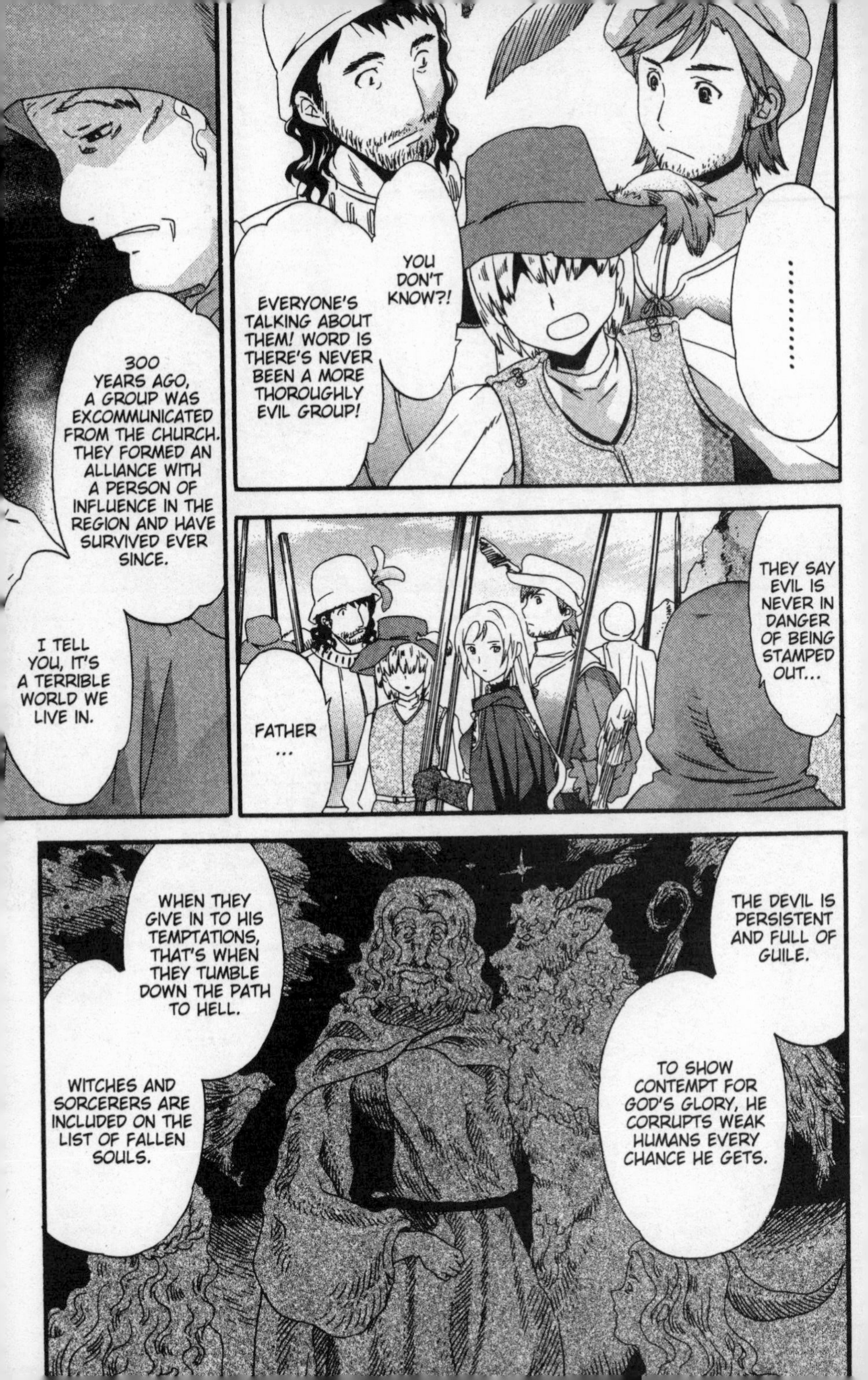
......
YOU DON'T KNOW?!
EVERYONE'S TALKING ABOUT THEM! WORD IS THERE'S NEVER BEEN A MORE THOROUGHLY EVIL GROUP!
THEY SAY EVIL IS NEVER IN DANGER OF BEING STAMPED OUT...
FATHER ...
300 YEARS AGO, A GROUP WAS EXCOMMUNICATED FROM THE CHURCH. THEY FORMED AN ALLIANCE WITH A PERSON OF INFLUENCE IN THE REGION AND HAVE SURVIVED EVER SINCE.
I TELL YOU, IT'S A TERRIBLE WORLD WE LIVE IN.
THE DEVIL IS PERSISTENT AND FULL OF GUILE.
TO SHOW CONTEMPT FOR GOD'S GLORY, HE CORRUPTS WEAK HUMANS EVERY CHANCE HE GETS.
WHEN THEY GIVE IN TO HIS TEMPTATIONS, THAT'S WHEN THEY TUMBLE DOWN THE PATH TO HELL.
WITCHES AND SORCERERS ARE INCLUDED ON THE LIST OF FALLEN SOULS.

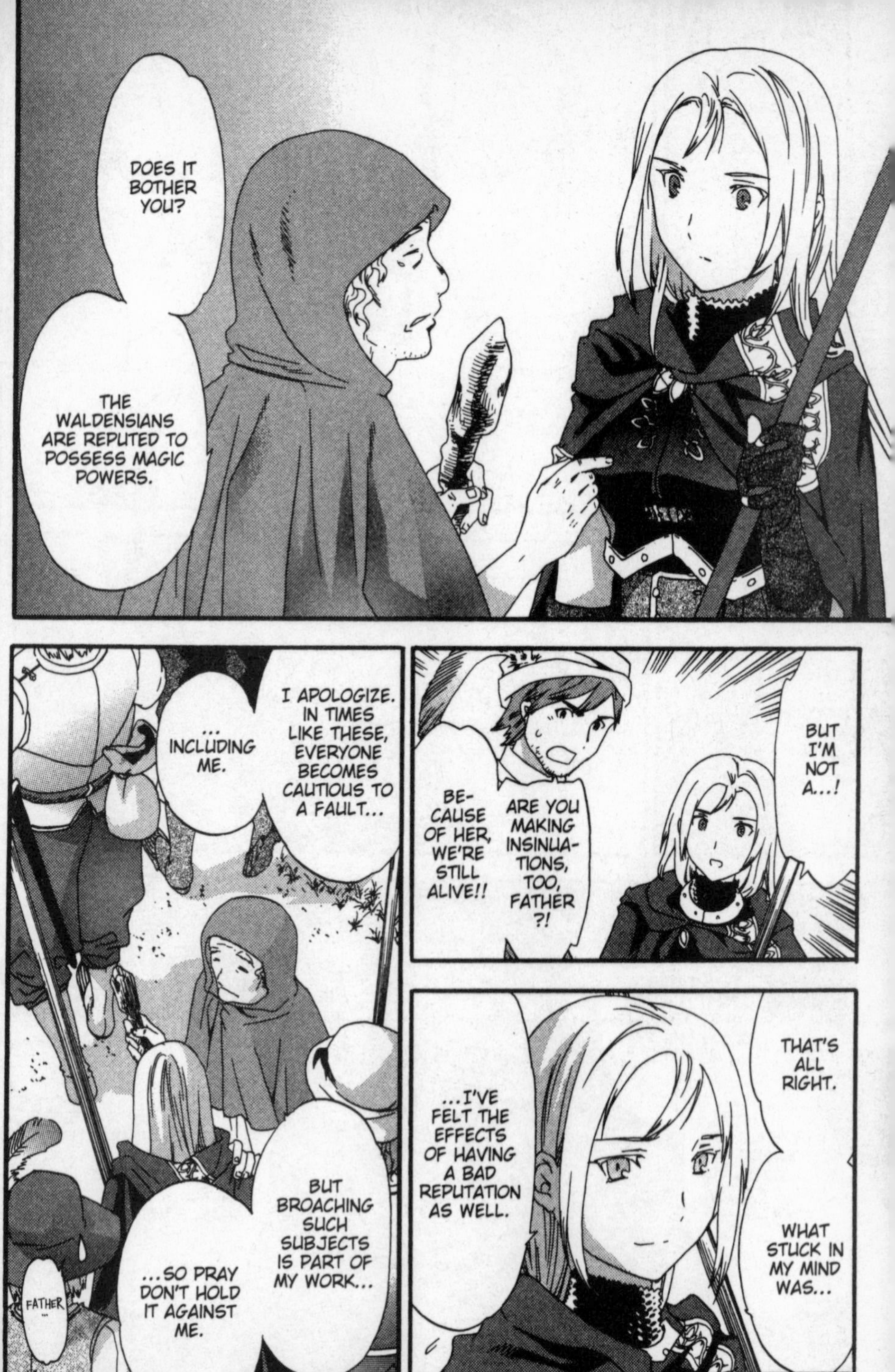
DOES IT BOTHER YOU?
THE WALDENSIANS ARE REPUTED TO POSSESS MAGIC POWERS.
BUT I'M NOT A...!
ARE YOU MAKING INSINUA-TIONS, TOO, FATHER?!
BE-CAUSE OF HER, WE'RE STILL ALIVE!!
THAT'S ALL RIGHT.
...I'VE FELT THE EFFECTS OF HAVING A BAD REPUTATION AS WELL.
WHAT STUCK IN MY MIND WAS...
I APOLOGIZE. IN TIMES LIKE THESE, EVERYONE BECOMES CAUTIOUS TO A FAULT...
... INCLUDING ME.
BUT BROACHING SUCH SUBJECTS IS PART OF MY WORK...
...SO PRAY DON'T HOLD IT AGAINST ME.
FATHER ...

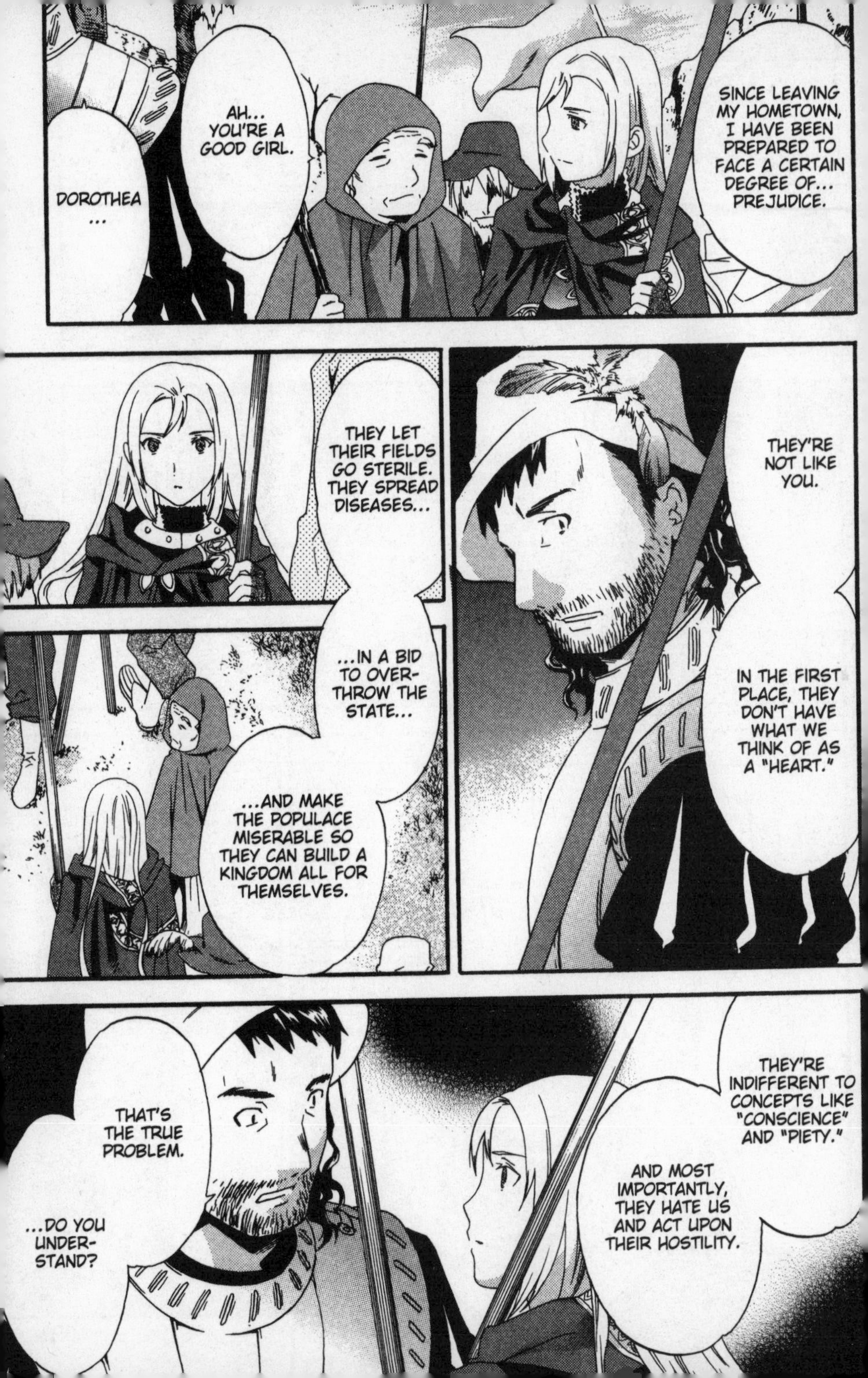
SINCE LEAVING MY HOMETOWN, I HAVE BEEN PREPARED TO FACE A CERTAIN DEGREE OF... PREJUDICE.
AH... YOU'RE A GOOD GIRL.
DOROTHEA...
THEY'RE NOT LIKE YOU.
IN THE FIRST PLACE, THEY DON'T HAVE WHAT WE THINK OF AS A "HEART."
THEY LET THEIR FIELDS GO STERILE. THEY SPREAD DISEASES...
...IN A BID TO OVER-THROW THE STATE...
...AND MAKE THE POPULACE MISERABLE SO THEY CAN BUILD A KINGDOM ALL FOR THEMSELVES.
THEY'RE INDIFFERENT TO CONCEPTS LIKE "CONSCIENCE" AND "PIETY."
AND MOST IMPORTANTLY, THEY HATE US AND ACT UPON THEIR HOSTILITY.
THAT'S THE TRUE PROBLEM.
...DO YOU UNDER-STAND?

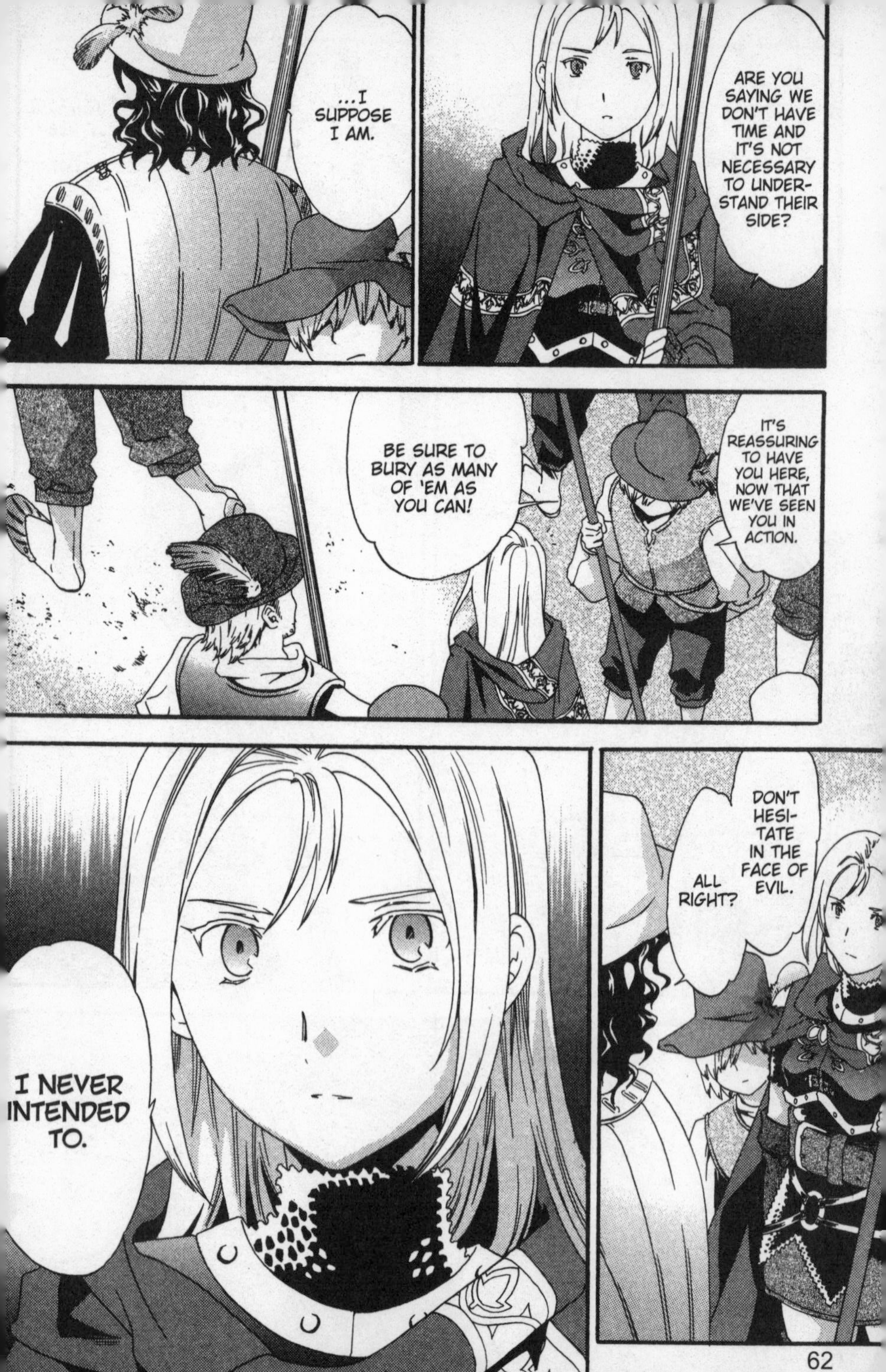
ARE YOU SAYING WE DON'T HAVE TIME AND IT'S NOT NECESSARY TO UNDER-STAND THEIR SIDE?
...I SUPPOSE I AM.
IT'S REASSURING TO HAVE YOU HERE, NOW THAT WE'VE SEEN YOU IN ACTION.
BE SURE TO BURY AS MANY OF 'EM AS YOU CAN!
DON'T HESI-TATE IN THE FACE OF EVIL.
ALL RIGHT?
I NEVER INTENDED TO.

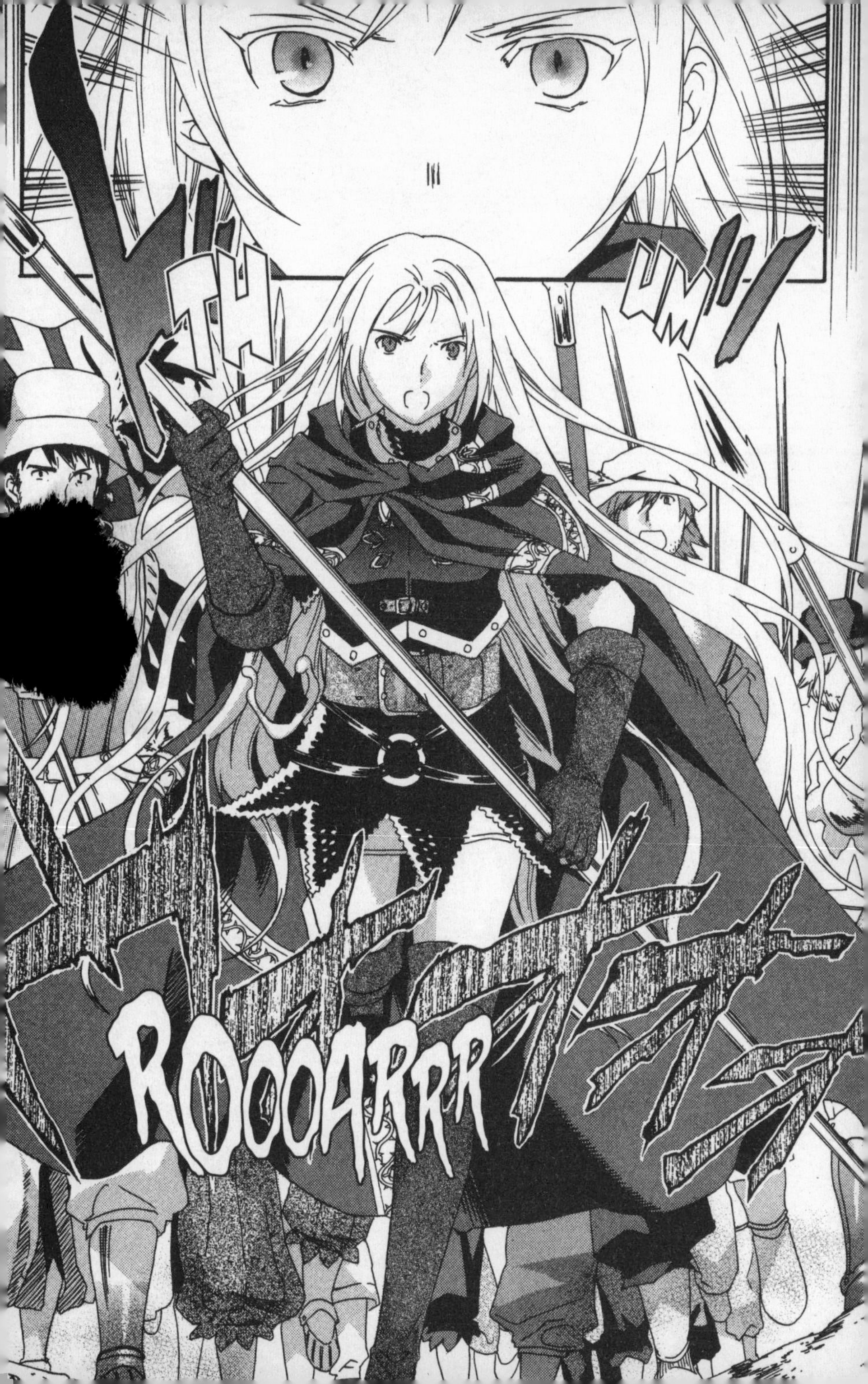
THUM
ROOOARRR

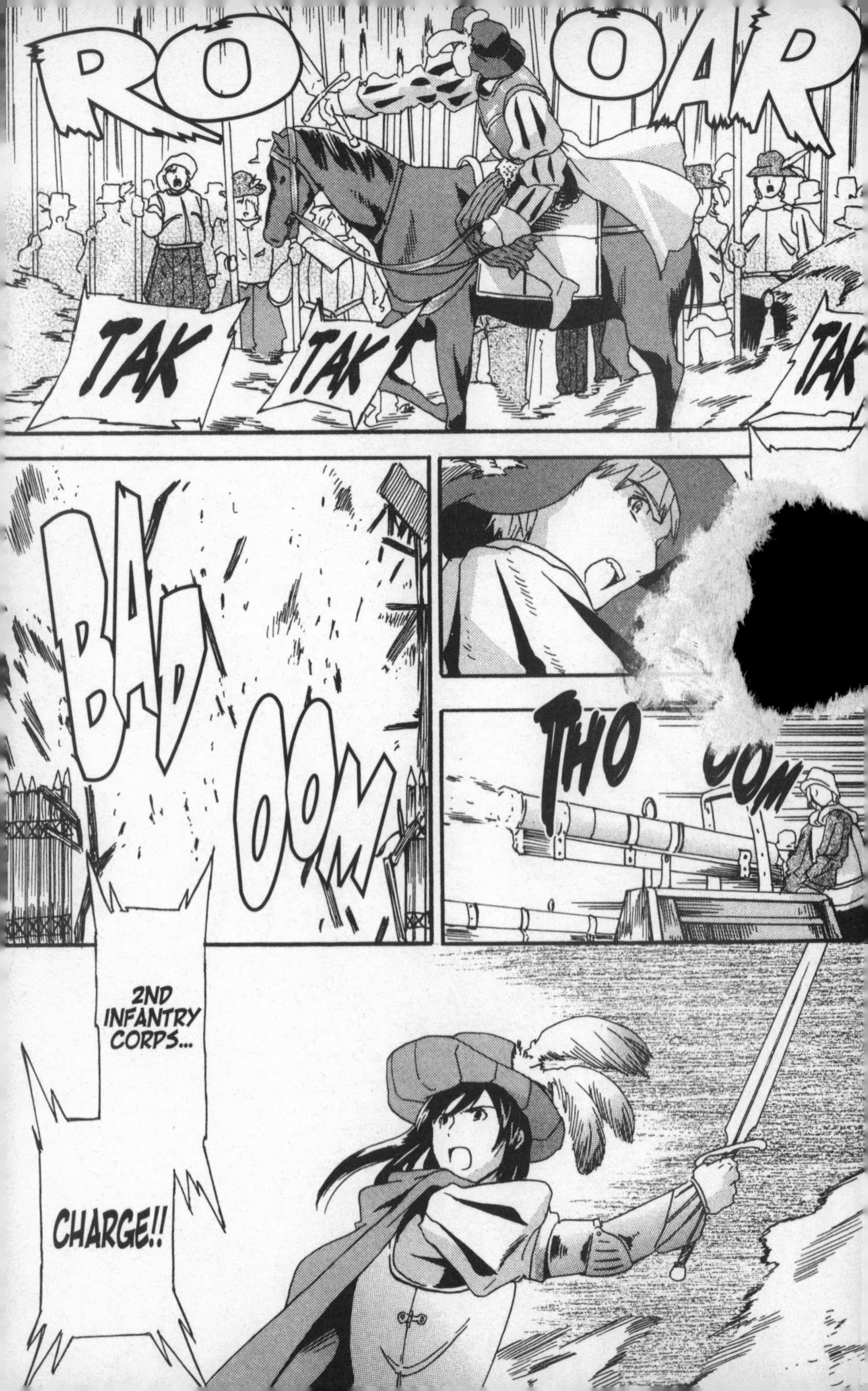
RO
OAR
TAK
TAK
TAK
THO
OOM
BA
DOOM
2ND INFANTRY CORPS...
CHARGE!!

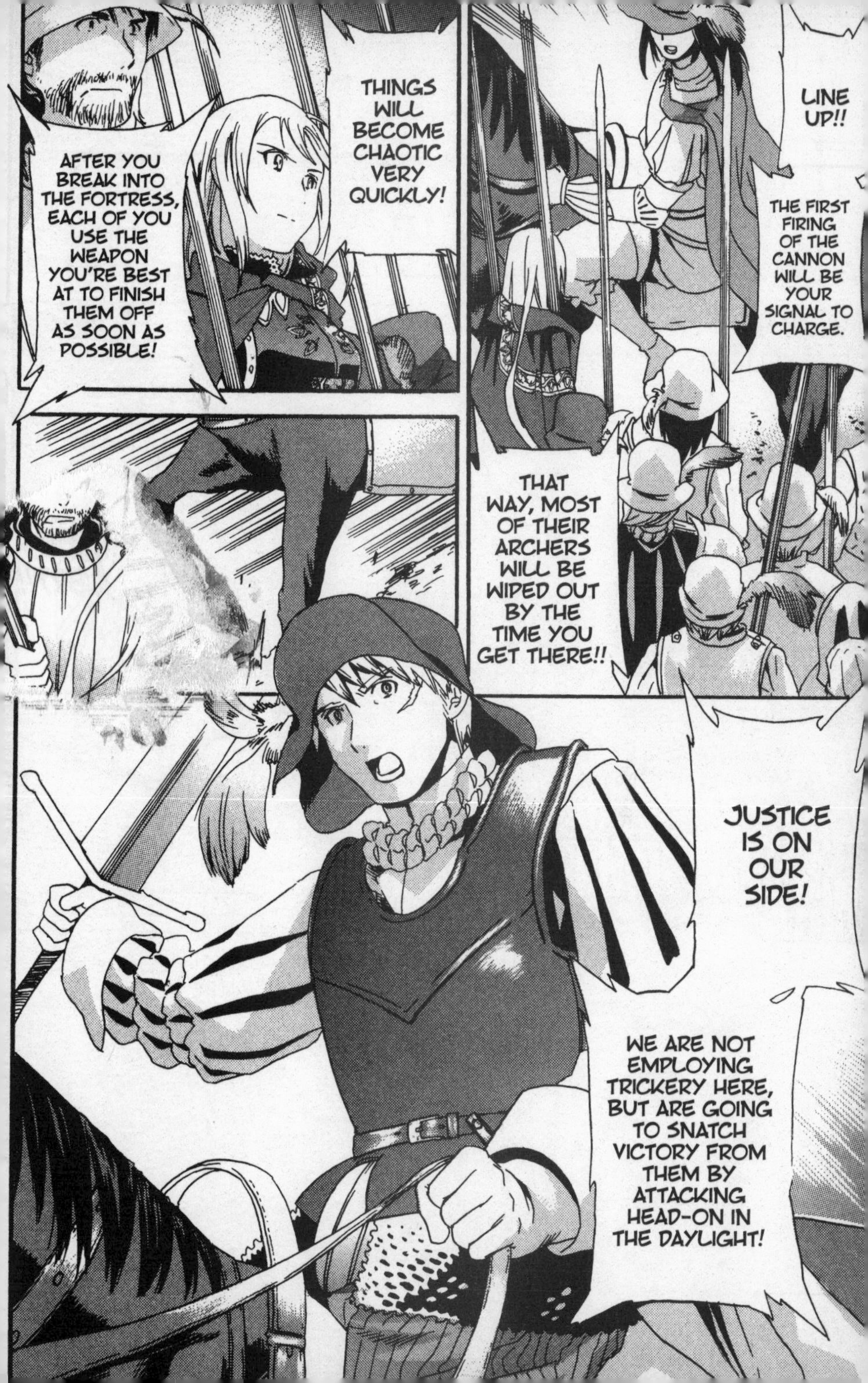
LINE UP!!
THE FIRST FIRING OF THE CANNON WILL BE YOUR SIGNAL TO CHARGE.
THAT WAY, MOST OF THEIR ARCHERS WILL BE WIPED OUT BY THE TIME YOU GET THERE!!
THINGS WILL BECOME CHAOTIC VERY QUICKLY!
AFTER YOU BREAK INTO THE FORTRESS, EACH OF YOU USE THE WEAPON YOU'RE BEST AT TO FINISH THEM OFF AS SOON AS POSSIBLE!
JUSTICE IS ON OUR SIDE!
WE ARE NOT EMPLOYING TRICKERY HERE, BUT ARE GOING TO SNATCH VICTORY FROM THEM BY ATTACKING HEAD-ON IN THE DAYLIGHT!

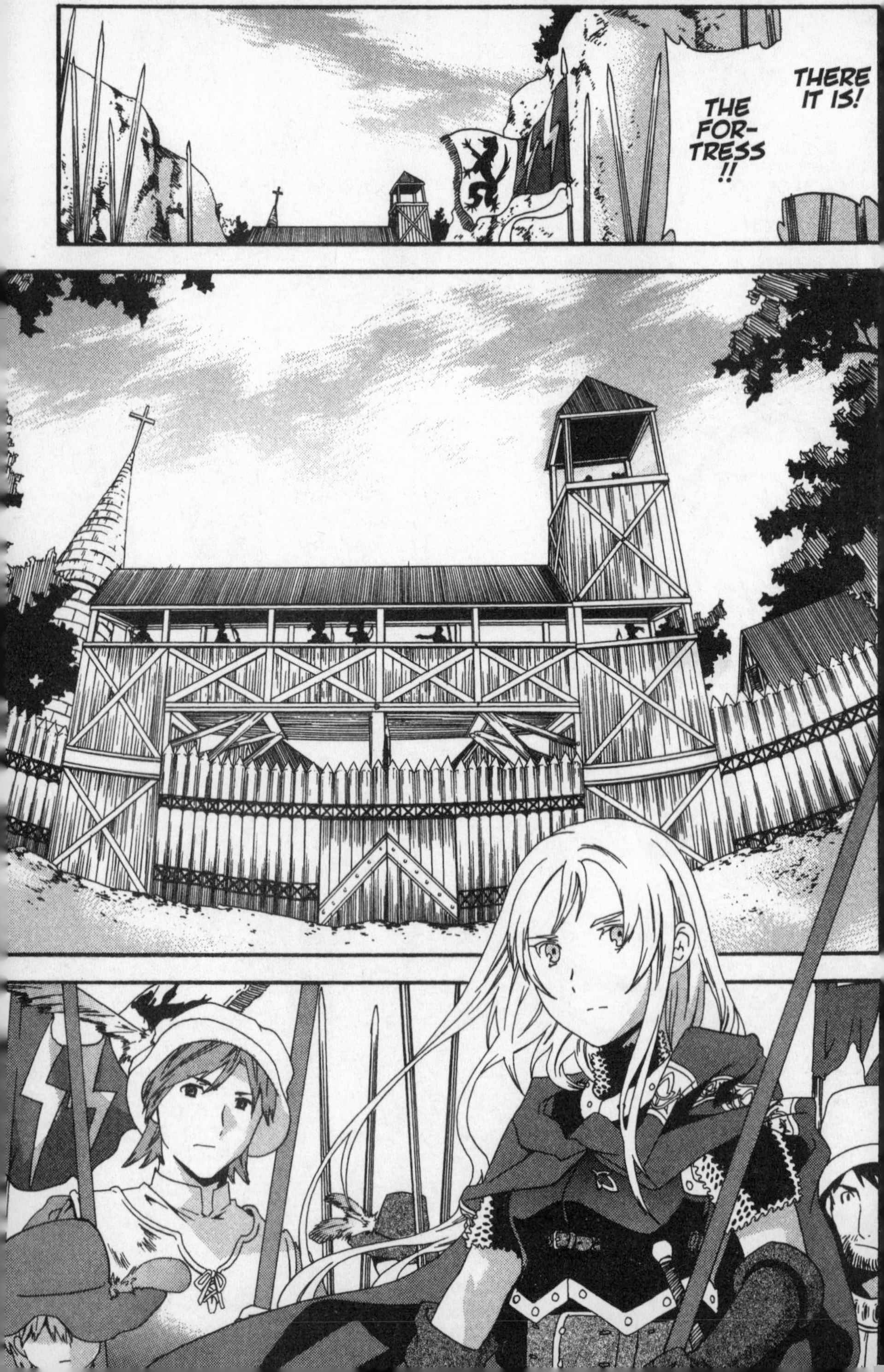
THERE IT IS!
THE FOR-TRESS !!

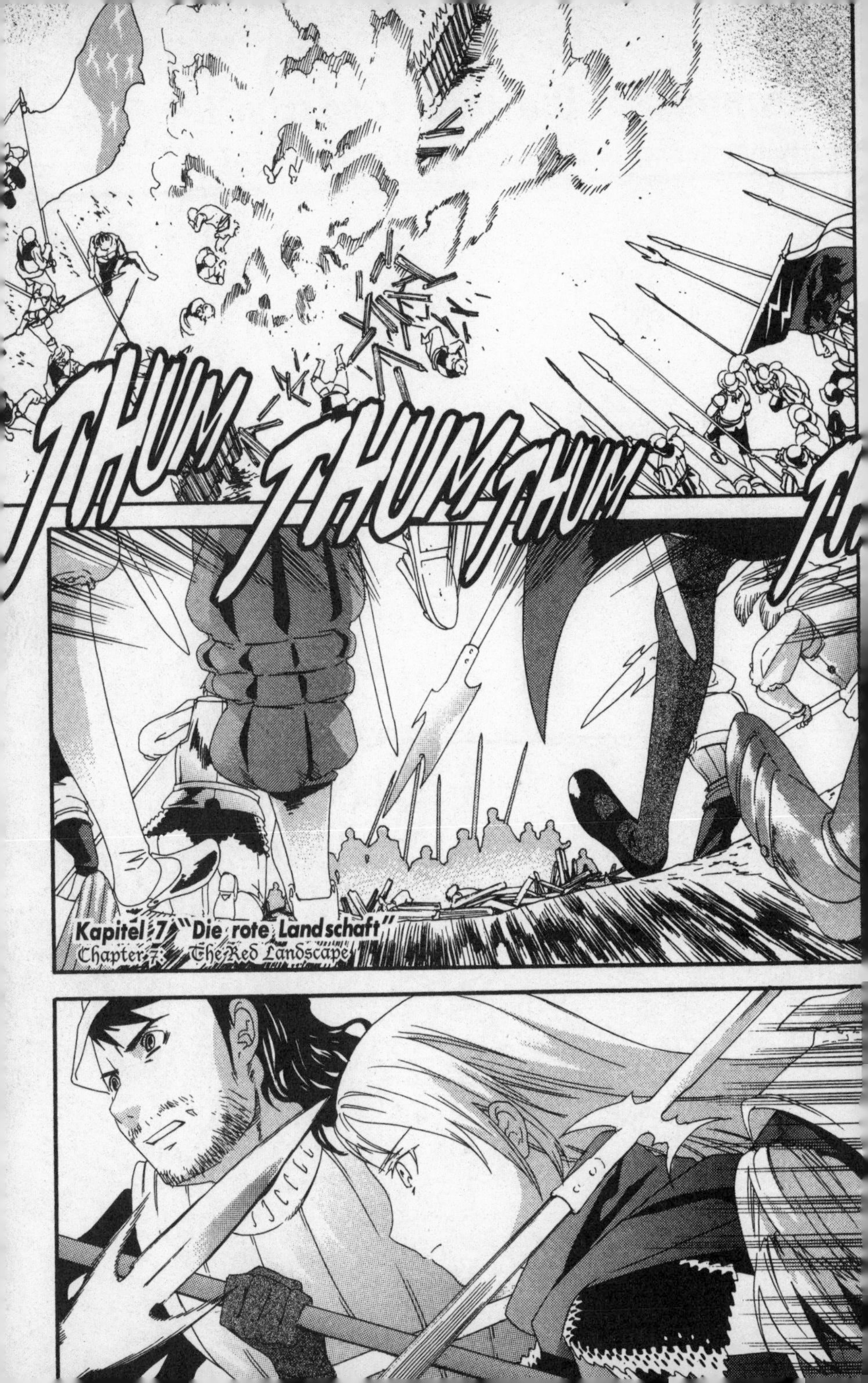
THUM
THUM
THUM
Kapitel 7 "Die rote Landschaft"
Chapter 7: The Red Landscape

Kapitel 7 "Die rote Landschaft"

Chapter 7: The Red Landscape

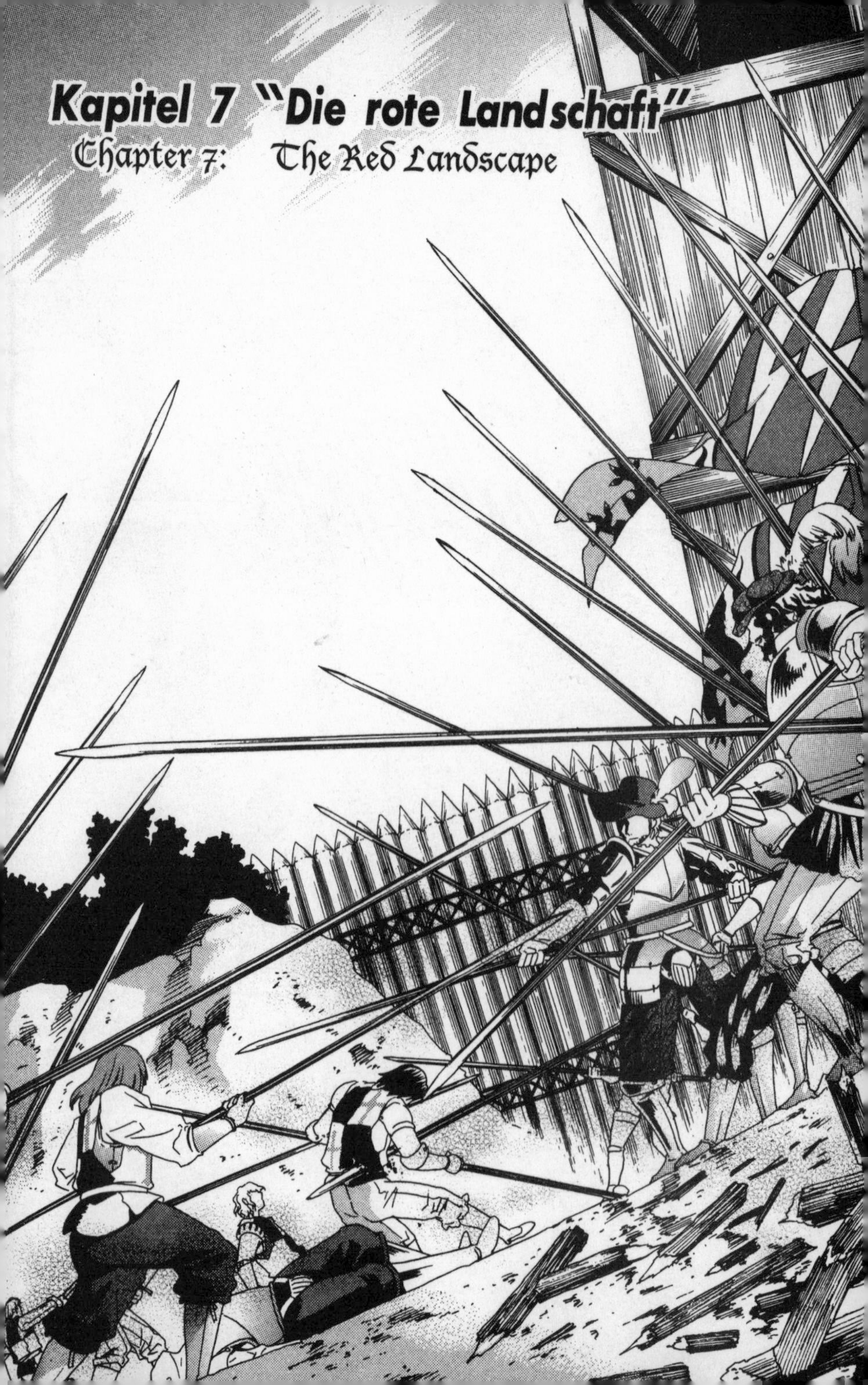

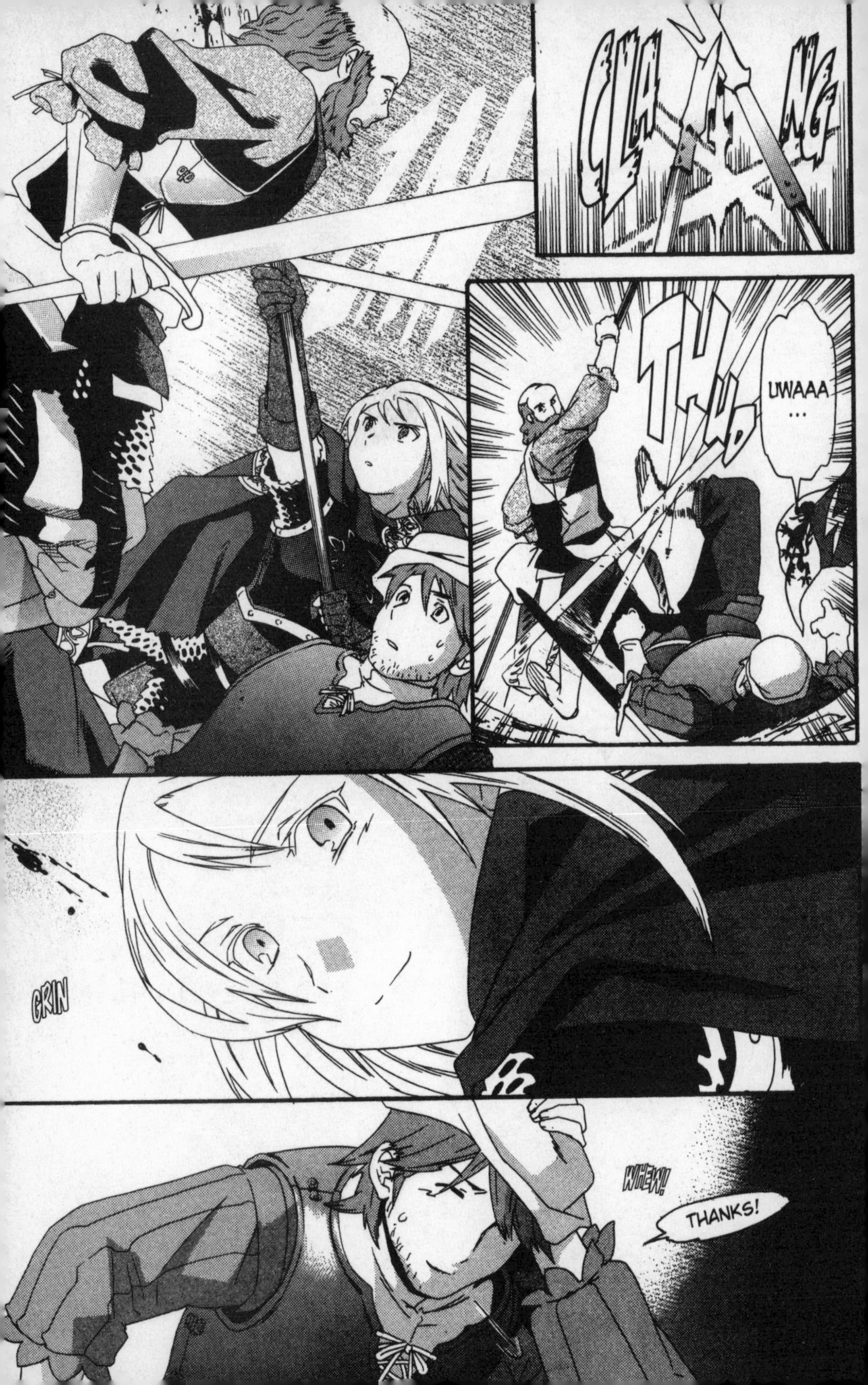
CLANG
THUD
UWAAA ...
GRIN
WHEW!
THANKS!

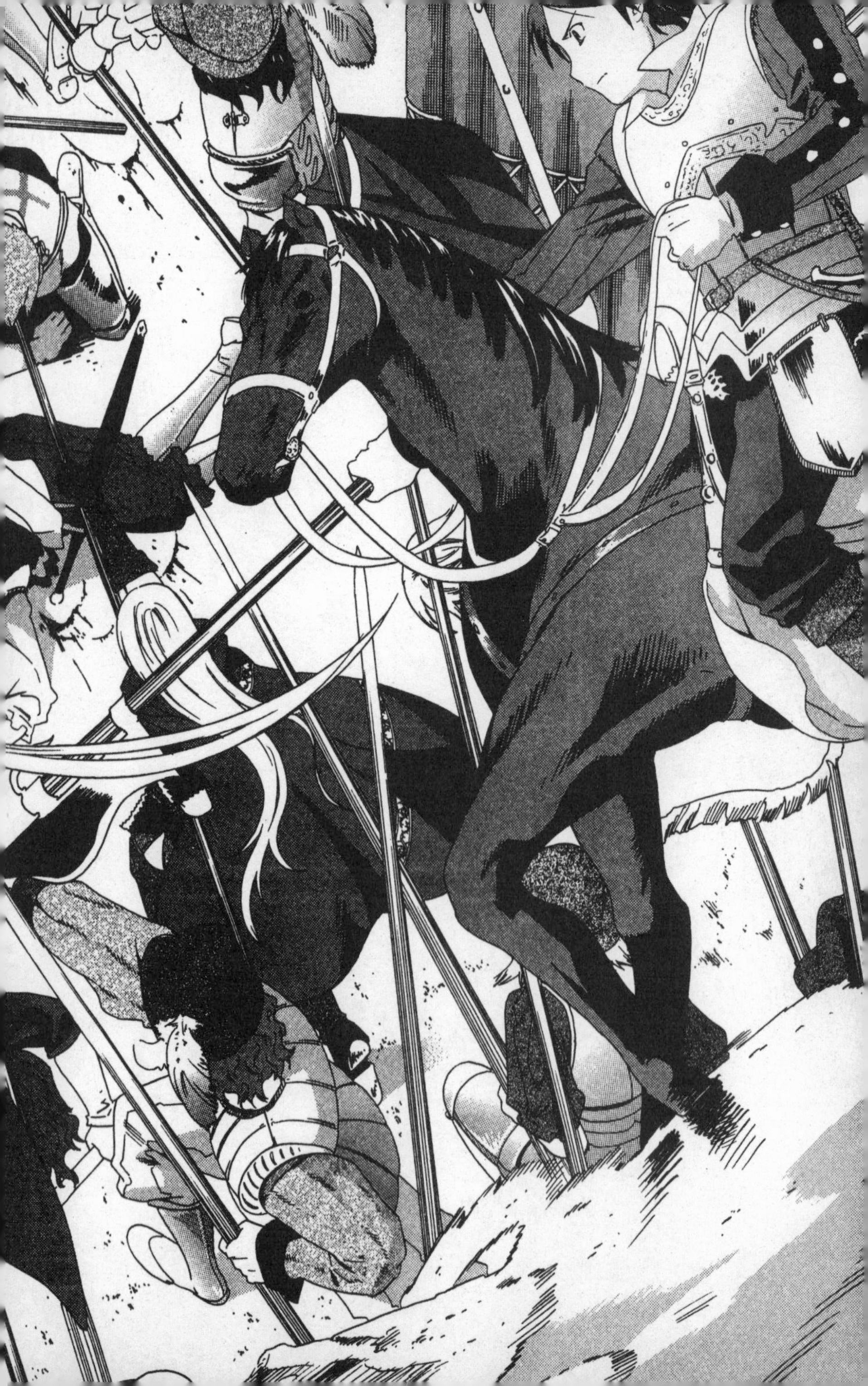

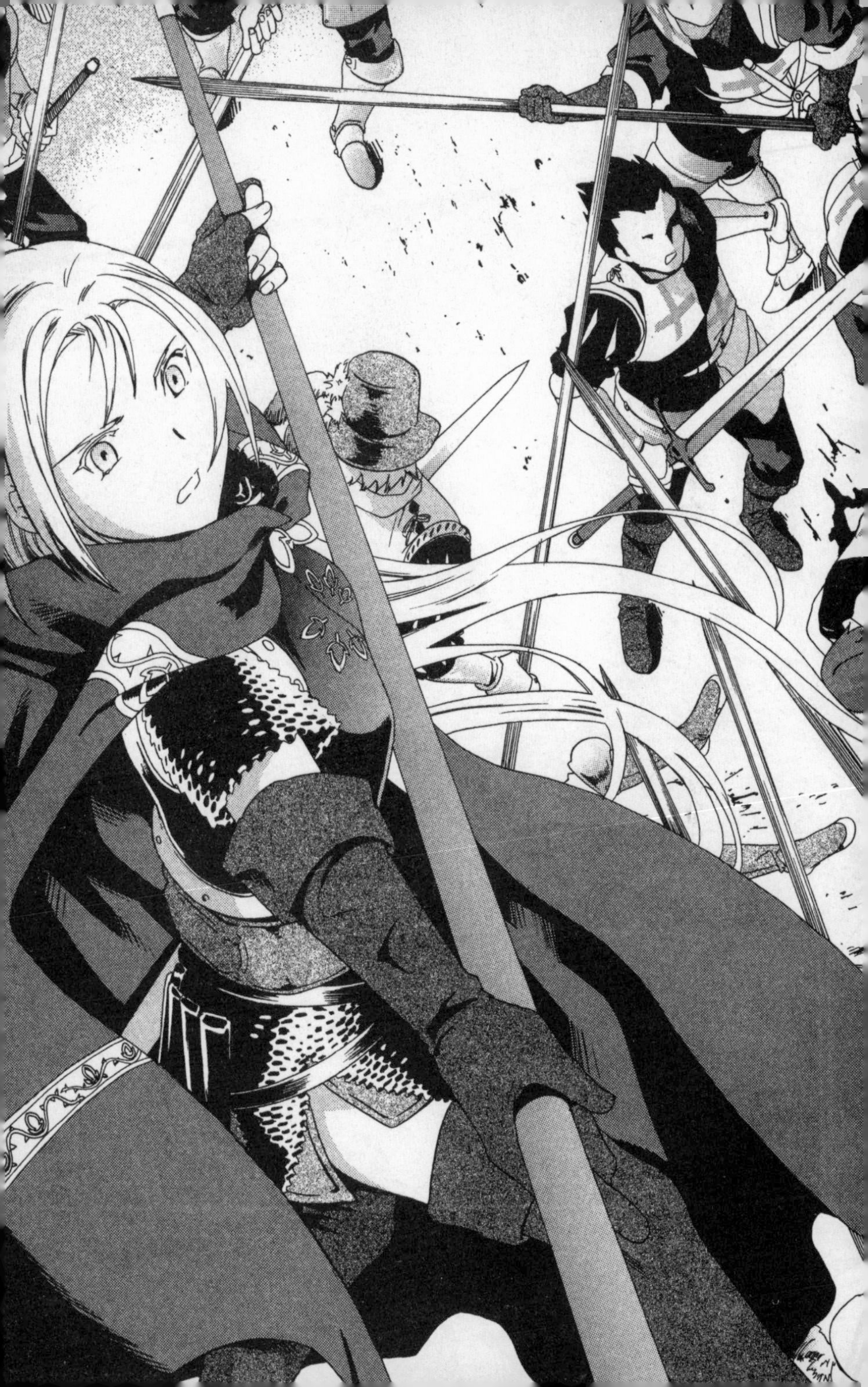

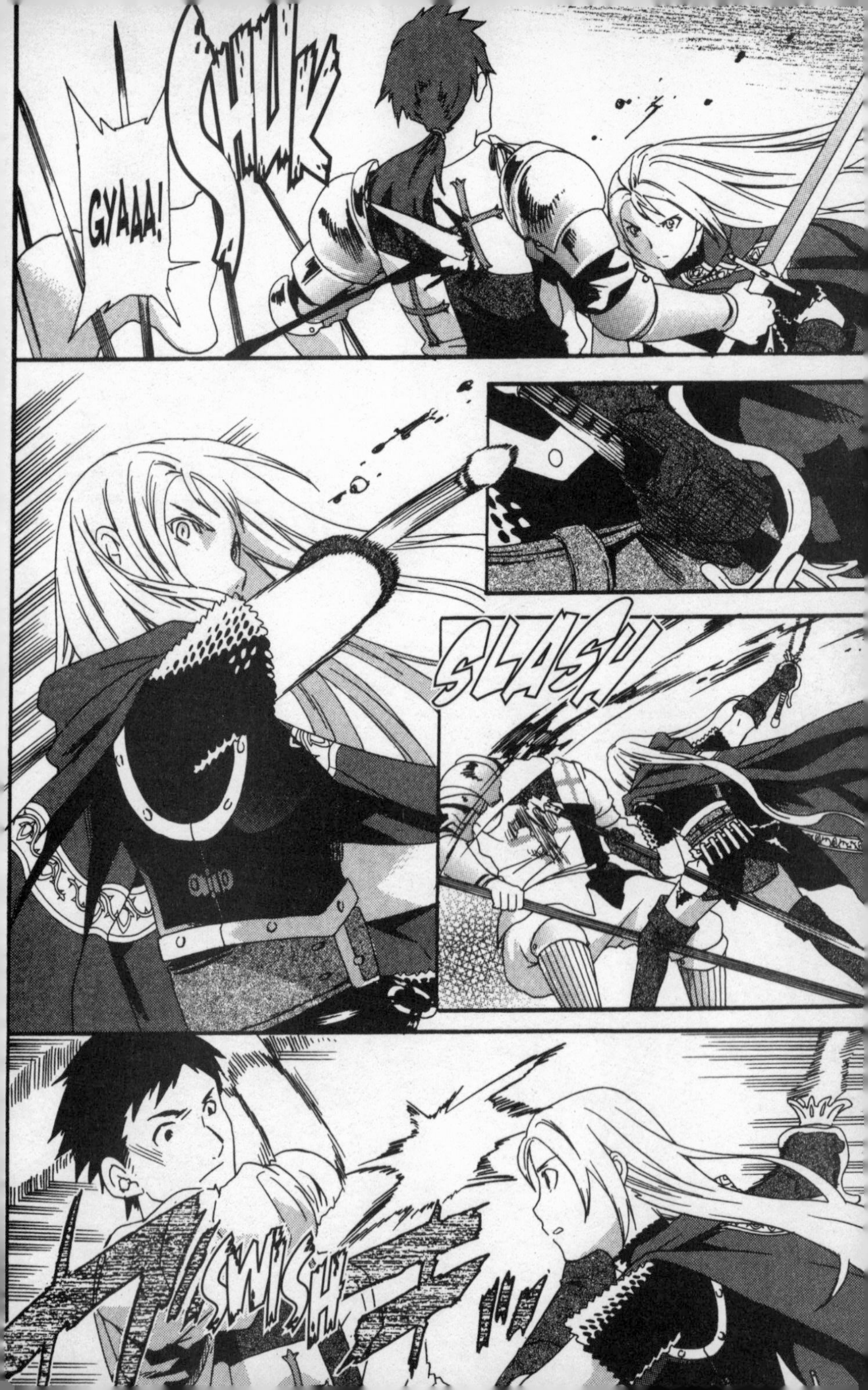
SHUK
GYAAA!
SLASH
SWISH

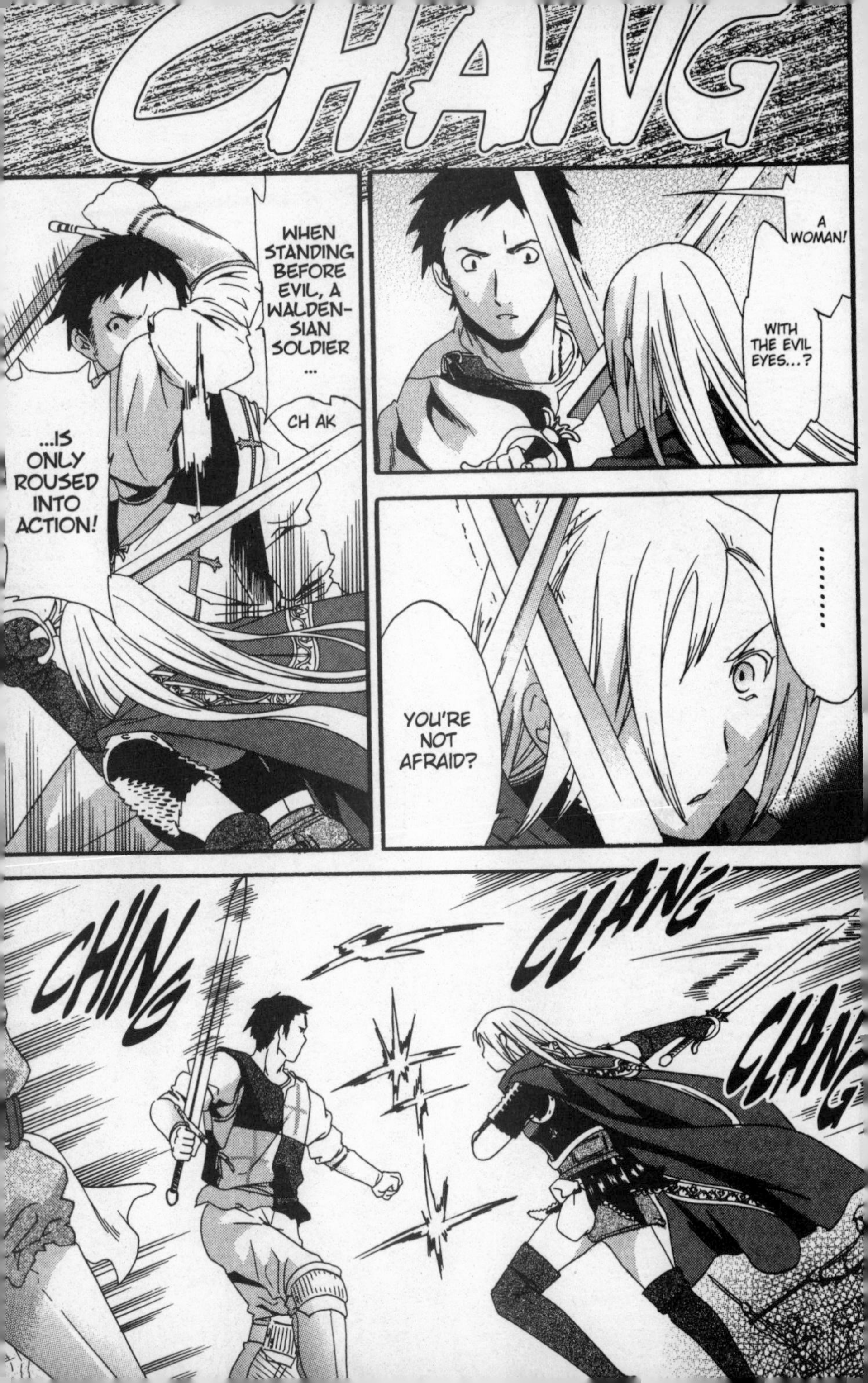
CHANG
A WOMAN!
WITH THE EVIL EYES...?
......
YOU'RE NOT AFRAID?
WHEN STANDING BEFORE EVIL, A WALDEN-SIAN SOLDIER ...
CH AK
...IS ONLY ROUSED INTO ACTION!
CLANG
CLANG
CHING

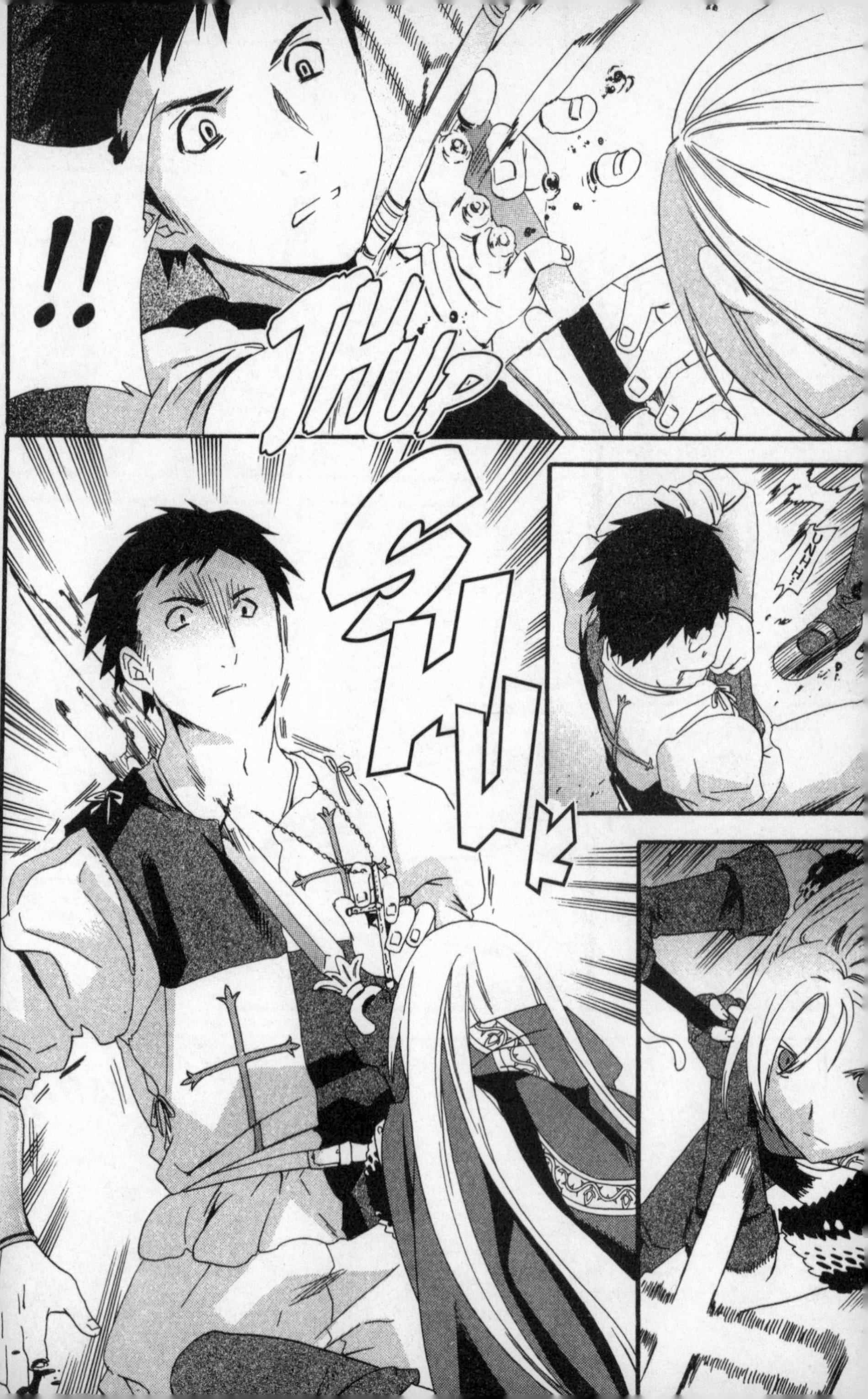
THUP
!!
UNH...
SHUNK

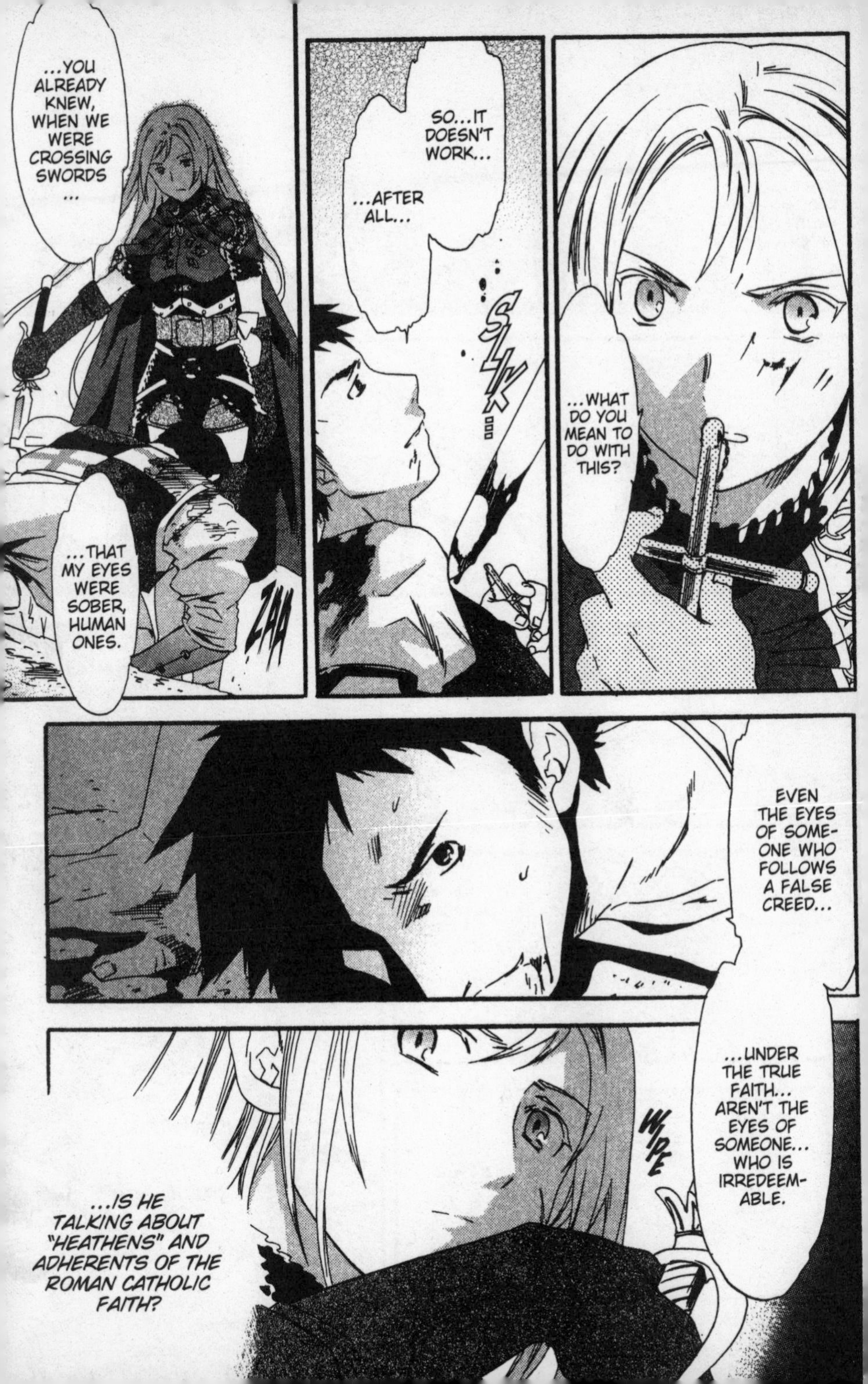
...WHAT DO YOU MEAN TO DO WITH THIS?
SO...IT DOESN'T WORK...
...AFTER ALL...
SLK...
...YOU ALREADY KNEW, WHEN WE WERE CROSSING SWORDS...
...THAT MY EYES WERE SOBER, HUMAN ONES.
ZAA
EVEN THE EYES OF SOME-ONE WHO FOLLOWS A FALSE CREED...
...UNDER THE TRUE FAITH... AREN'T THE EYES OF SOMEONE... WHO IS IRREDEEM-ABLE.
WIPE
...IS HE TALKING ABOUT "HEATHENS" AND ADHERENTS OF THE ROMAN CATHOLIC FAITH?

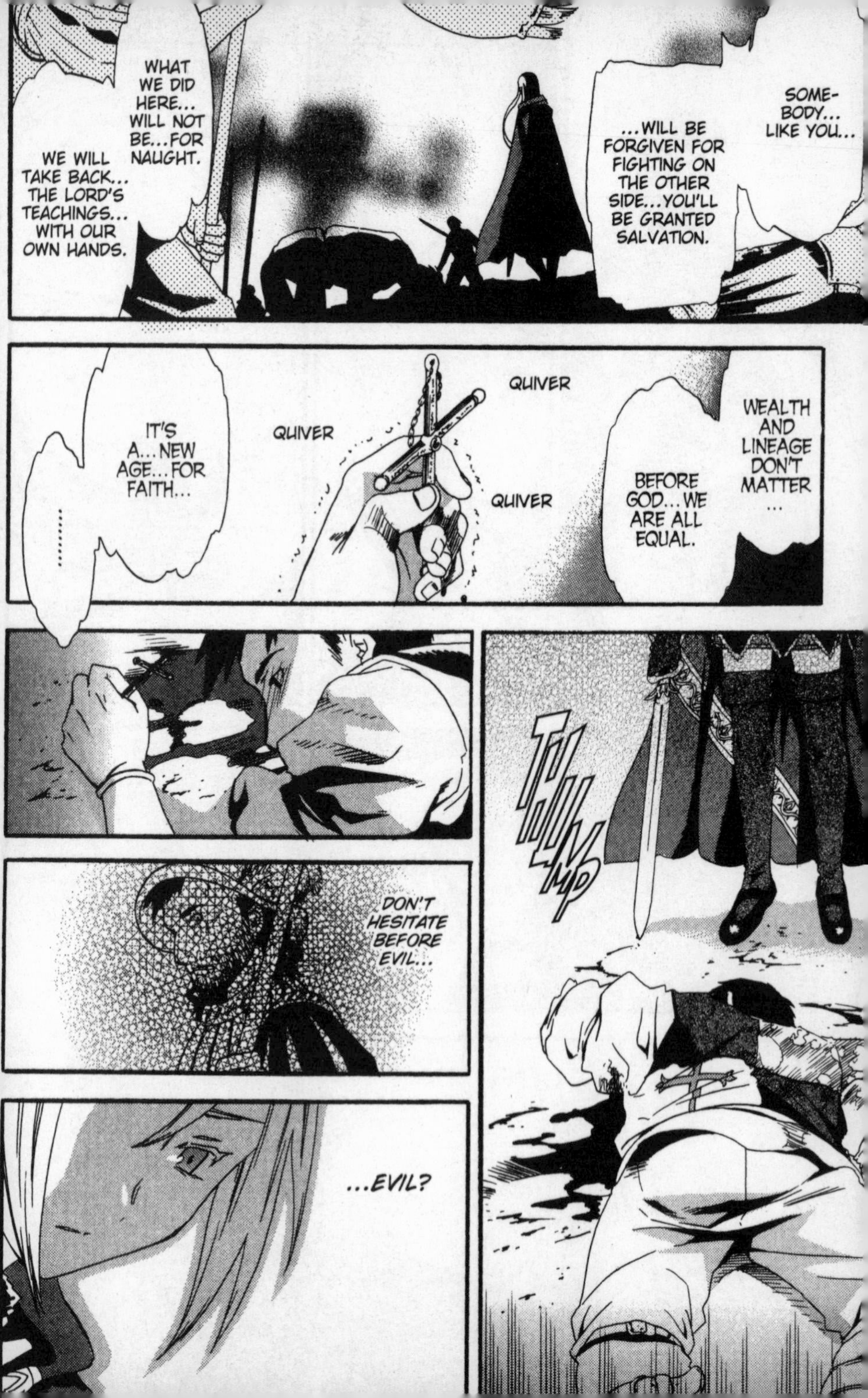
SOME-BODY... LIKE YOU...
...WILL BE FORGIVEN FOR FIGHTING ON THE OTHER SIDE...YOU'LL BE GRANTED SALVATION.
WHAT WE DID HERE... WILL NOT BE...FOR NAUGHT.
WE WILL TAKE BACK... THE LORD'S TEACHINGS... WITH OUR OWN HANDS.
WEALTH AND LINEAGE DON'T MATTER...
BEFORE GOD...WE ARE ALL EQUAL.
QUIVER
QUIVER
QUIVER
IT'S A...NEW AGE...FOR FAITH...
......
THUMP
DON'T HESITATE BEFORE EVIL...
...EVIL?

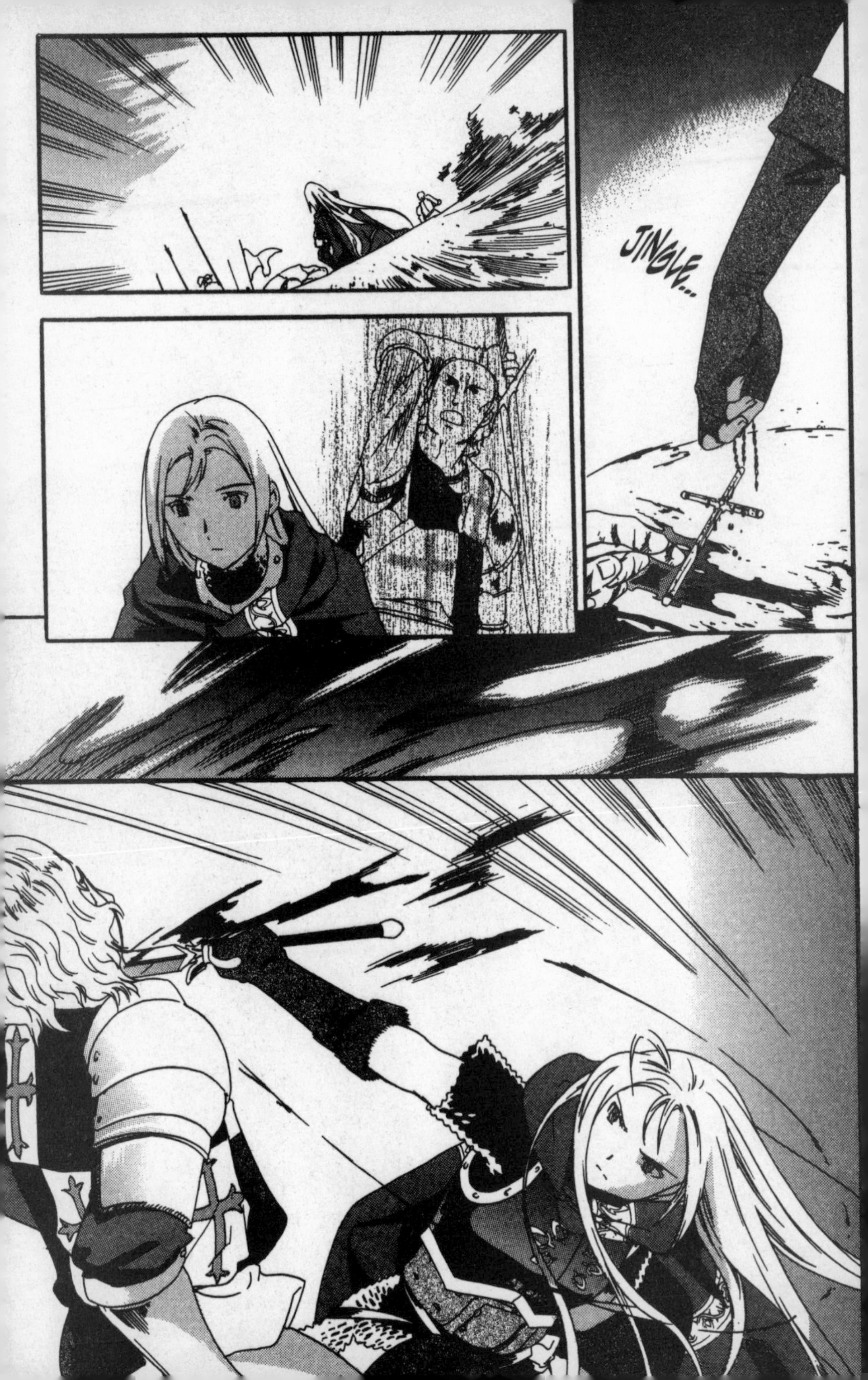
JINGLE...

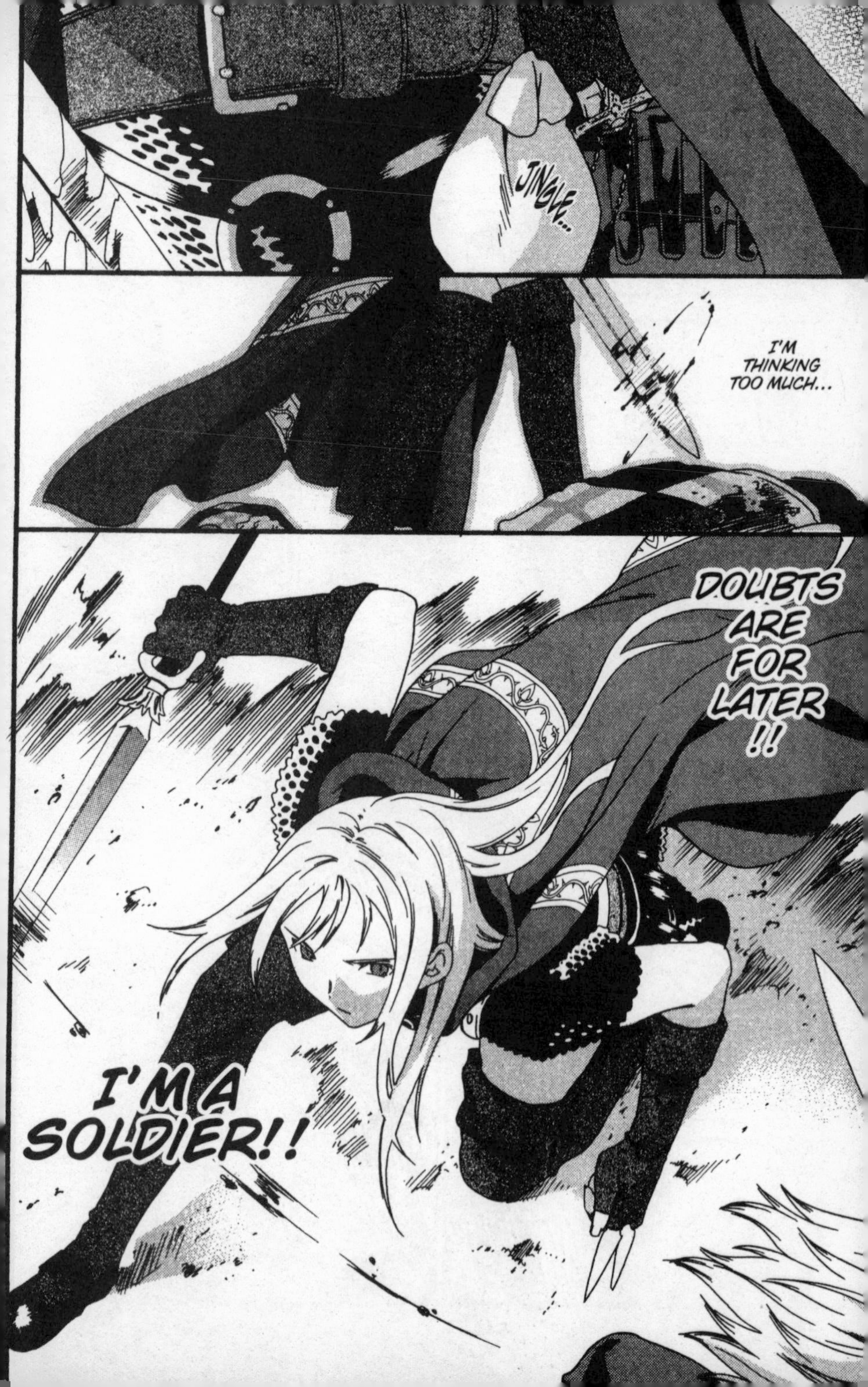
JINGLE...
I'M THINKING TOO MUCH...
DOUBTS ARE FOR LATER!!
I'M A SOLDIER!!

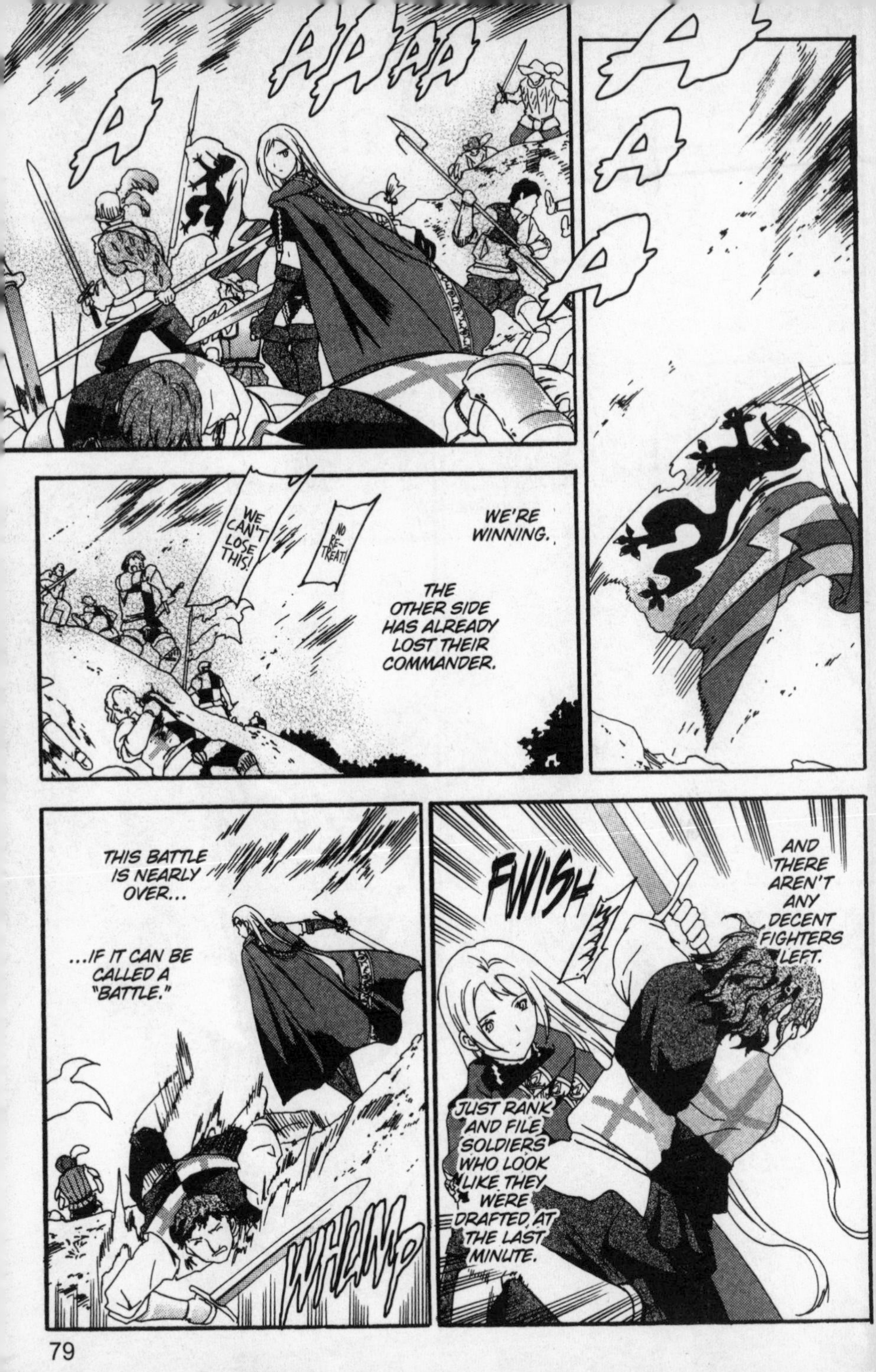

A
AAAA
WE CAN'T LOSE THIS!
NO RETREAT!
WE'RE WINNING.
THE OTHER SIDE HAS ALREADY LOST THEIR COMMANDER.
A
A
A
THIS BATTLE IS NEARLY OVER...
...IF IT CAN BE CALLED A "BATTLE."
WHUMP
FWISH
WAAA
AND THERE AREN'T ANY DECENT FIGHTERS LEFT.
JUST RANK AND FILE SOLDIERS WHO LOOK LIKE THEY WERE DRAFTED AT THE LAST MINUTE.

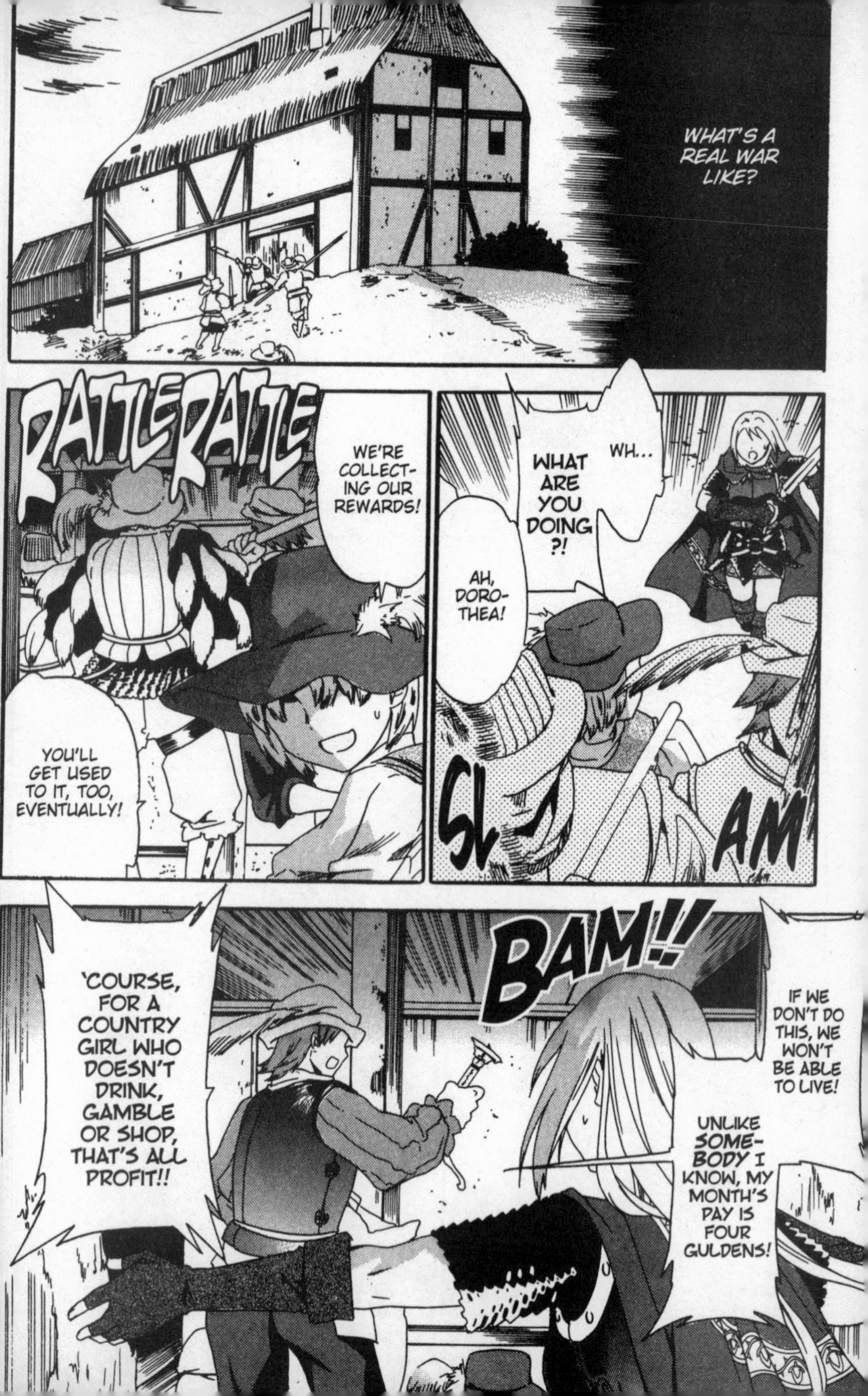
WHAT'S A REAL WAR LIKE?
WH...
WHAT ARE YOU DOING?!
AH, DOROTHEA!
SL AM
RATTLE RATTLE
WE'RE COLLECTING OUR REWARDS!
YOU'LL GET USED TO IT, TOO, EVENTUALLY!
IF WE DON'T DO THIS, WE WON'T BE ABLE TO LIVE!
BAM!!
UNLIKE *SOMEBODY* I KNOW, MY MONTH'S PAY IS FOUR GULDENS!
'COURSE, FOR A COUNTRY GIRL WHO DOESN'T DRINK, GAMBLE OR SHOP, THAT'S ALL PROFIT!!

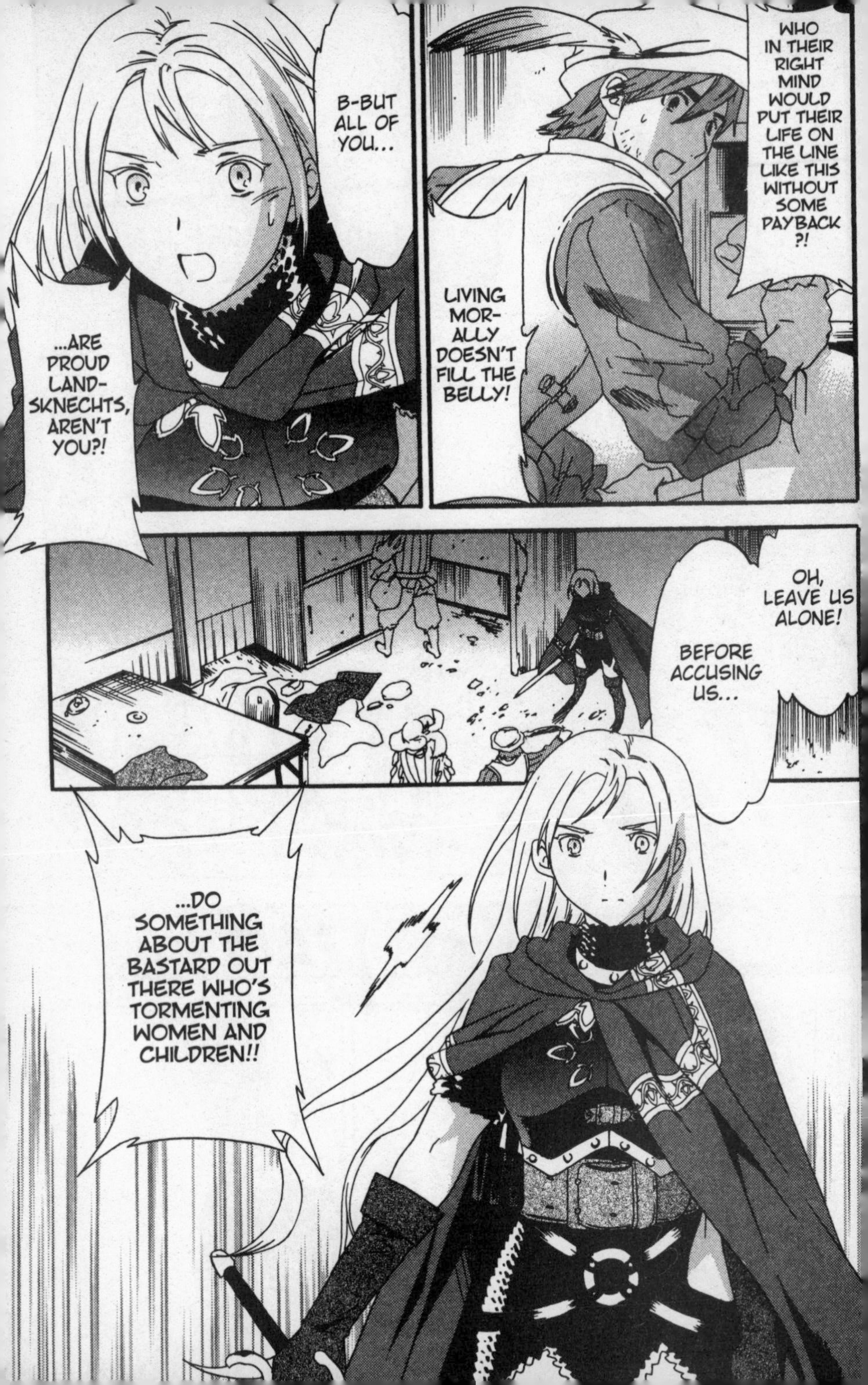

WHO IN THEIR RIGHT MIND WOULD PUT THEIR LIFE ON THE LINE LIKE THIS WITHOUT SOME PAYBACK?!
LIVING MOR-ALLY DOESN'T FILL THE BELLY!
B-BUT ALL OF YOU...
...ARE PROUD LAND-SKNECHTS, AREN'T YOU?!
OH, LEAVE US ALONE!
BEFORE ACCUSING US...
...DO SOMETHING ABOUT THE BASTARD OUT THERE WHO'S TORMENTING WOMEN AND CHILDREN!!

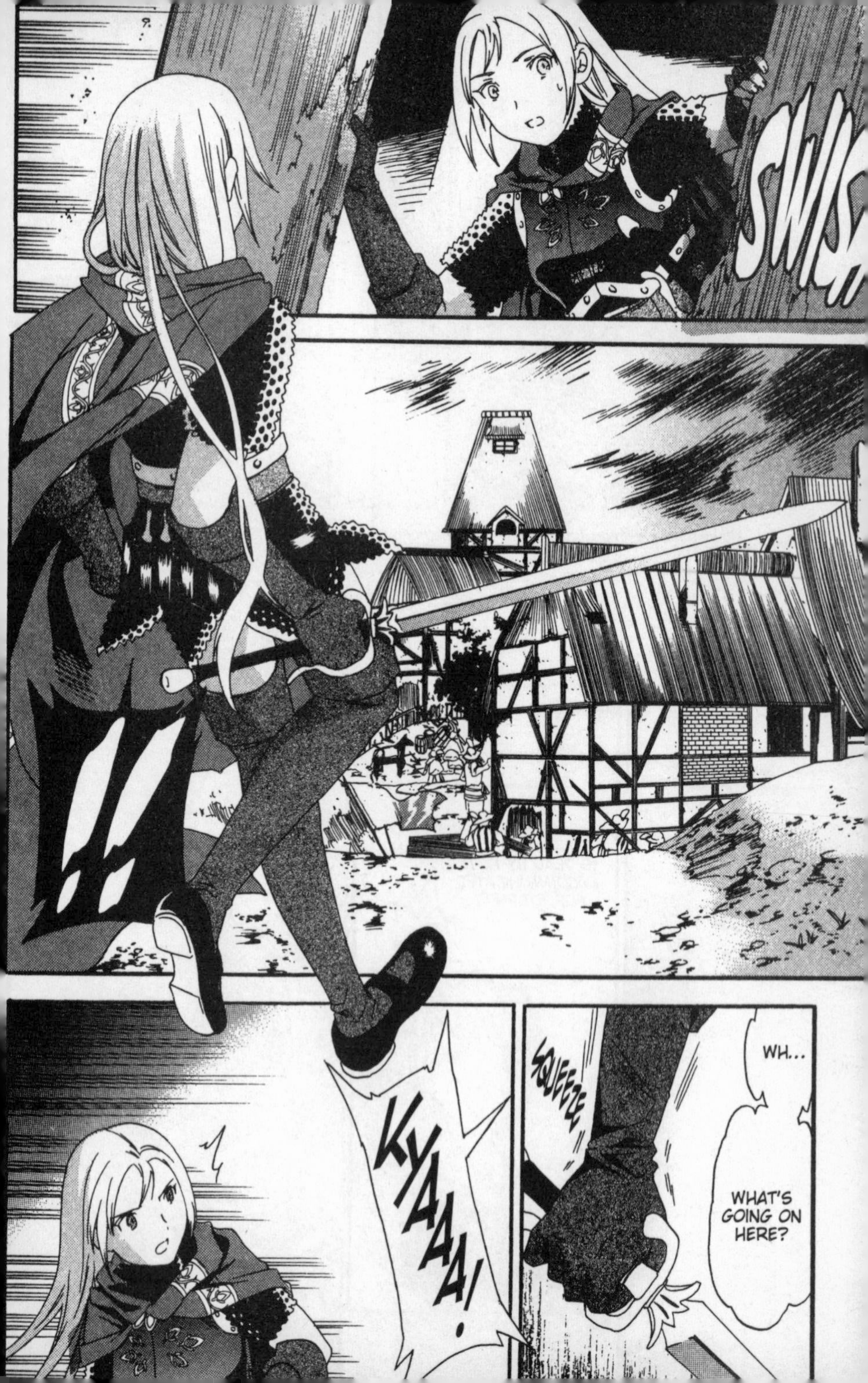
SWISH
WH...
WHAT'S GOING ON HERE?
SQUEEZE
KYAAAA!

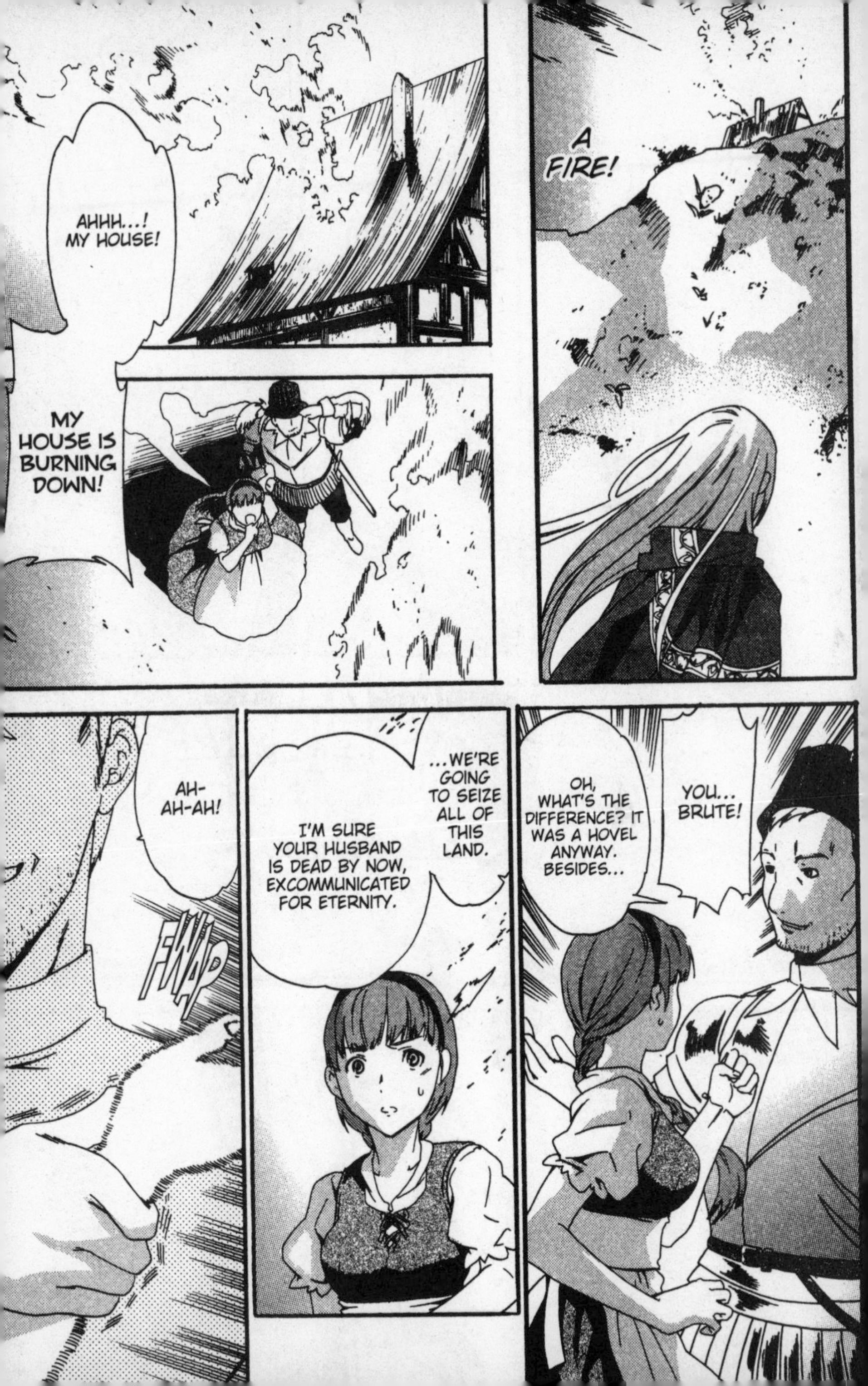
A FIRE!
AHHH...! MY HOUSE!
MY HOUSE IS BURNING DOWN!
YOU... BRUTE!
OH, WHAT'S THE DIFFERENCE? IT WAS A HOVEL ANYWAY. BESIDES...
...WE'RE GOING TO SEIZE ALL OF THIS LAND.
I'M SURE YOUR HUSBAND IS DEAD BY NOW, EXCOMMUNICATED FOR ETERNITY.
AH-AH-AH!
FWAP

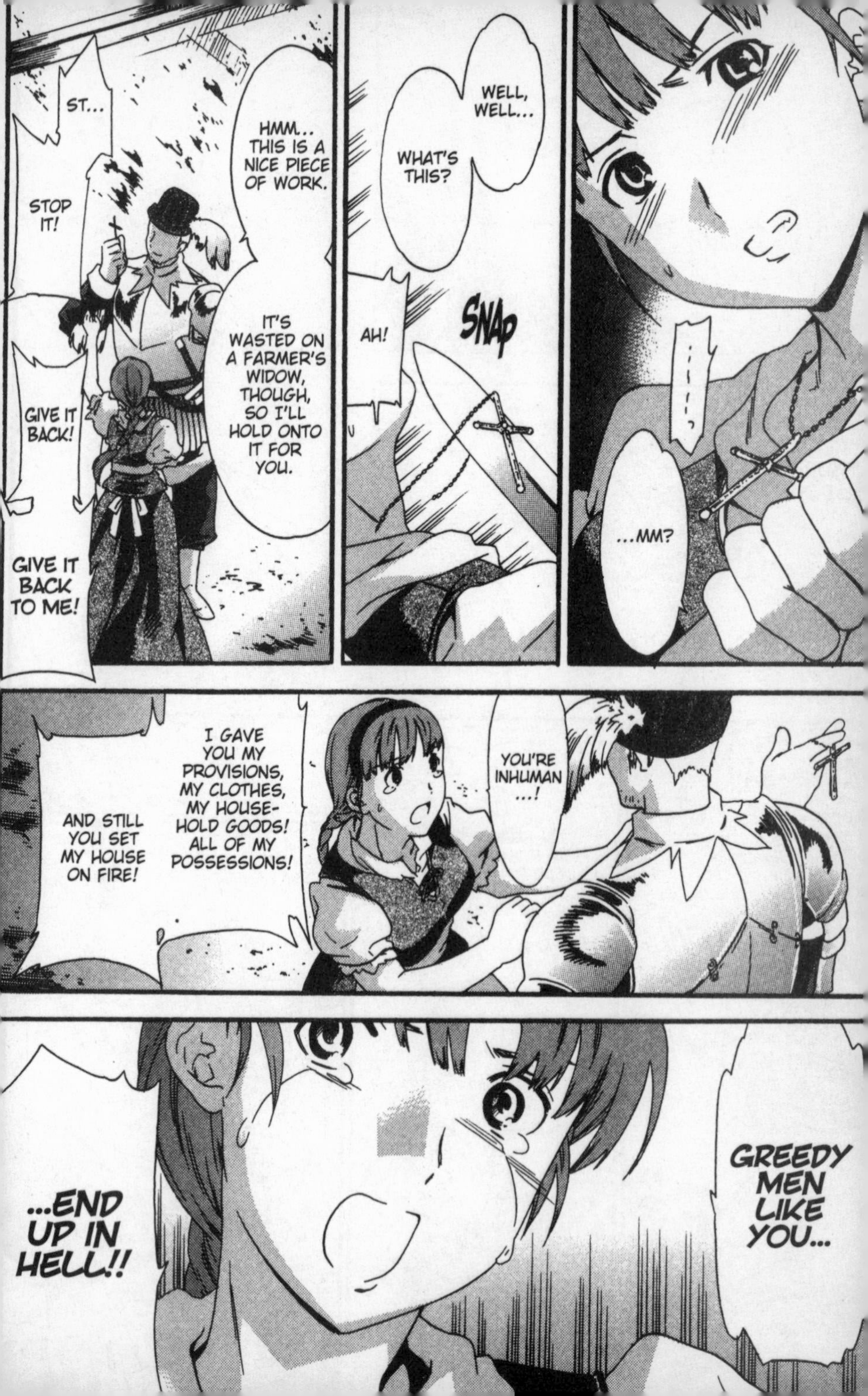
...MM?
WELL, WELL...
WHAT'S THIS?
SNAP
AH!
HMM... THIS IS A NICE PIECE OF WORK.
IT'S WASTED ON A FARMER'S WIDOW, THOUGH, SO I'LL HOLD ONTO IT FOR YOU.
ST...
STOP IT!
GIVE IT BACK!
GIVE IT BACK TO ME!
YOU'RE INHUMAN ...!
I GAVE YOU MY PROVISIONS, MY CLOTHES, MY HOUSE-HOLD GOODS! ALL OF MY POSSESSIONS!
AND STILL YOU SET MY HOUSE ON FIRE!
GREEDY MEN LIKE YOU...
...END UP IN HELL!!

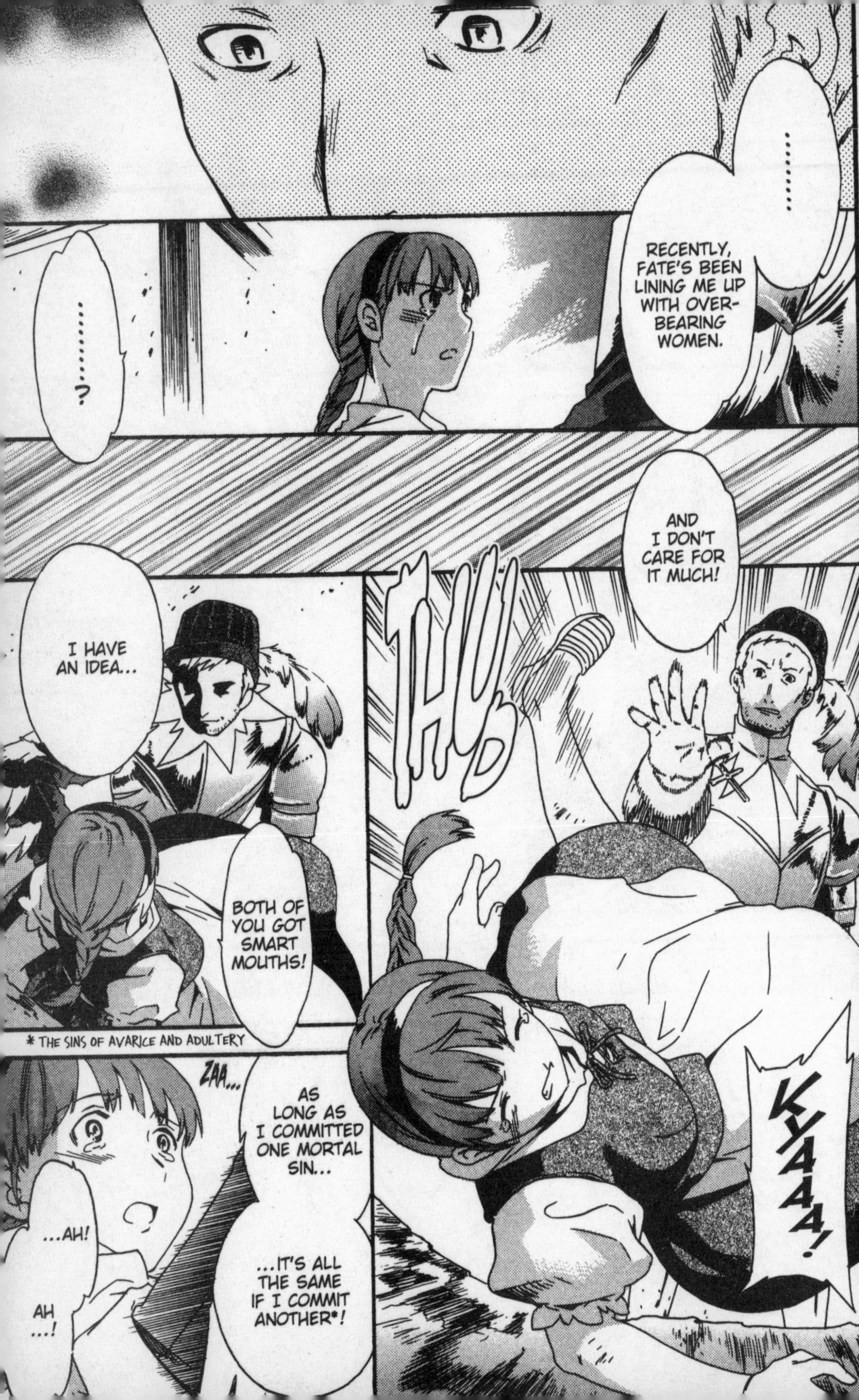
......
RECENTLY, FATE'S BEEN LINING ME UP WITH OVER-BEARING WOMEN.
......?
AND I DON'T CARE FOR IT MUCH!
THUD
KYAAA!
I HAVE AN IDEA...
BOTH OF YOU GOT SMART MOUTHS!
AS LONG AS I COMMITTED ONE MORTAL SIN...
...IT'S ALL THE SAME IF I COMMIT ANOTHER*!
ZAA...
...AH!
AH ...!
* THE SINS OF AVARICE AND ADULTERY

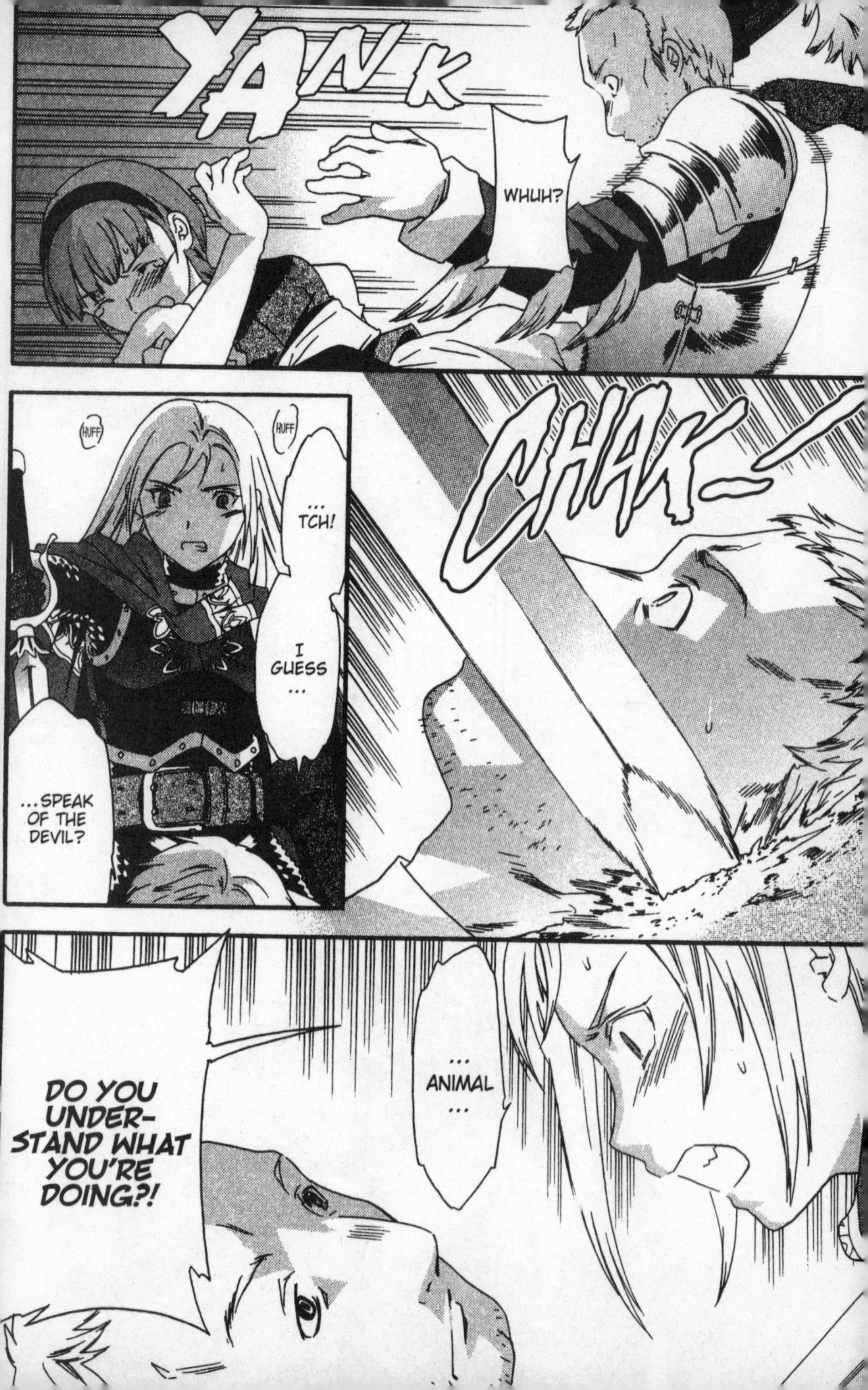
YANK
WHUH?
CHAK--!
HUFF
HUFF
...TCH!
I GUESS...
...SPEAK OF THE DEVIL?
...ANIMAL...
DO YOU UNDER-STAND WHAT YOU'RE DOING?!

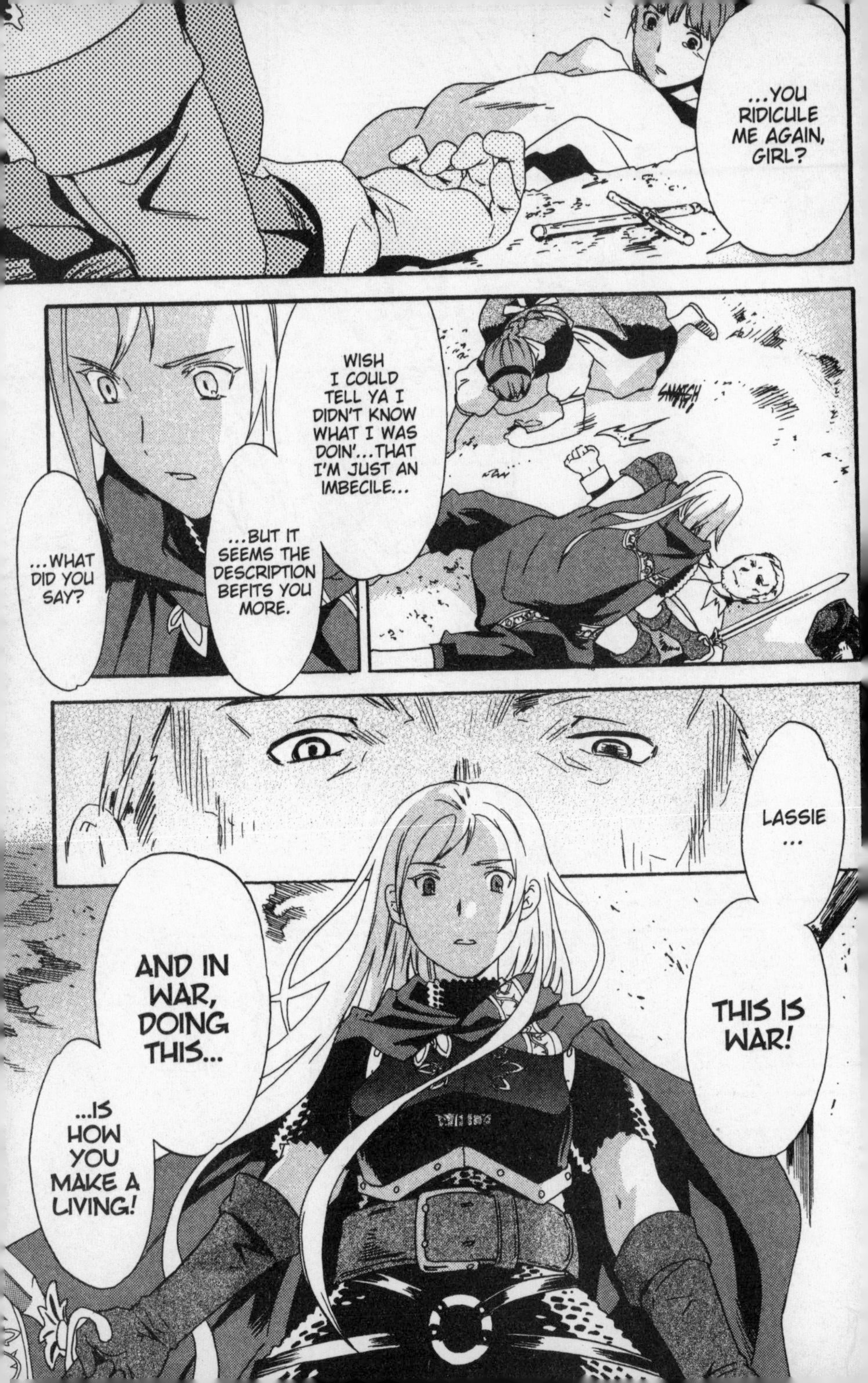
...YOU RIDICULE ME AGAIN, GIRL?
SMASH
WISH I COULD TELL YA I DIDN'T KNOW WHAT I WAS DOIN'...THAT I'M JUST AN IMBECILE...
...BUT IT SEEMS THE DESCRIPTION BEFITS YOU MORE.
...WHAT DID YOU SAY?
LASSIE...
THIS IS WAR!
AND IN WAR, DOING THIS...
...IS HOW YOU MAKE A LIVING!

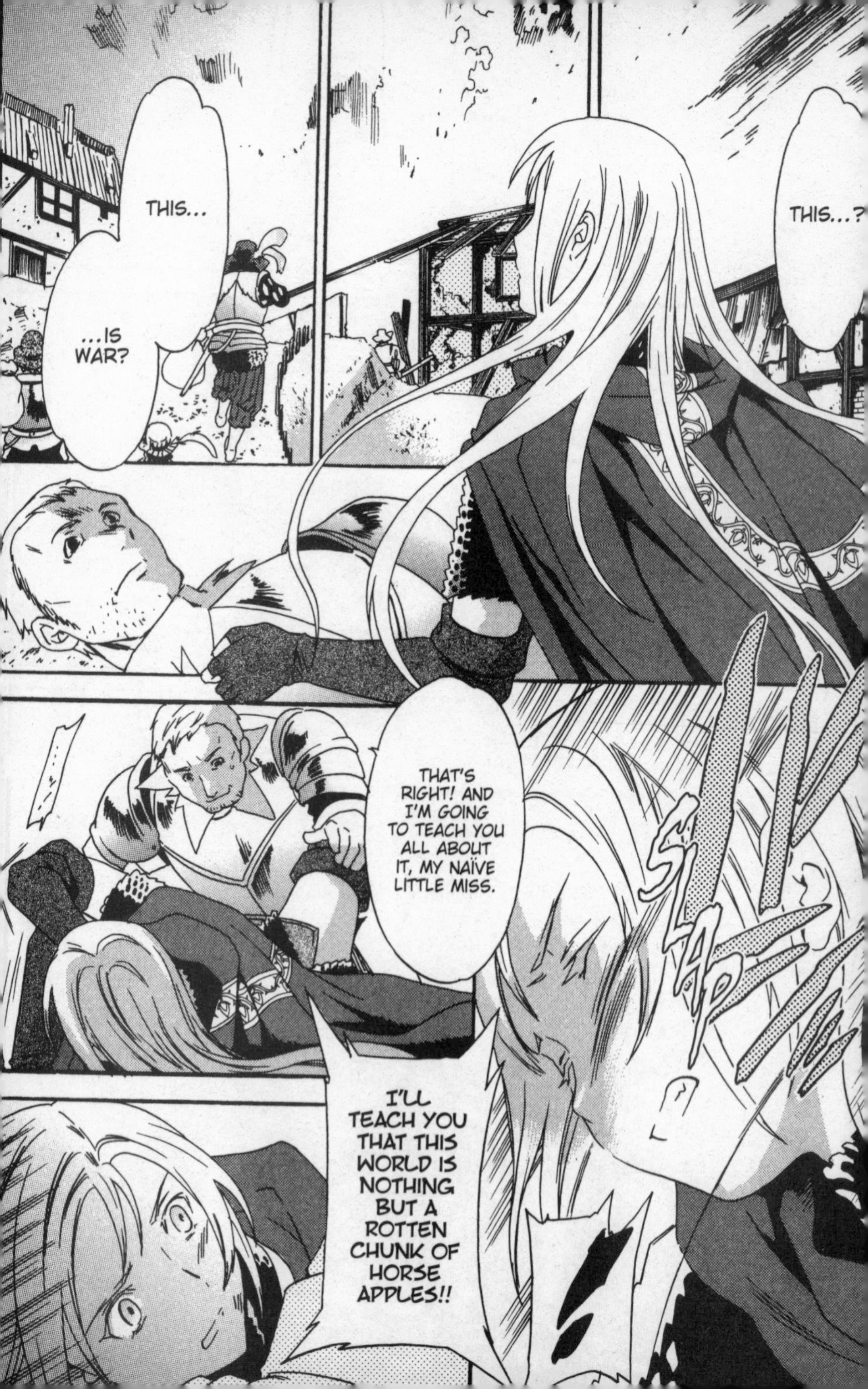
THIS...?
THIS...
...IS WAR?
SLAP
THAT'S RIGHT! AND I'M GOING TO TEACH YOU ALL ABOUT IT, MY NAÏVE LITTLE MISS.
I'LL TEACH YOU THAT THIS WORLD IS NOTHING BUT A ROTTEN CHUNK OF HORSE APPLES!!

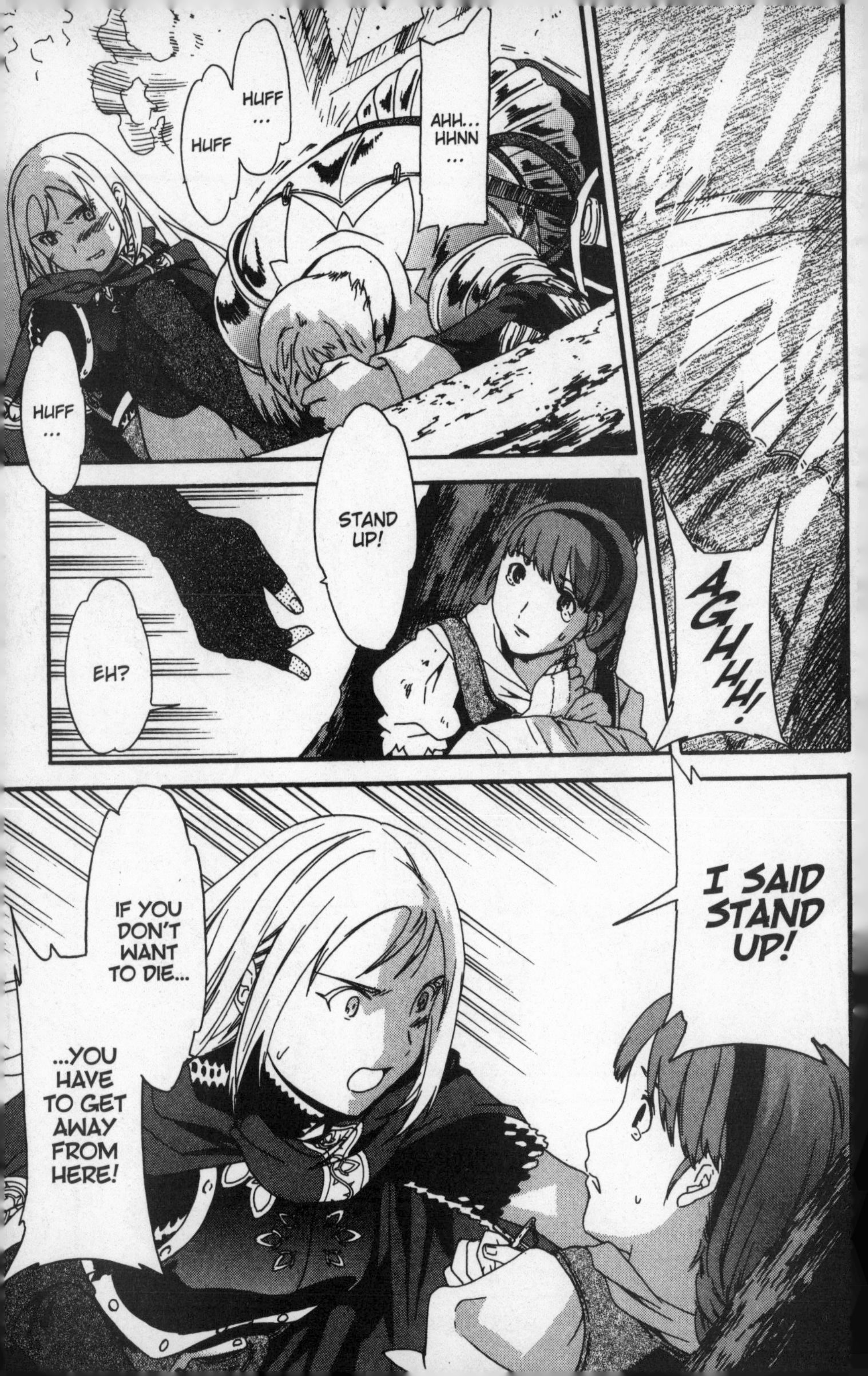
AGHHH!
AHH... HHNN ...
HUFF ... HUFF
HUFF ...
STAND UP!
EH?
I SAID STAND UP!
IF YOU DON'T WANT TO DIE...
...YOU HAVE TO GET AWAY FROM HERE!

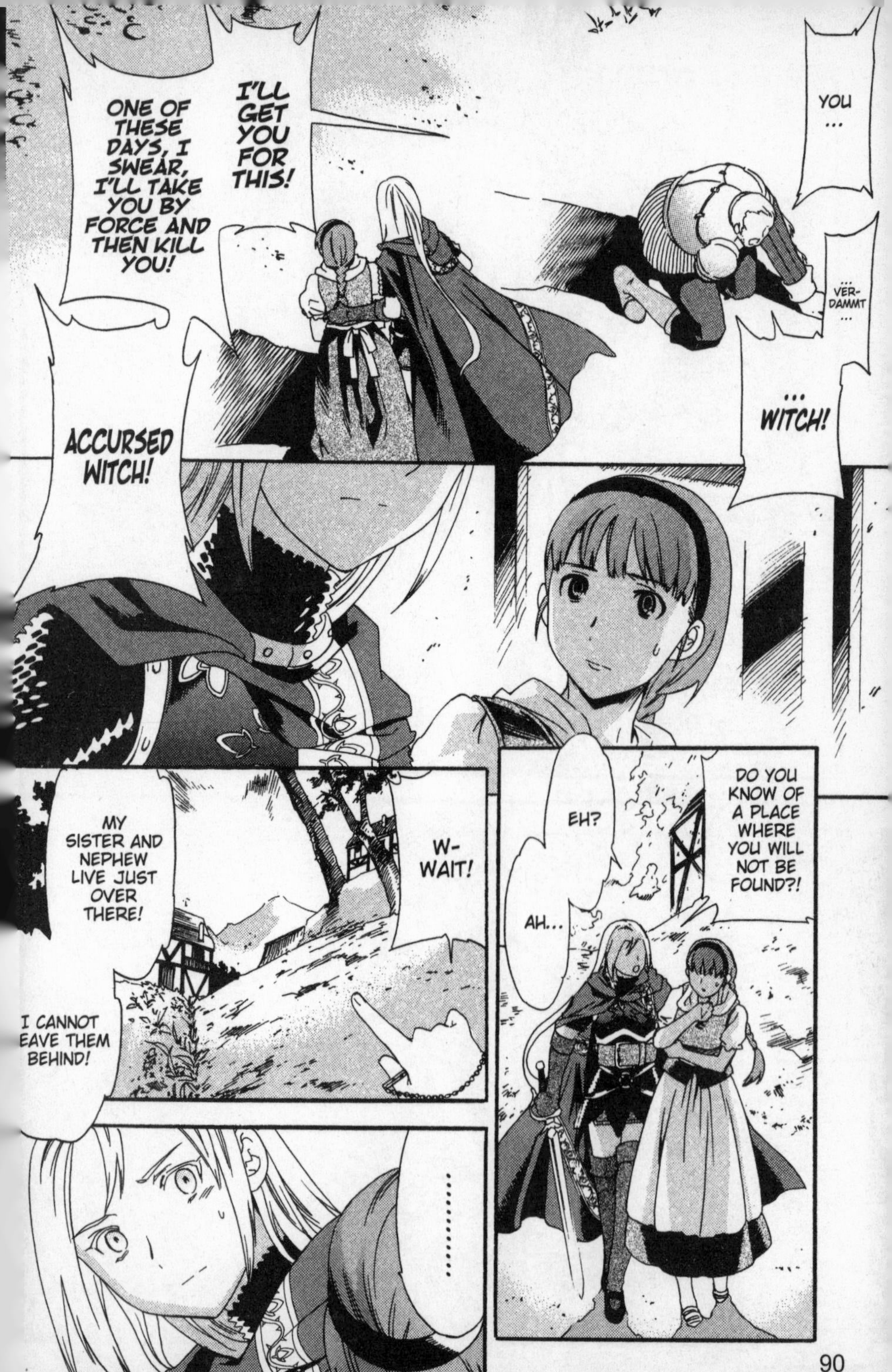
YOU ...
... VERDAMMT ...
... WITCH!
I'LL GET YOU FOR THIS!
ONE OF THESE DAYS, I SWEAR, I'LL TAKE YOU BY FORCE AND THEN KILL YOU!
ACCURSED WITCH!
DO YOU KNOW OF A PLACE WHERE YOU WILL NOT BE FOUND?!
EH?
AH...
W-WAIT!
MY SISTER AND NEPHEW LIVE JUST OVER THERE!
I CANNOT EAVE THEM BEHIND!
......

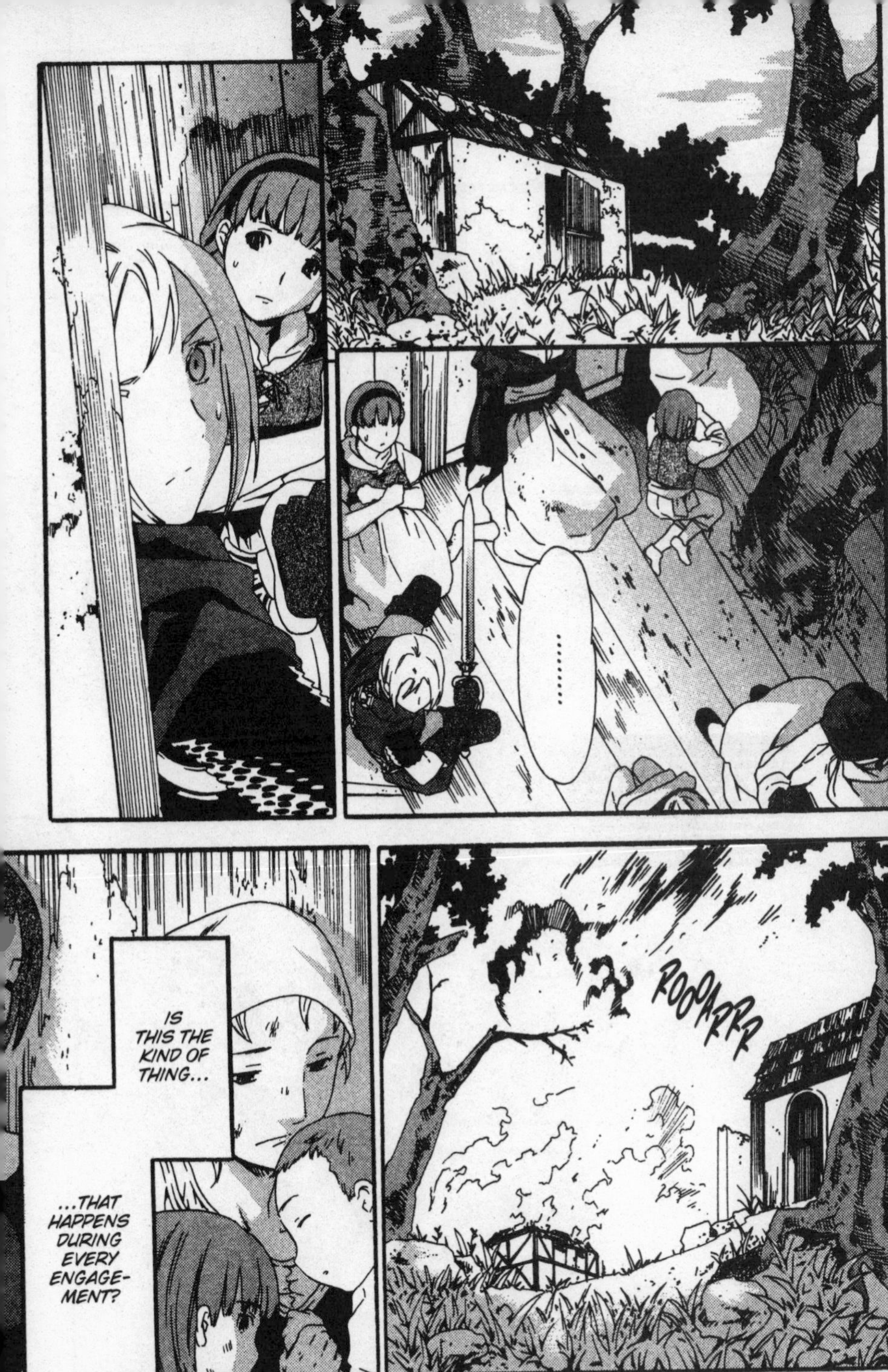
......
ROOOARRR
IS THIS THE KIND OF THING...
...THAT HAPPENS DURING EVERY ENGAGEMENT?

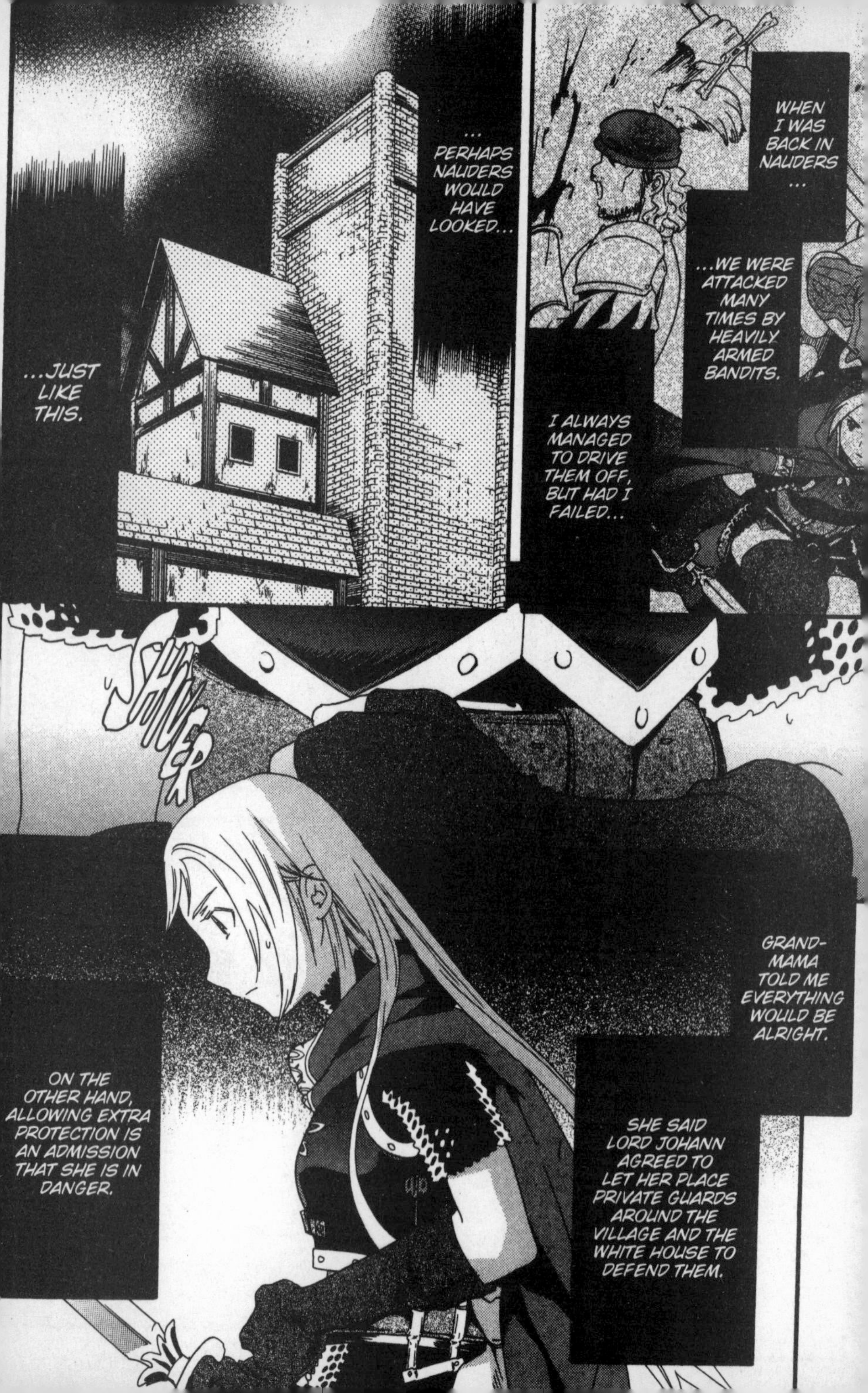

WHEN I WAS BACK IN NAUDERS...
...WE WERE ATTACKED MANY TIMES BY HEAVILY ARMED BANDITS.
I ALWAYS MANAGED TO DRIVE THEM OFF, BUT HAD I FAILED...
...PERHAPS NAUDERS WOULD HAVE LOOKED...
...JUST LIKE THIS.
SHIVER
GRAND-MAMA TOLD ME EVERYTHING WOULD BE ALRIGHT.
SHE SAID LORD JOHANN AGREED TO LET HER PLACE PRIVATE GUARDS AROUND THE VILLAGE AND THE WHITE HOUSE TO DEFEND THEM.
ON THE OTHER HAND, ALLOWING EXTRA PROTECTION IS AN ADMISSION THAT SHE IS IN DANGER.

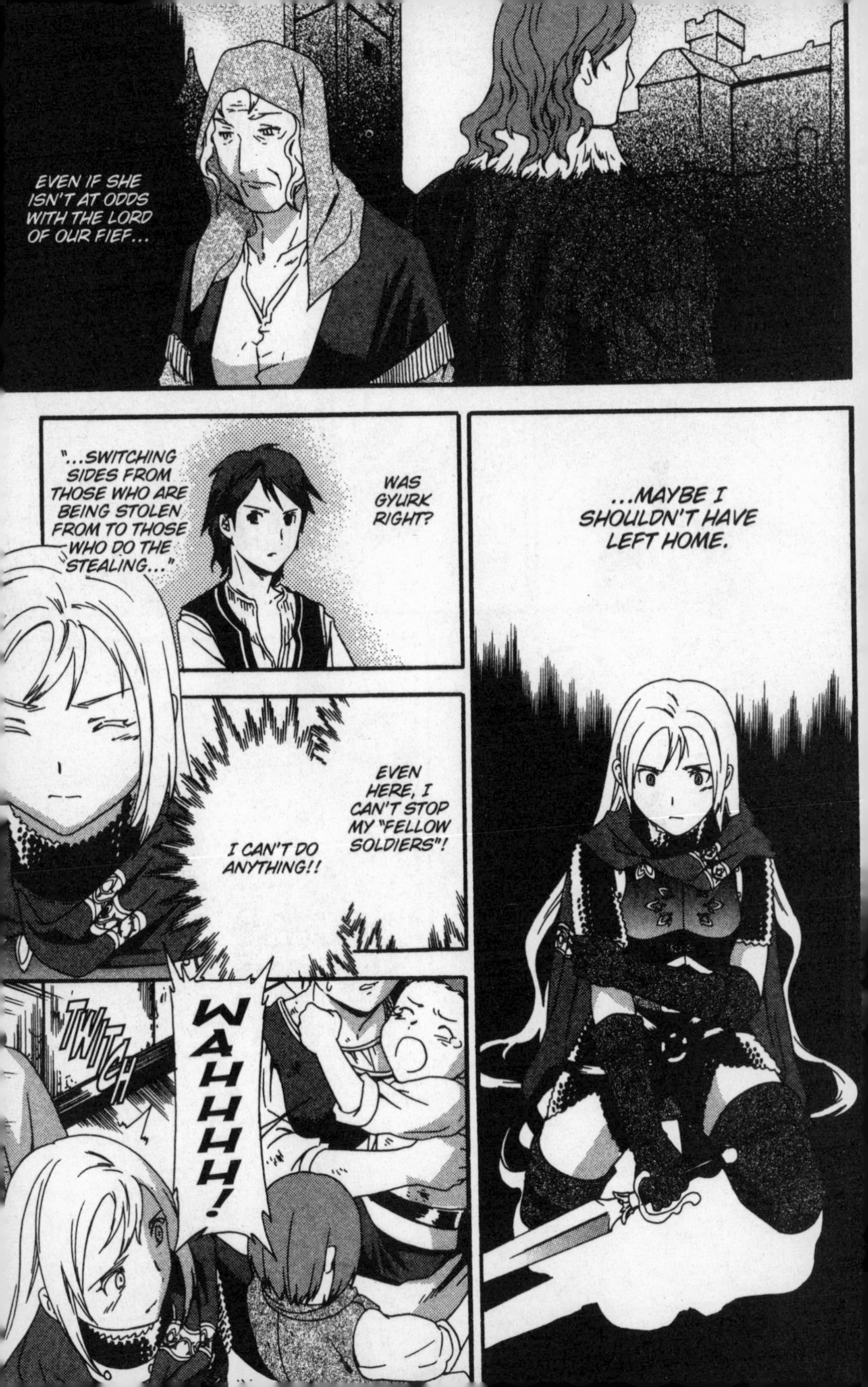
EVEN IF SHE ISN'T AT ODDS WITH THE LORD OF OUR FIEF...
"...SWITCHING SIDES FROM THOSE WHO ARE BEING STOLEN FROM TO THOSE WHO DO THE STEALING..."
WAS GYURK RIGHT?
I CAN'T DO ANYTHING!!
EVEN HERE, I CAN'T STOP MY "FELLOW SOLDIERS"!
TWITCH
WAHHHH!
...MAYBE I SHOULDN'T HAVE LEFT HOME.

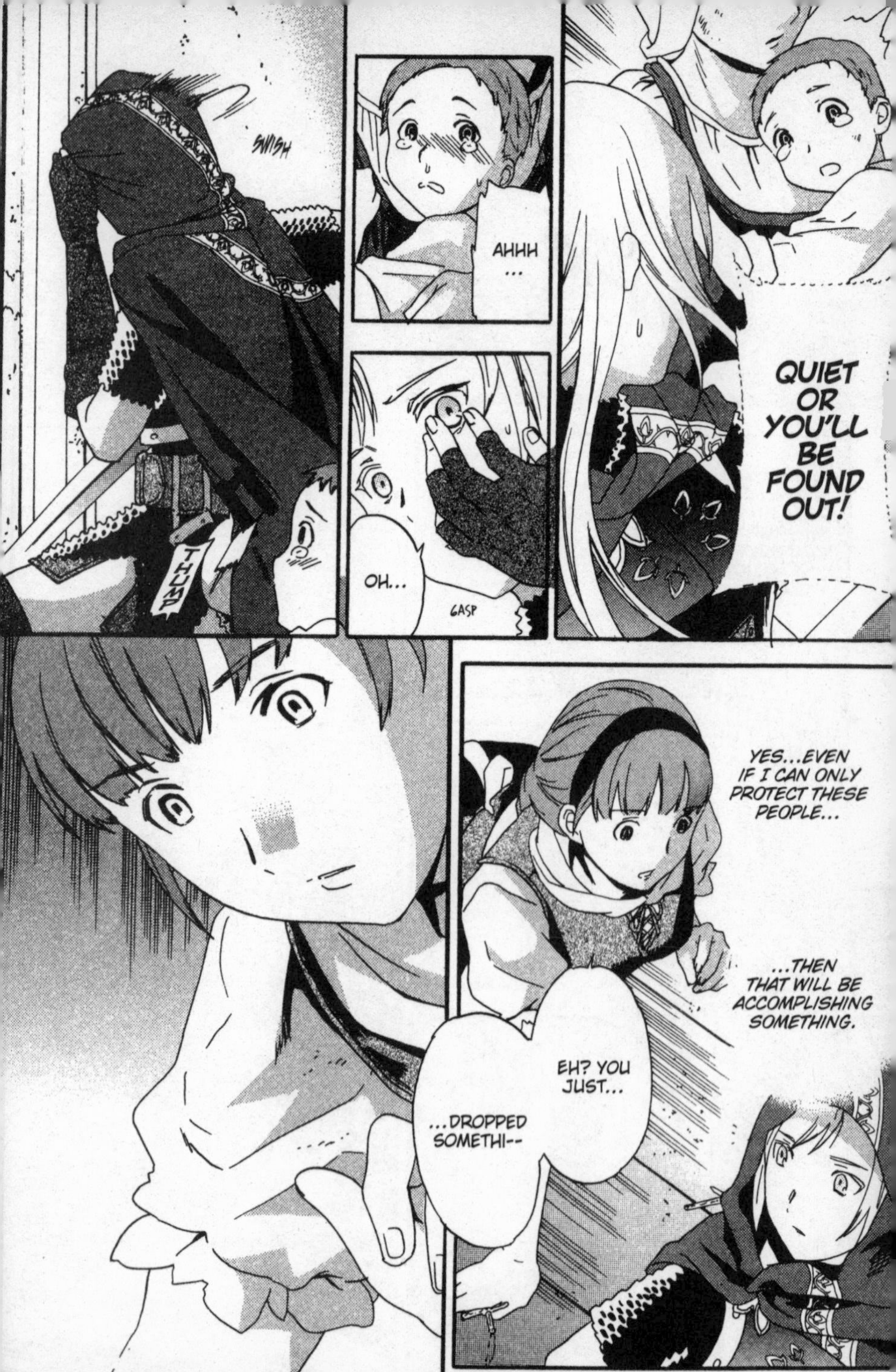
QUIET OR YOU'LL BE FOUND OUT!
AHHH ...
OH...
GASP
SWISH
THUMP
YES...EVEN IF I CAN ONLY PROTECT THESE PEOPLE...
...THEN THAT WILL BE ACCOMPLISHING SOMETHING.
EH? YOU JUST...
...DROPPED SOMETHI--

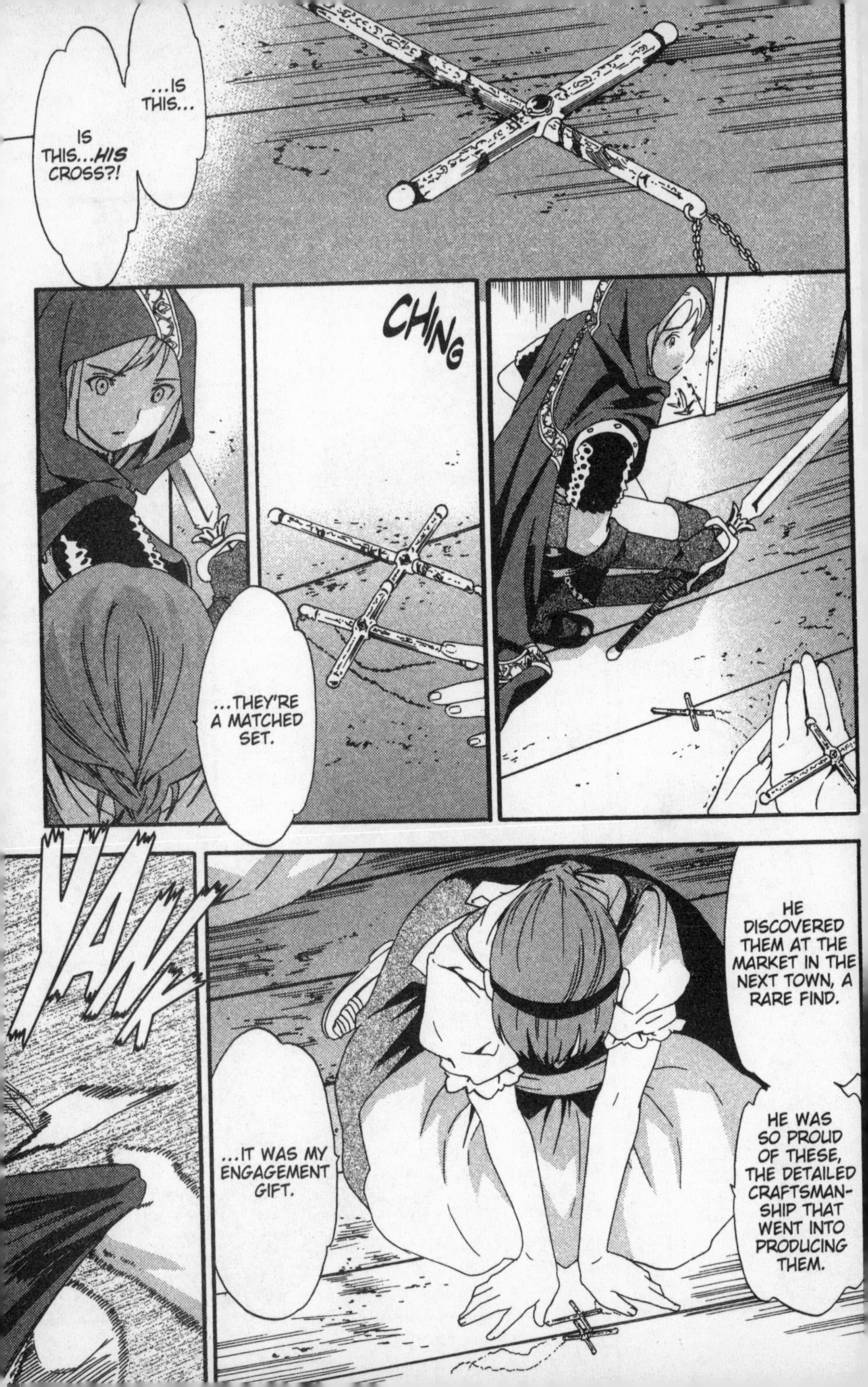
...IS THIS...
IS THIS...*HIS* CROSS?!
CHING
...THEY'RE A MATCHED SET.
HE DISCOVERED THEM AT THE MARKET IN THE NEXT TOWN, A RARE FIND.
HE WAS SO PROUD OF THESE, THE DETAILED CRAFTSMANSHIP THAT WENT INTO PRODUCING THEM.
...IT WAS MY ENGAGEMENT GIFT.
YANK

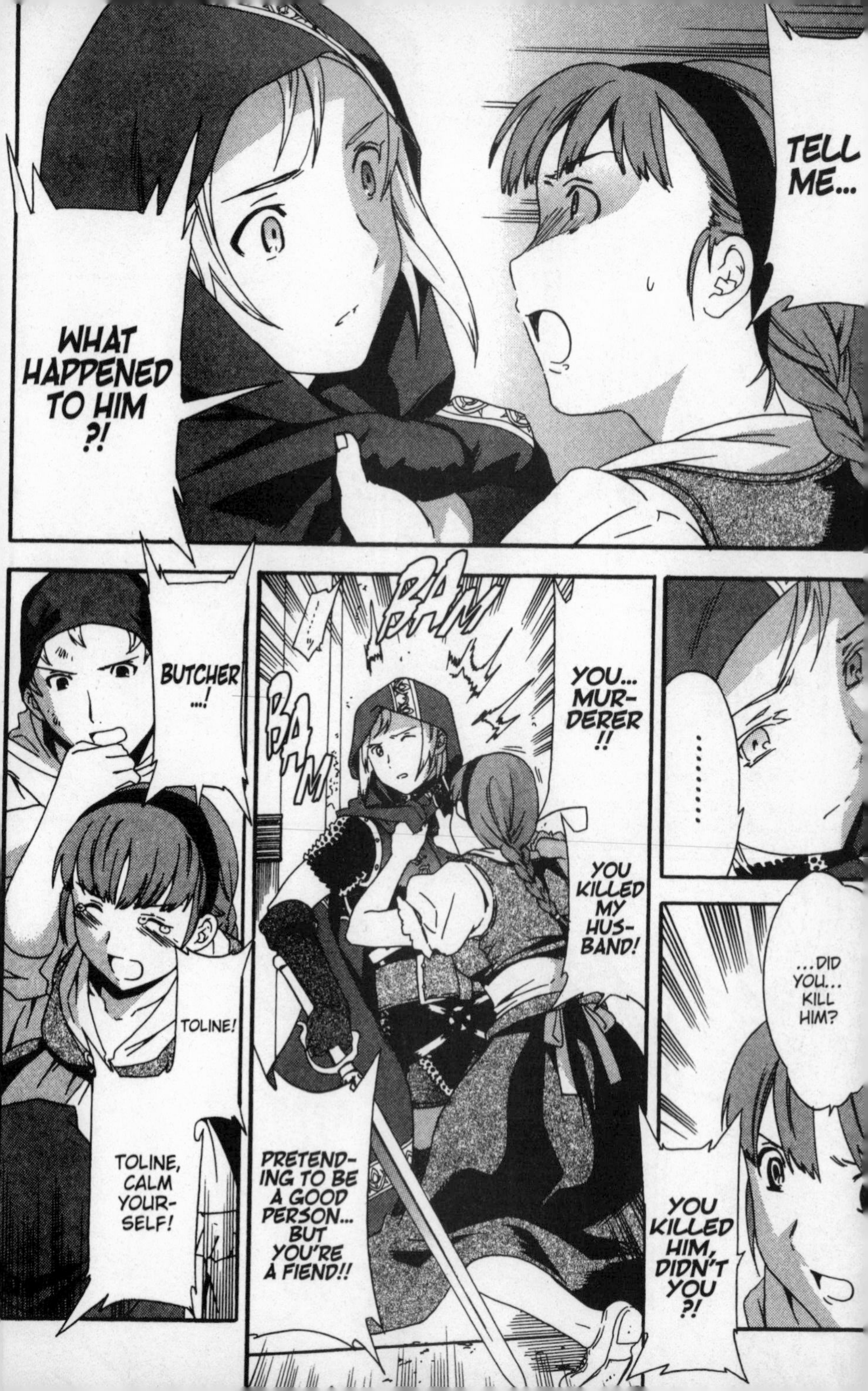
TELL ME...
WHAT HAPPENED TO HIM ?!
......
...DID YOU... KILL HIM?
YOU KILLED HIM, DIDN'T YOU ?!
BAM
BAM
YOU... MUR-DERER !!
YOU KILLED MY HUS-BAND!
PRETEND-ING TO BE A GOOD PERSON... BUT YOU'RE A FIEND!!
BUTCHER ...!
TOLINE!
TOLINE, CALM YOUR-SELF!

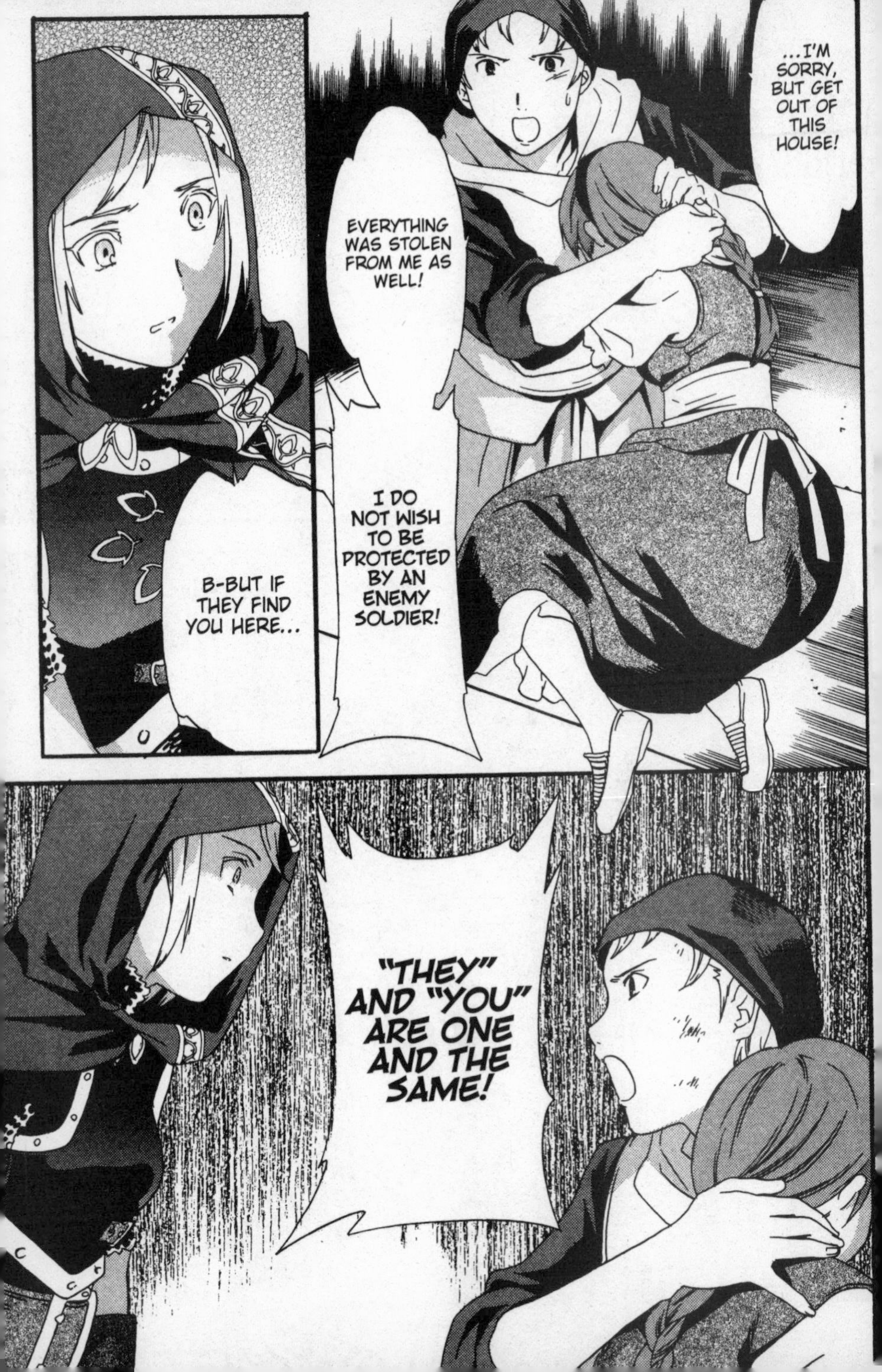
...I'M SORRY, BUT GET OUT OF THIS HOUSE!
B-BUT IF THEY FIND YOU HERE...
EVERYTHING WAS STOLEN FROM ME AS WELL!
I DO NOT WISH TO BE PROTECTED BY AN ENEMY SOLDIER!
"THEY" AND "YOU" ARE ONE AND THE SAME!

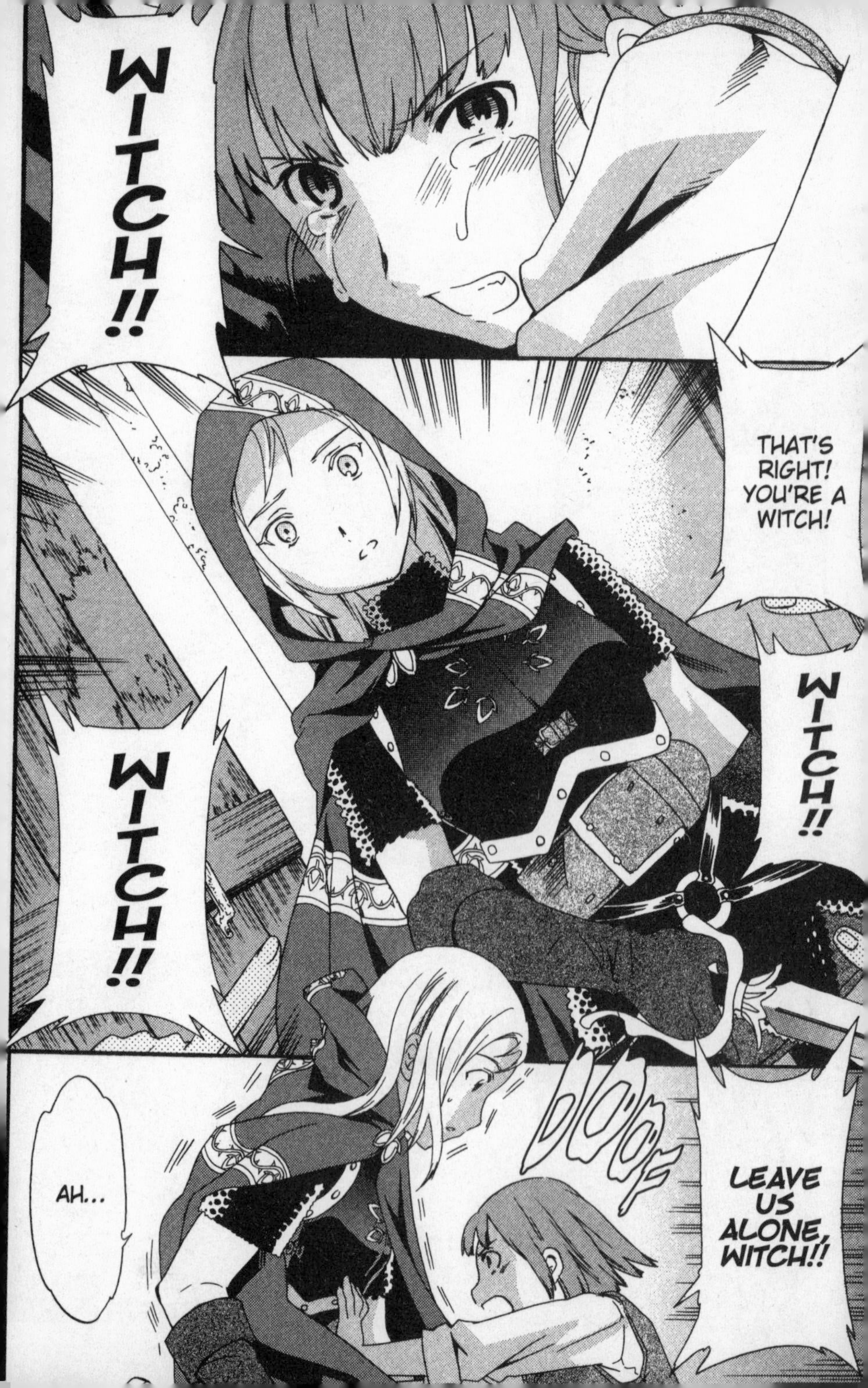
WITCH!!
THAT'S RIGHT! YOU'RE A WITCH!
WITCH!!
WITCH!!
LEAVE US ALONE, WITCH!!
AH...

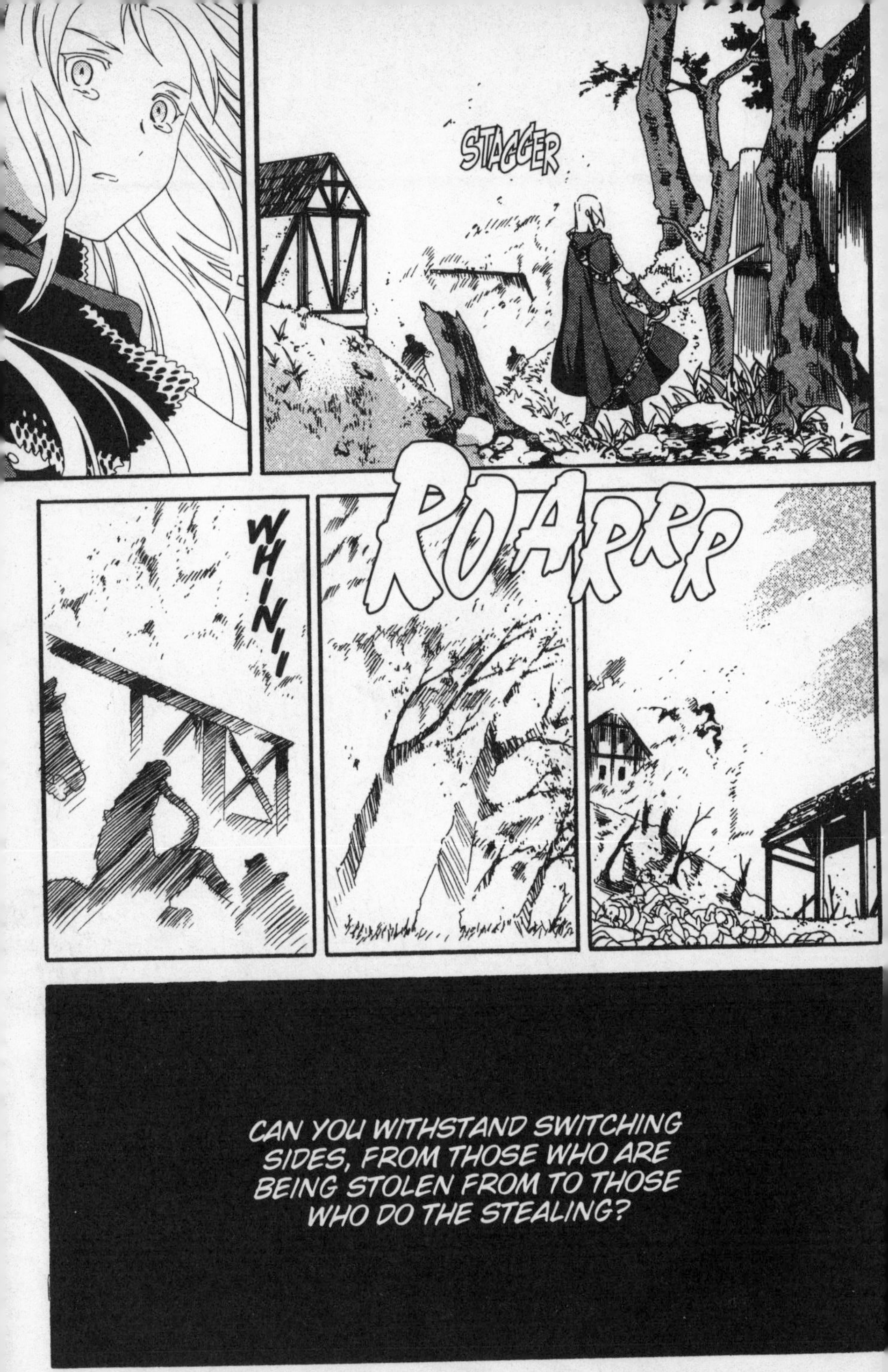
STAGGER
ROARRR
WHINIII
CAN YOU WITHSTAND SWITCHING SIDES, FROM THOSE WHO ARE BEING STOLEN FROM TO THOSE WHO DO THE STEALING?

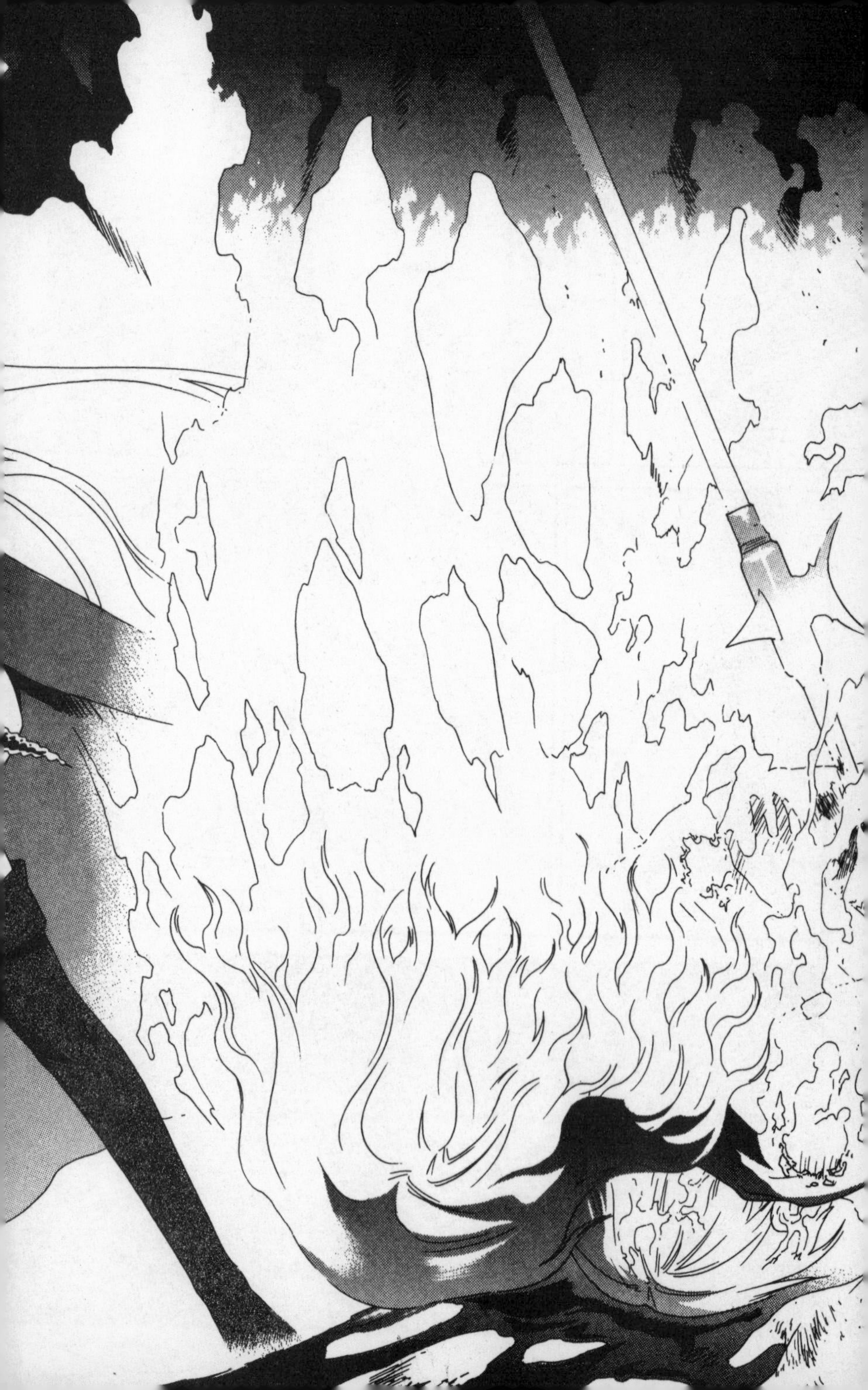

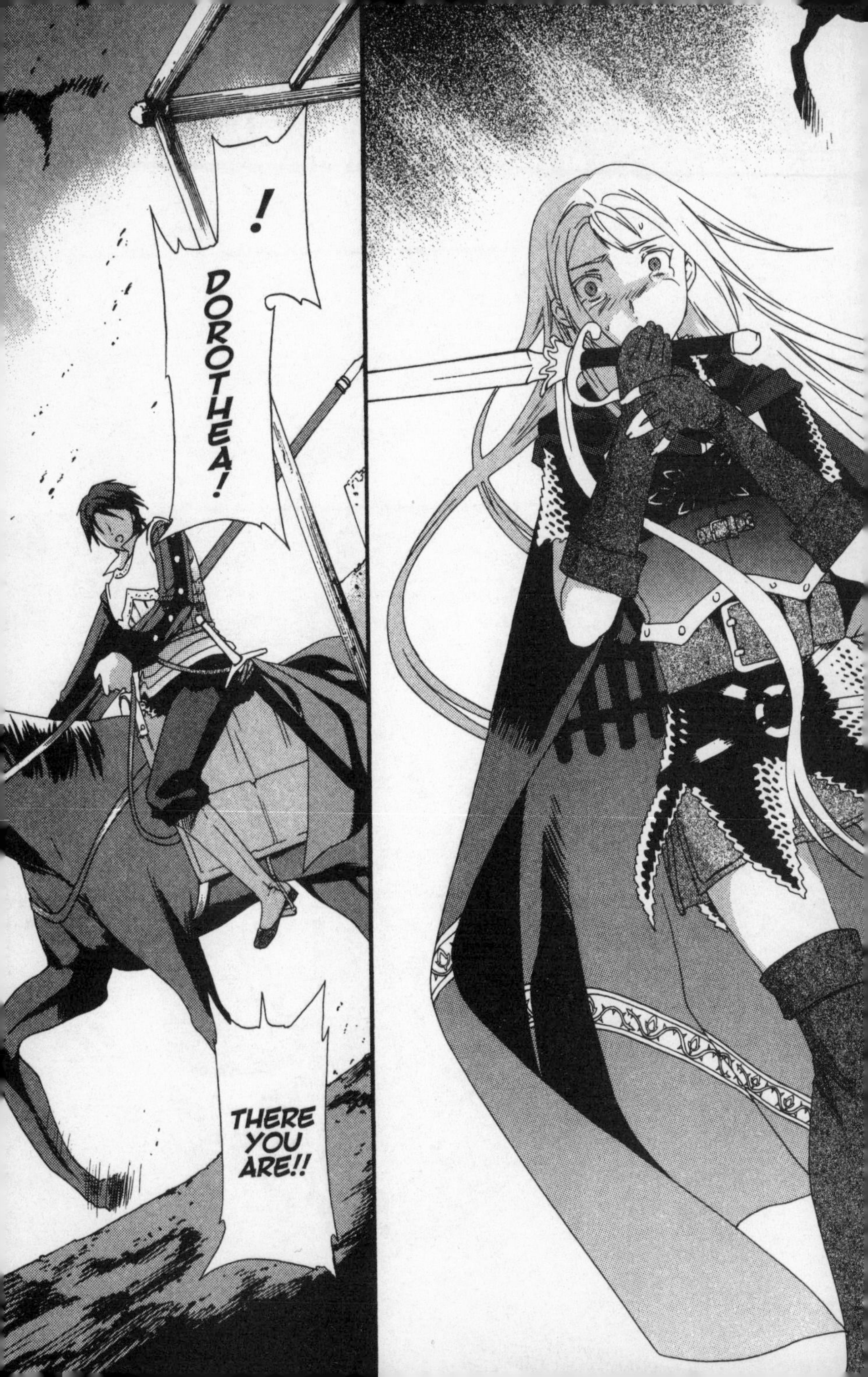
!
DOROTHEA!
THERE YOU ARE!!

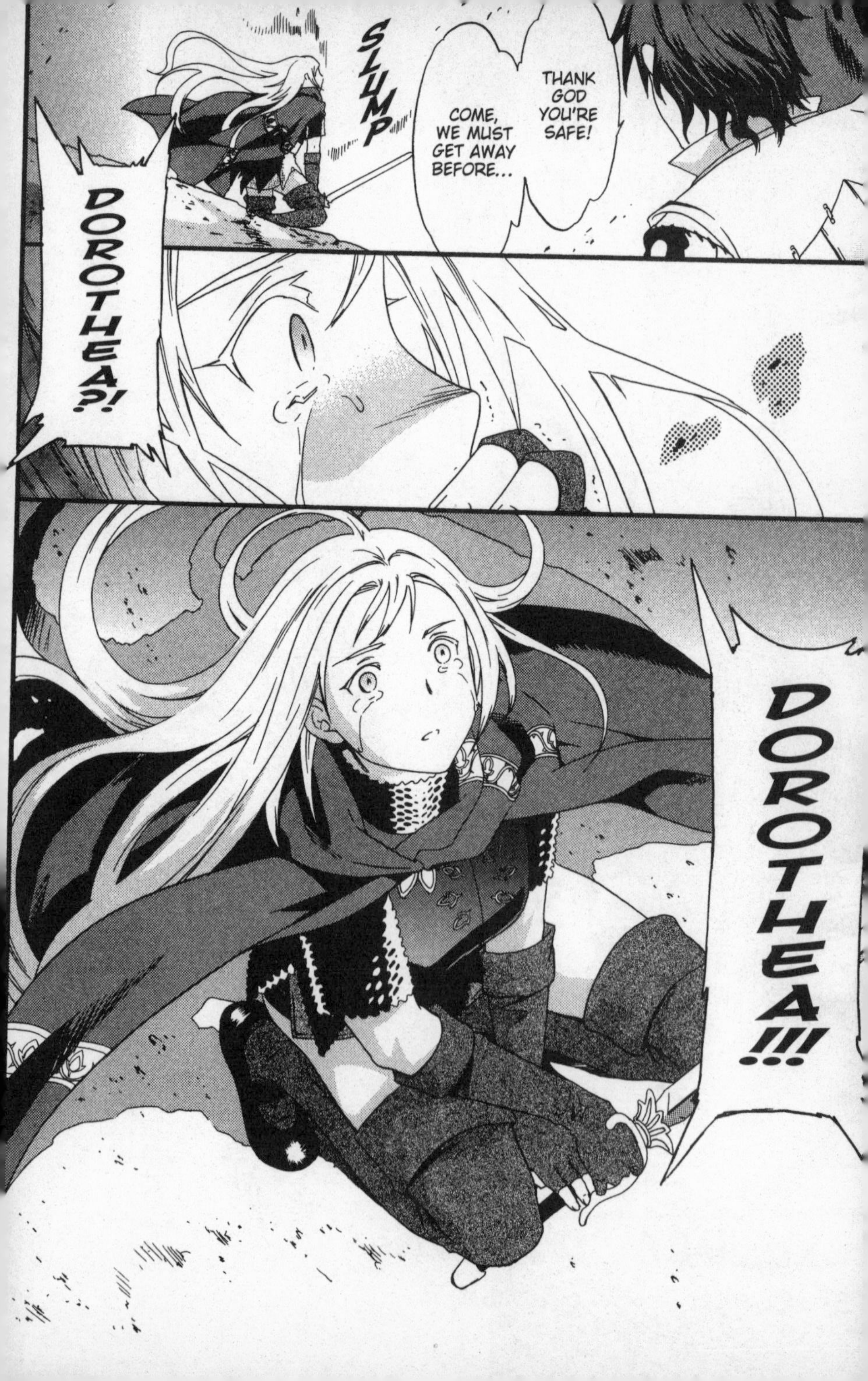
THANK GOD YOU'RE SAFE!
COME, WE MUST GET AWAY BEFORE...
SLUMP
DOROTHEA?!
DOROTHEA!!!

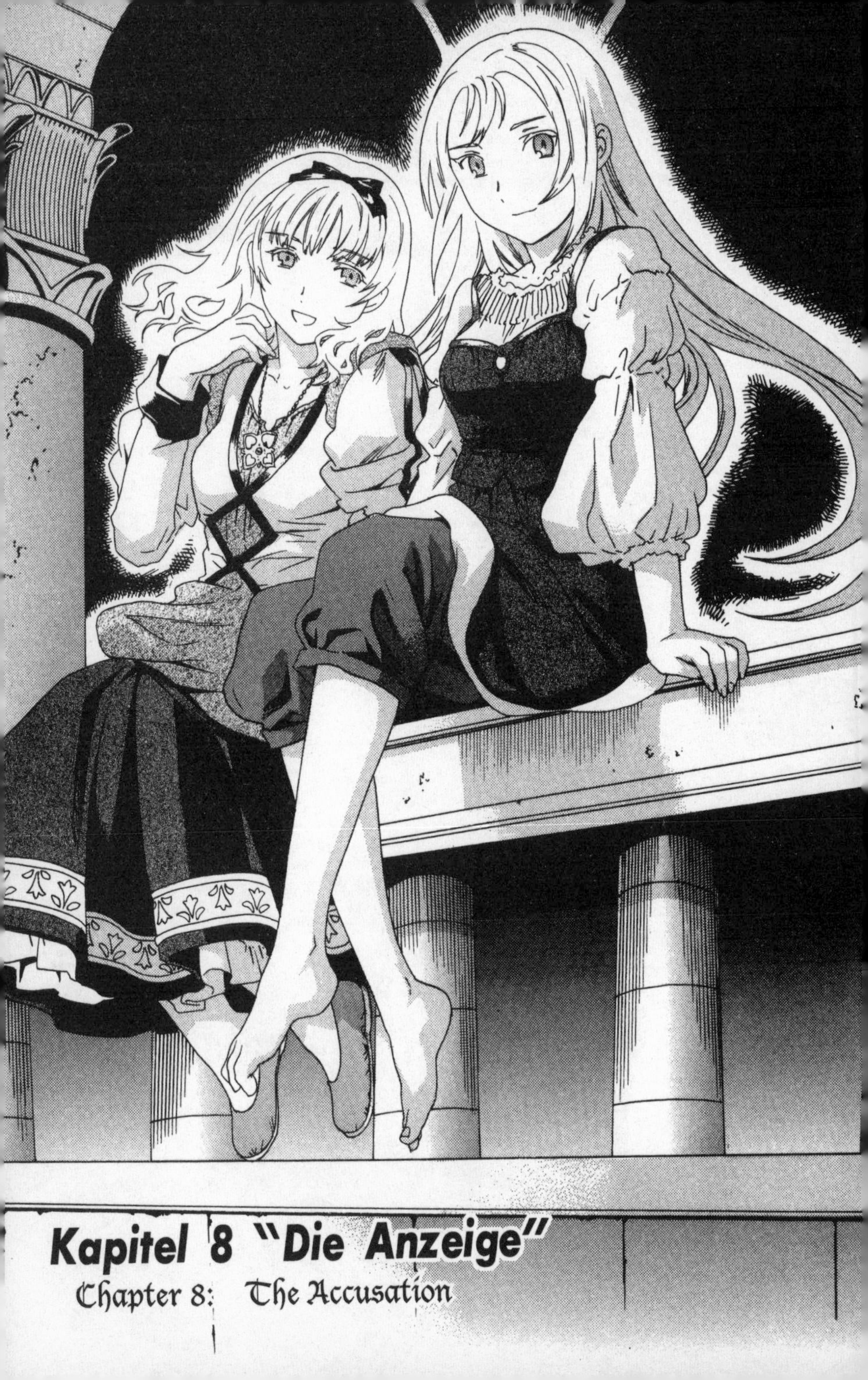

Kapitel 8 "Die Anzeige"

Chapter 8: The Accusation

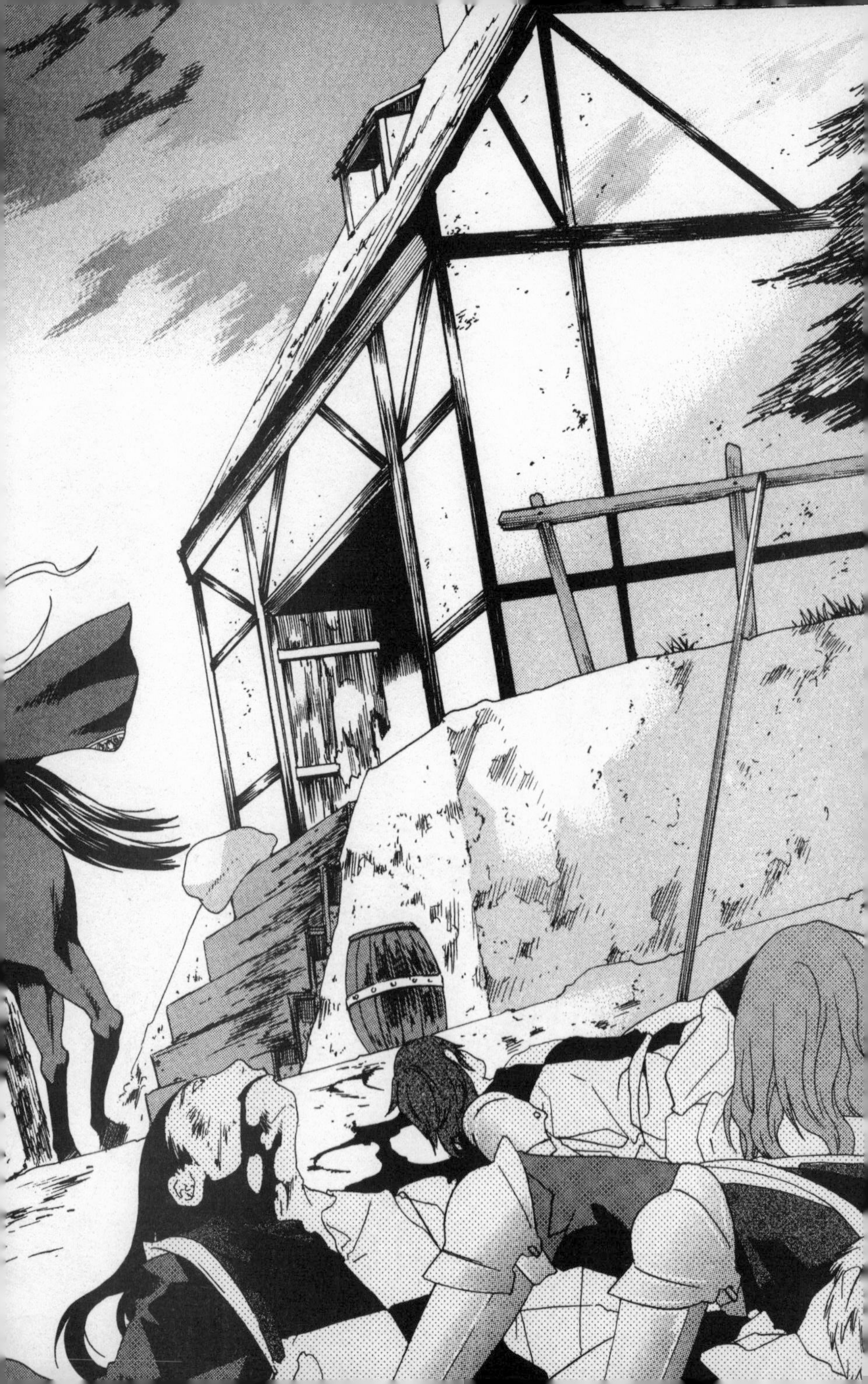

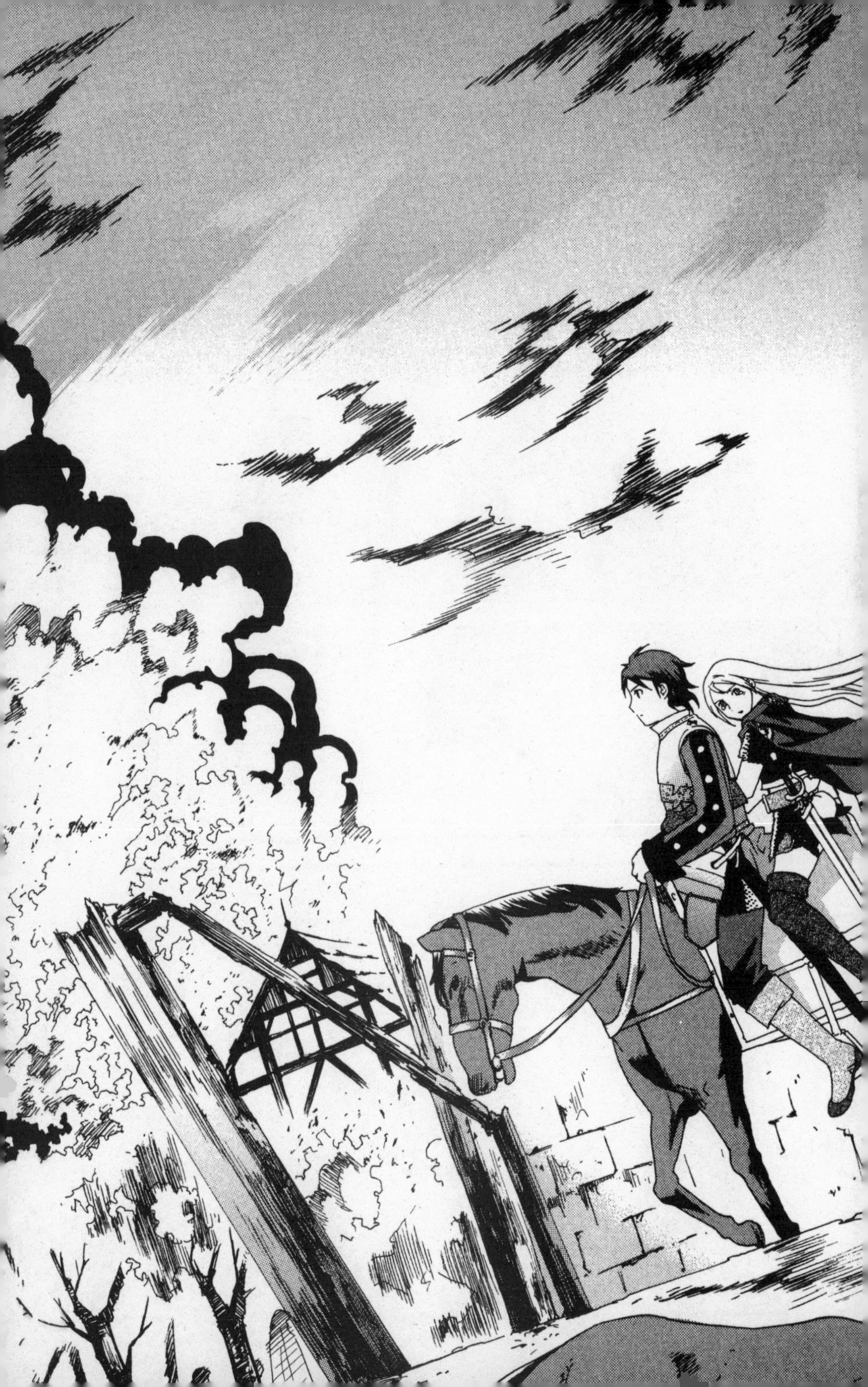

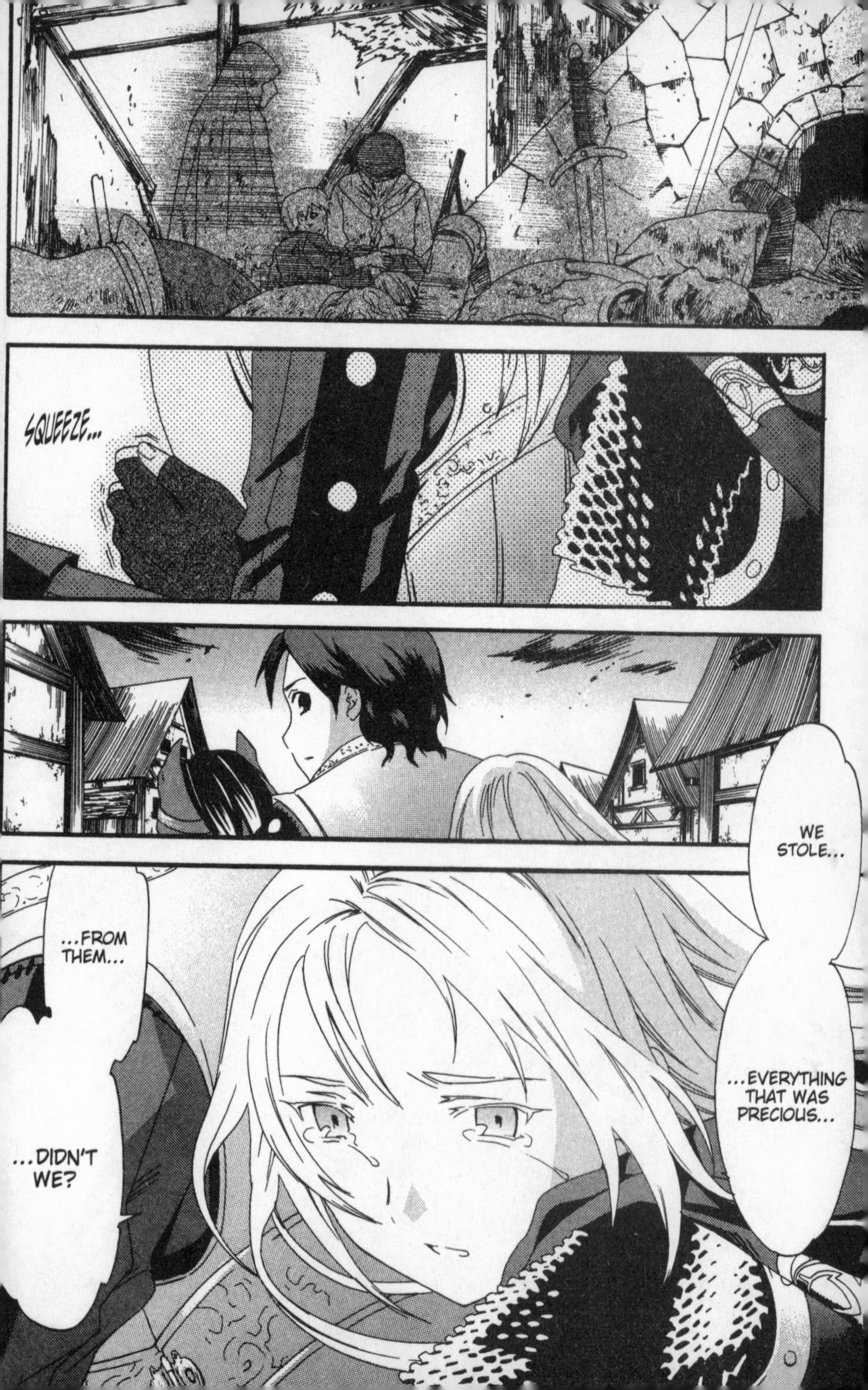
SQUEEZE...
WE STOLE...
...FROM THEM...
...EVERYTHING THAT WAS PRECIOUS...
...DIDN'T WE?

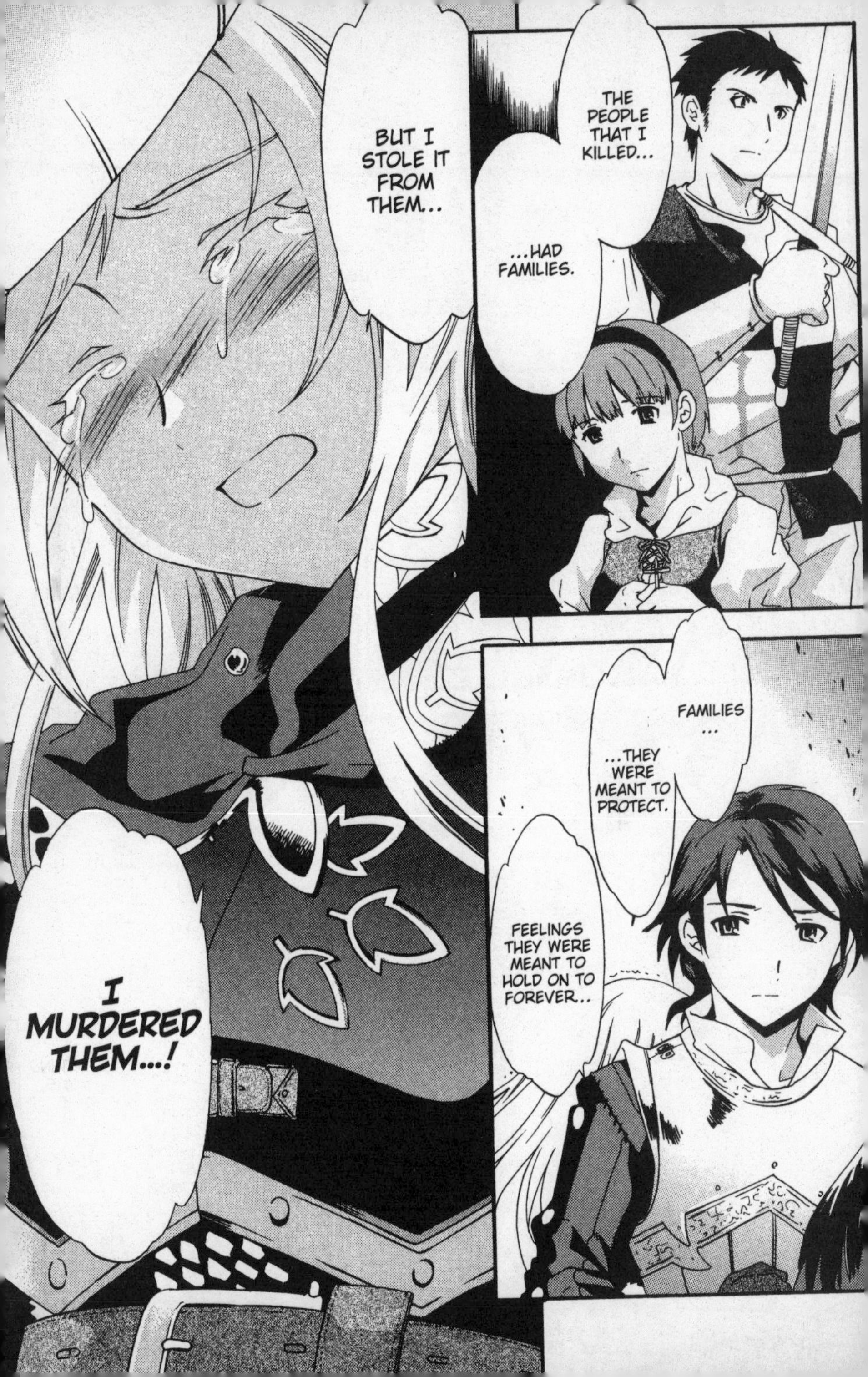
THE PEOPLE THAT I KILLED...
...HAD FAMILIES.
FAMILIES ...
...THEY WERE MEANT TO PROTECT.
FEELINGS THEY WERE MEANT TO HOLD ON TO FOREVER...
BUT I STOLE IT FROM THEM...
I MURDERED THEM...!

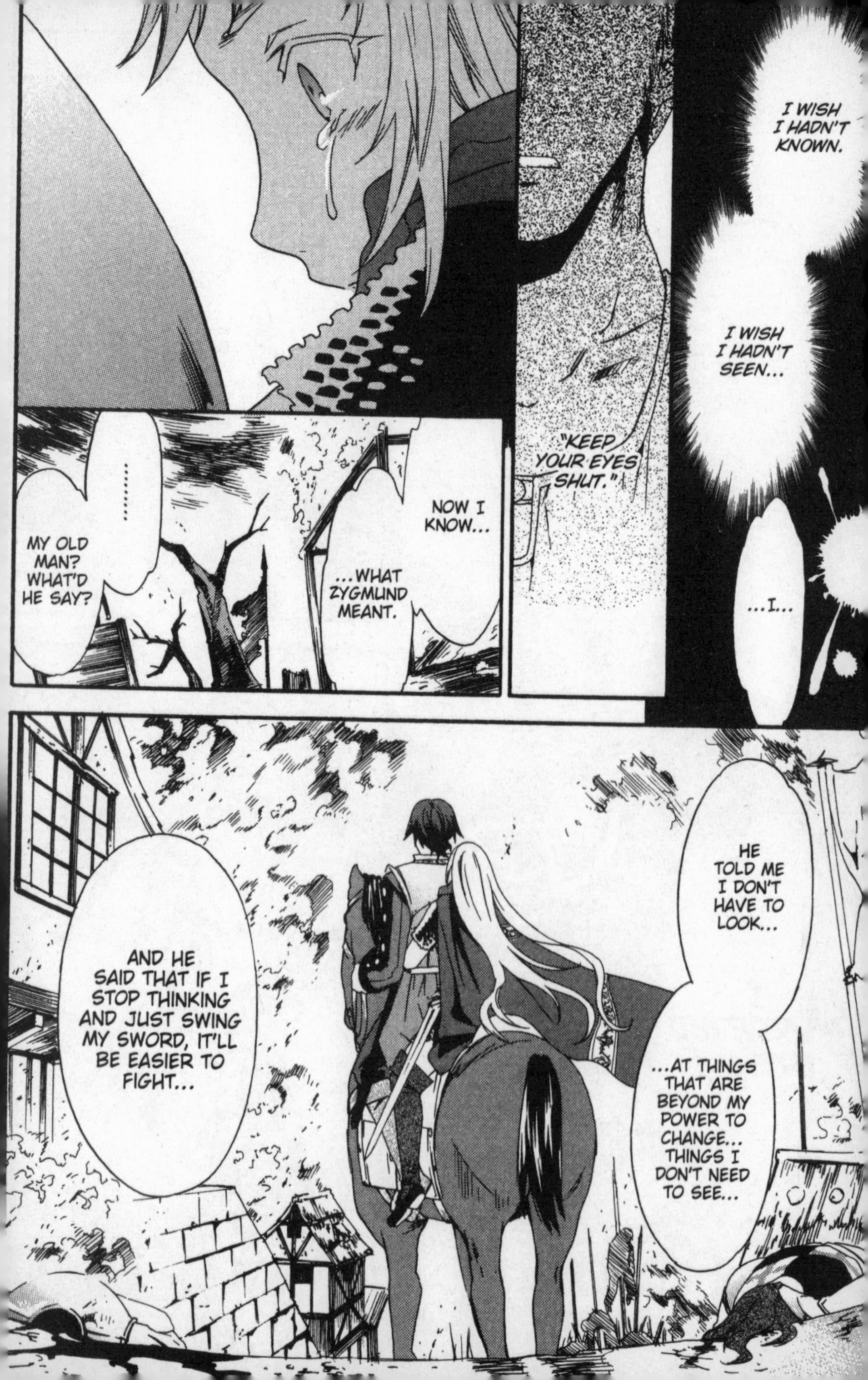
I WISH I HADN'T KNOWN.
I WISH I HADN'T SEEN...
...I...
"KEEP YOUR EYES SHUT."
NOW I KNOW...
...WHAT ZYGMUND MEANT.
......
MY OLD MAN? WHAT'D HE SAY?
HE TOLD ME I DON'T HAVE TO LOOK...
...AT THINGS THAT ARE BEYOND MY POWER TO CHANGE... THINGS I DON'T NEED TO SEE...
AND HE SAID THAT IF I STOP THINKING AND JUST SWING MY SWORD, IT'LL BE EASIER TO FIGHT...

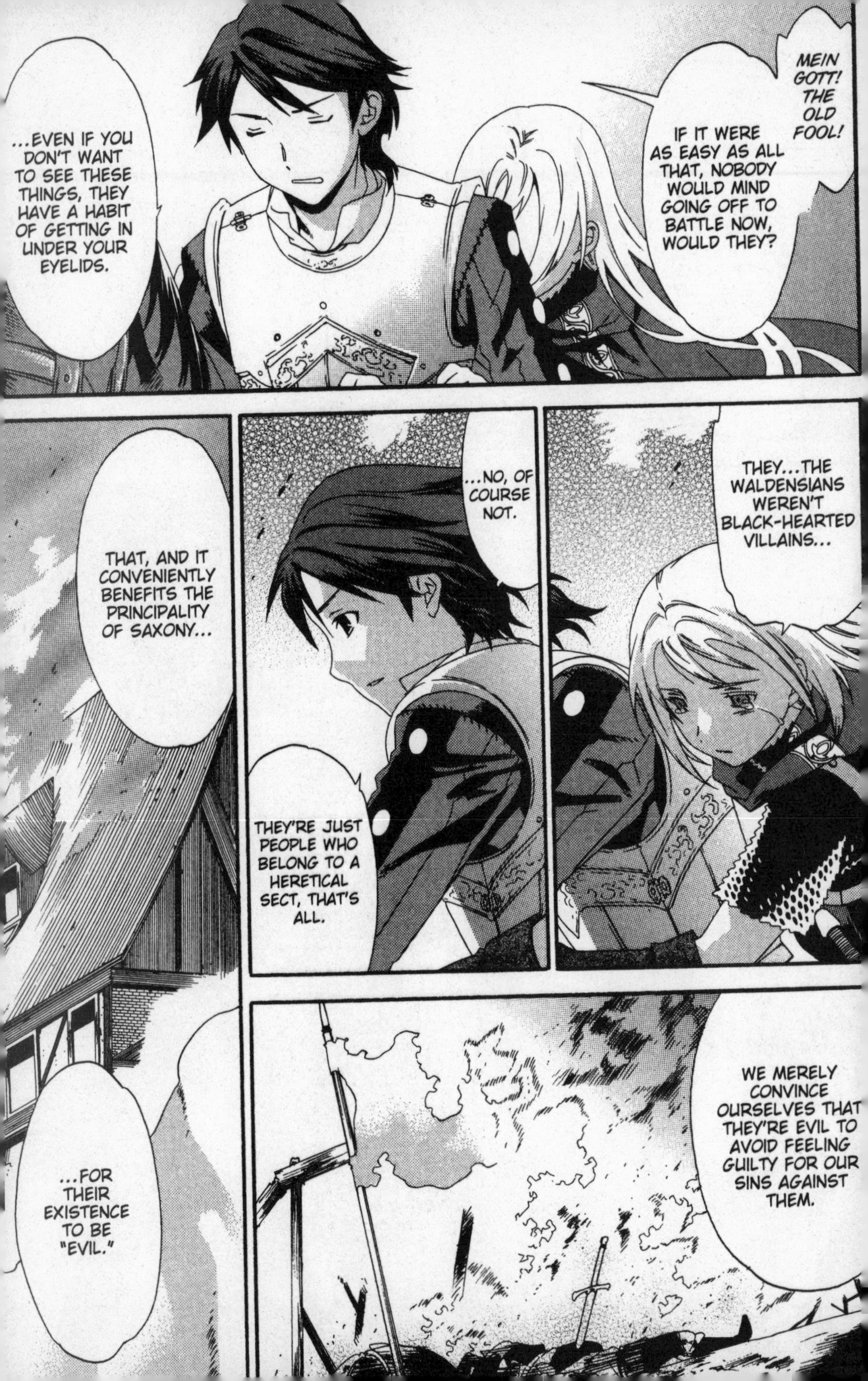
MEIN GOTT! THE OLD FOOL!
IF IT WERE AS EASY AS ALL THAT, NOBODY WOULD MIND GOING OFF TO BATTLE NOW, WOULD THEY?
...EVEN IF YOU DON'T WANT TO SEE THESE THINGS, THEY HAVE A HABIT OF GETTING IN UNDER YOUR EYELIDS.
THEY...THE WALDENSIANS WEREN'T BLACK-HEARTED VILLAINS...
...NO, OF COURSE NOT.
THEY'RE JUST PEOPLE WHO BELONG TO A HERETICAL SECT, THAT'S ALL.
WE MERELY CONVINCE OURSELVES THAT THEY'RE EVIL TO AVOID FEELING GUILTY FOR OUR SINS AGAINST THEM.
THAT, AND IT CONVENIENTLY BENEFITS THE PRINCIPALITY OF SAXONY...
...FOR THEIR EXISTENCE TO BE "EVIL."

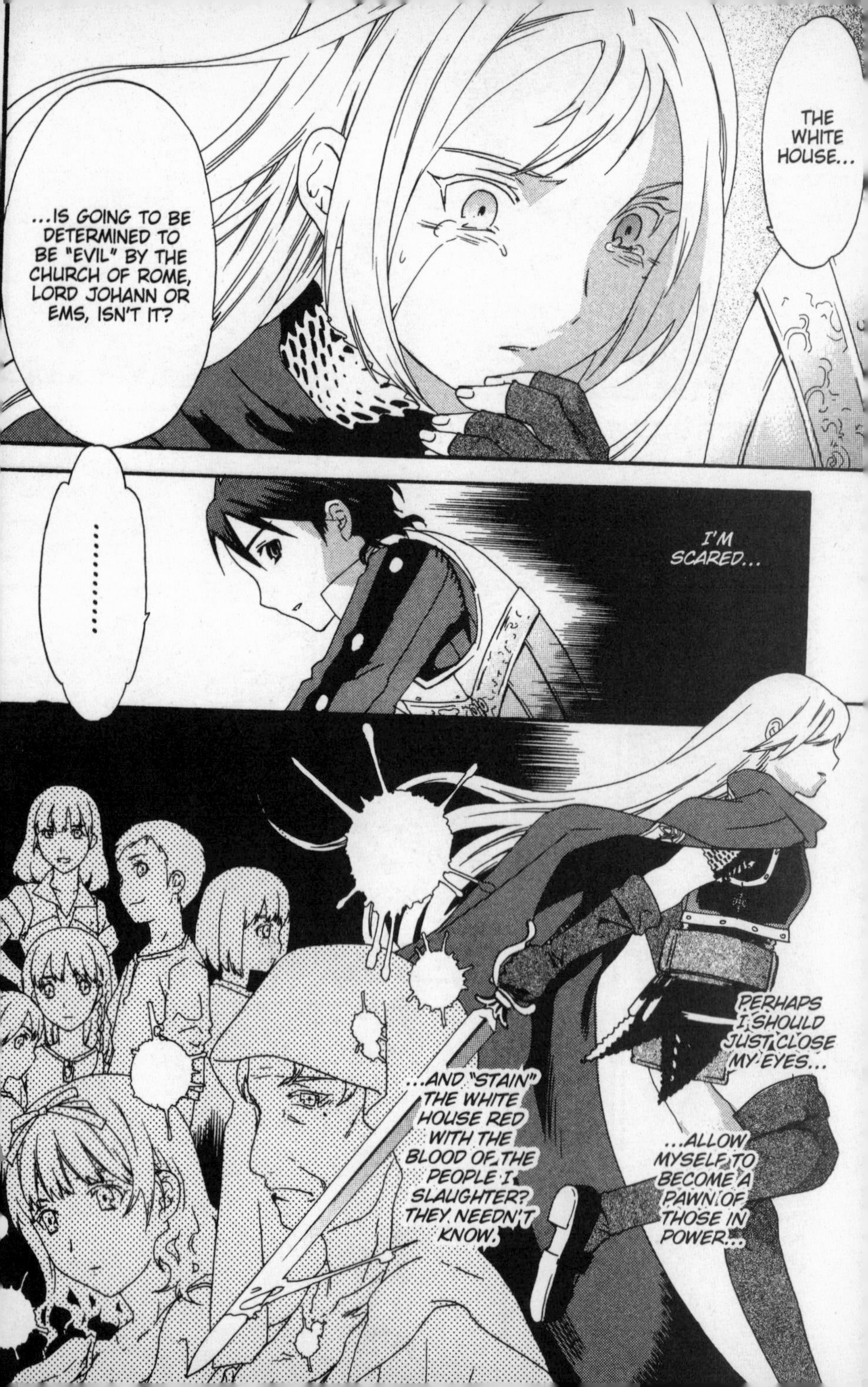
THE WHITE HOUSE...
...IS GOING TO BE DETERMINED TO BE "EVIL" BY THE CHURCH OF ROME, LORD JOHANN OR EMS, ISN'T IT?
I'M SCARED...
....
PERHAPS I SHOULD JUST CLOSE MY EYES...
...ALLOW MYSELF TO BECOME A PAWN OF THOSE IN POWER...
...AND "STAIN" THE WHITE HOUSE RED WITH THE BLOOD OF THE PEOPLE I SLAUGHTER? THEY NEEDN'T KNOW.

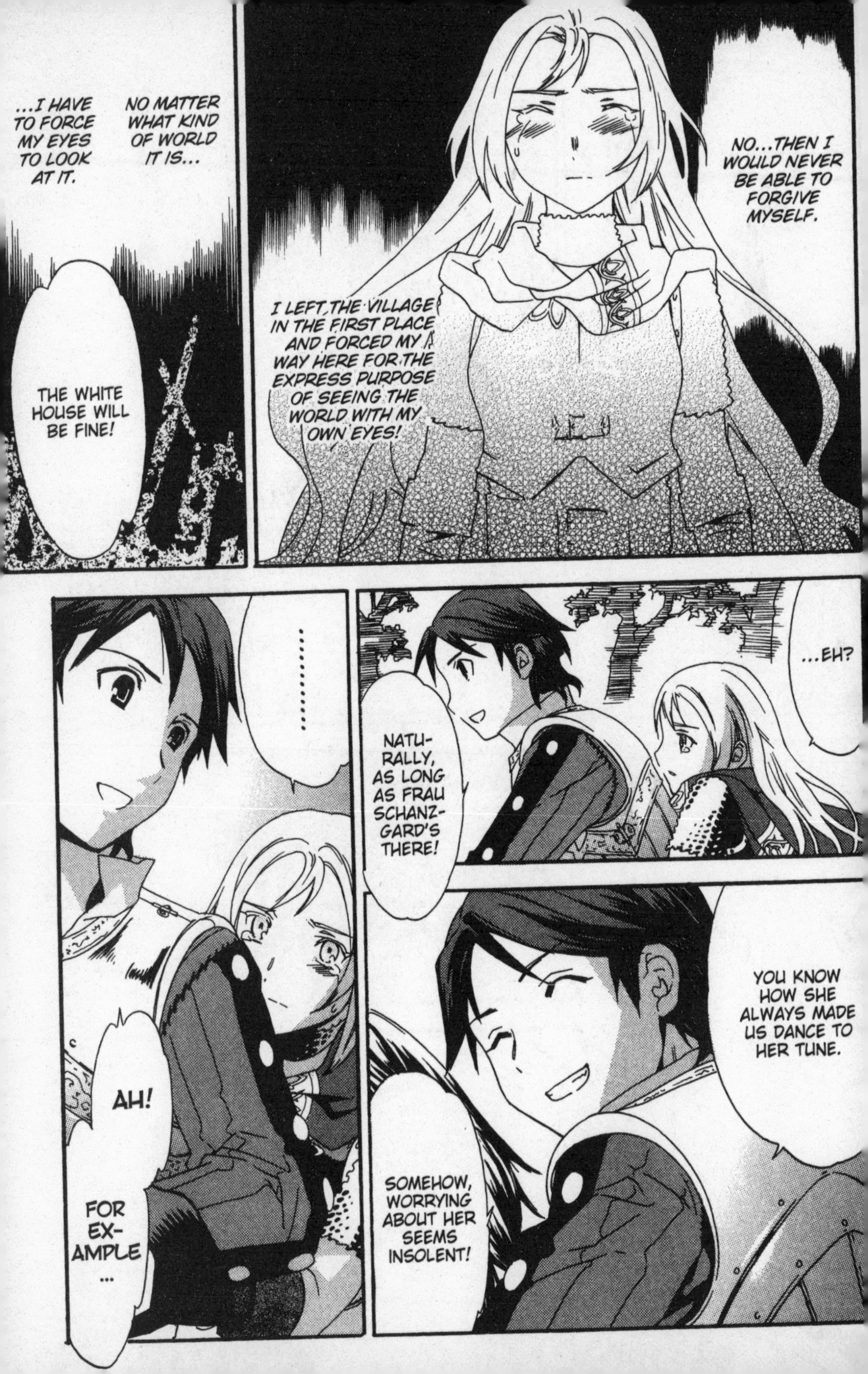

NO...THEN I WOULD NEVER BE ABLE TO FORGIVE MYSELF.
I LEFT THE VILLAGE IN THE FIRST PLACE AND FORCED MY WAY HERE FOR THE EXPRESS PURPOSE OF SEEING THE WORLD WITH MY OWN EYES!
NO MATTER WHAT KIND OF WORLD IT IS...
...I HAVE TO FORCE MY EYES TO LOOK AT IT.
THE WHITE HOUSE WILL BE FINE!
...EH?
NATU-RALLY, AS LONG AS FRAU SCHANZ-GARD'S THERE!
YOU KNOW HOW SHE ALWAYS MADE US DANCE TO HER TUNE.
SOMEHOW, WORRYING ABOUT HER SEEMS INSOLENT!
......
AH!
FOR EX-AMPLE ...

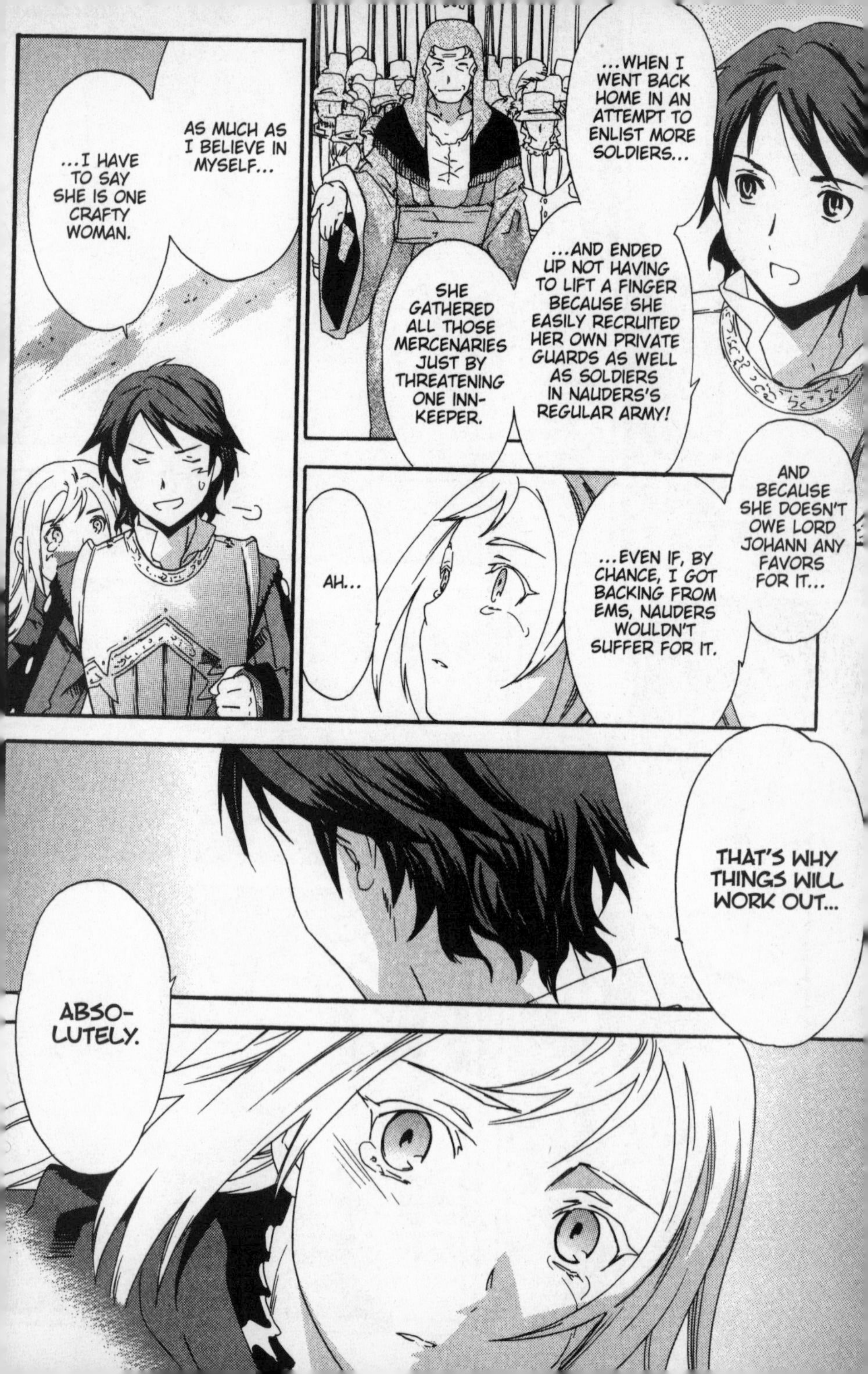

...WHEN I WENT BACK HOME IN AN ATTEMPT TO ENLIST MORE SOLDIERS...
...AND ENDED UP NOT HAVING TO LIFT A FINGER BECAUSE SHE EASILY RECRUITED HER OWN PRIVATE GUARDS AS WELL AS SOLDIERS IN NAUDERS'S REGULAR ARMY!
SHE GATHERED ALL THOSE MERCENARIES JUST BY THREATENING ONE INN-KEEPER.
AND BECAUSE SHE DOESN'T OWE LORD JOHANN ANY FAVORS FOR IT...
...EVEN IF, BY CHANCE, I GOT BACKING FROM EMS, NAUDERS WOULDN'T SUFFER FOR IT.
AH...
AS MUCH AS I BELIEVE IN MYSELF...
...I HAVE TO SAY SHE IS ONE CRAFTY WOMAN.
THAT'S WHY THINGS WILL WORK OUT...
ABSO-LUTELY.

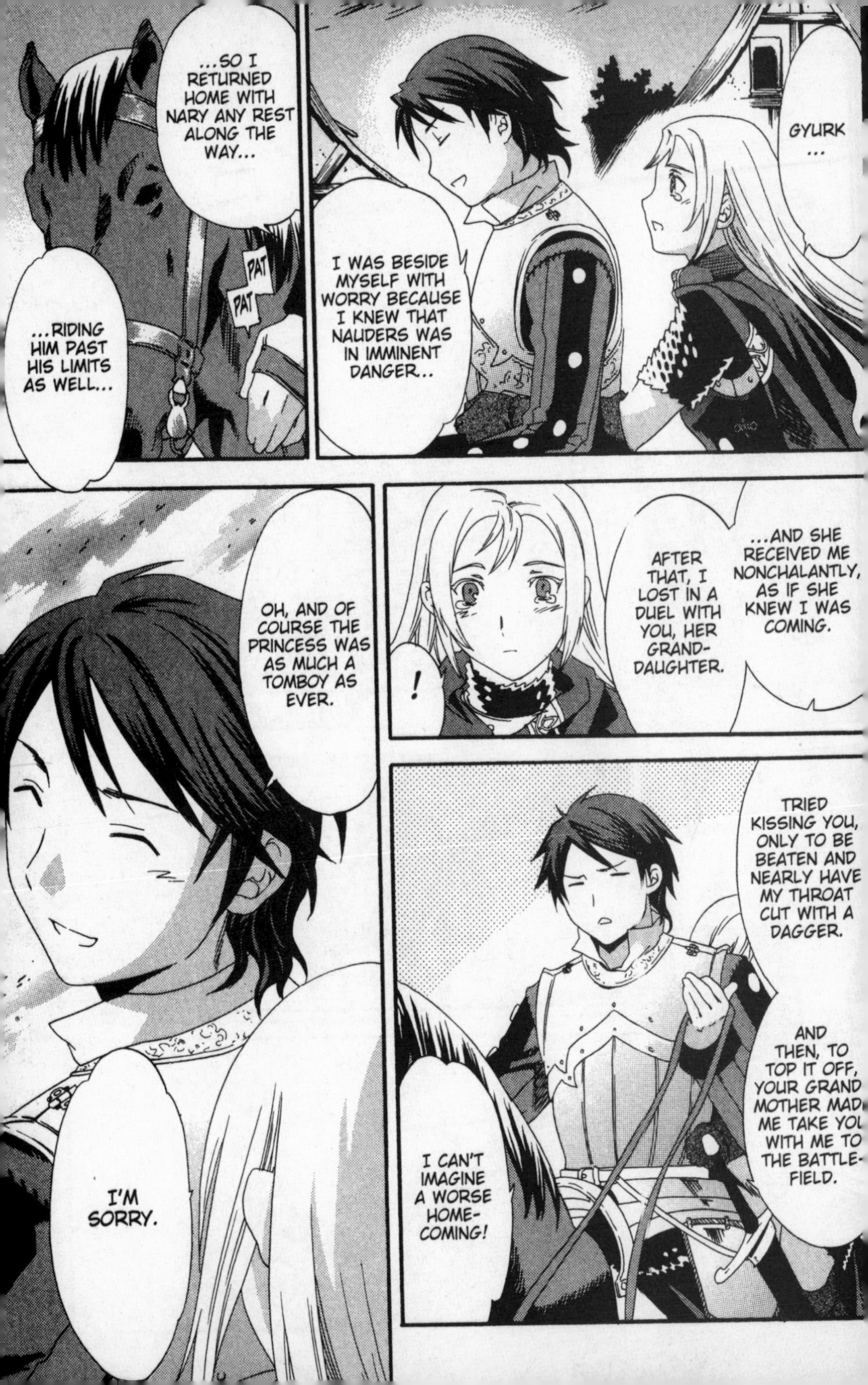
GYURK ...
I WAS BESIDE MYSELF WITH WORRY BECAUSE I KNEW THAT NAUDERS WAS IN IMMINENT DANGER...
...SO I RETURNED HOME WITH NARY ANY REST ALONG THE WAY...
PAT
PAT
...RIDING HIM PAST HIS LIMITS AS WELL...
...AND SHE RECEIVED ME NONCHALANTLY, AS IF SHE KNEW I WAS COMING.
AFTER THAT, I LOST IN A DUEL WITH YOU, HER GRAND-DAUGHTER.
!
TRIED KISSING YOU, ONLY TO BE BEATEN AND NEARLY HAVE MY THROAT CUT WITH A DAGGER.
AND THEN, TO TOP IT OFF, YOUR GRAND MOTHER MAD ME TAKE YO WITH ME TO THE BATTLE-FIELD.
I CAN'T IMAGINE A WORSE HOME-COMING!
OH, AND OF COURSE THE PRINCESS WAS AS MUCH A TOMBOY AS EVER.
I'M SORRY.

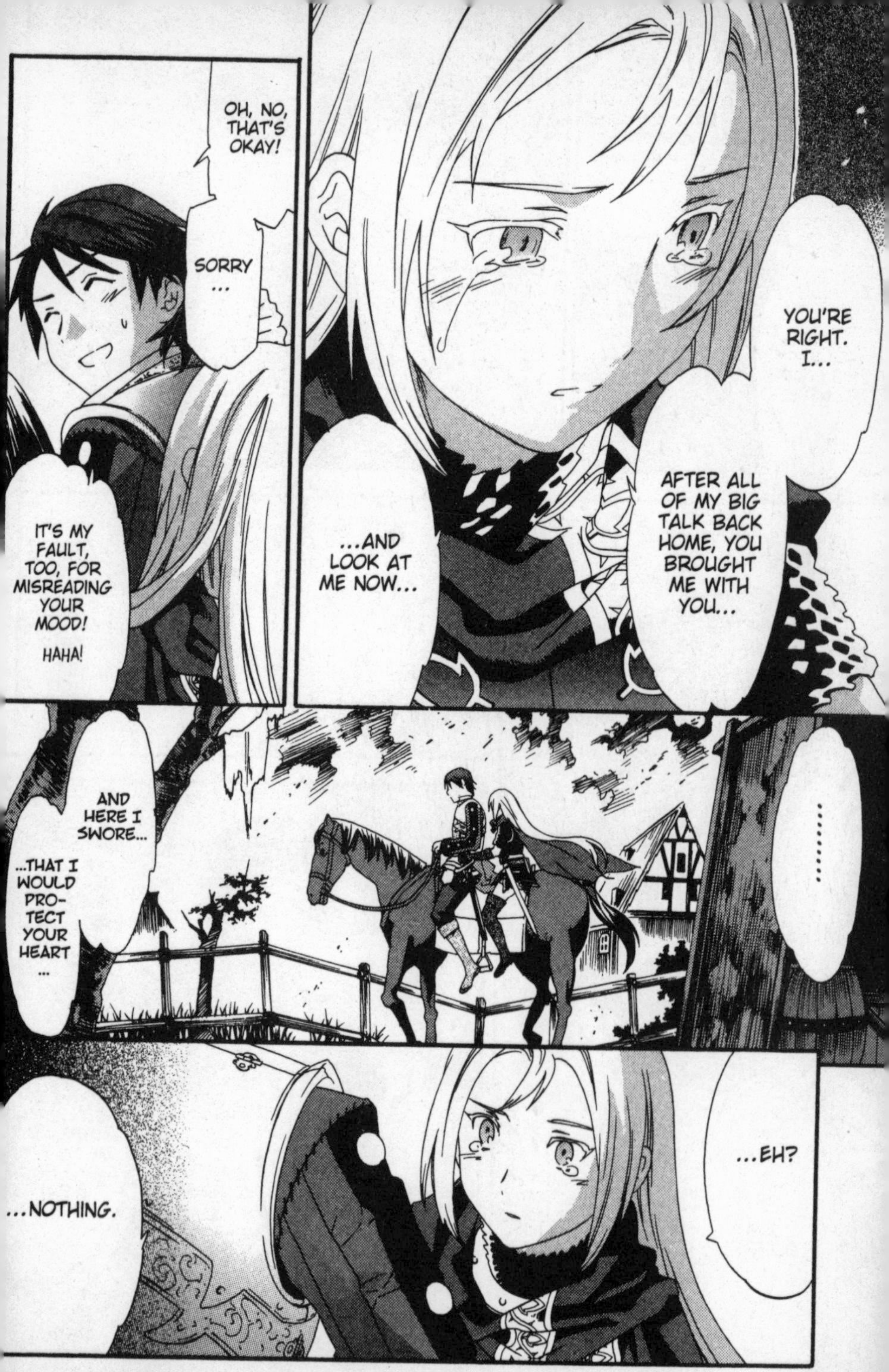
YOU'RE RIGHT. I...
AFTER ALL OF MY BIG TALK BACK HOME, YOU BROUGHT ME WITH YOU...
...AND LOOK AT ME NOW...
OH, NO, THAT'S OKAY!
SORRY ...
IT'S MY FAULT, TOO, FOR MISREADING YOUR MOOD!
HAHA!
......
AND HERE I SWORE...
...THAT I WOULD PRO-TECT YOUR HEART ...
...EH?
...NOTHING.

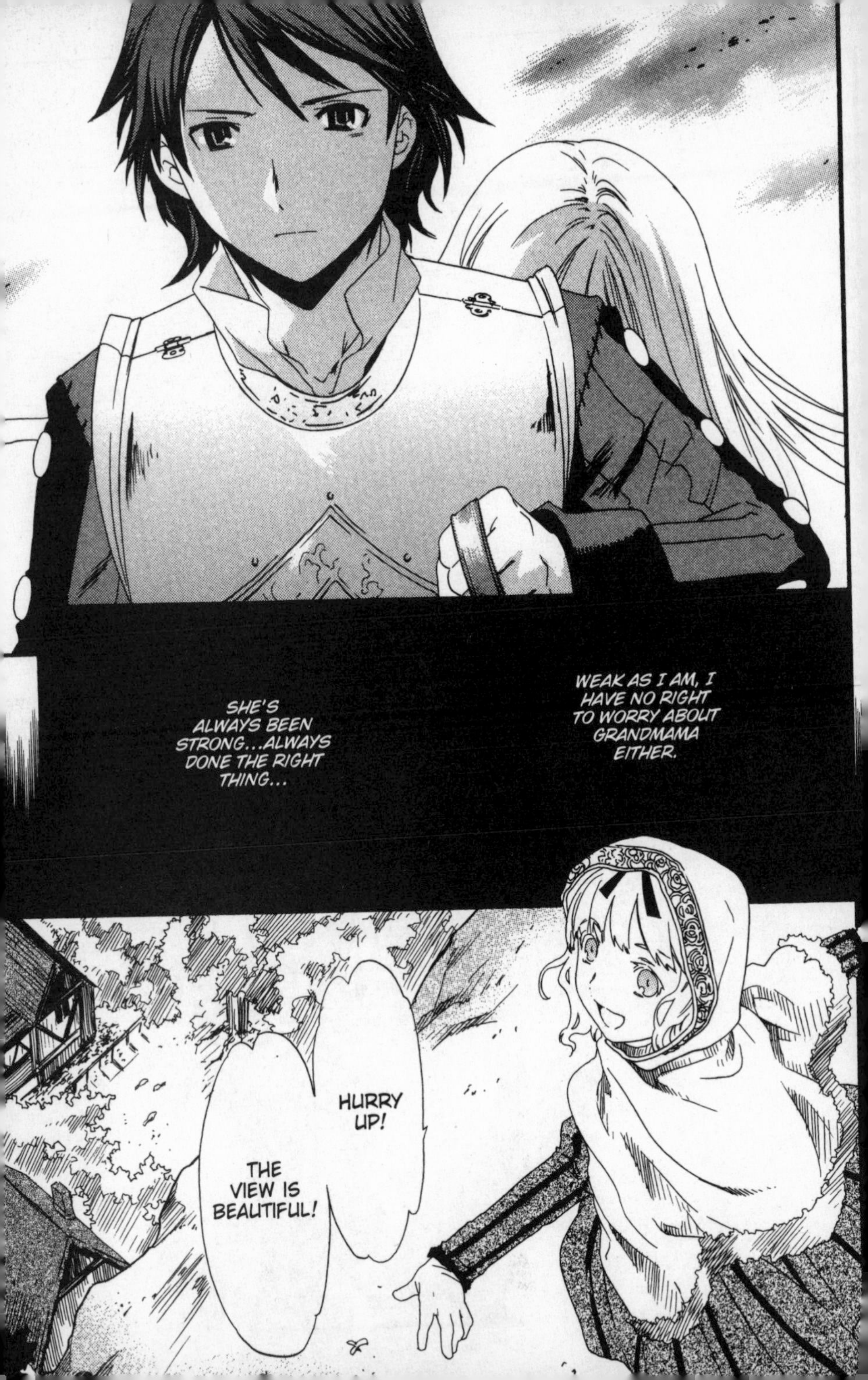
WEAK AS I AM, I HAVE NO RIGHT TO WORRY ABOUT GRANDMAMA EITHER.
SHE'S ALWAYS BEEN STRONG...ALWAYS DONE THE RIGHT THING...
HURRY UP!
THE VIEW IS BEAUTIFUL!

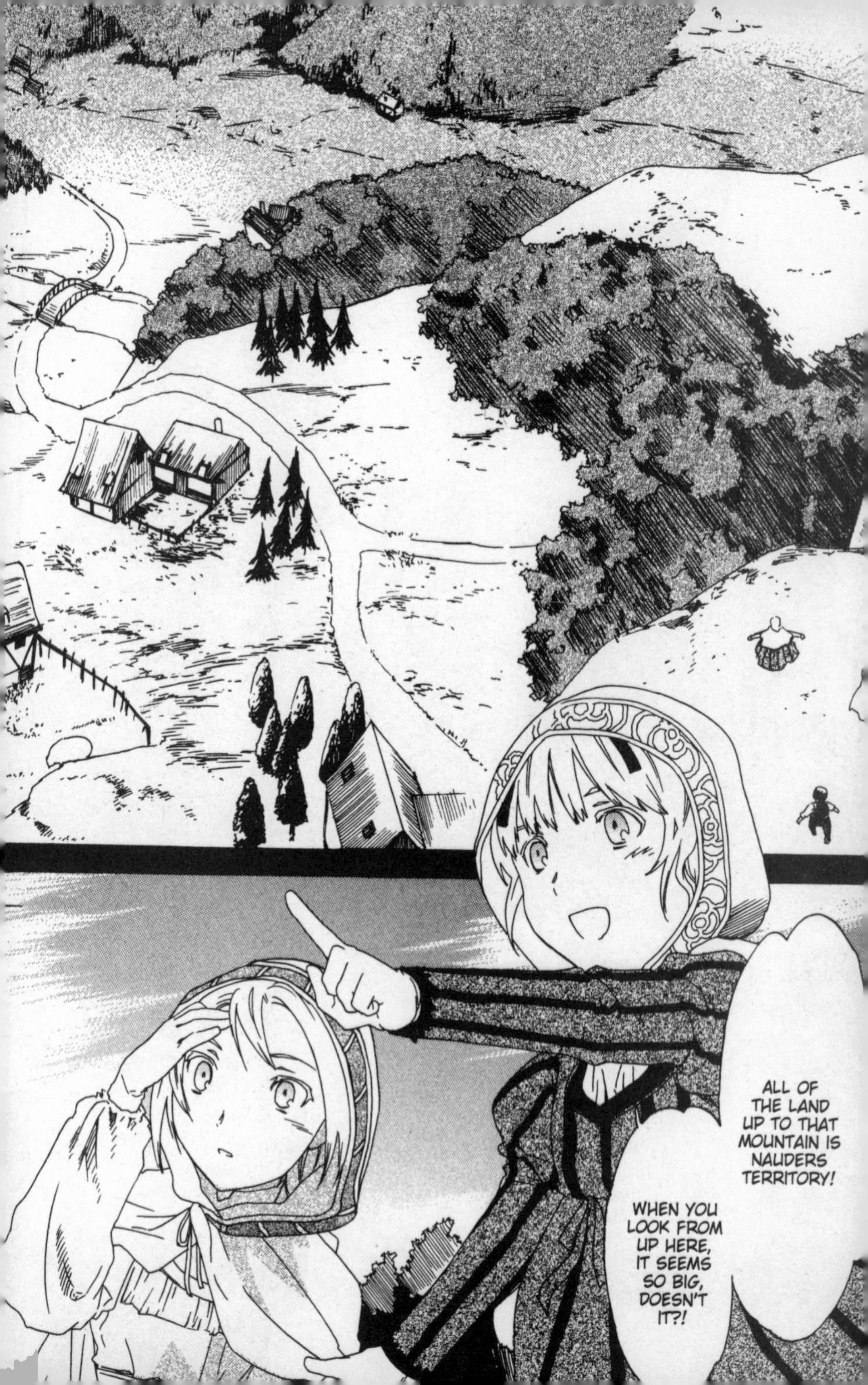
ALL OF THE LAND UP TO THAT MOUNTAIN IS NAUDERS TERRITORY!
WHEN YOU LOOK FROM UP HERE, IT SEEMS SO BIG, DOESN'T IT?!

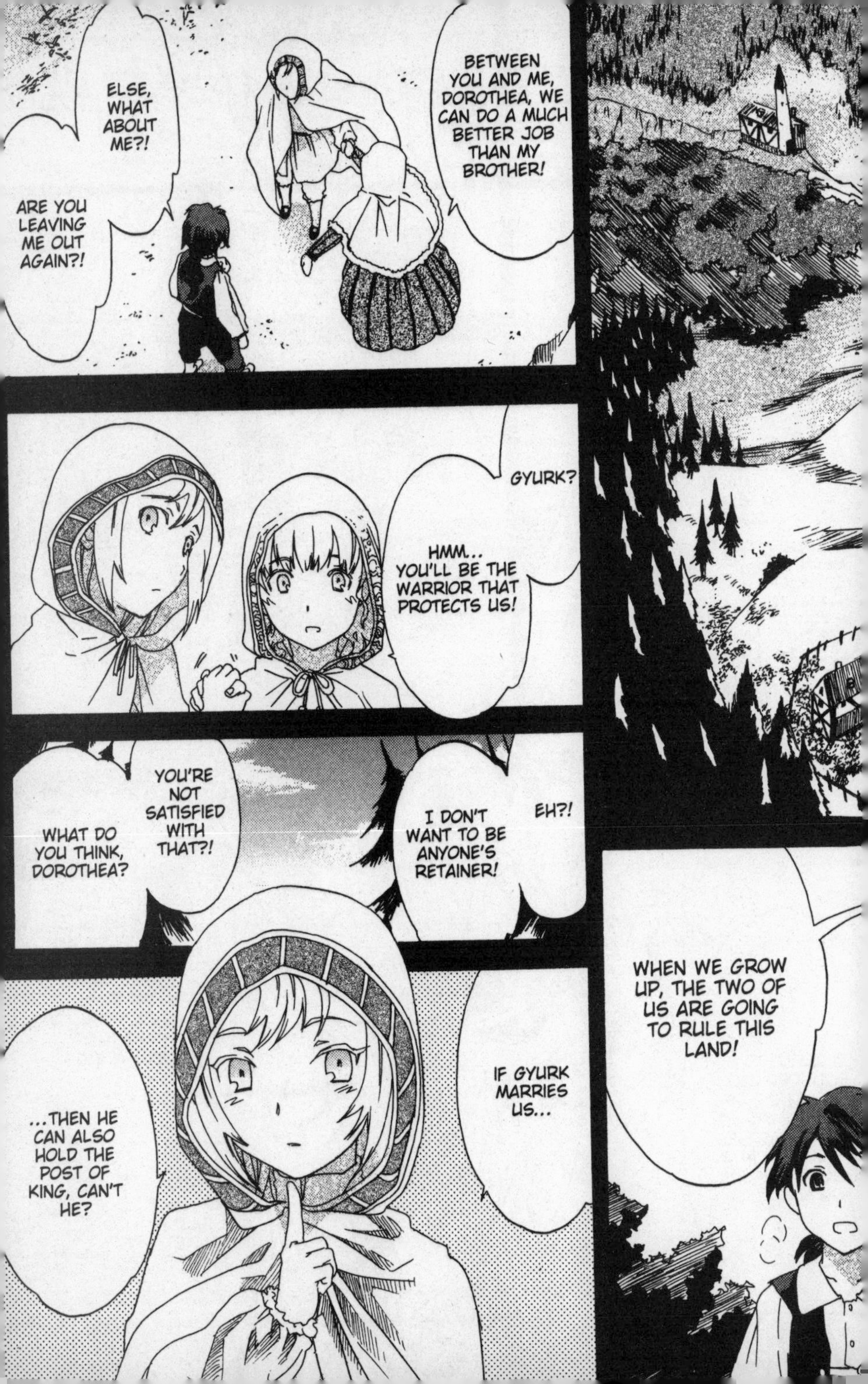
BETWEEN YOU AND ME, DOROTHEA, WE CAN DO A MUCH BETTER JOB THAN MY BROTHER!
ELSE, WHAT ABOUT ME?!
ARE YOU LEAVING ME OUT AGAIN?!
GYURK?
HMM... YOU'LL BE THE WARRIOR THAT PROTECTS US!
EH?!
I DON'T WANT TO BE ANYONE'S RETAINER!
YOU'RE NOT SATISFIED WITH THAT?!
WHAT DO YOU THINK, DOROTHEA?
WHEN WE GROW UP, THE TWO OF US ARE GOING TO RULE THIS LAND!
IF GYURK MARRIES US...
...THEN HE CAN ALSO HOLD THE POST OF KING, CAN'T HE?

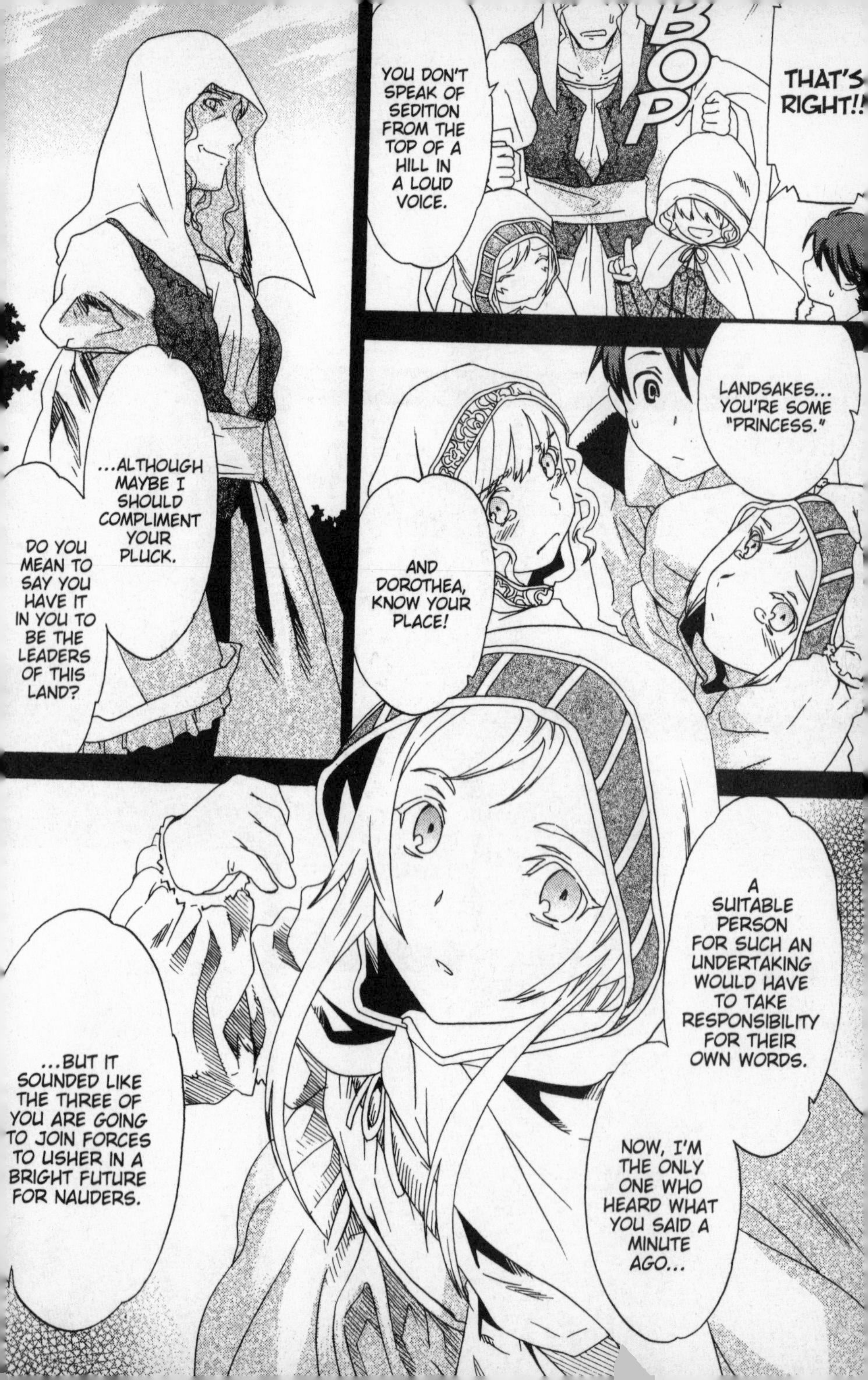
THAT'S RIGHT!!
BOP
YOU DON'T SPEAK OF SEDITION FROM THE TOP OF A HILL IN A LOUD VOICE.
LANDSAKES... YOU'RE SOME "PRINCESS."
AND DOROTHEA, KNOW YOUR PLACE!
...ALTHOUGH MAYBE I SHOULD COMPLIMENT YOUR PLUCK.
DO YOU MEAN TO SAY YOU HAVE IT IN YOU TO BE THE LEADERS OF THIS LAND?
A SUITABLE PERSON FOR SUCH AN UNDERTAKING WOULD HAVE TO TAKE RESPONSIBILITY FOR THEIR OWN WORDS.
NOW, I'M THE ONLY ONE WHO HEARD WHAT YOU SAID A MINUTE AGO...
...BUT IT SOUNDED LIKE THE THREE OF YOU ARE GOING TO JOIN FORCES TO USHER IN A BRIGHT FUTURE FOR NAUDERS.

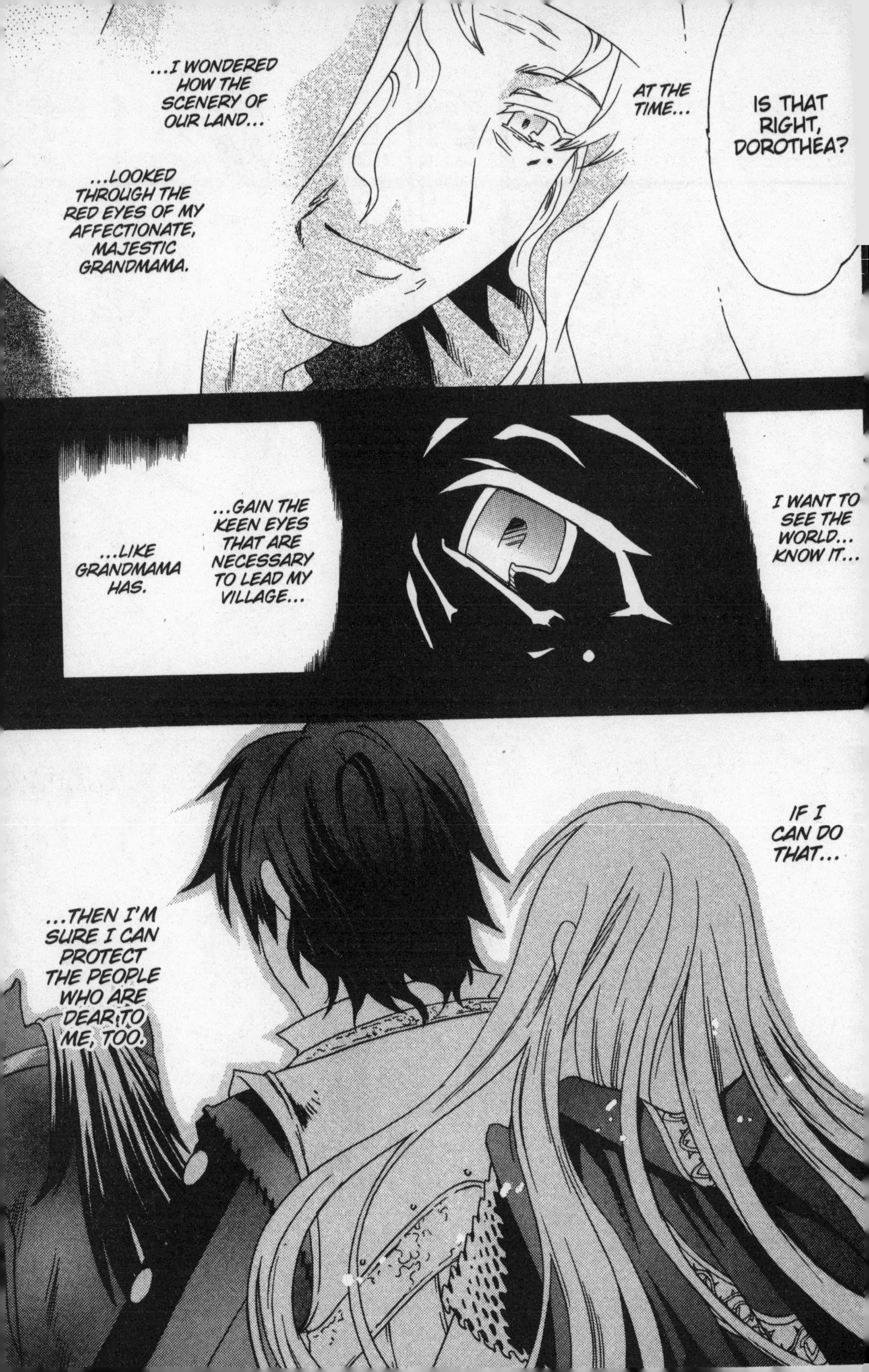
IS THAT RIGHT, DOROTHEA?
AT THE TIME...
...I WONDERED HOW THE SCENERY OF OUR LAND...
...LOOKED THROUGH THE RED EYES OF MY AFFECTIONATE, MAJESTIC GRANDMAMA.
I WANT TO SEE THE WORLD... KNOW IT...
...GAIN THE KEEN EYES THAT ARE NECESSARY TO LEAD MY VILLAGE...
...LIKE GRANDMAMA HAS.
IF I CAN DO THAT...
...THEN I'M SURE I CAN PROTECT THE PEOPLE WHO ARE DEAR TO ME, TOO.

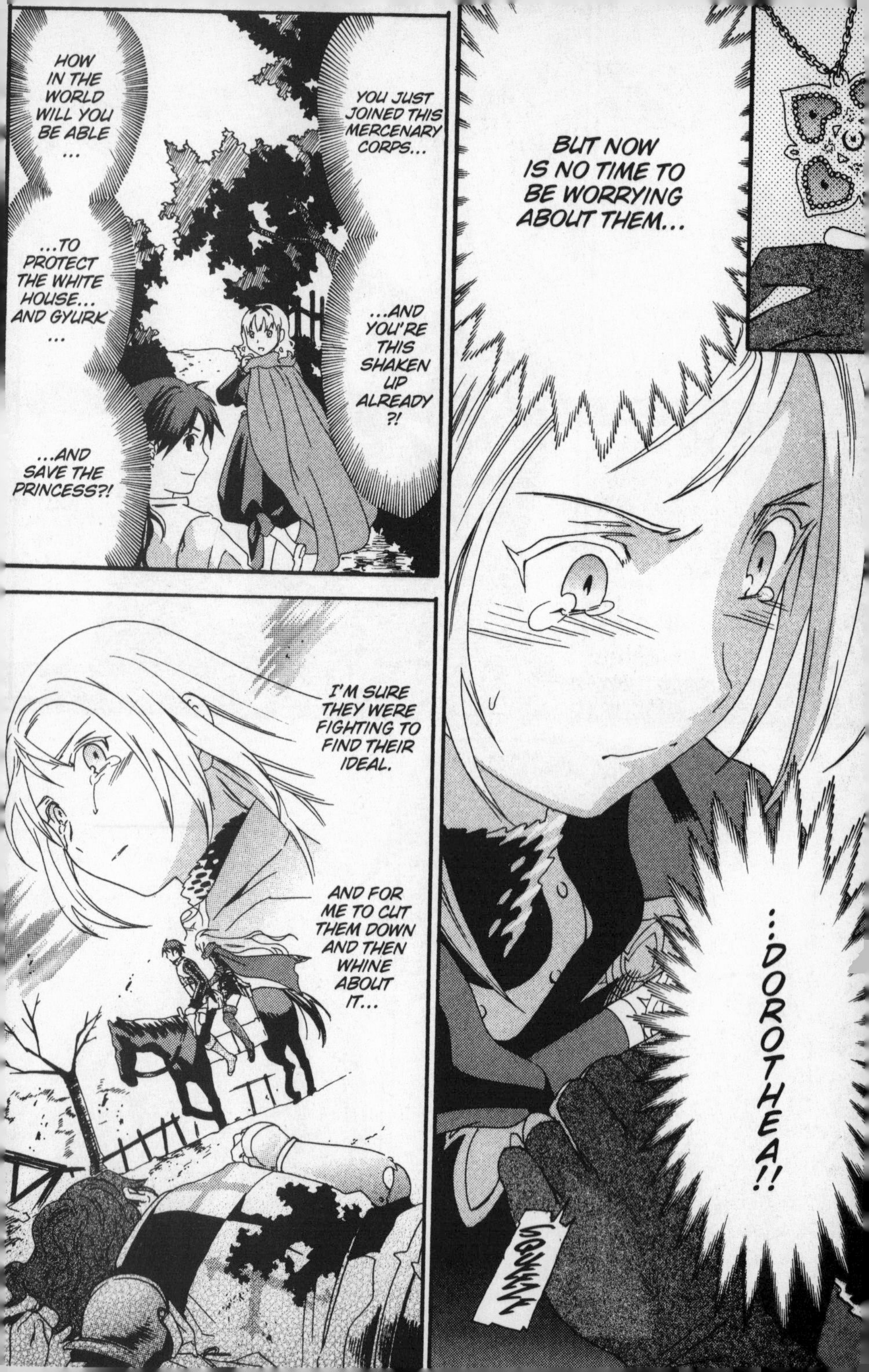
BUT NOW IS NO TIME TO BE WORRYING ABOUT THEM...
...DOROTHEA!!
SQUEEZE
HOW IN THE WORLD WILL YOU BE ABLE ...
...TO PROTECT THE WHITE HOUSE... AND GYURK ...
...AND SAVE THE PRINCESS?!
YOU JUST JOINED THIS MERCENARY CORPS...
...AND YOU'RE THIS SHAKEN UP ALREADY ?!
I'M SURE THEY WERE FIGHTING TO FIND THEIR IDEAL.
AND FOR ME TO CUT THEM DOWN AND THEN WHINE ABOUT IT...

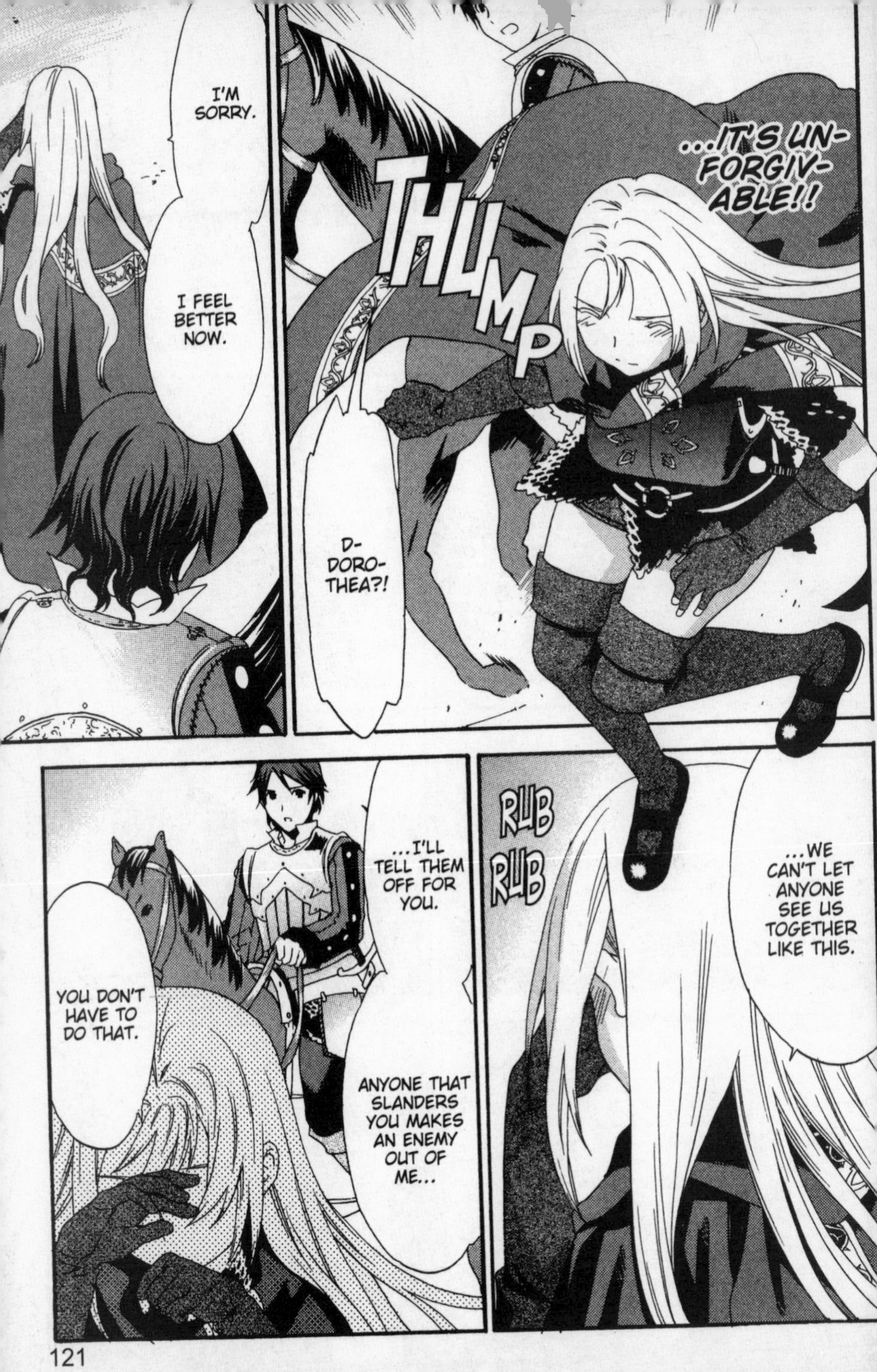
...IT'S UN-FORGIV-ABLE!!
THUMP
D-DORO-THEA?!
I'M SORRY.
I FEEL BETTER NOW.
RUB
RUB
...WE CAN'T LET ANYONE SEE US TOGETHER LIKE THIS.
...I'LL TELL THEM OFF FOR YOU.
ANYONE THAT SLANDERS YOU MAKES AN ENEMY OUT OF ME...
YOU DON'T HAVE TO DO THAT.

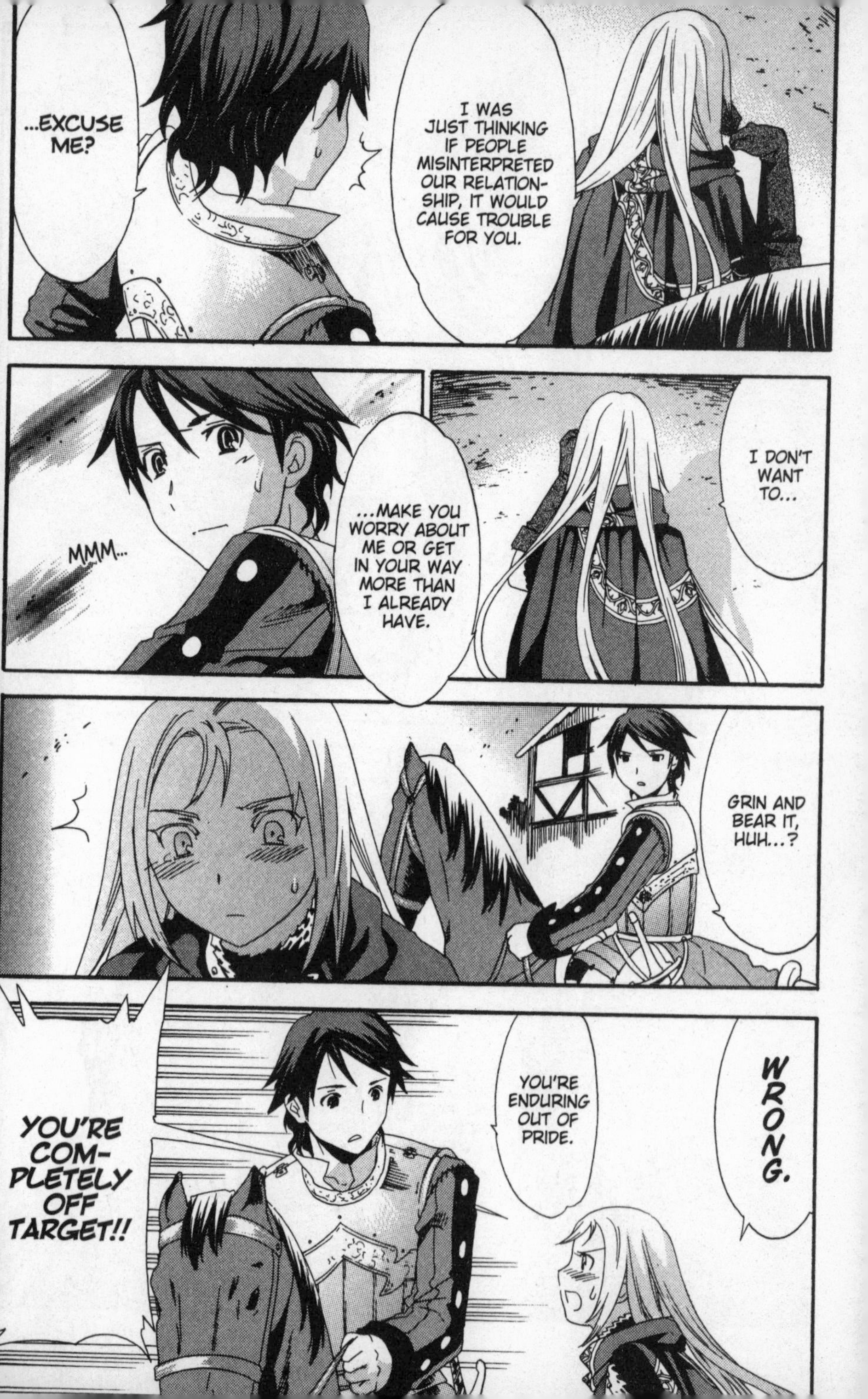
I WAS JUST THINKING IF PEOPLE MISINTERPRETED OUR RELATION-SHIP, IT WOULD CAUSE TROUBLE FOR YOU.
...EXCUSE ME?
I DON'T WANT TO...
...MAKE YOU WORRY ABOUT ME OR GET IN YOUR WAY MORE THAN I ALREADY HAVE.
MMM...
GRIN AND BEAR IT, HUH...?
WRONG.
YOU'RE ENDURING OUT OF PRIDE.
YOU'RE COM-PLETELY OFF TARGET!!

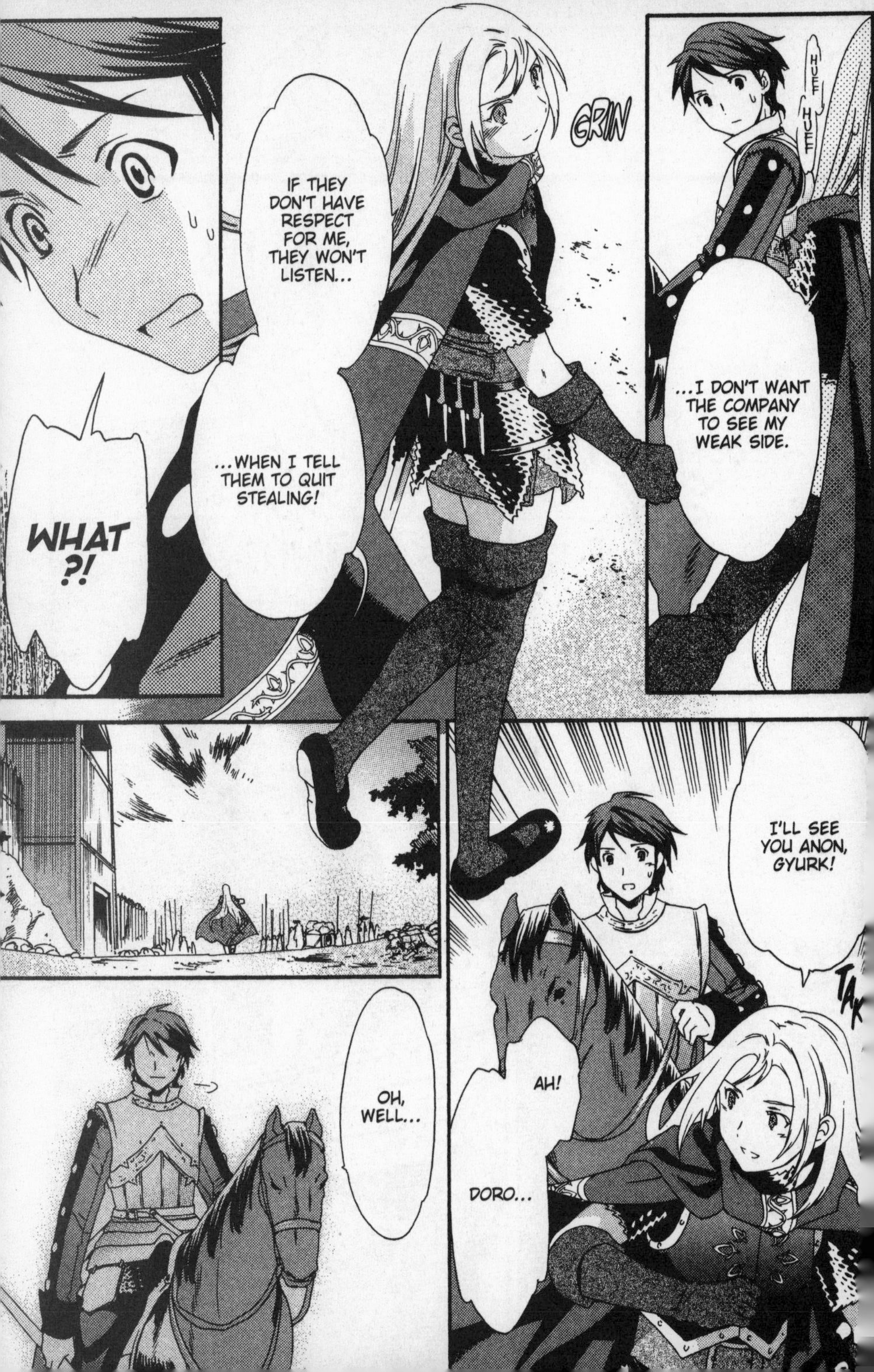
HUFF HUFF
...I DON'T WANT THE COMPANY TO SEE MY WEAK SIDE.
GRIN
IF THEY DON'T HAVE RESPECT FOR ME, THEY WON'T LISTEN...
...WHEN I TELL THEM TO QUIT STEALING!
WHAT ?!
I'LL SEE YOU ANON, GYURK!
TAK
AH!
DORO...
OH, WELL...

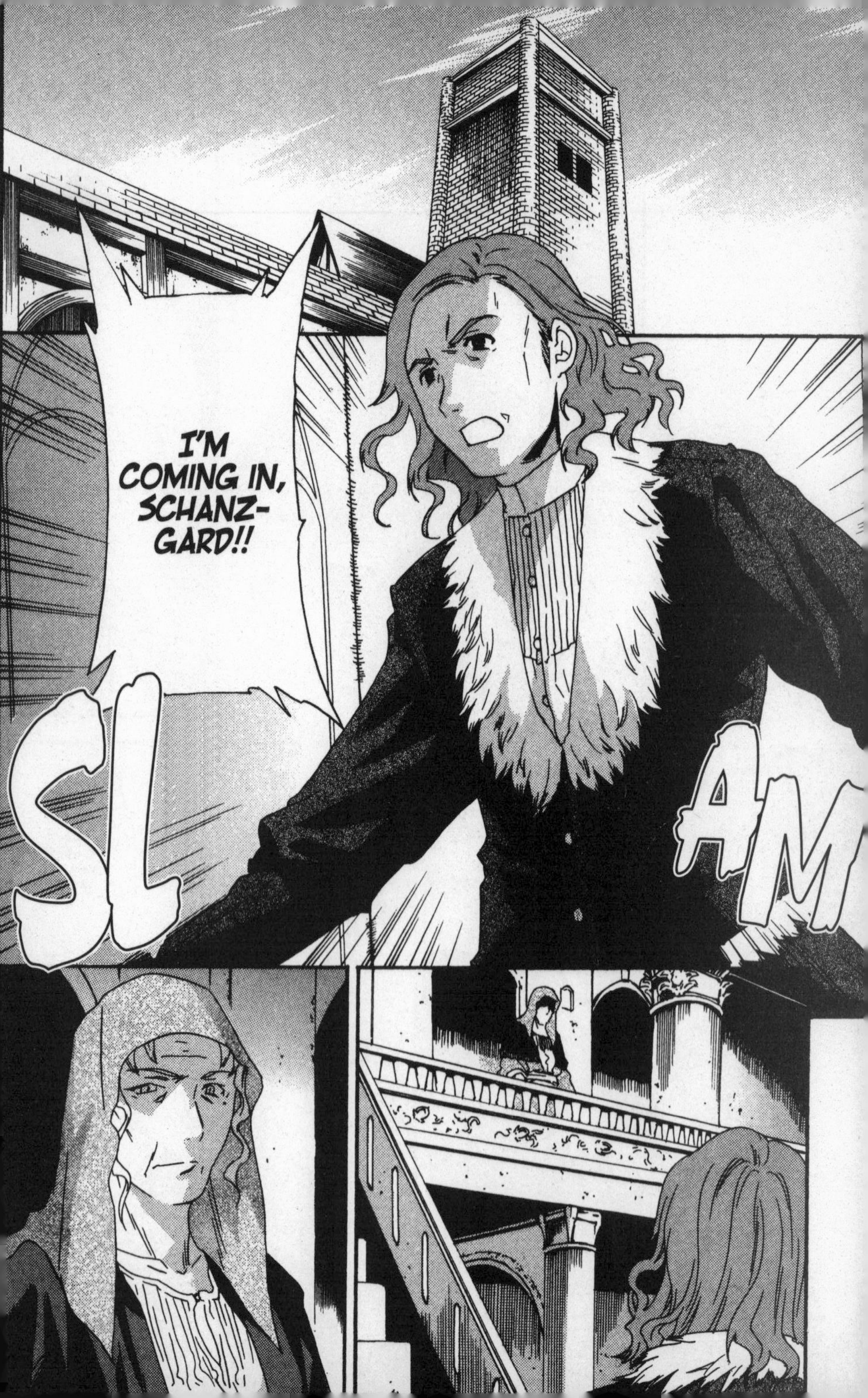
I'M COMING IN, SCHANZ-GARD!!
SLAM

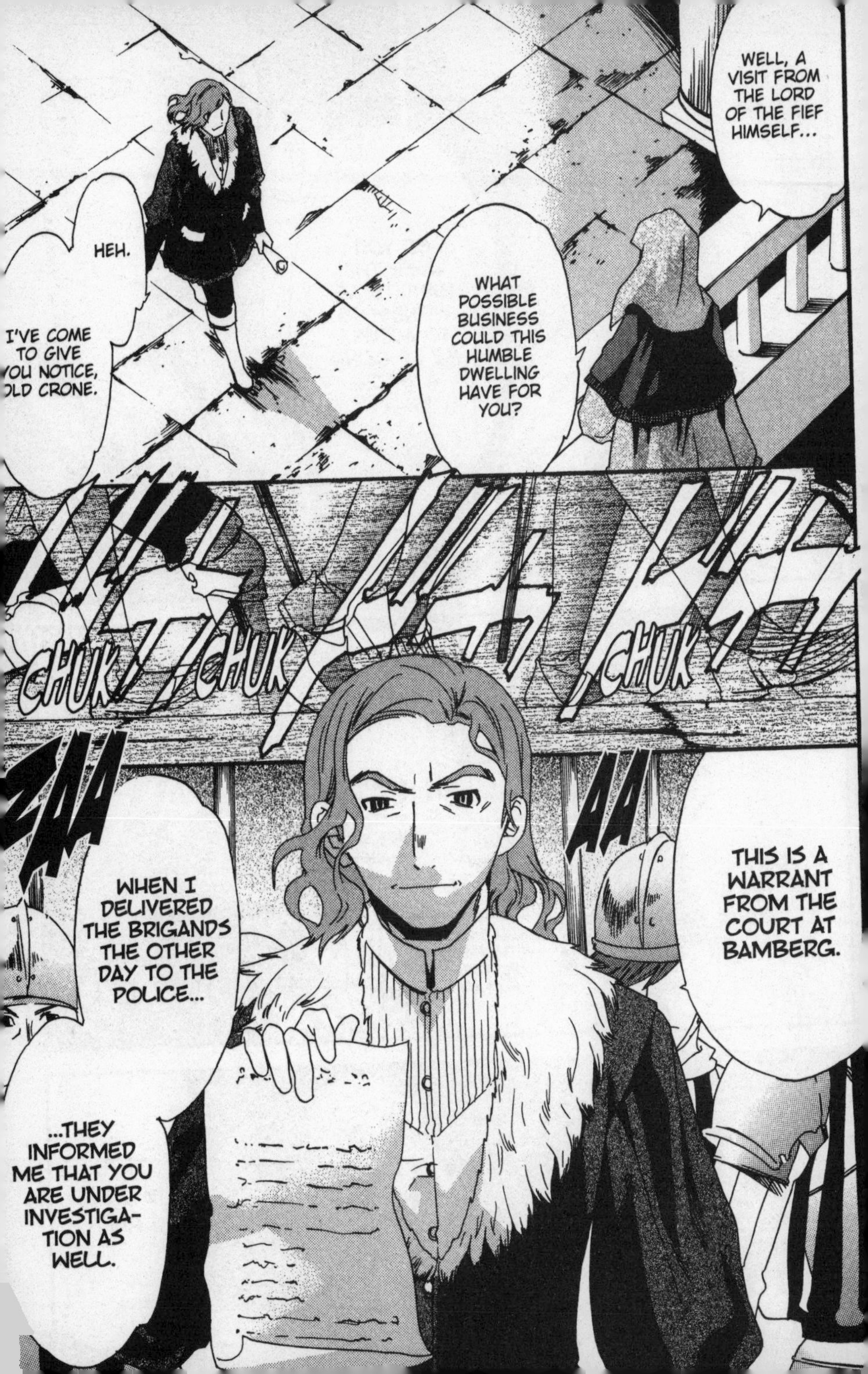

WELL, A VISIT FROM THE LORD OF THE FIEF HIMSELF...
WHAT POSSIBLE BUSINESS COULD THIS HUMBLE DWELLING HAVE FOR YOU?
HEH.
I'VE COME TO GIVE YOU NOTICE, OLD CRONE.
CHUK
CHUK
CHUK
ZAA
AA
THIS IS A WARRANT FROM THE COURT AT BAMBERG.
WHEN I DELIVERED THE BRIGANDS THE OTHER DAY TO THE POLICE...
...THEY INFORMED ME THAT YOU ARE UNDER INVESTIGATION AS WELL.

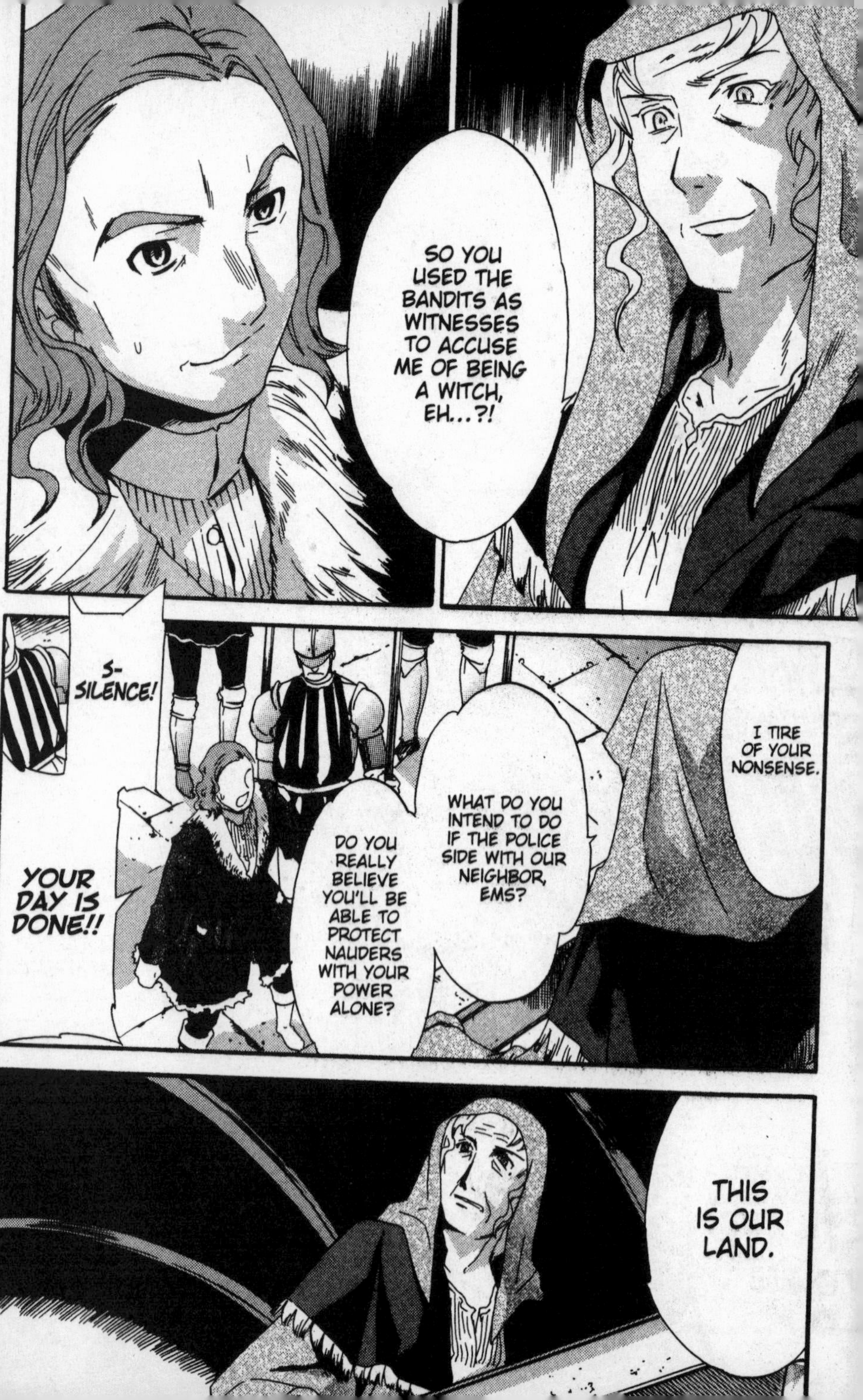
SO YOU USED THE BANDITS AS WITNESSES TO ACCUSE ME OF BEING A WITCH, EH...?!
I TIRE OF YOUR NONSENSE.
WHAT DO YOU INTEND TO DO IF THE POLICE SIDE WITH OUR NEIGHBOR, EMS?
DO YOU REALLY BELIEVE YOU'LL BE ABLE TO PROTECT NAUDERS WITH YOUR POWER ALONE?
S-SILENCE!
YOUR DAY IS DONE!!
THIS IS OUR LAND.

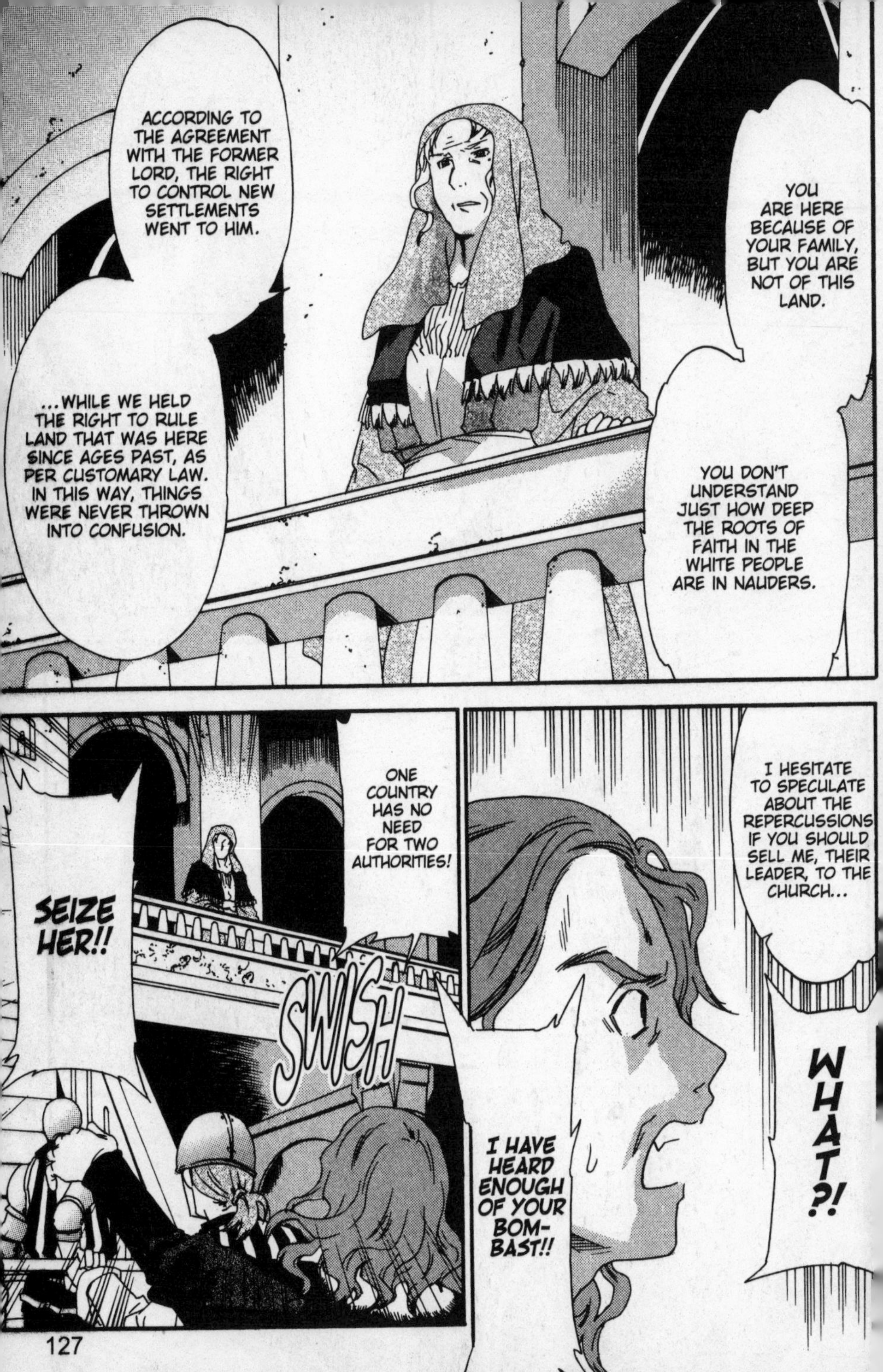
YOU ARE HERE BECAUSE OF YOUR FAMILY, BUT YOU ARE NOT OF THIS LAND.
ACCORDING TO THE AGREEMENT WITH THE FORMER LORD, THE RIGHT TO CONTROL NEW SETTLEMENTS WENT TO HIM.
YOU DON'T UNDERSTAND JUST HOW DEEP THE ROOTS OF FAITH IN THE WHITE PEOPLE ARE IN NAUDERS.
...WHILE WE HELD THE RIGHT TO RULE LAND THAT WAS HERE SINCE AGES PAST, AS PER CUSTOMARY LAW. IN THIS WAY, THINGS WERE NEVER THROWN INTO CONFUSION.
I HESITATE TO SPECULATE ABOUT THE REPERCUSSIONS IF YOU SHOULD SELL ME, THEIR LEADER, TO THE CHURCH...
WHAT?!
I HAVE HEARD ENOUGH OF YOUR BOM-BAST!!
ONE COUNTRY HAS NO NEED FOR TWO AUTHORITIES!
SEIZE HER!!
SWISH

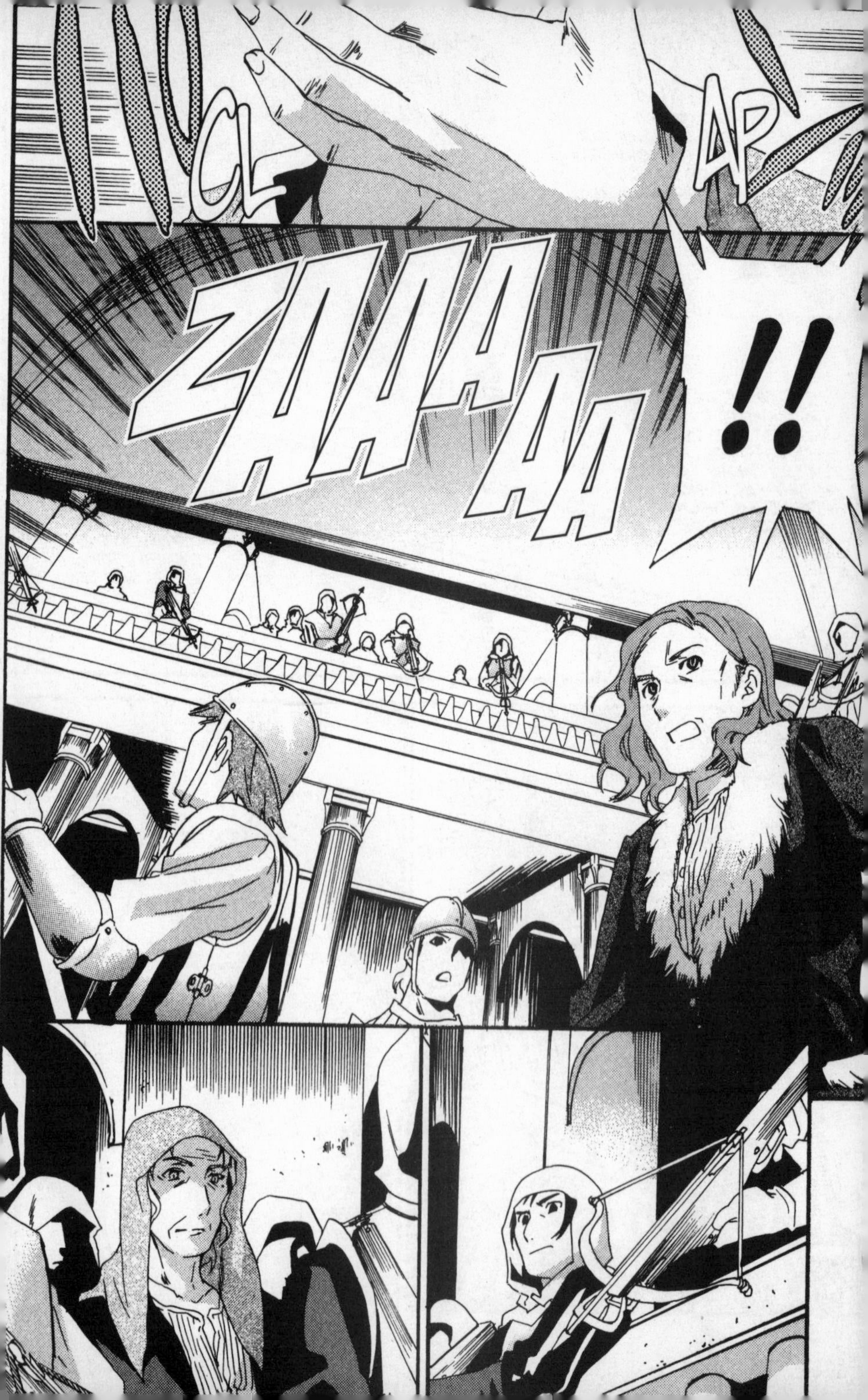
CLAP
ZAAAAA!!

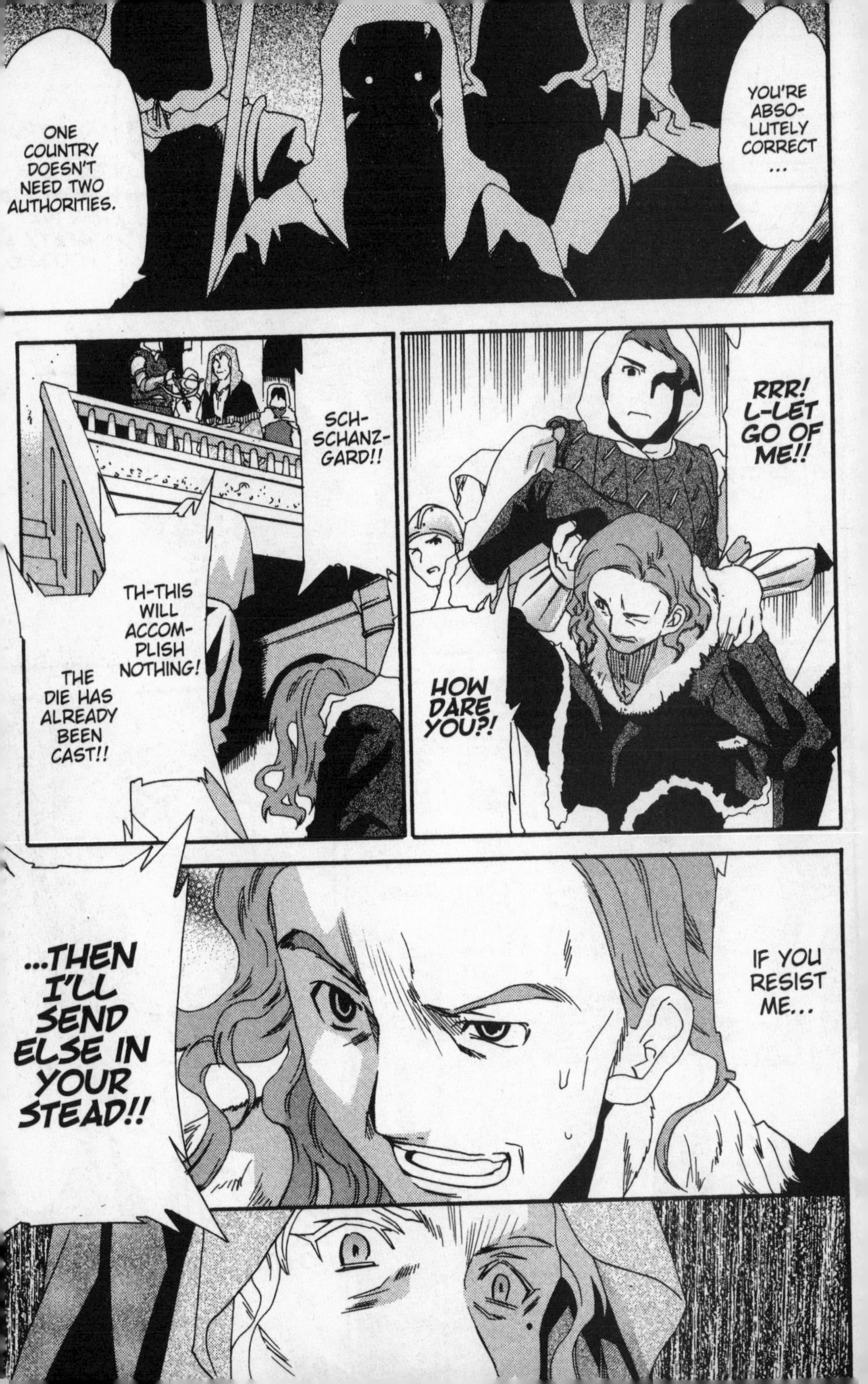
YOU'RE ABSOLUTELY CORRECT...
ONE COUNTRY DOESN'T NEED TWO AUTHORITIES.
RRR! L-LET GO OF ME!!
HOW DARE YOU?!
SCH-SCHANZGARD!!
TH-THIS WILL ACCOMPLISH NOTHING!
THE DIE HAS ALREADY BEEN CAST!!
IF YOU RESIST ME...
...THEN I'LL SEND ELSE IN YOUR STEAD!!

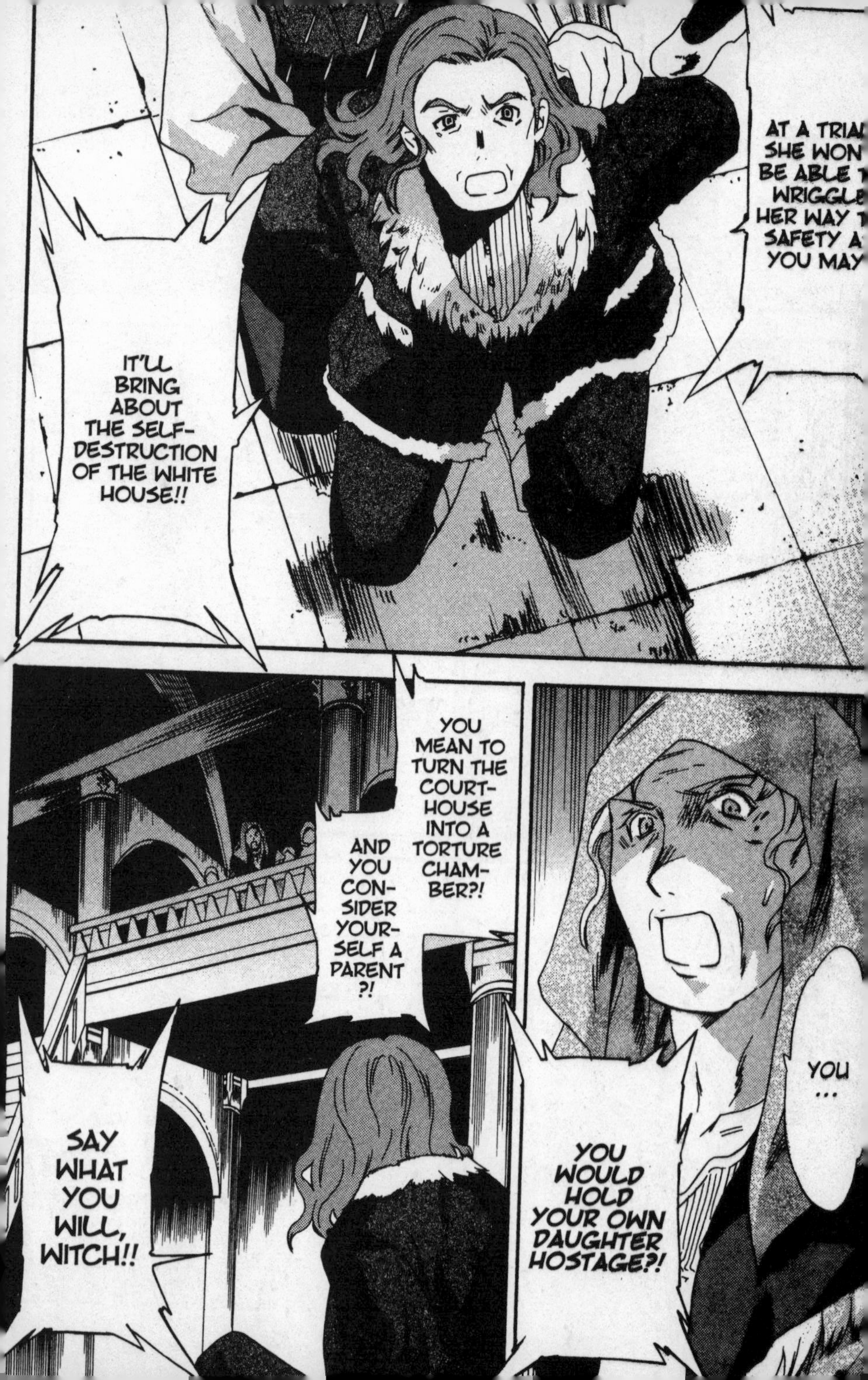
AT A TRIA SHE WON BE ABLE WRIGGLE HER WAY SAFETY A YOU MAY
IT'LL BRING ABOUT THE SELF-DESTRUCTION OF THE WHITE HOUSE!!
YOU ...
YOU WOULD HOLD YOUR OWN DAUGHTER HOSTAGE?!
YOU MEAN TO TURN THE COURT-HOUSE INTO A TORTURE CHAM-BER?!
AND YOU CON-SIDER YOUR-SELF A PARENT?!
SAY WHAT YOU WILL, WITCH!!

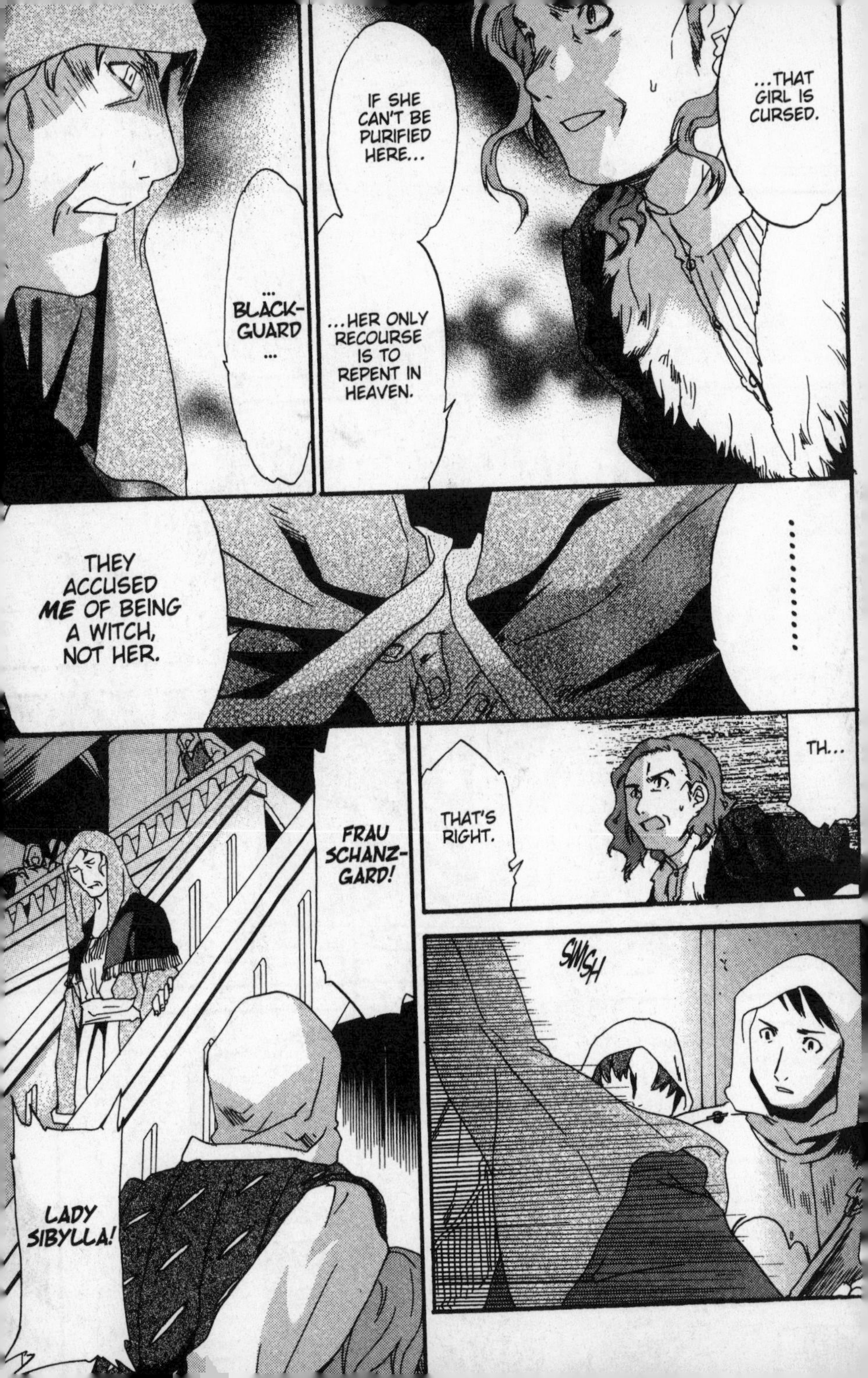
...THAT GIRL IS CURSED.
IF SHE CAN'T BE PURIFIED HERE...
...HER ONLY RECOURSE IS TO REPENT IN HEAVEN.
...BLACKGUARD...
....
THEY ACCUSED *ME* OF BEING A WITCH, NOT HER.
TH...
THAT'S RIGHT.
SMSH
FRAU SCHANZGARD!
LADY SIBYLLA!

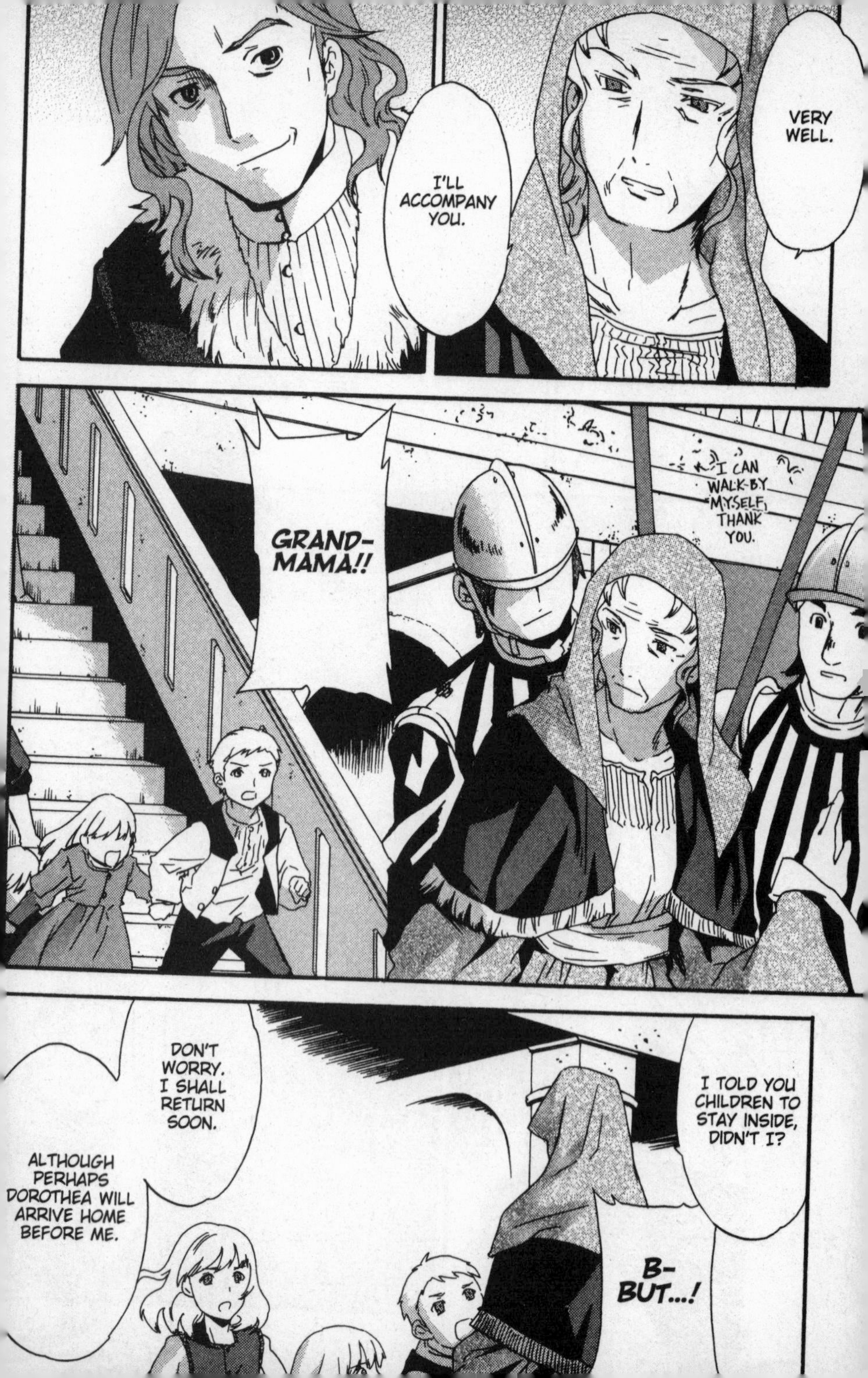
VERY WELL.
I'LL ACCOMPANY YOU.
I CAN WALK BY MYSELF, THANK YOU.
GRAND-MAMA!!
I TOLD YOU CHILDREN TO STAY INSIDE, DIDN'T I?
B-BUT...!
DON'T WORRY. I SHALL RETURN SOON.
ALTHOUGH PERHAPS DOROTHEA WILL ARRIVE HOME BEFORE ME.

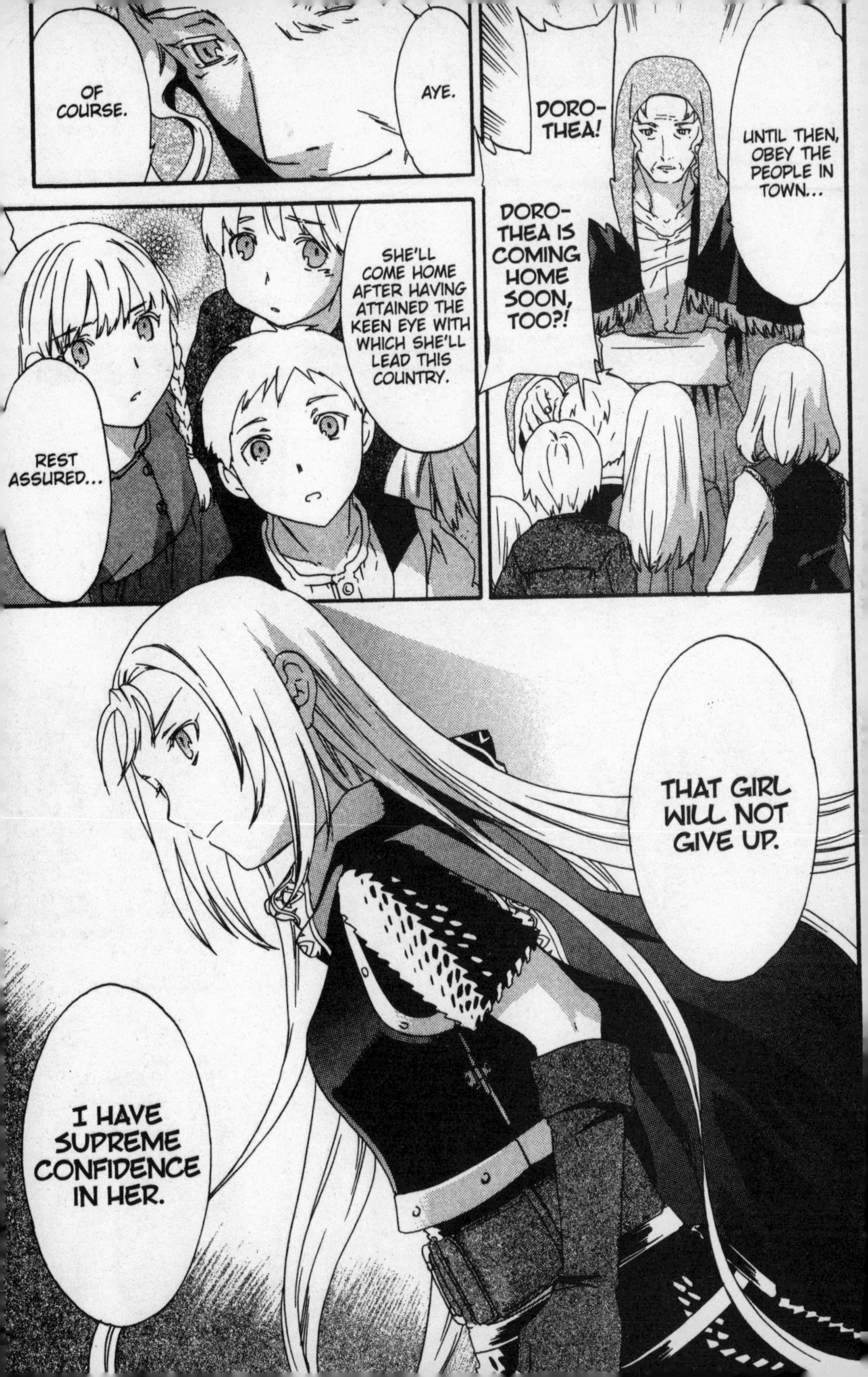
UNTIL THEN, OBEY THE PEOPLE IN TOWN...
DORO-THEA!
DORO-THEA IS COMING HOME SOON, TOO?!
AYE.
OF COURSE.
SHE'LL COME HOME AFTER HAVING ATTAINED THE KEEN EYE WITH WHICH SHE'LL LEAD THIS COUNTRY.
REST ASSURED...
THAT GIRL WILL NOT GIVE UP.
I HAVE SUPREME CONFIDENCE IN HER.

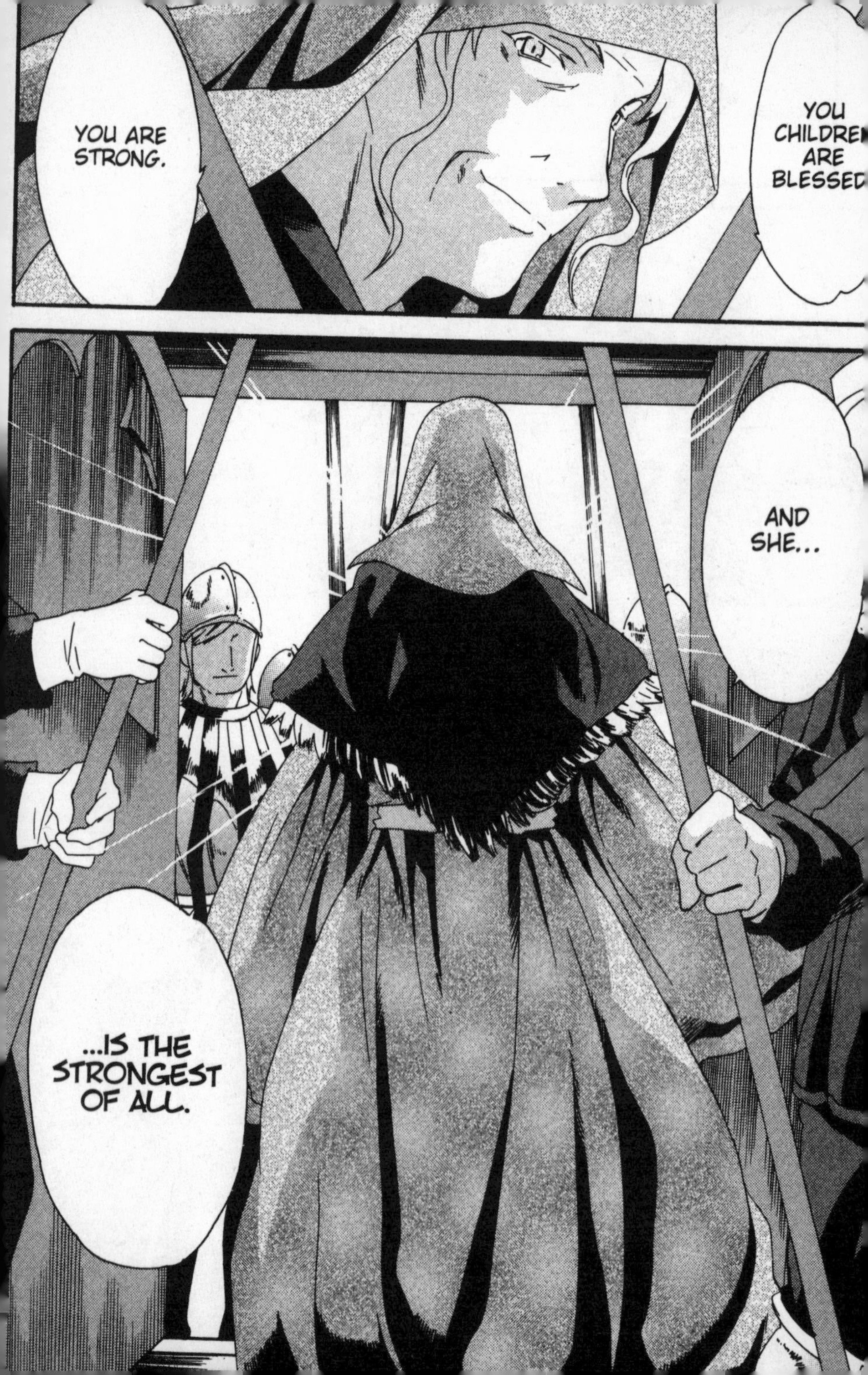
YOU CHILDREN ARE BLESSED
YOU ARE STRONG.
AND SHE...
...IS THE STRONGEST OF ALL.

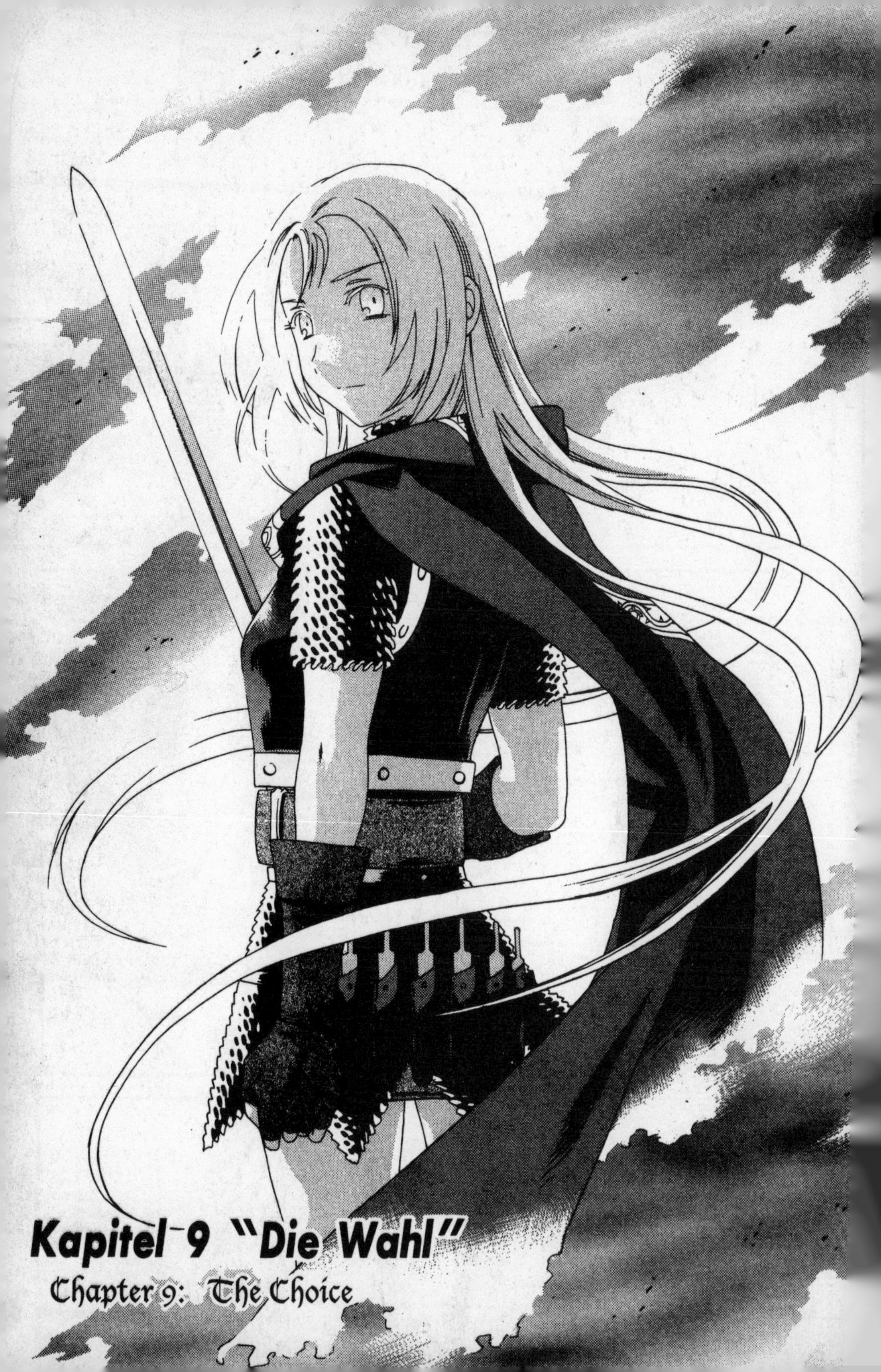

Kapitel 9 "Die Wahl"

Chapter 9: The Choice

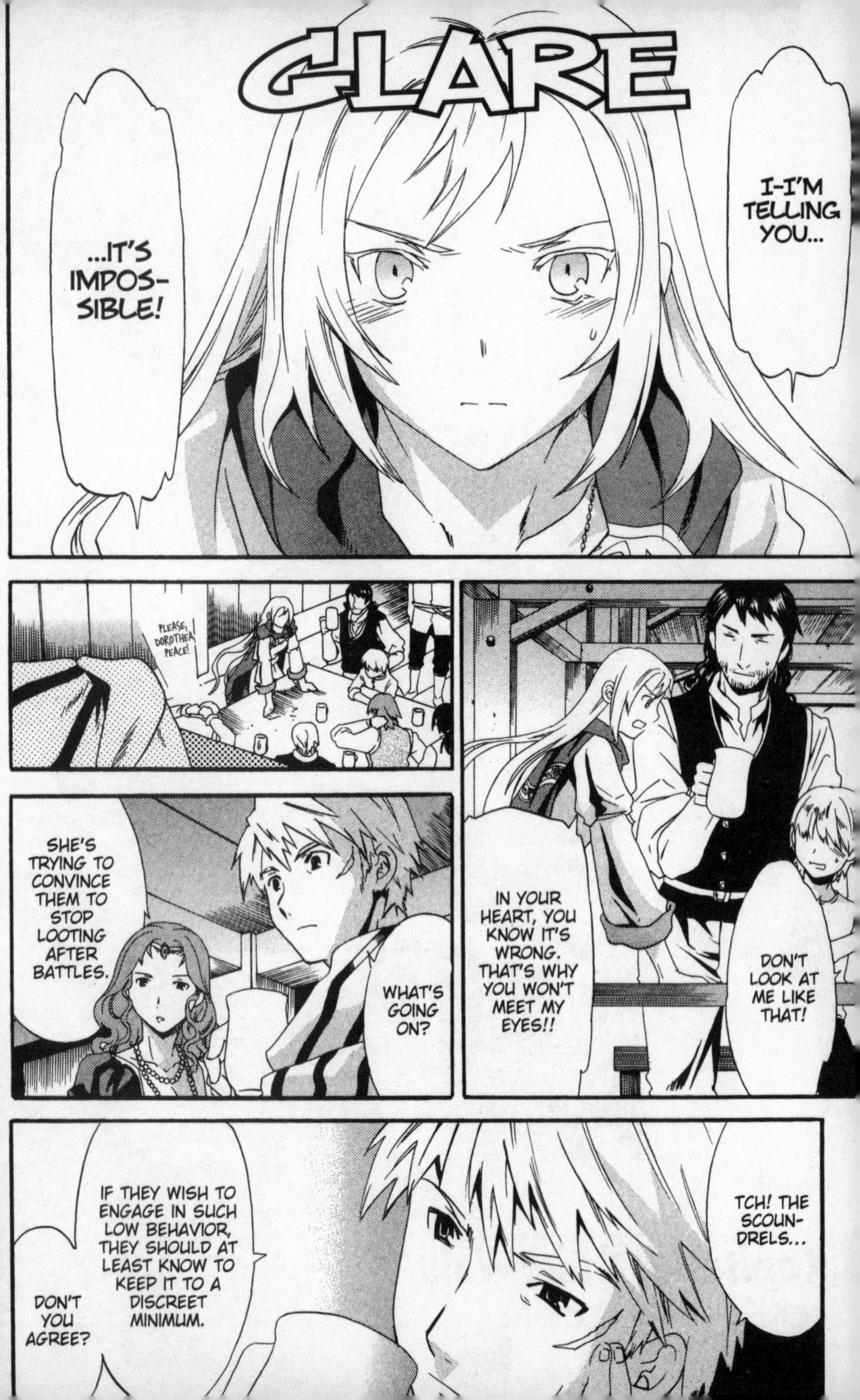
CLARE
I-I'M TELLING YOU...
...IT'S IMPOS-SIBLE!
IN YOUR HEART, YOU KNOW IT'S WRONG. THAT'S WHY YOU WON'T MEET MY EYES!!
DON'T LOOK AT ME LIKE THAT!
PLEASE, DOROTHEA! PEACE!
WHAT'S GOING ON?
SHE'S TRYING TO CONVINCE THEM TO STOP LOOTING AFTER BATTLES.
TCH! THE SCOUN-DRELS...
IF THEY WISH TO ENGAGE IN SUCH LOW BEHAVIOR, THEY SHOULD AT LEAST KNOW TO KEEP IT TO A DISCREET MINIMUM.
DON'T YOU AGREE?

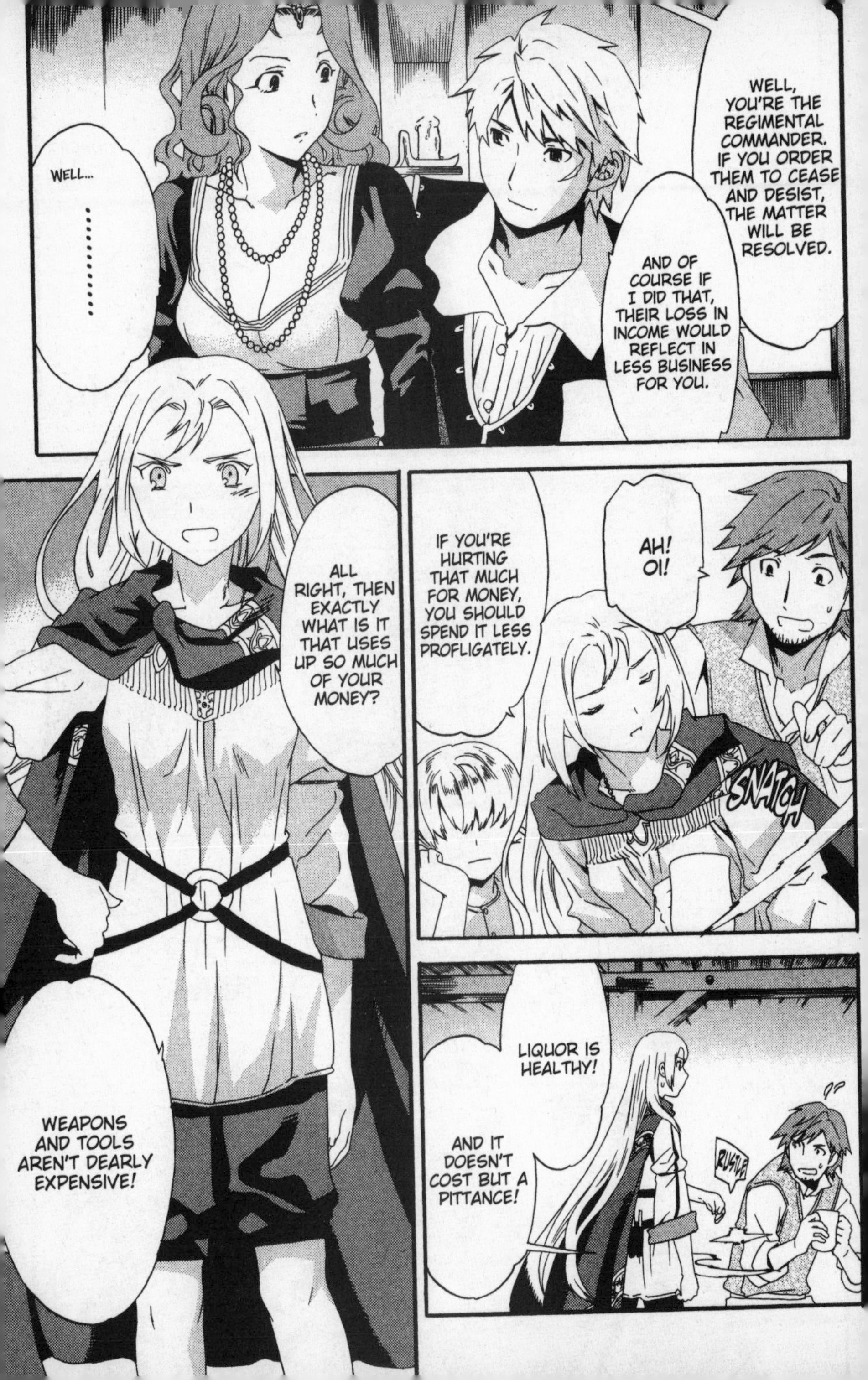
WELL, YOU'RE THE REGIMENTAL COMMANDER. IF YOU ORDER THEM TO CEASE AND DESIST, THE MATTER WILL BE RESOLVED.
AND OF COURSE IF I DID THAT, THEIR LOSS IN INCOME WOULD REFLECT IN LESS BUSINESS FOR YOU.
WELL...
......
AH! OI!
IF YOU'RE HURTING THAT MUCH FOR MONEY, YOU SHOULD SPEND IT LESS PROFLIGATELY.
SNATCH
LIQUOR IS HEALTHY!
AND IT DOESN'T COST BUT A PITTANCE!
RUSTLE
ALL RIGHT, THEN EXACTLY WHAT IS IT THAT USES UP SO MUCH OF YOUR MONEY?
WEAPONS AND TOOLS AREN'T DEARLY EXPENSIVE!

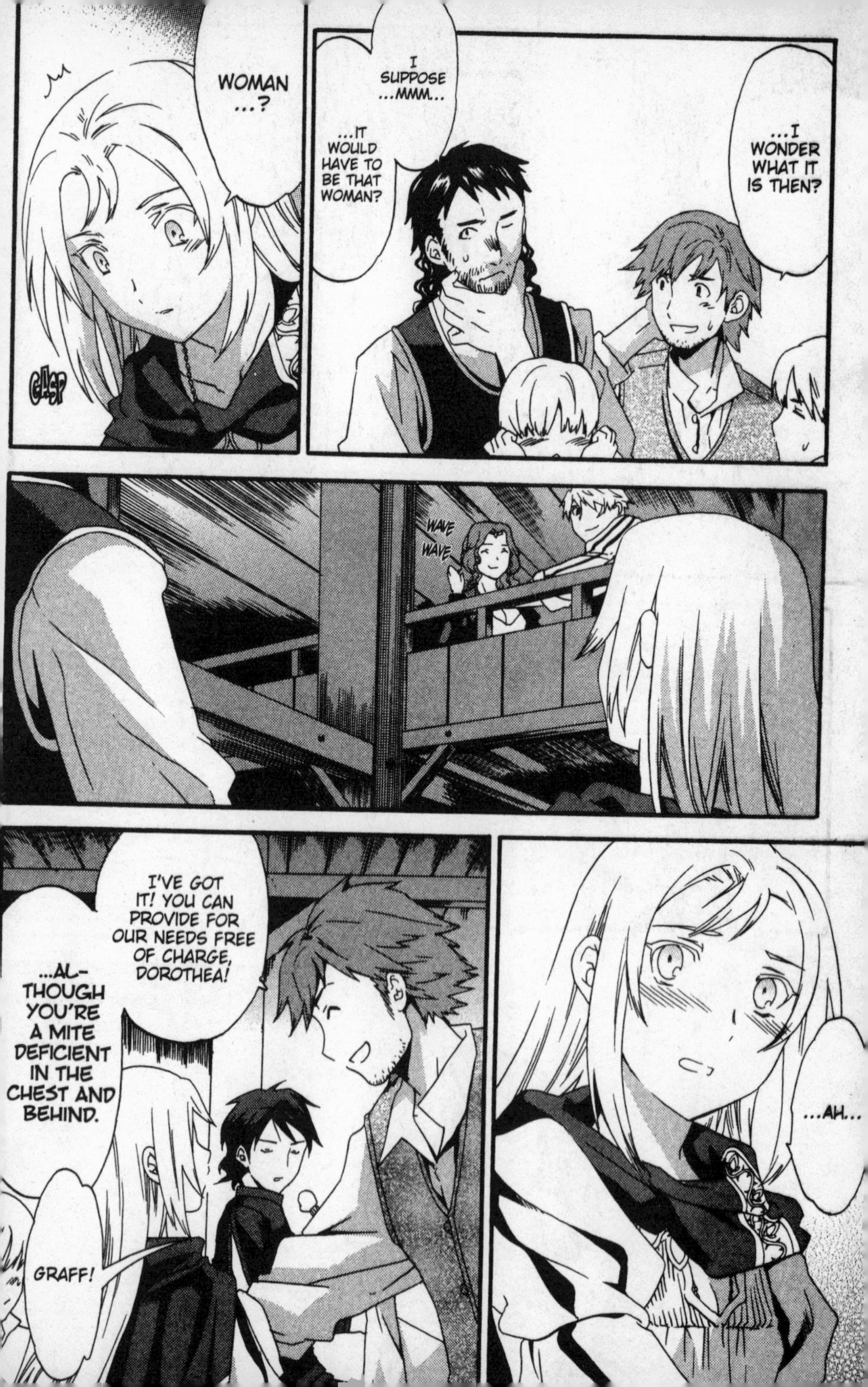

...I WONDER WHAT IT IS THEN?
I SUPPOSE ...MMM...
...IT WOULD HAVE TO BE THAT WOMAN?
WOMAN ...?
GASP
WAVE
WAVE
...AH...
I'VE GOT IT! YOU CAN PROVIDE FOR OUR NEEDS FREE OF CHARGE, DOROTHEA!
...AL-THOUGH YOU'RE A MITE DEFICIENT IN THE CHEST AND BEHIND.
GRAFF!

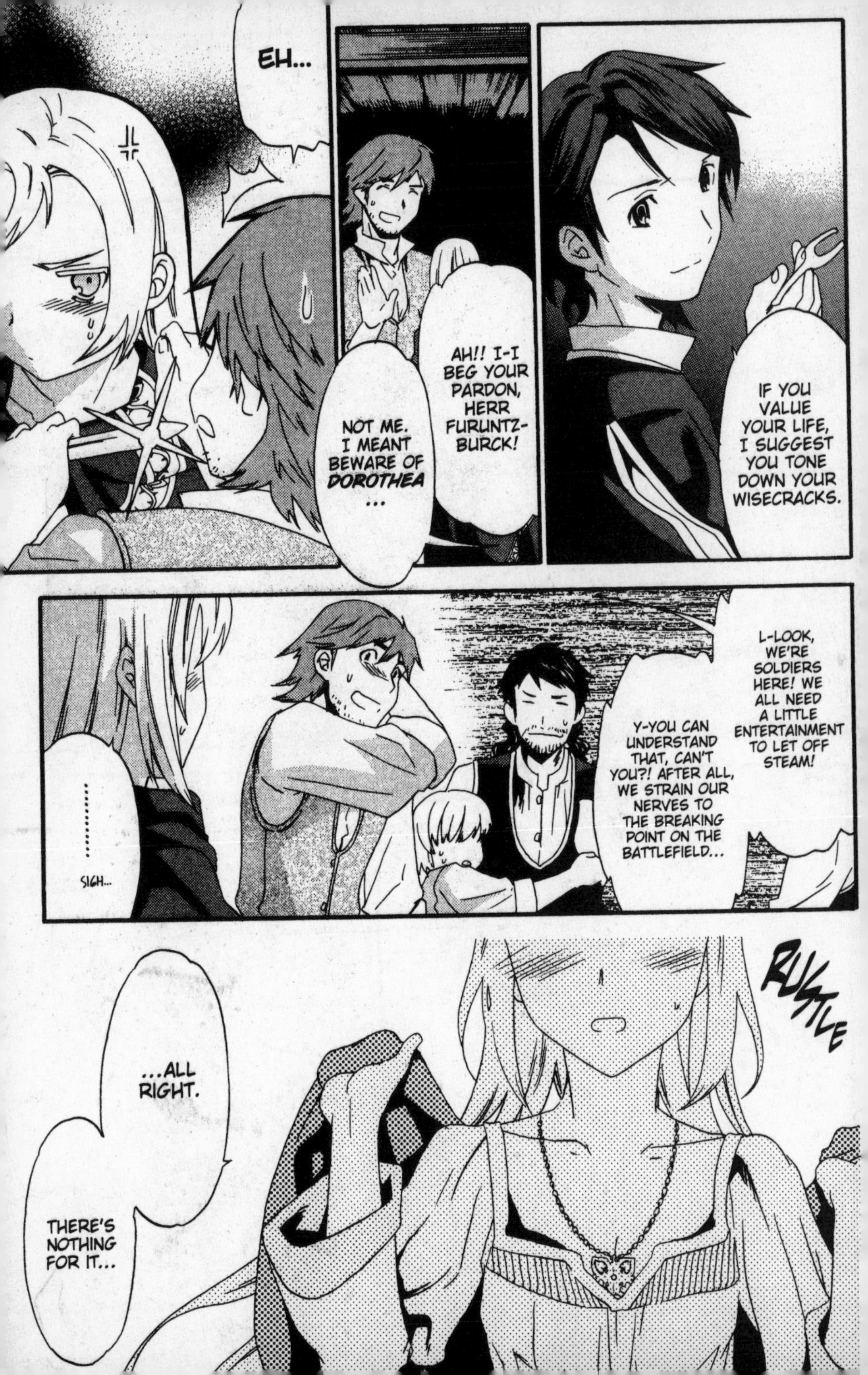
IF YOU VALUE YOUR LIFE, I SUGGEST YOU TONE DOWN YOUR WISECRACKS.
AH!! I-I BEG YOUR PARDON, HERR FURUNTZ-BURCK!
NOT ME. I MEANT BEWARE OF DOROTHEA ...
EH...
L-LOOK, WE'RE SOLDIERS HERE! WE ALL NEED A LITTLE ENTERTAINMENT TO LET OFF STEAM!
Y-YOU CAN UNDERSTAND THAT, CAN'T YOU?! AFTER ALL, WE STRAIN OUR NERVES TO THE BREAKING POINT ON THE BATTLEFIELD...
....
SIGH...
RUSTLE
...ALL RIGHT.
THERE'S NOTHING FOR IT...

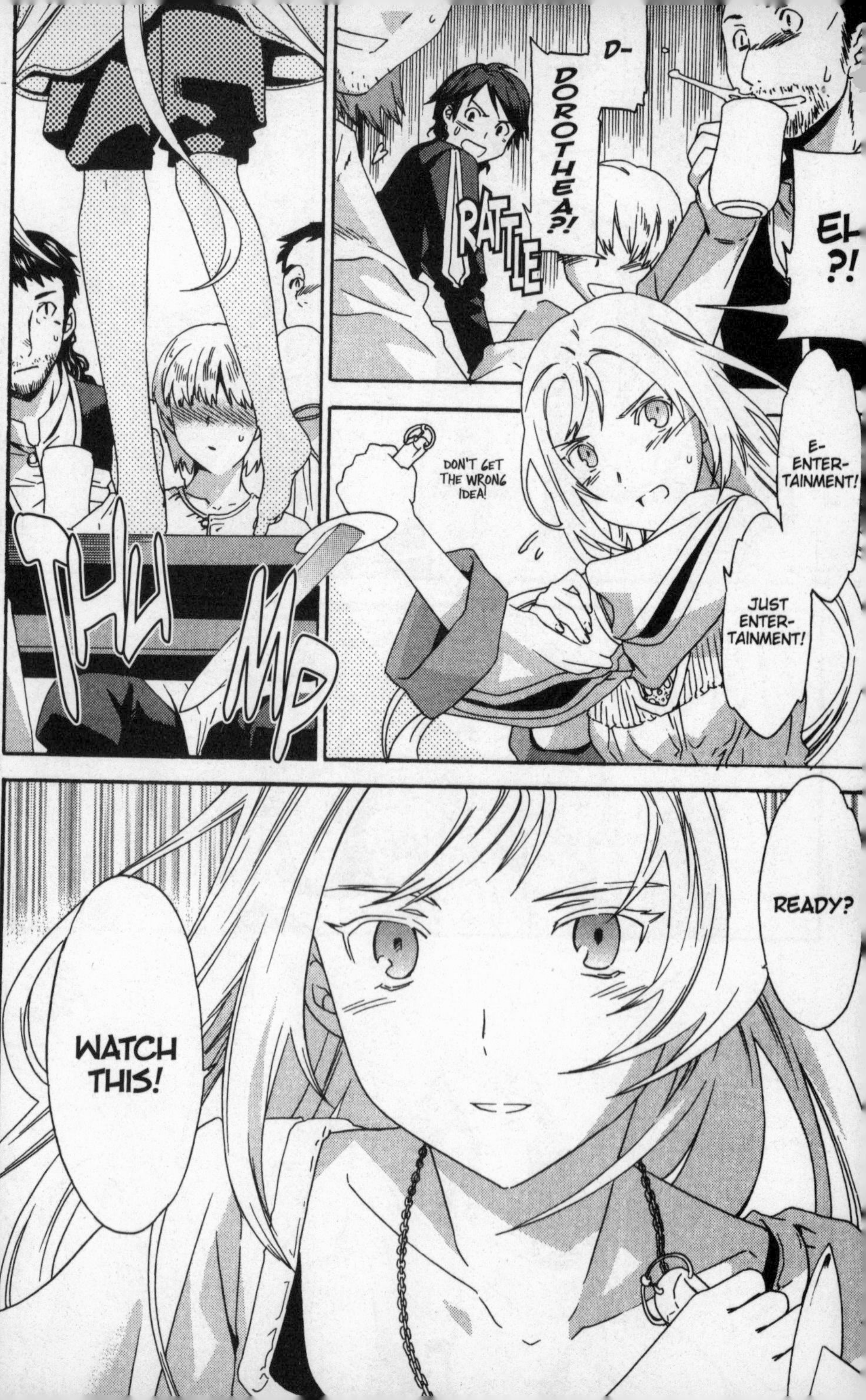
D- DOROTHEA?!
RATTLE
EH ?!
E- ENTERTAINMENT!
JUST ENTERTAINMENT!
DON'T GET THE WRONG IDEA!
THUMP
READY?
WATCH THIS!

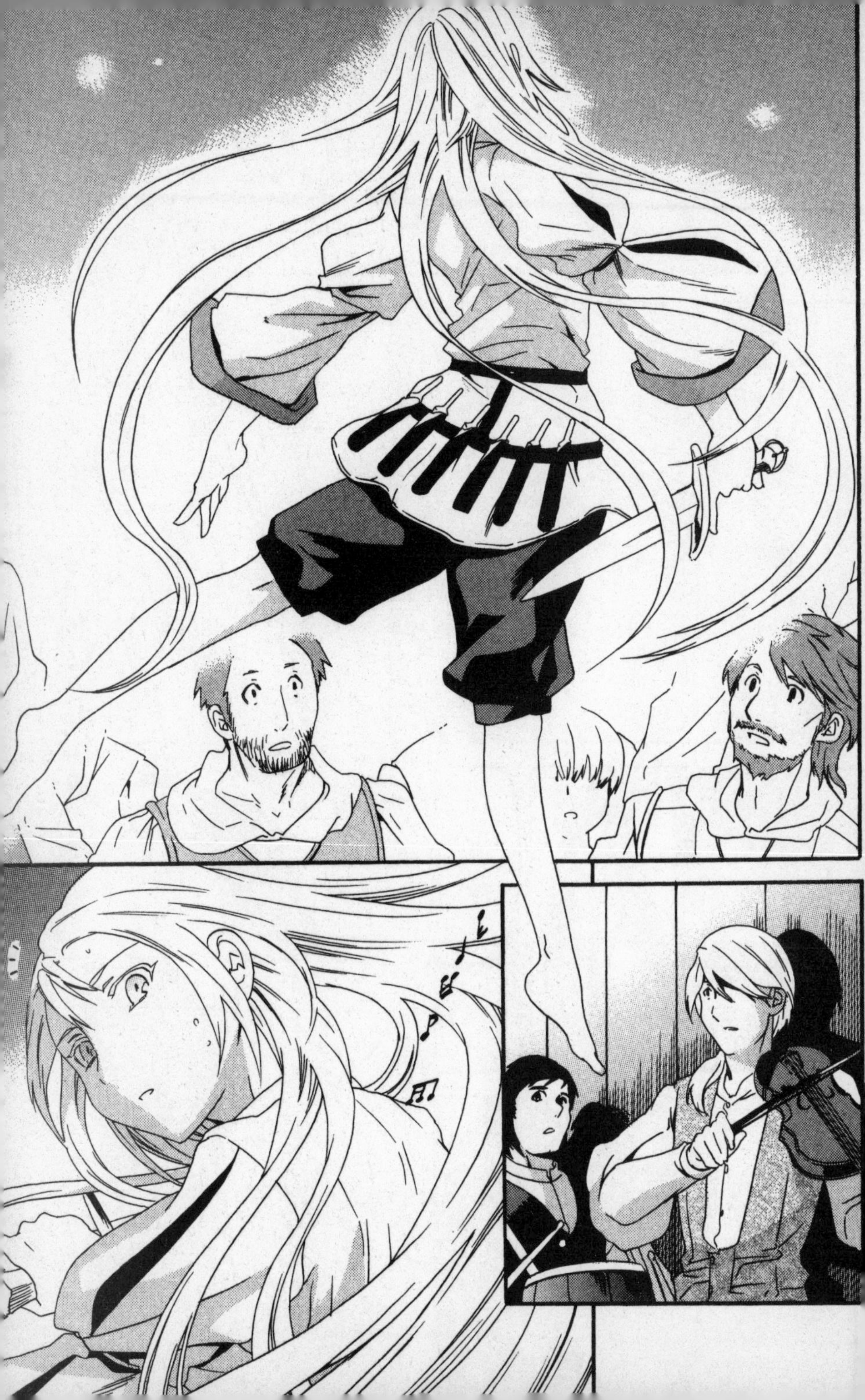

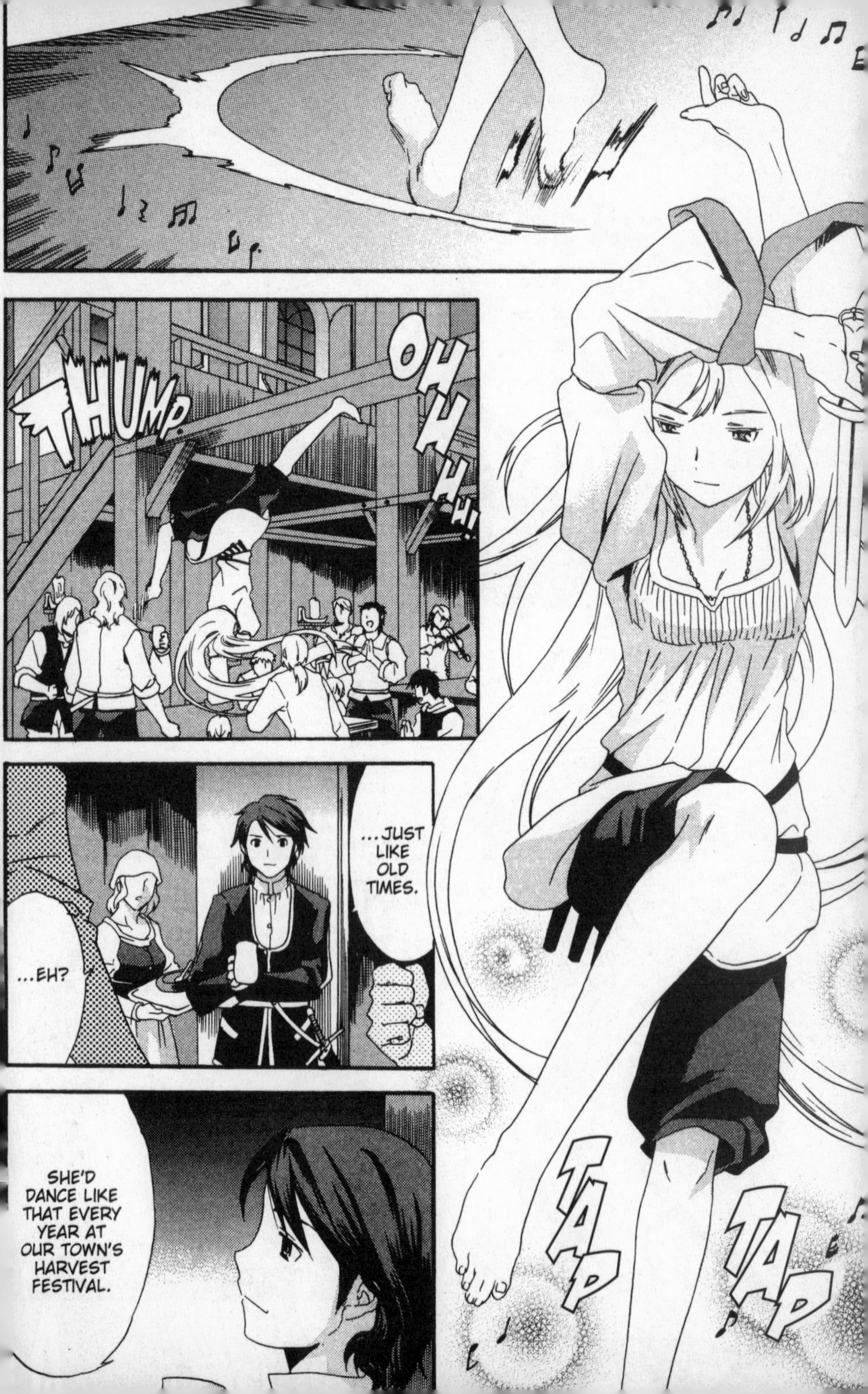
TAP
TAP
OHHHH!!
THUMP
...JUST LIKE OLD TIMES.
...EH?
SHE'D DANCE LIKE THAT EVERY YEAR AT OUR TOWN'S HARVEST FESTIVAL.

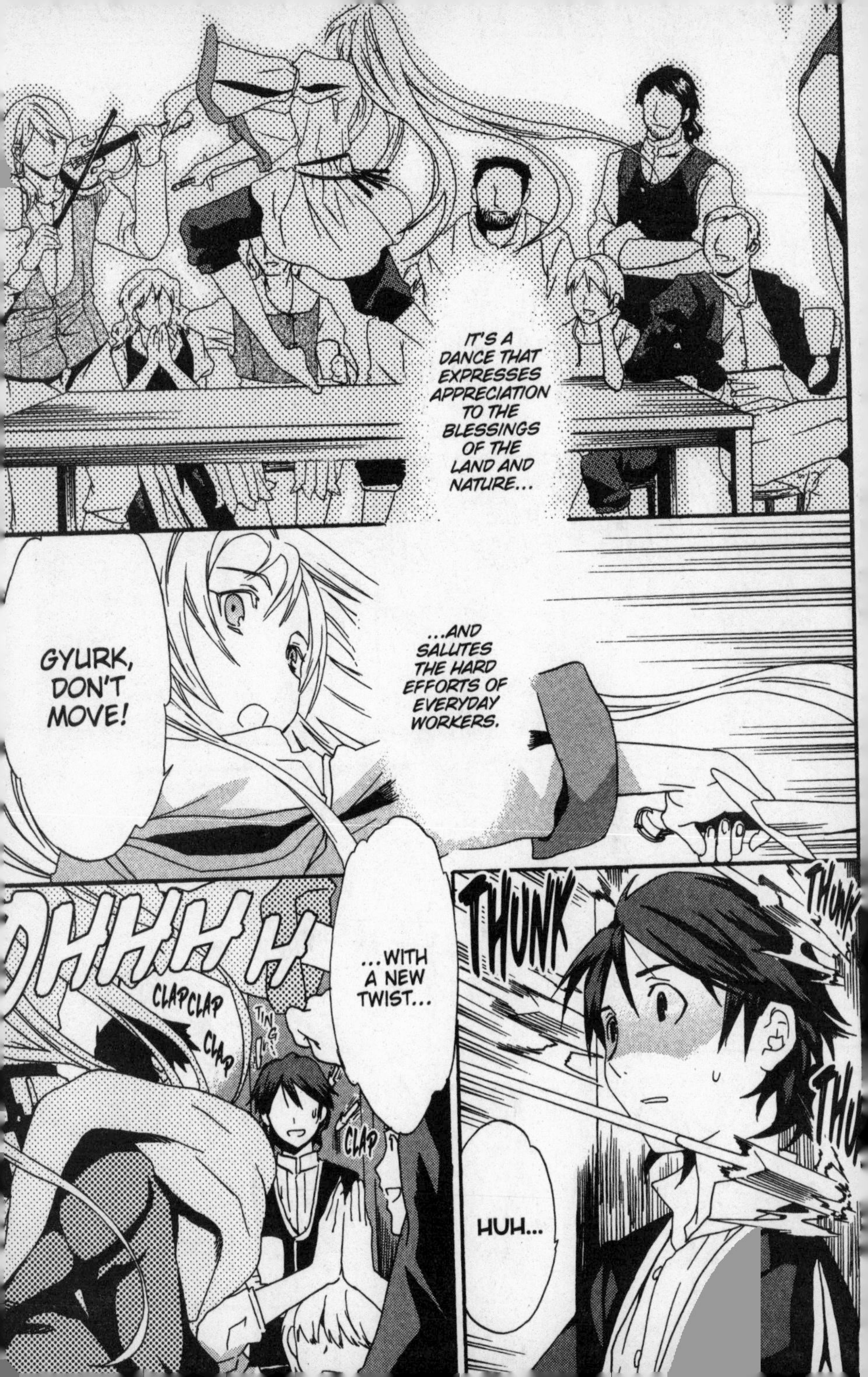
IT'S A DANCE THAT EXPRESSES APPRECIATION TO THE BLESSINGS OF THE LAND AND NATURE...
...AND SALUTES THE HARD EFFORTS OF EVERYDAY WORKERS.
GYURK, DON'T MOVE!
THUNK
THUNK
HUH...
...WITH A NEW TWIST...
CLAPCLAP
CLAP
CLAP

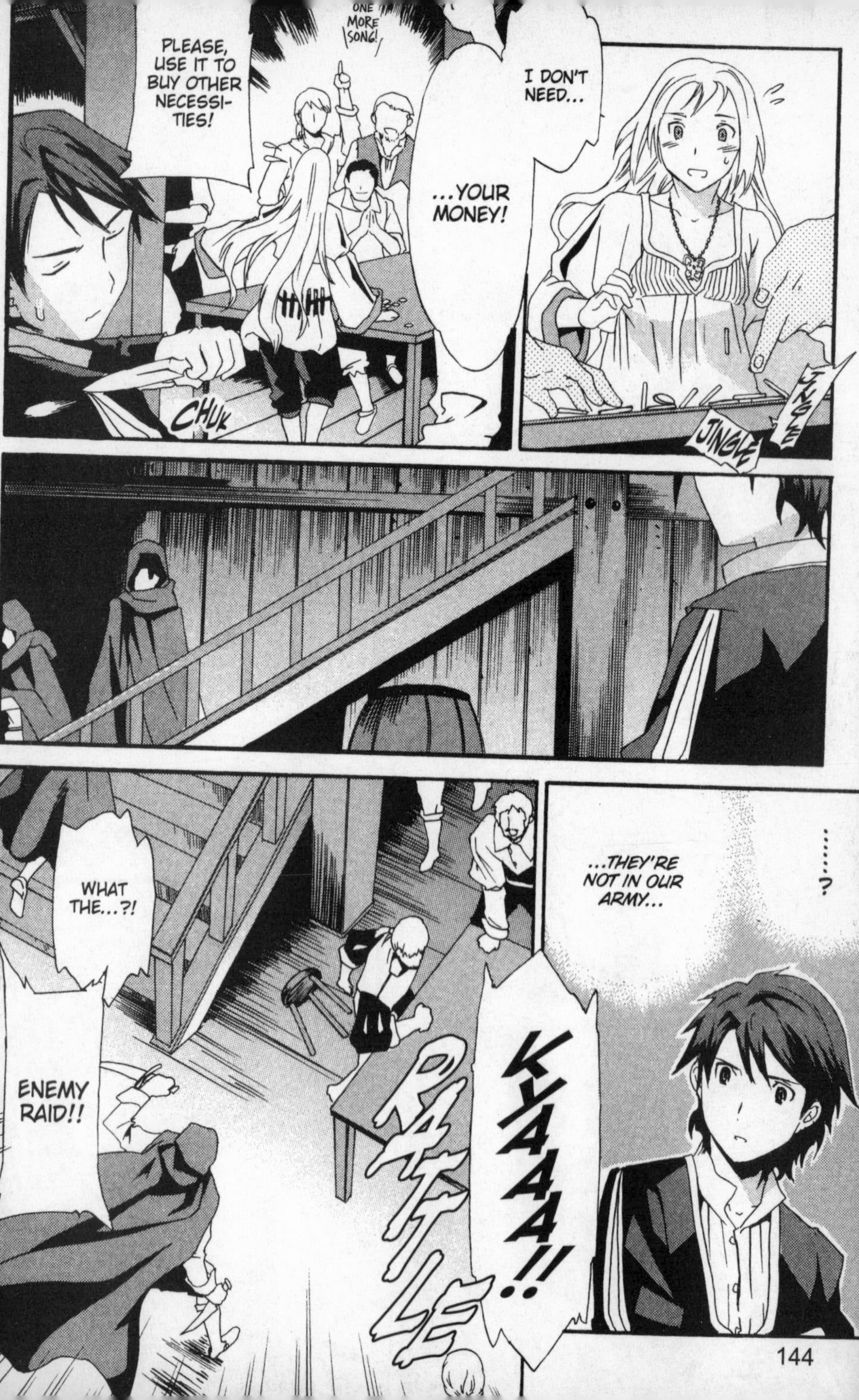
I DON'T NEED...
...YOUR MONEY!
JINGLE
JINGLE
ONE MORE SONG!
PLEASE, USE IT TO BUY OTHER NECESSI-TIES!
CHUK
......?
...THEY'RE NOT IN OUR ARMY...
KYAAAA!!
RATTLE
WHAT THE...?!
ENEMY RAID!!

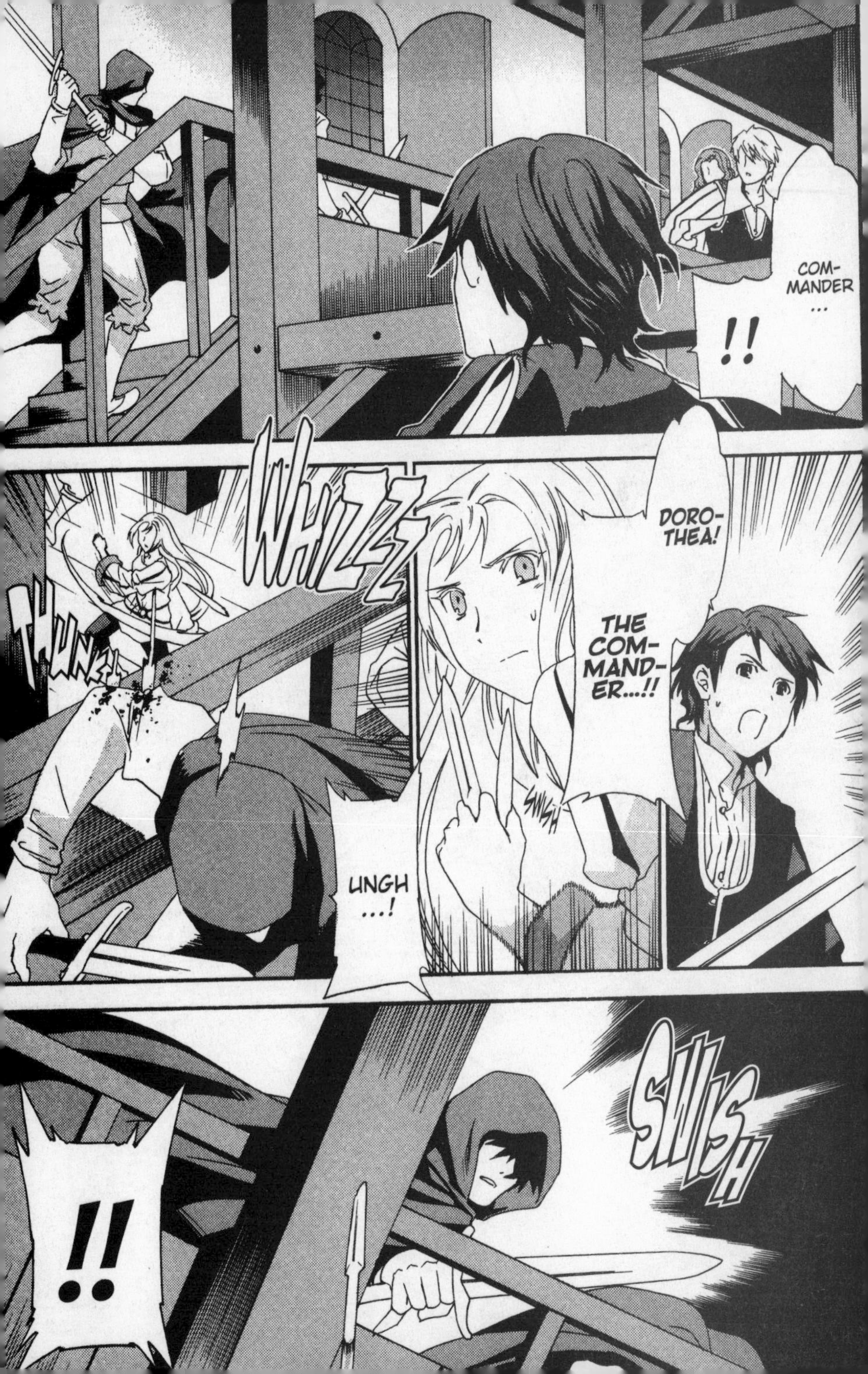
COM-MANDER ...
!!
DORO-THEA!
THE COM-MAND-ER...!!
SWISH
WHIZZZ
THUNK
UNGH ...!
SWISH
!!

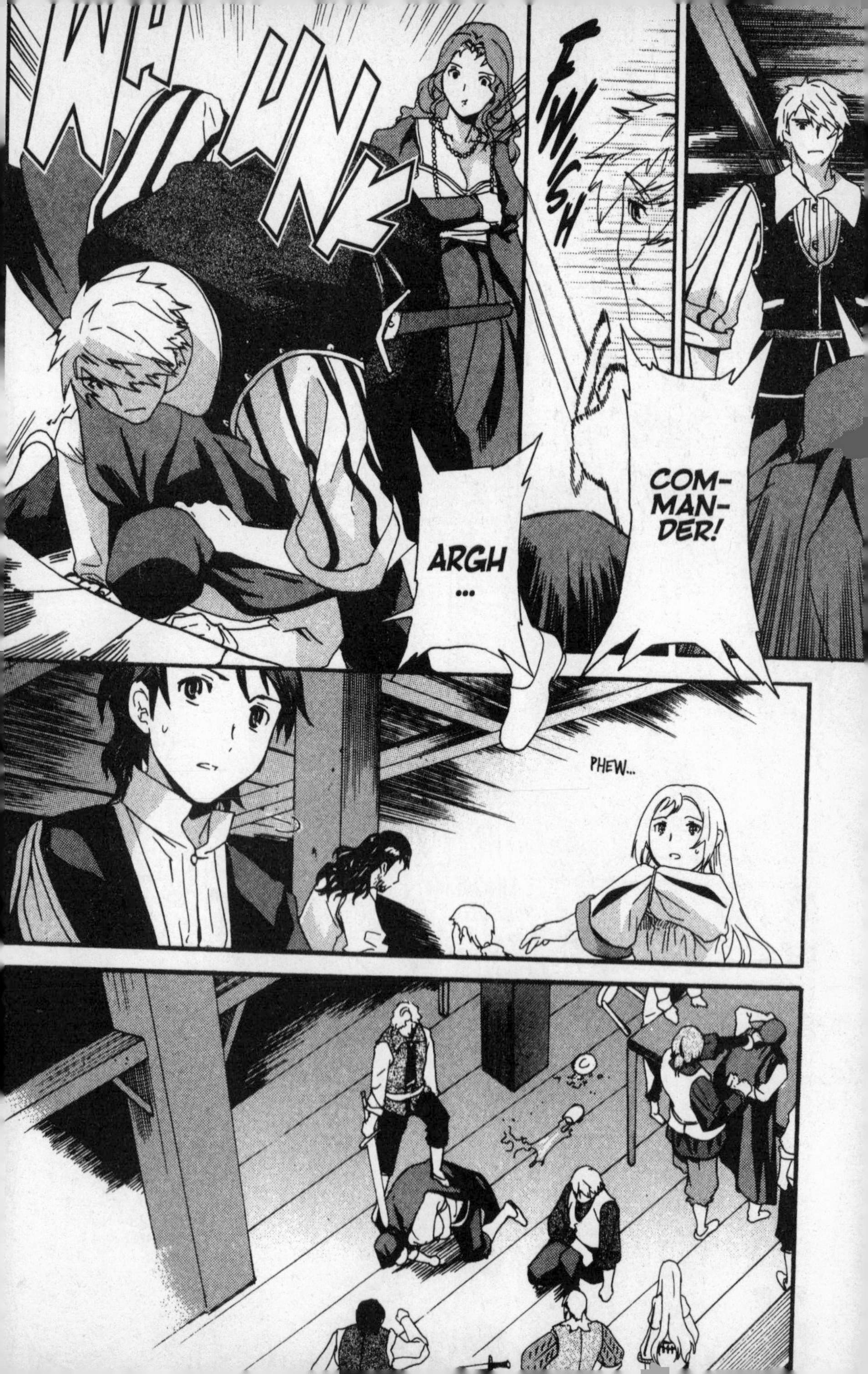
FWISH
COM-MAN-DER!
WHUNK
ARGH...
PHEW...

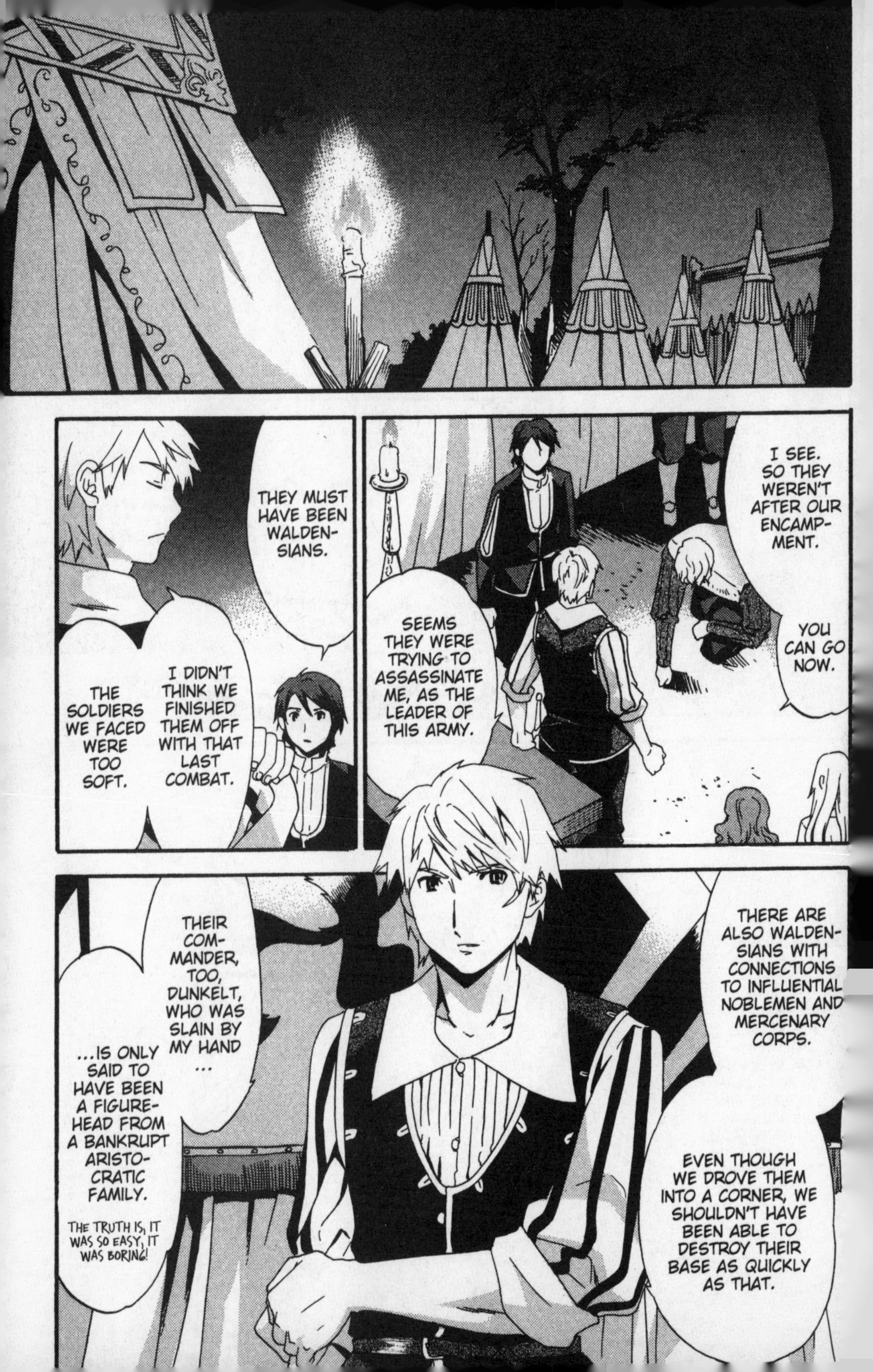
I SEE. SO THEY WEREN'T AFTER OUR ENCAMPMENT.
YOU CAN GO NOW.
SEEMS THEY WERE TRYING TO ASSASSINATE ME, AS THE LEADER OF THIS ARMY.
THEY MUST HAVE BEEN WALDENSIANS.
I DIDN'T THINK WE FINISHED THEM OFF WITH THAT LAST COMBAT.
THE SOLDIERS WE FACED WERE TOO SOFT.
THERE ARE ALSO WALDENSIANS WITH CONNECTIONS TO INFLUENTIAL NOBLEMEN AND MERCENARY CORPS.
EVEN THOUGH WE DROVE THEM INTO A CORNER, WE SHOULDN'T HAVE BEEN ABLE TO DESTROY THEIR BASE AS QUICKLY AS THAT.
THEIR COMMANDER, TOO, DUNKELT, WHO WAS SLAIN BY MY HAND ...
...IS ONLY SAID TO HAVE BEEN A FIGUREHEAD FROM A BANKRUPT ARISTOCRATIC FAMILY.
THE TRUTH IS, IT WAS SO EASY, IT WAS BORING!

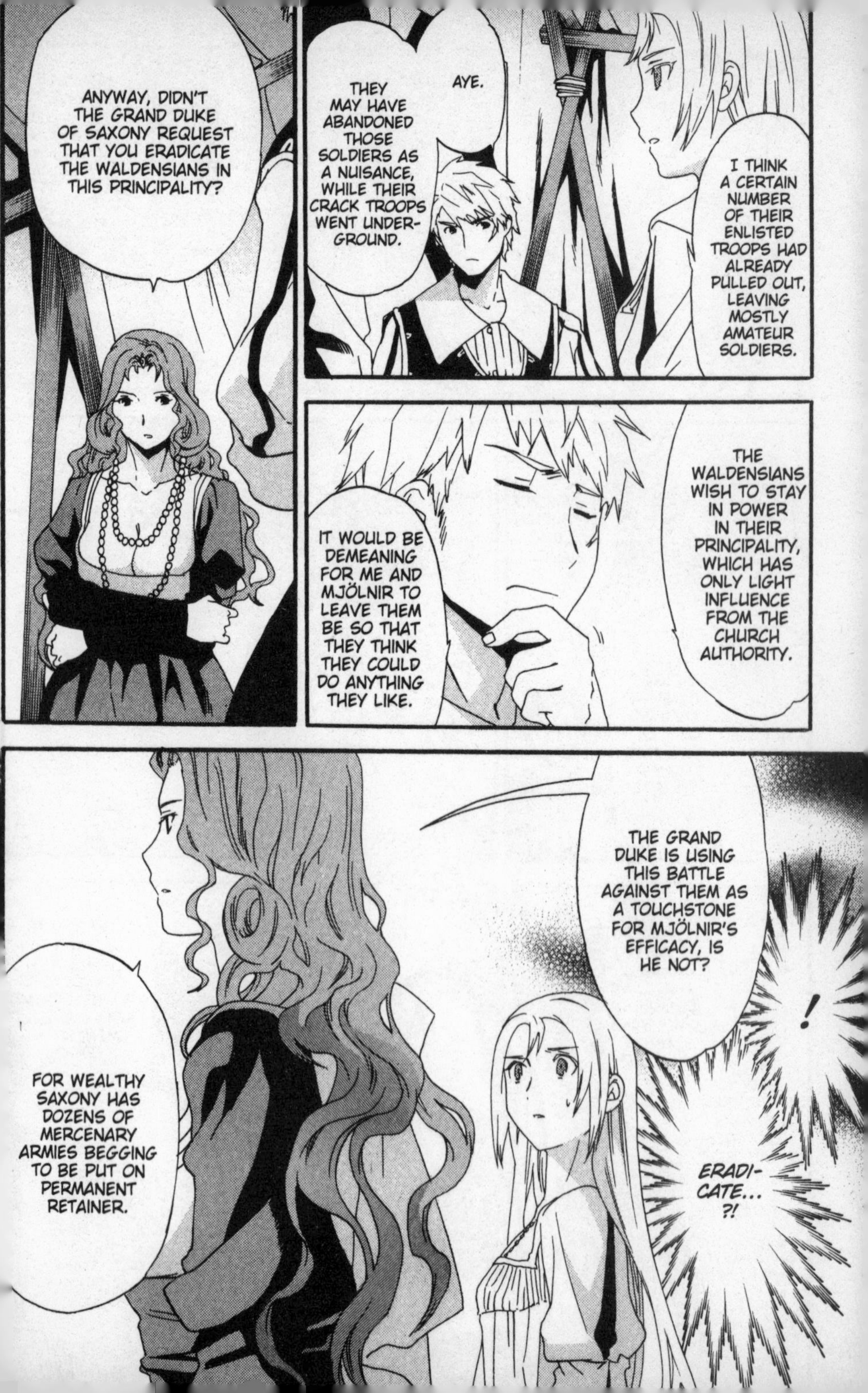
I THINK A CERTAIN NUMBER OF THEIR ENLISTED TROOPS HAD ALREADY PULLED OUT, LEAVING MOSTLY AMATEUR SOLDIERS.
AYE. THEY MAY HAVE ABANDONED THOSE SOLDIERS AS A NUISANCE, WHILE THEIR CRACK TROOPS WENT UNDER-GROUND.
THE WALDENSIANS WISH TO STAY IN POWER IN THEIR PRINCIPALITY, WHICH HAS ONLY LIGHT INFLUENCE FROM THE CHURCH AUTHORITY.
IT WOULD BE DEMEANING FOR ME AND MJÖLNIR TO LEAVE THEM BE SO THAT THEY THINK THEY COULD DO ANYTHING THEY LIKE.
ANYWAY, DIDN'T THE GRAND DUKE OF SAXONY REQUEST THAT YOU ERADICATE THE WALDENSIANS IN THIS PRINCIPALITY?
THE GRAND DUKE IS USING THIS BATTLE AGAINST THEM AS A TOUCHSTONE FOR MJÖLNIR'S EFFICACY, IS HE NOT?
!
ERADI-CATE... ?!
FOR WEALTHY SAXONY HAS DOZENS OF MERCENARY ARMIES BEGGING TO BE PUT ON PERMANENT RETAINER.

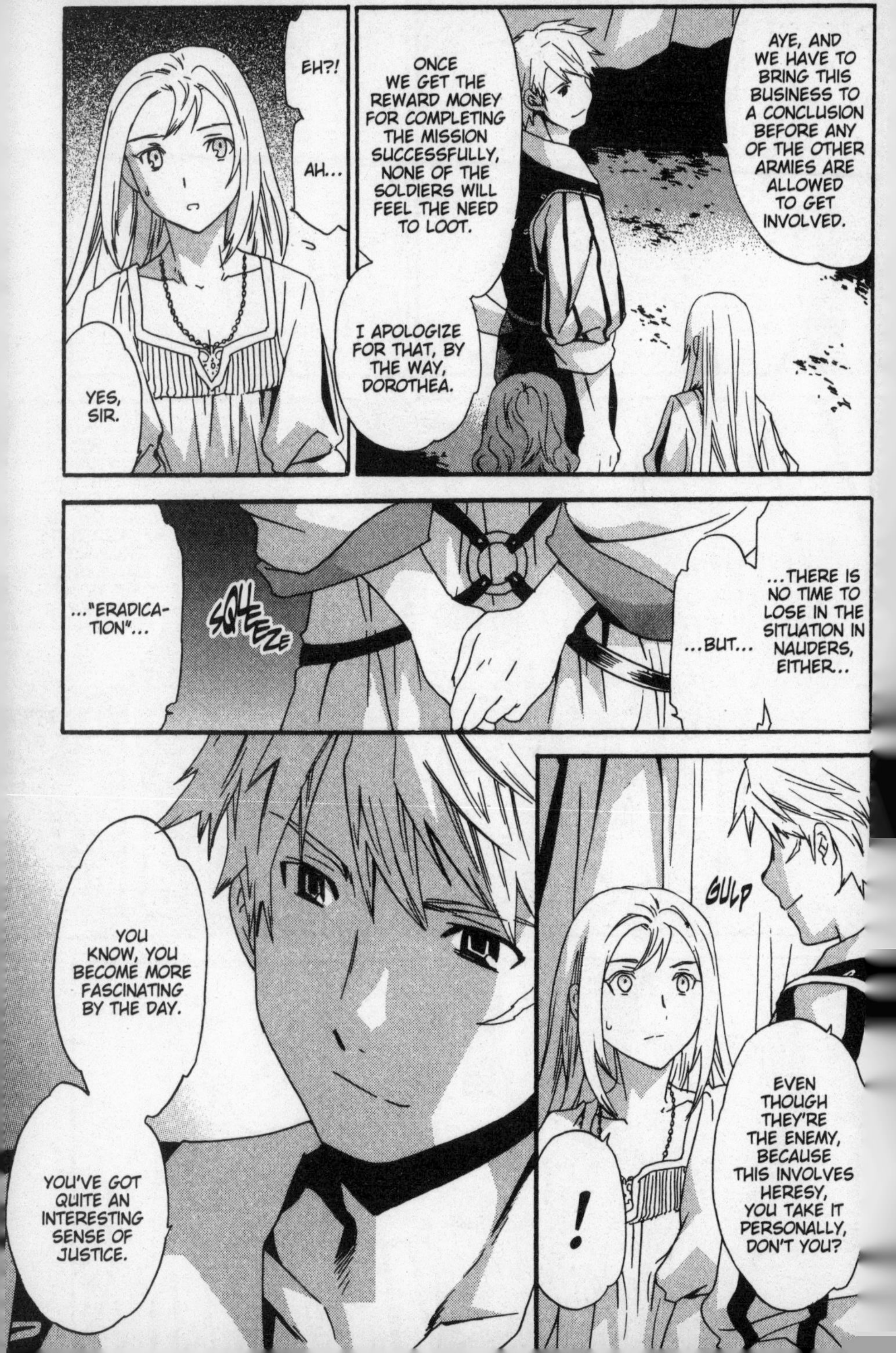
AYE, AND WE HAVE TO BRING THIS BUSINESS TO A CONCLUSION BEFORE ANY OF THE OTHER ARMIES ARE ALLOWED TO GET INVOLVED.
ONCE WE GET THE REWARD MONEY FOR COMPLETING THE MISSION SUCCESSFULLY, NONE OF THE SOLDIERS WILL FEEL THE NEED TO LOOT.
I APOLOGIZE FOR THAT, BY THE WAY, DOROTHEA.
EH?!
AH...
YES, SIR.
...THERE IS NO TIME TO LOSE IN THE SITUATION IN NAUDERS, EITHER...
...BUT...
SQUEEZE
..."ERADICATION"...
GULP
EVEN THOUGH THEY'RE THE ENEMY, BECAUSE THIS INVOLVES HERESY, YOU TAKE IT PERSONALLY, DON'T YOU?
!
YOU KNOW, YOU BECOME MORE FASCINATING BY THE DAY.
YOU'VE GOT QUITE AN INTERESTING SENSE OF JUSTICE.

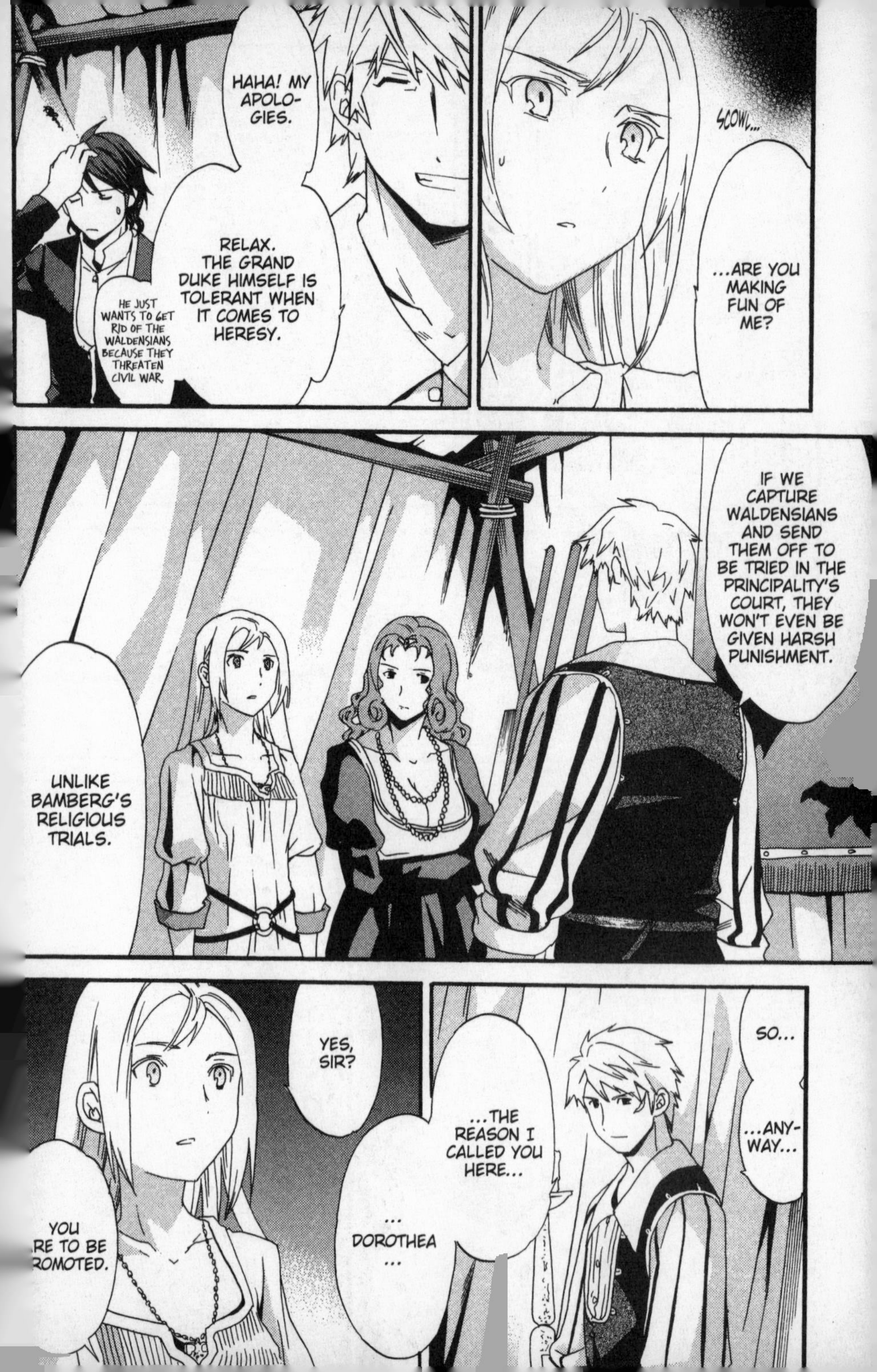
SCOWL...
...ARE YOU MAKING FUN OF ME?
HAHA! MY APOLOGIES.
RELAX. THE GRAND DUKE HIMSELF IS TOLERANT WHEN IT COMES TO HERESY.
HE JUST WANTS TO GET RID OF THE WALDENSIANS BECAUSE THEY THREATEN CIVIL WAR.
IF WE CAPTURE WALDENSIANS AND SEND THEM OFF TO BE TRIED IN THE PRINCIPALITY'S COURT, THEY WON'T EVEN BE GIVEN HARSH PUNISHMENT.
UNLIKE BAMBERG'S RELIGIOUS TRIALS.
SO...
...ANYWAY...
...THE REASON I CALLED YOU HERE...
...DOROTHEA...
YES, SIR?
YOU RE TO BE ROMOTED.

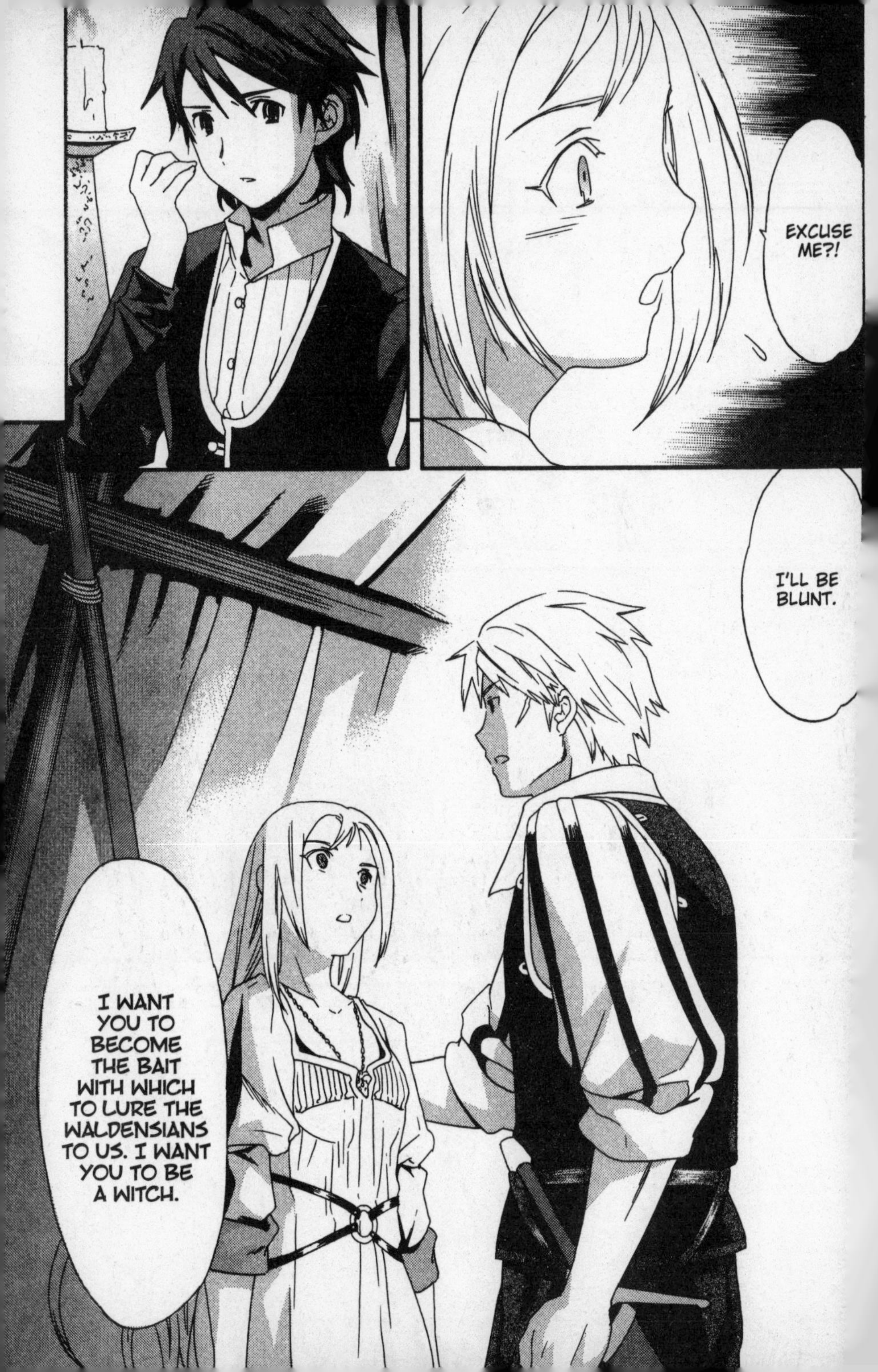
EXCUSE ME?!
I'LL BE BLUNT.
I WANT YOU TO BECOME THE BAIT WITH WHICH TO LURE THE WALDENSIANS TO US. I WANT YOU TO BE A WITCH.

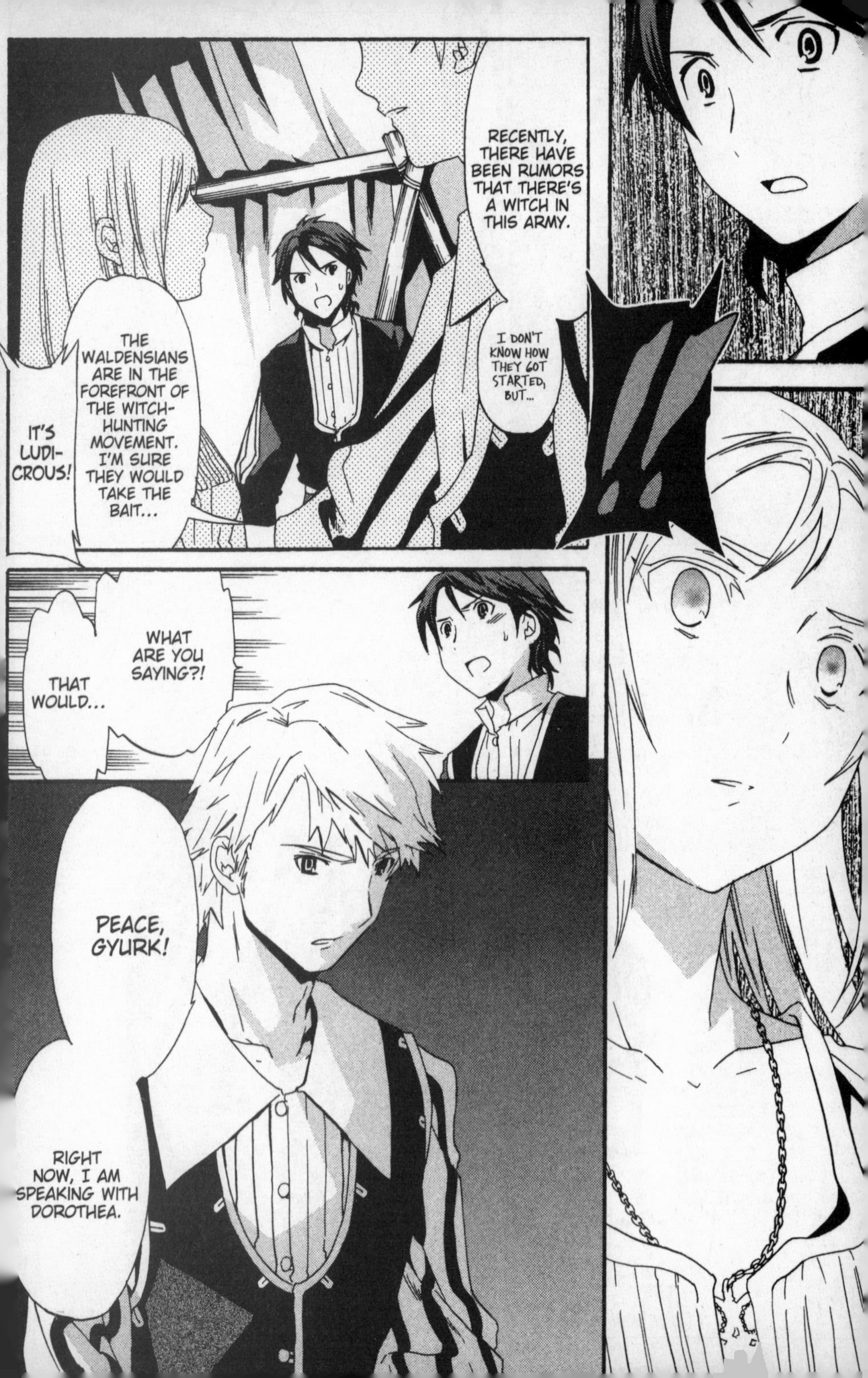
RECENTLY, THERE HAVE BEEN RUMORS THAT THERE'S A WITCH IN THIS ARMY.
I DON'T KNOW HOW THEY GOT STARTED, BUT...
THE WALDENSIANS ARE IN THE FOREFRONT OF THE WITCH-HUNTING MOVEMENT. I'M SURE THEY WOULD TAKE THE BAIT...
IT'S LUDI-CROUS!
WHAT ARE YOU SAYING?!
THAT WOULD...
PEACE, GYURK!
RIGHT NOW, I AM SPEAKING WITH DOROTHEA.

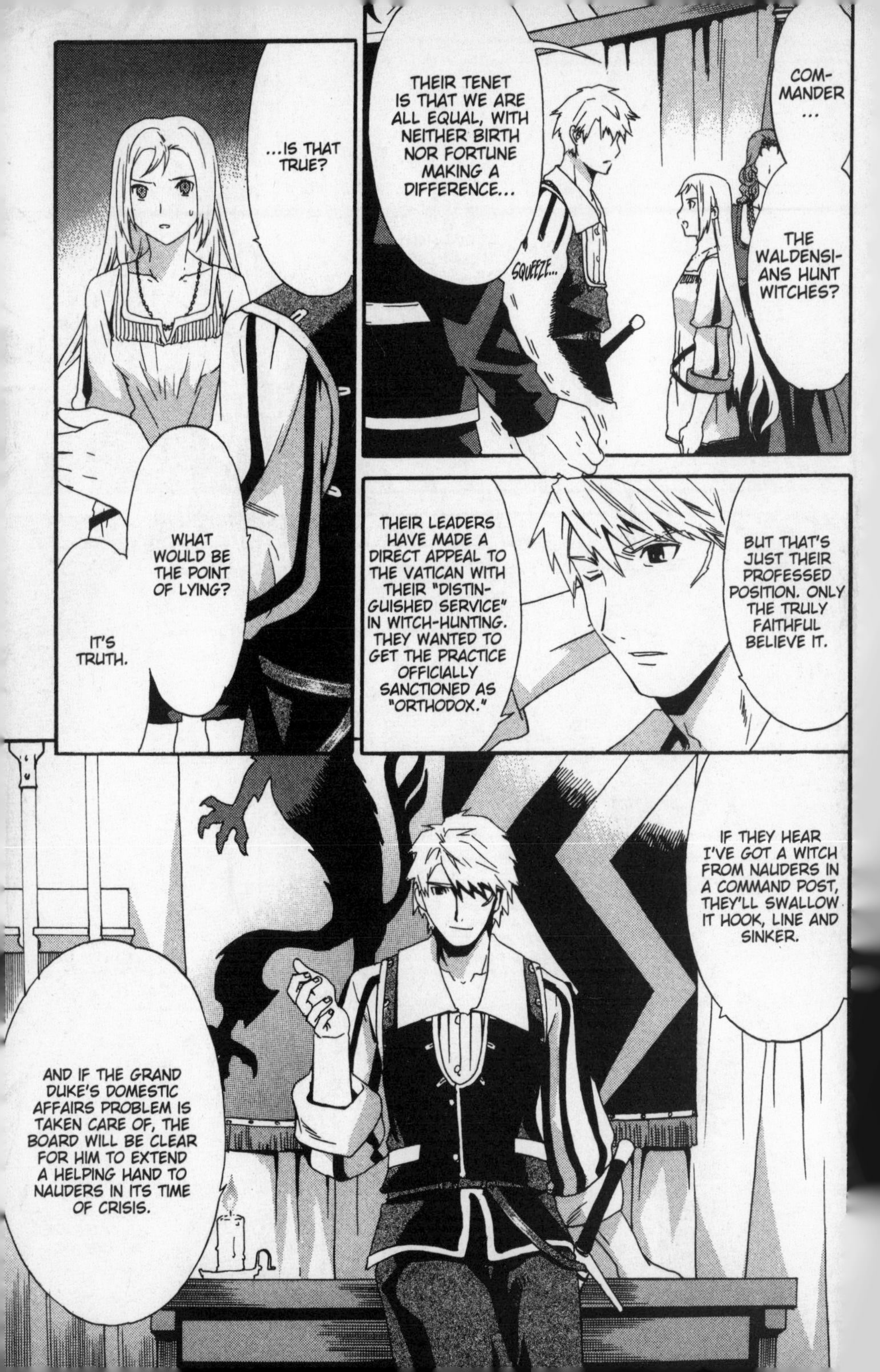
COM-MANDER...
THE WALDENSI-ANS HUNT WITCHES?
THEIR TENET IS THAT WE ARE ALL EQUAL, WITH NEITHER BIRTH NOR FORTUNE MAKING A DIFFERENCE...
SQUEEZE...
BUT THAT'S JUST THEIR PROFESSED POSITION. ONLY THE TRULY FAITHFUL BELIEVE IT.
THEIR LEADERS HAVE MADE A DIRECT APPEAL TO THE VATICAN WITH THEIR "DISTIN-GUISHED SERVICE" IN WITCH-HUNTING. THEY WANTED TO GET THE PRACTICE OFFICIALLY SANCTIONED AS "ORTHODOX."
...IS THAT TRUE?
WHAT WOULD BE THE POINT OF LYING?
IT'S TRUTH.
IF THEY HEAR I'VE GOT A WITCH FROM NAUDERS IN A COMMAND POST, THEY'LL SWALLOW IT HOOK, LINE AND SINKER.
AND IF THE GRAND DUKE'S DOMESTIC AFFAIRS PROBLEM IS TAKEN CARE OF, THE BOARD WILL BE CLEAR FOR HIM TO EXTEND A HELPING HAND TO NAUDERS IN ITS TIME OF CRISIS.

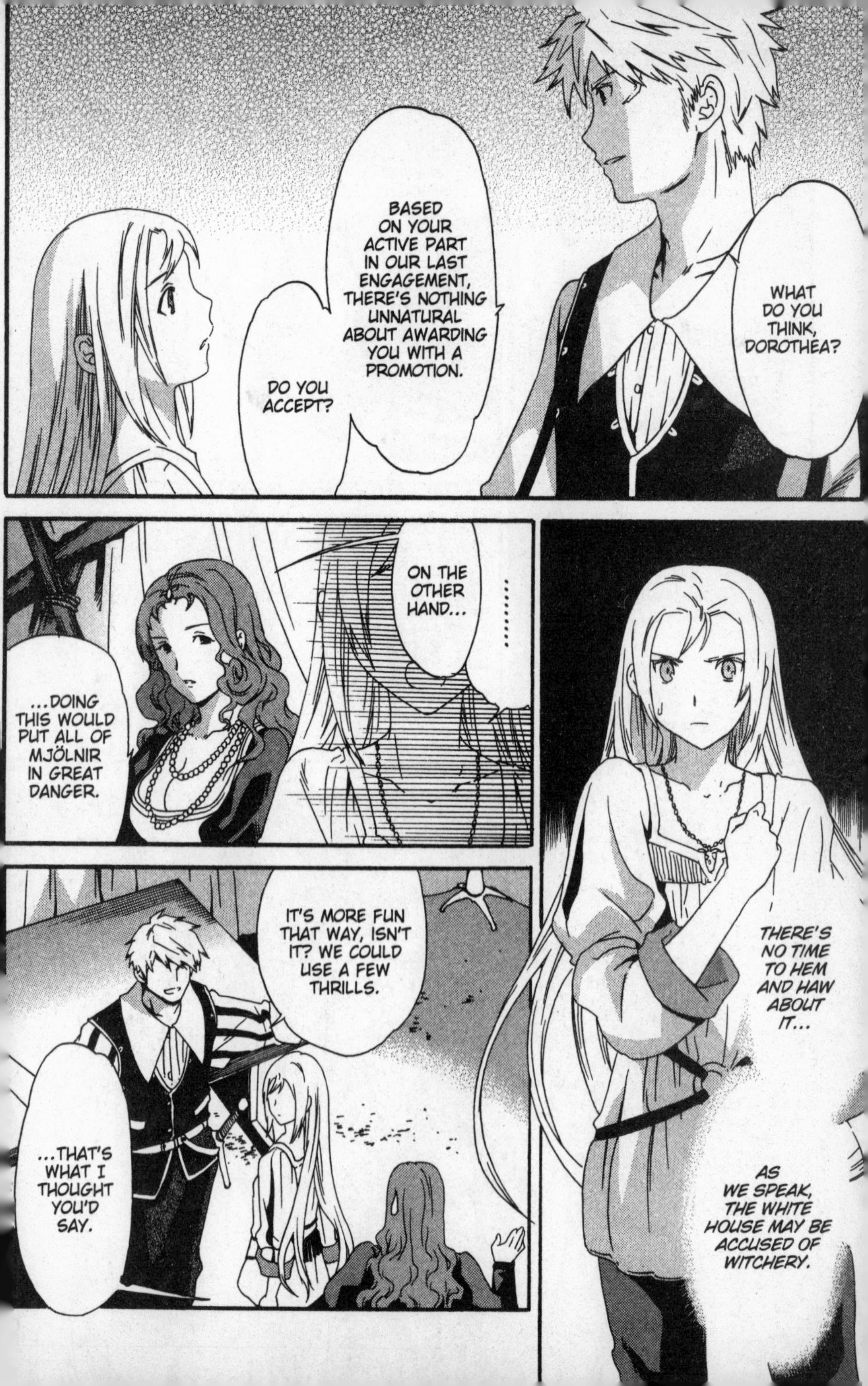
WHAT DO YOU THINK, DOROTHEA?
BASED ON YOUR ACTIVE PART IN OUR LAST ENGAGEMENT, THERE'S NOTHING UNNATURAL ABOUT AWARDING YOU WITH A PROMOTION.
DO YOU ACCEPT?
THERE'S NO TIME TO HEM AND HAW ABOUT IT...
AS WE SPEAK, THE WHITE HOUSE MAY BE ACCUSED OF WITCHERY.
......
ON THE OTHER HAND...
...DOING THIS WOULD PUT ALL OF MJÖLNIR IN GREAT DANGER.
IT'S MORE FUN THAT WAY, ISN'T IT? WE COULD USE A FEW THRILLS.
...THAT'S WHAT I THOUGHT YOU'D SAY.

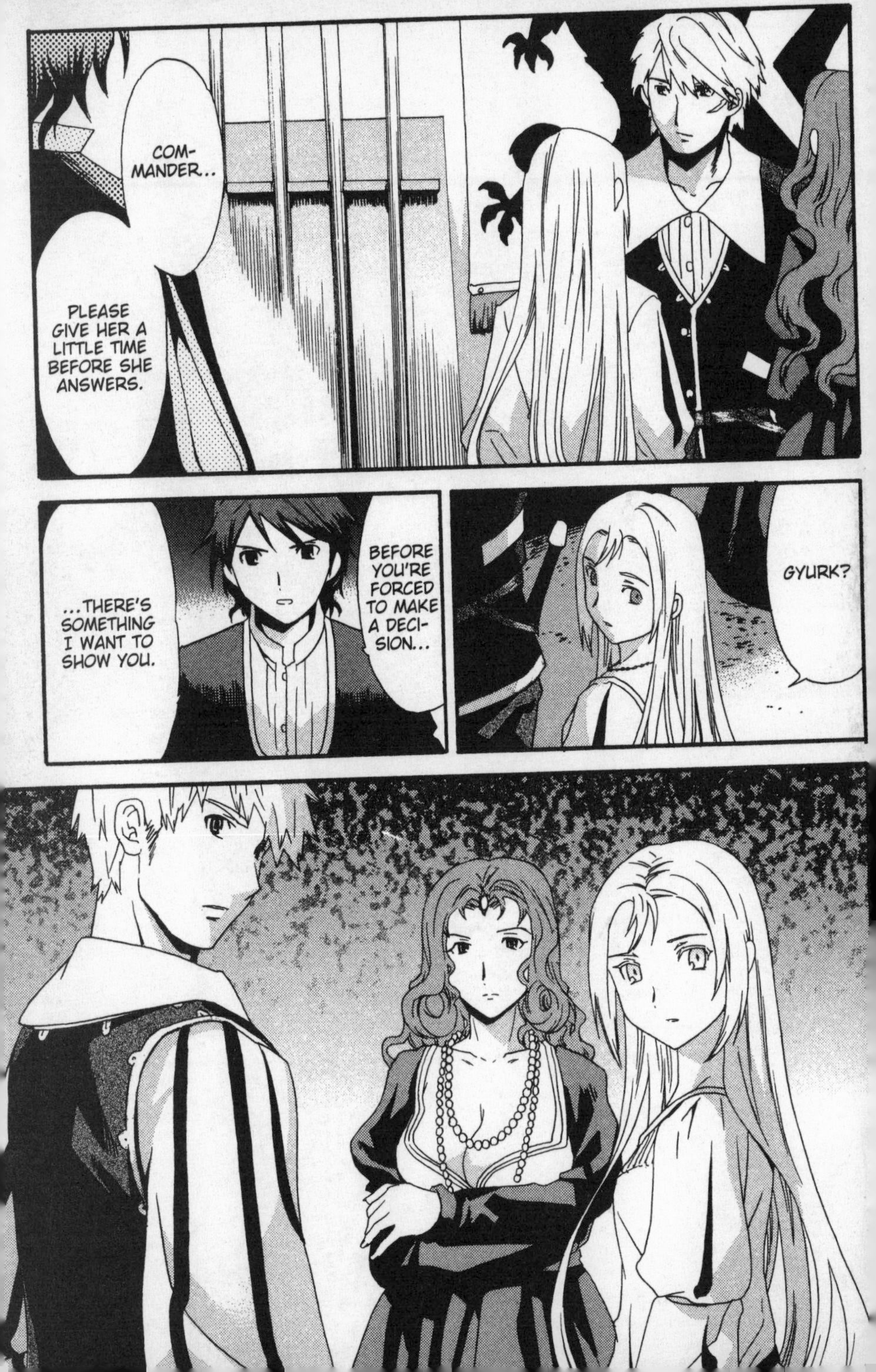
COM-MANDER...
PLEASE GIVE HER A LITTLE TIME BEFORE SHE ANSWERS.
GYURK?
BEFORE YOU'RE FORCED TO MAKE A DECI-SION...
...THERE'S SOMETHING I WANT TO SHOW YOU.

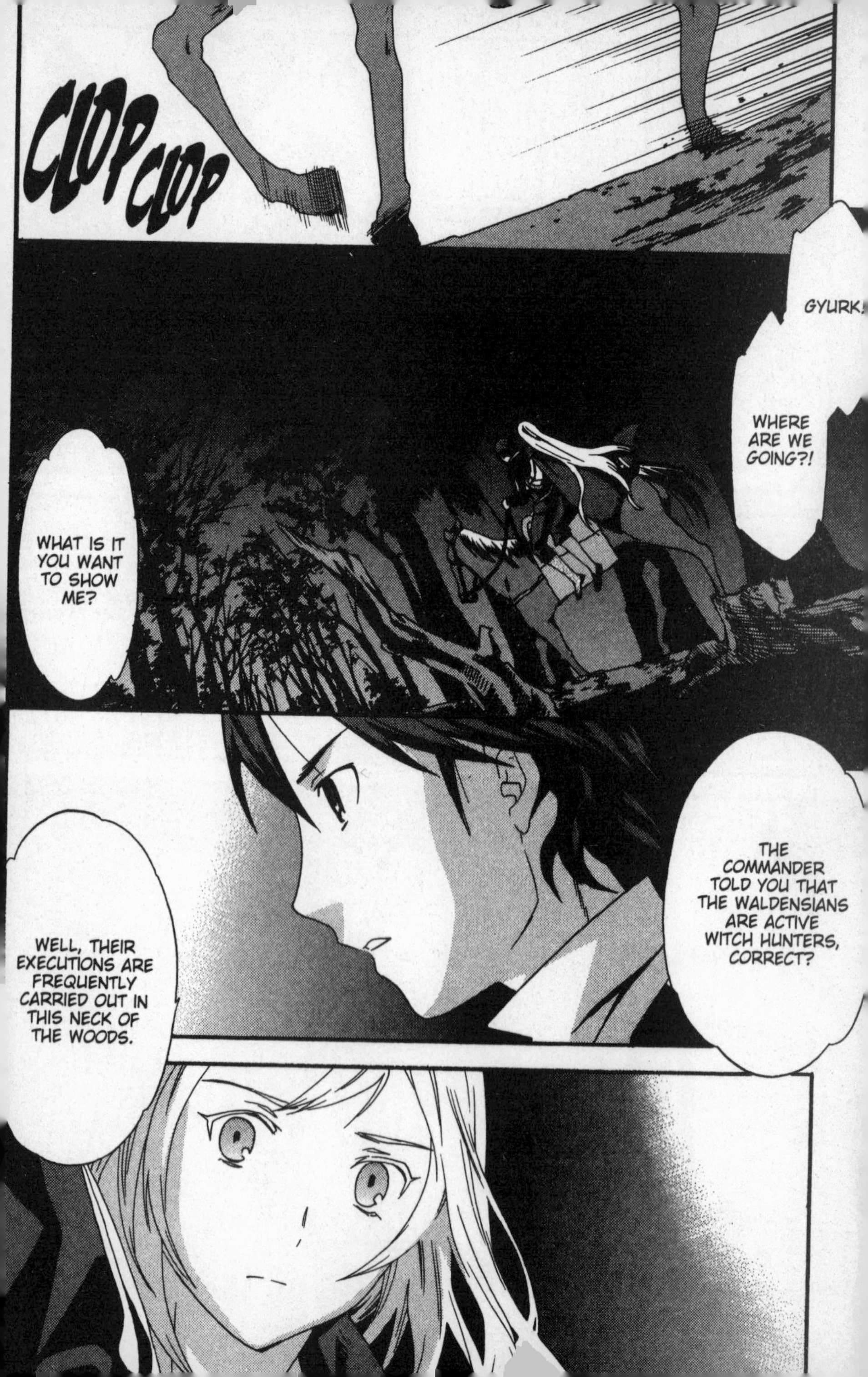
CLOP CLOP
GYURK!
WHERE ARE WE GOING?!
WHAT IS IT YOU WANT TO SHOW ME?
THE COMMANDER TOLD YOU THAT THE WALDENSIANS ARE ACTIVE WITCH HUNTERS, CORRECT?
WELL, THEIR EXECUTIONS ARE FREQUENTLY CARRIED OUT IN THIS NECK OF THE WOODS.

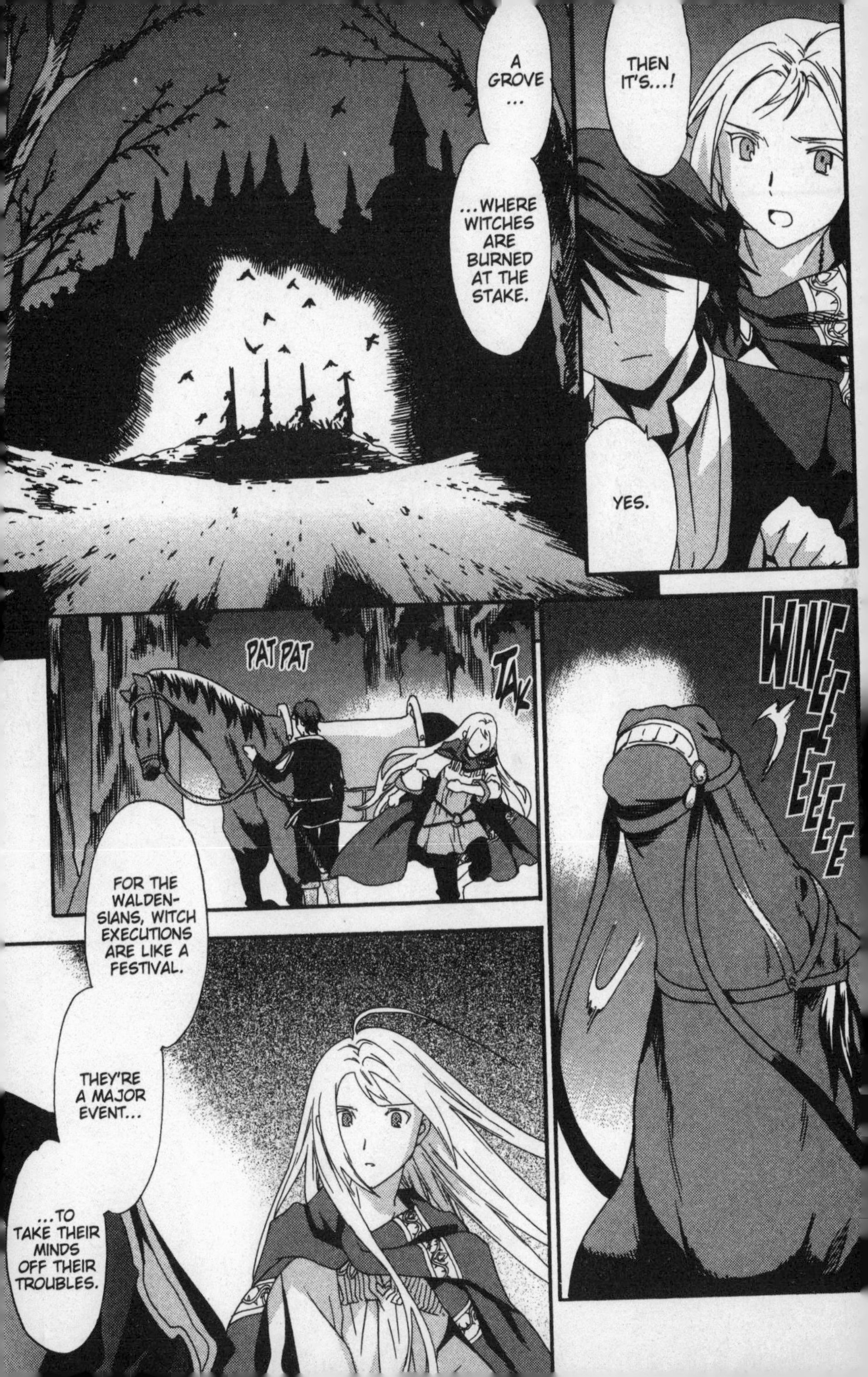
THEN IT'S...!
A GROVE...
...WHERE WITCHES ARE BURNED AT THE STAKE.
YES.
WINEEEEEEE
TAK
PAT PAT
FOR THE WALDEN-SIANS, WITCH EXECUTIONS ARE LIKE A FESTIVAL.
THEY'RE A MAJOR EVENT...
...TO TAKE THEIR MINDS OFF THEIR TROUBLES.

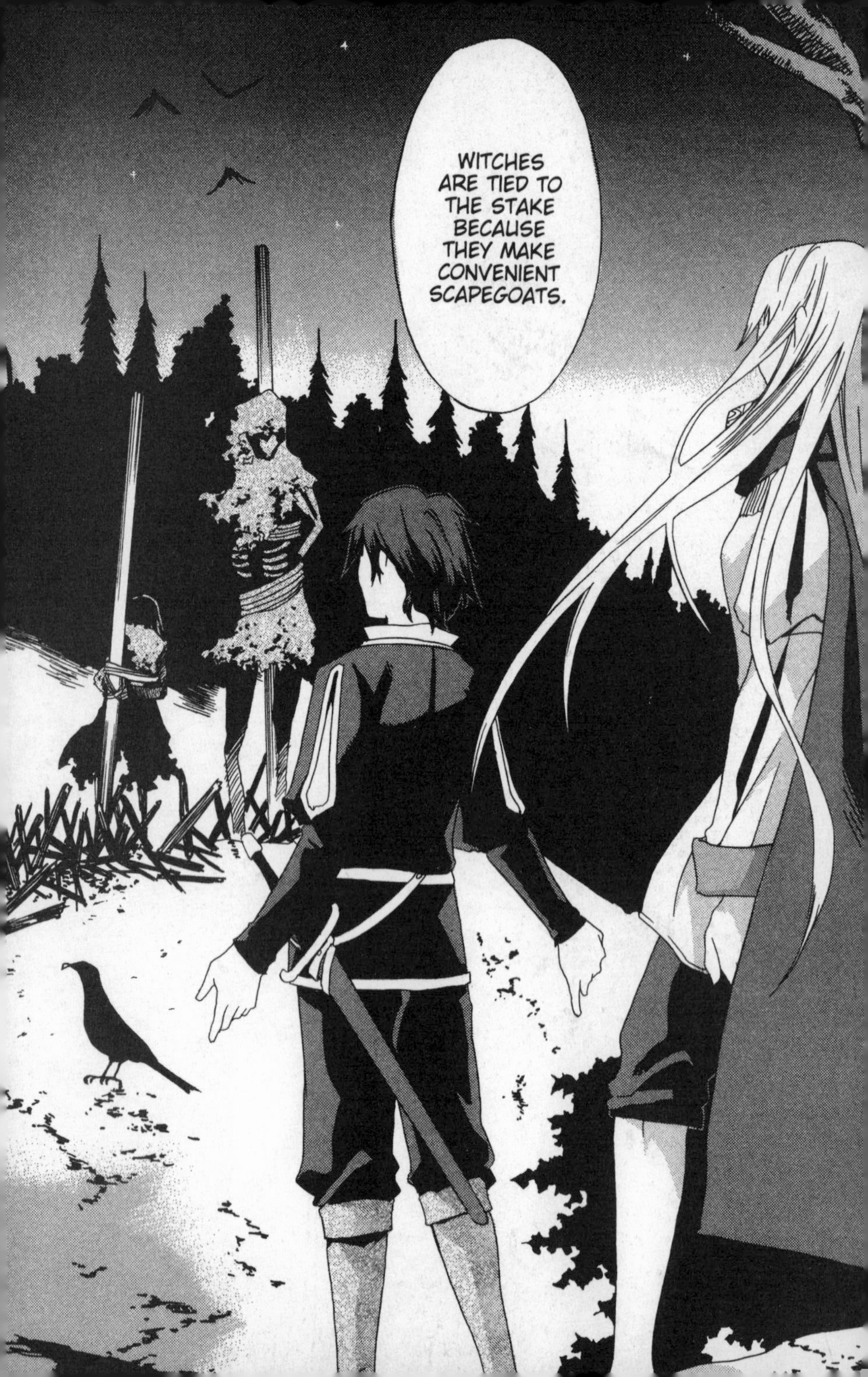
WITCHES ARE TIED TO THE STAKE BECAUSE THEY MAKE CONVENIENT SCAPEGOATS.

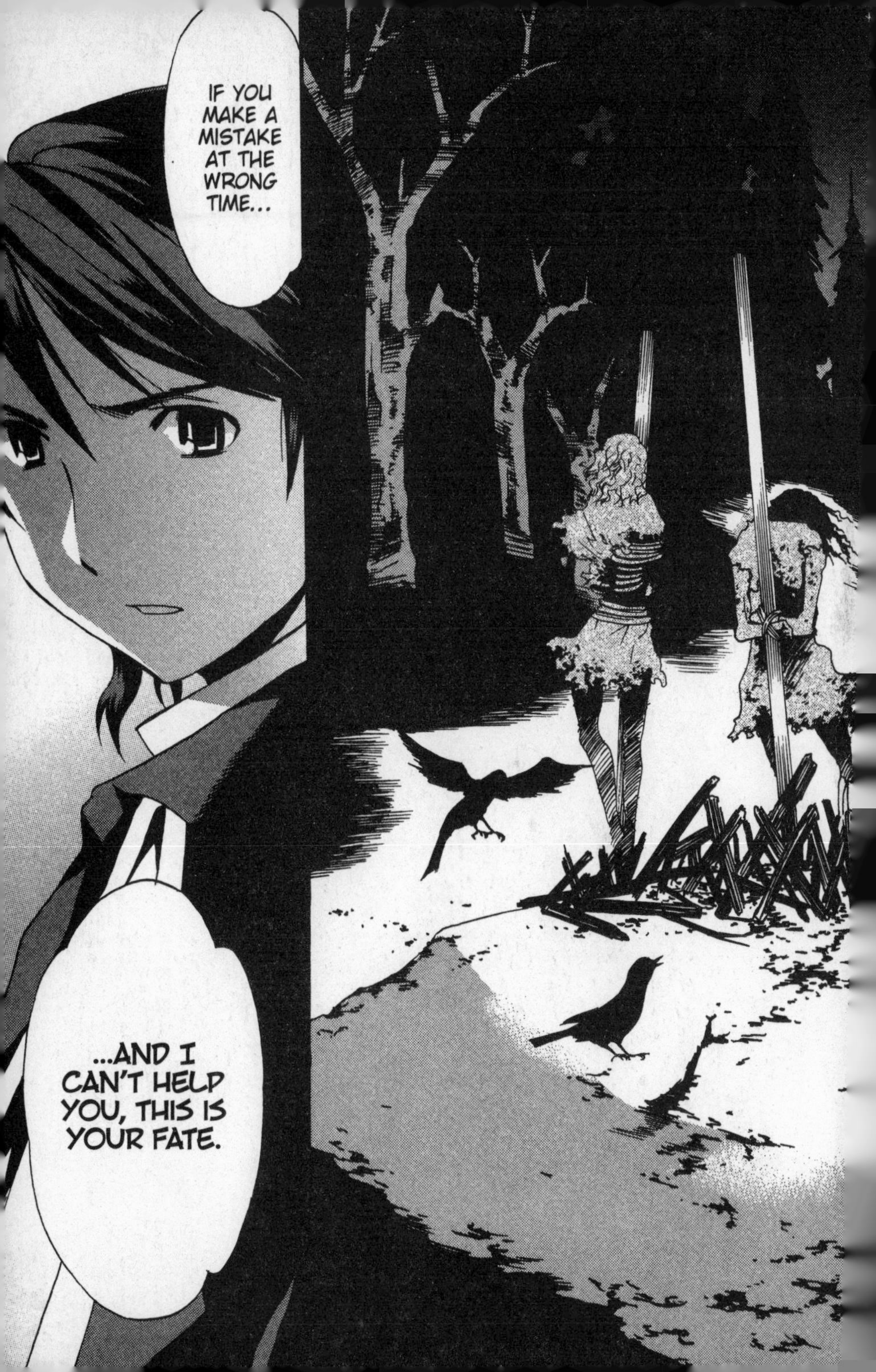
IF YOU MAKE A MISTAKE AT THE WRONG TIME...
...AND I CAN'T HELP YOU, THIS IS YOUR FATE.

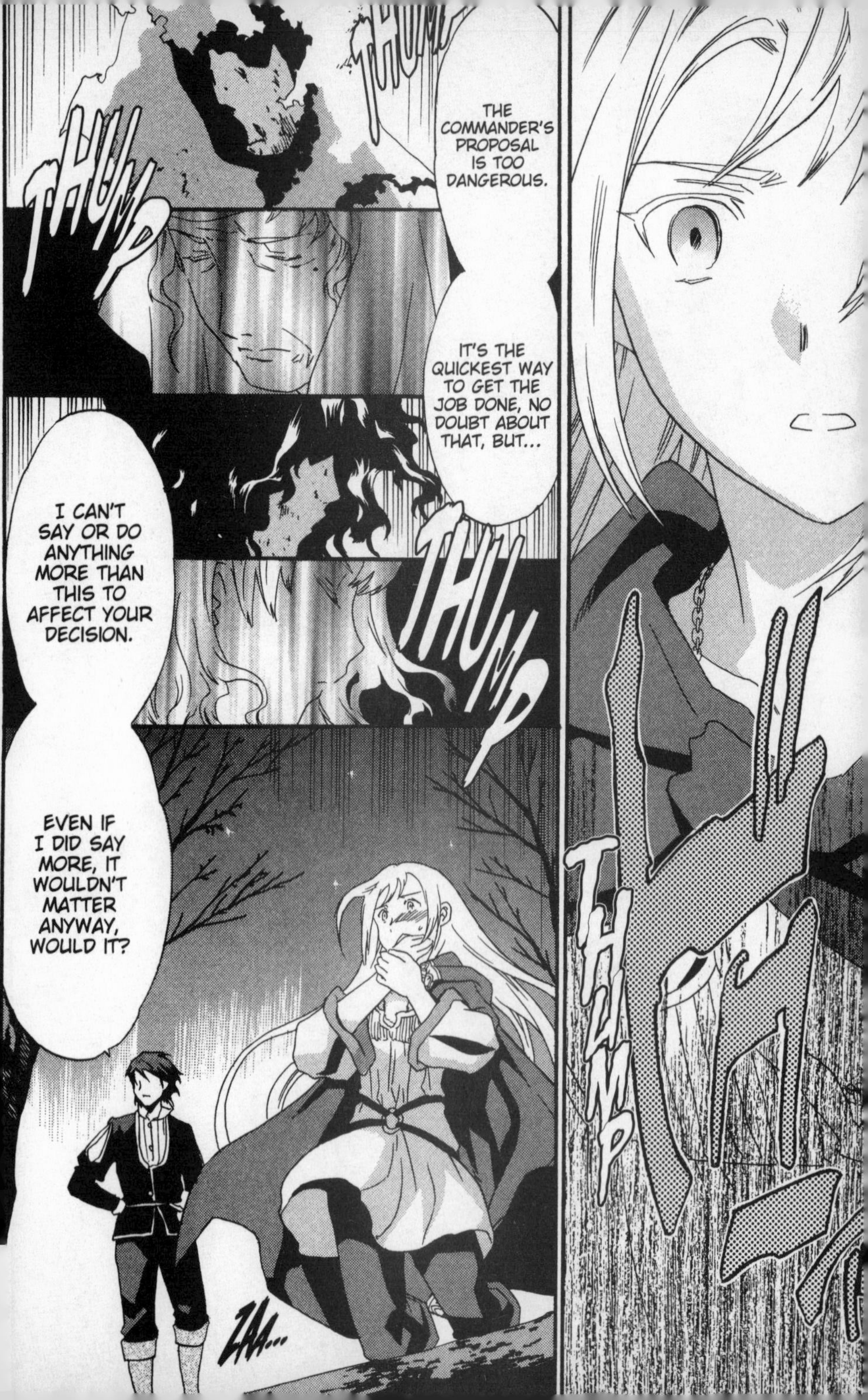
THUMP
THUMP
THUMP
THE COMMANDER'S PROPOSAL IS TOO DANGEROUS.
IT'S THE QUICKEST WAY TO GET THE JOB DONE, NO DOUBT ABOUT THAT, BUT...
THUMP
I CAN'T SAY OR DO ANYTHING MORE THAN THIS TO AFFECT YOUR DECISION.
EVEN IF I DID SAY MORE, IT WOULDN'T MATTER ANYWAY, WOULD IT?
ZAA...

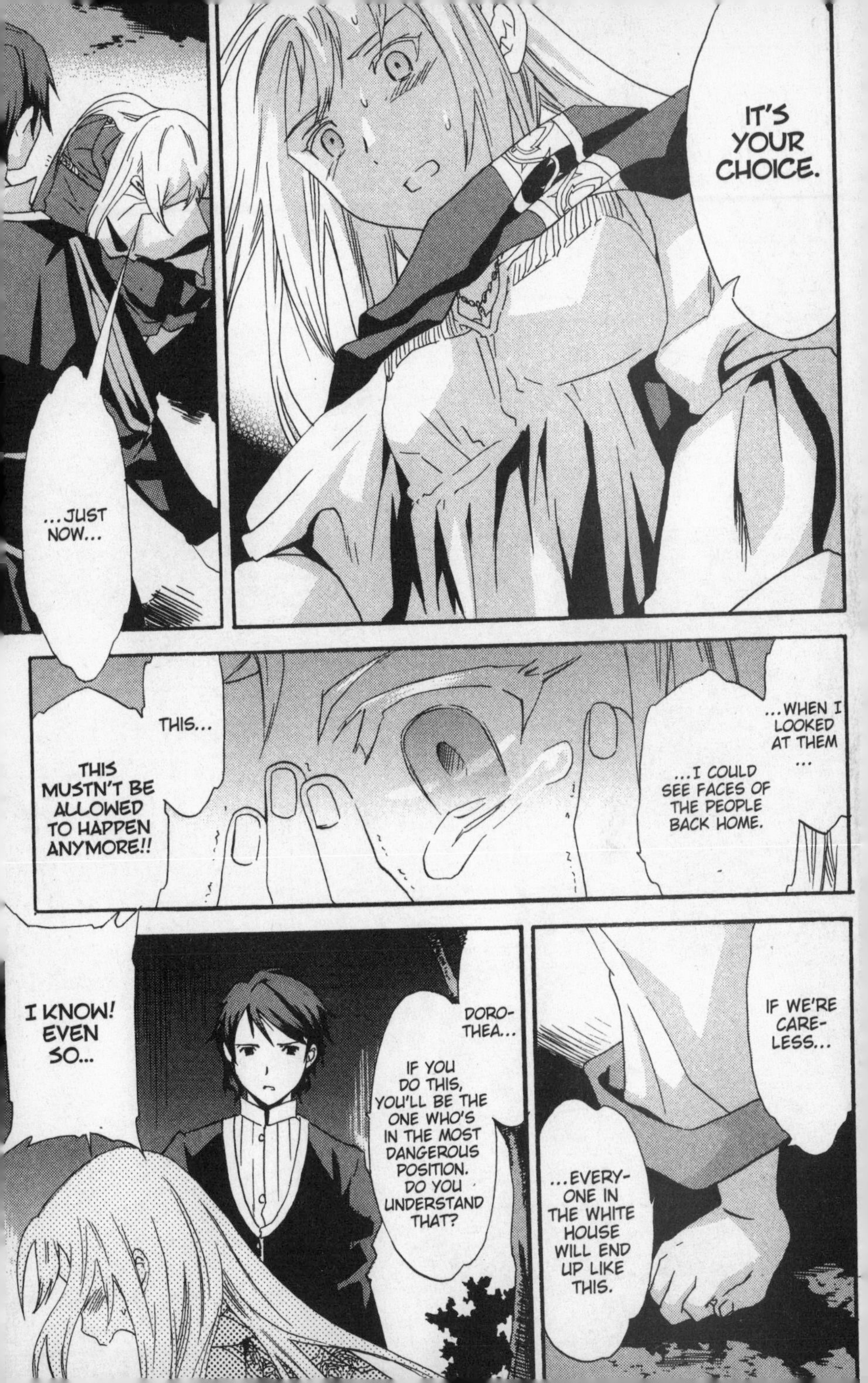
IT'S YOUR CHOICE.
...JUST NOW...
...WHEN I LOOKED AT THEM ...
...I COULD SEE FACES OF THE PEOPLE BACK HOME.
THIS...
THIS MUSTN'T BE ALLOWED TO HAPPEN ANYMORE!!
IF WE'RE CARE-LESS...
...EVERY-ONE IN THE WHITE HOUSE WILL END UP LIKE THIS.
DORO-THEA...
IF YOU DO THIS, YOU'LL BE THE ONE WHO'S IN THE MOST DANGEROUS POSITION. DO YOU UNDERSTAND THAT?
I KNOW! EVEN SO...

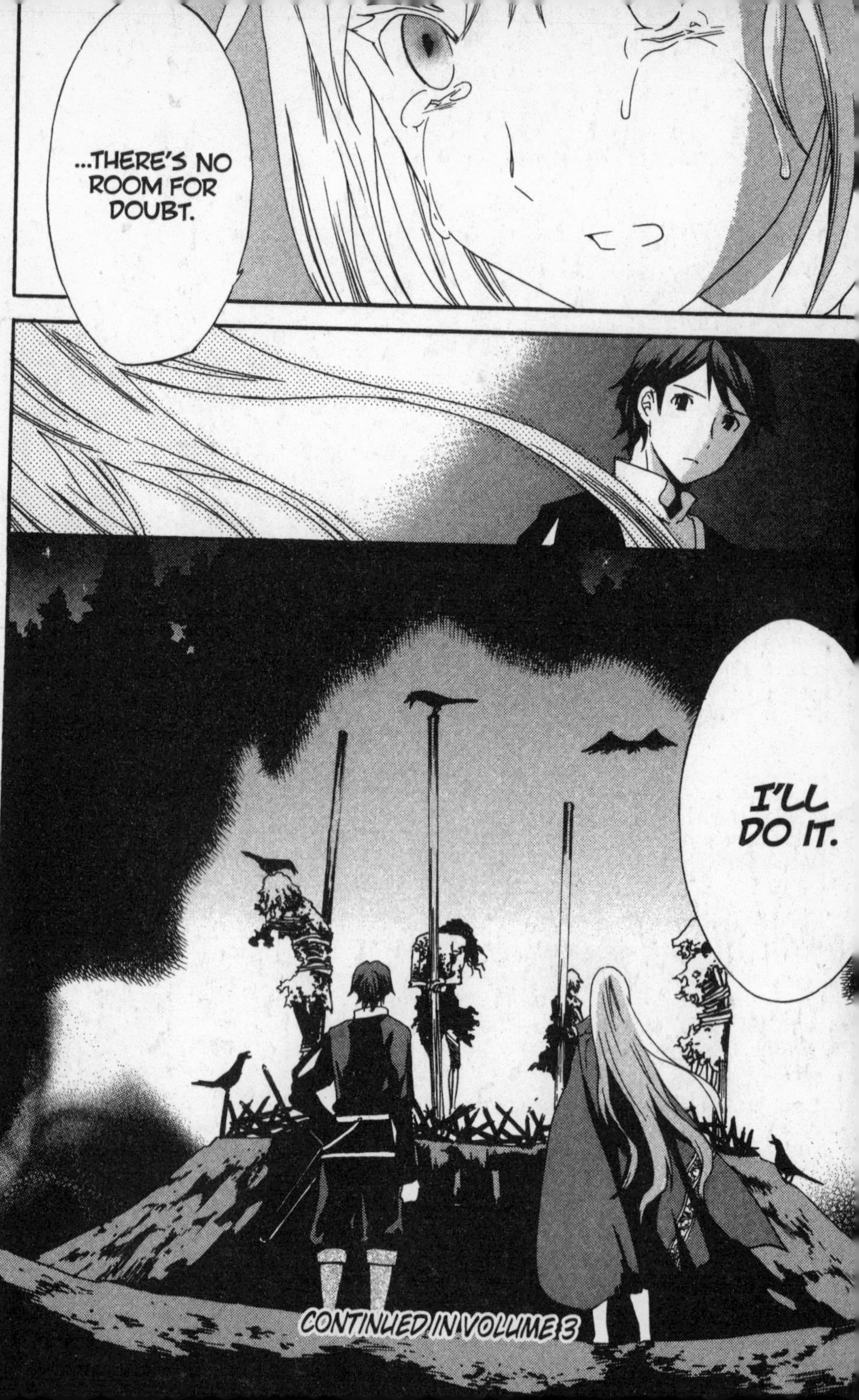
...THERE'S NO ROOM FOR DOUBT.
I'LL DO IT.
CONTINUED IN VOLUME 3

◆DOROTHEA ♯2

◆STAFF

N.HARA
K.YAMADA
H.SUGIMOTO
M.FUJI

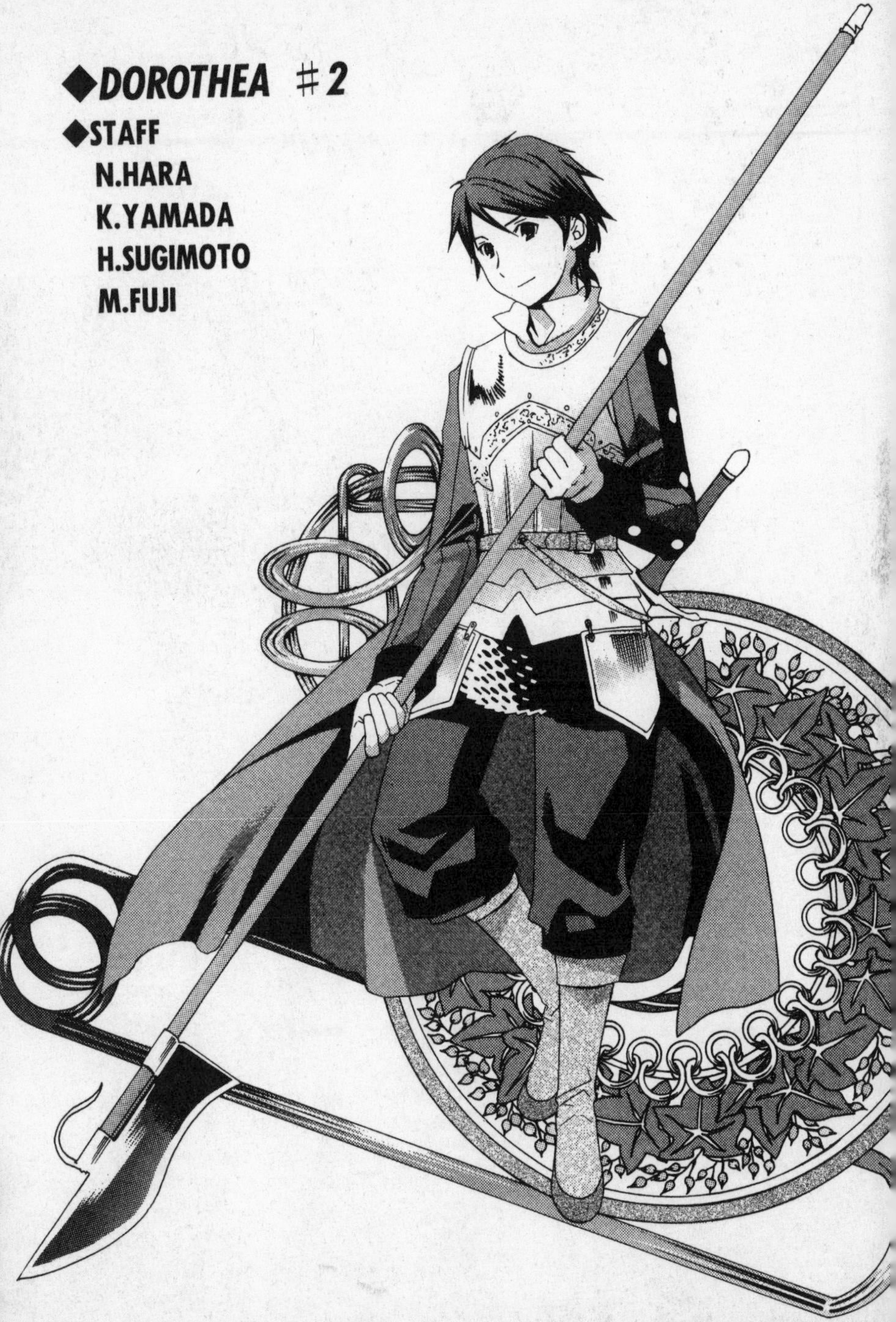

DOROTHEA MIGHT BE IN OVER HER HEAD! COMING IN OCTOBER.

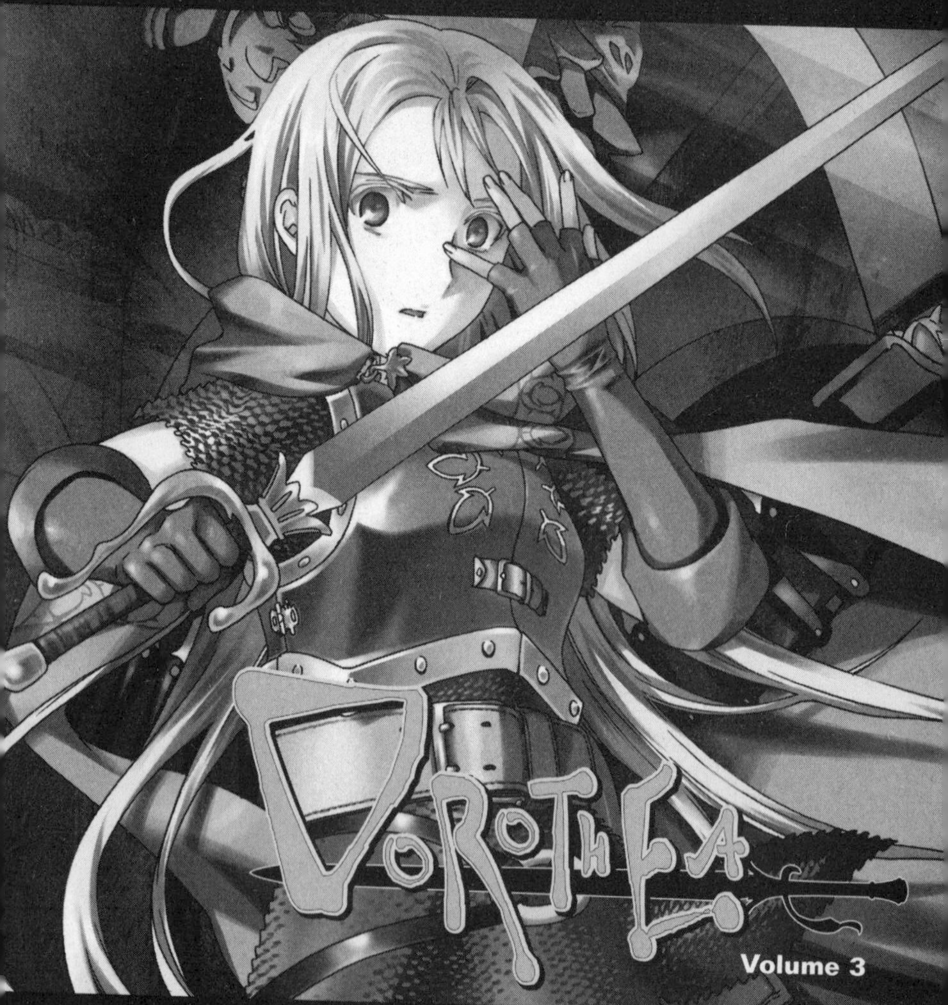
DOROTHEA
Volume 3

By Cuvie. Dorothea has agreed to serve as a decoy for the army's zealot enemies. The commander hopes that they can draw their opponents into the open and confront them head on. But their plan may prove to be riskier than they thought. Dorothea runs afoul of a knight who's burned 99 witches at the stake…and he wants to make Dorothea number 100! This knight may prove to be the deadliest adversary

TENJHO TENGE

Volume 17

By Oh! great. This is it! The Imperial Martial Arts Election Tournament is on at Todo High. Through their recent traumas, the members of the Juken Club have certainly gained a lot of experience and maturity. But will that be enough to help the fractured group pull themselves together without Maya, their natural leader? And what tricks does the wheelchair-bound Mitsuomi have up his sleeve?

KIKAIDER IS BACK FOR ONE FINAL BATTLE!

KIKAIDERO2
CODE ZERO TWO
Volume 7

Cover not final.

By Shotaro Ishinomori and MEIMU. In a bleak, future world, a young man named Jiro is really the robot called Kikaider. Created by a scientist who built robots for an evil organization, Jiro was given a special, humanizing chip to keep him from being used for destructive purposes. This sequel picks up on the fast-paced robot action of the cult CMX series and addresses some unanswered questions.

By Yoshito Usui. More crude adventures with the star of the hit anime series. Shin's parents may find him embarrassing, but that's obviously not his view in "I, Shin, Am A Very Good Boy!" Then Shin spreads the joy to teachers and fellow students in "I'm The Most Popular Kid in Kindergarten." Being foul has never been so fun.

CRAYON SHINCHAN Vol. 3 © Yoshito Usui 1990/Futabasha.

WANT TO TRY A NEW SERIES?
START HERE!

KYUBANME NO MUSASHI © 1996 Miyuki Takahashi/AKITASHOTEN.

By Miyuki Takahashi
15 Volumes Available

EROICA YORI AI WO KOMETE © 1976 Yasuko Aoike/AKITASHOTEN.

By Yasuko Aoike
13 Volumes Available

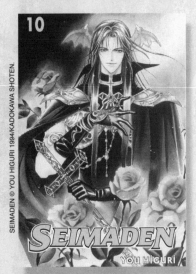

SEIMADEN © YOU HIGURI 1994/KADOKAWA SHOTEN.

By You Higuri
All 10 Volumes Available

GON © 1992 Masashi Tanaka/Kodansha Ltd.

By Masashi Tanaka
4 Volumes Available

DON'T MISS THESE OTHER GREAT SERIES!

MOON CHILD © 1988 Reiko Shimizu/HAKUSENSHA, INC.

By Reiko Shimizu
11 Volumes Available

CIPHER © 1984 Minako Narita/HAKUSENSHA, INC.

By Minako Narita
All 11 Volumes Available

SEKAI DE ICHIBAN DAIKIRAI © 1997 Banri Hidaka/HAKUSENSHA, INC.

By Banri Hidaka
4 Volumes Available

PENGUIN KAKUMEI © 2004 Sakura Tsukuba/HAKUSENSHA, INC.

By Sakura Tsukuba
5 Volumes Available

For more information and sneak previews, visit cmxmanga.com.
Call 1-888-COMIC BOOK for the nearest comics shop or head
to your local book store.

DOROTHEA - MAJYO NO TETTSUI Vol. 2 © 2006 Cuvie. First
Published in Japan in 2006 by FUJIMISHOBO CO., LTD., Tokyo.

DOROTHEA, Volume 2, published by WildStorm Productions, an
imprint of DC Comics, 888 Prospect St. #240, La Jolla, CA
92037. English Translation © 2008. All Rights Reserved. English
translation rights in U.S.A. arranged with KADOKAWA SHOTEN
PUBLISHING CO., LTD., Tokyo, through TUTTLE-MORI
AGENCY, INC., Tokyo. CMX is a trademark of DC Comics. The
stories, characters, and incidents mentioned in this magazine
are entirely fictional. Printed on recyclable paper. WildStorm
does not read or accept unsolicited submissions of ideas,
stories or artwork. Printed in Canada.

DC Comics, A Warner Bros. Entertainment Company.

Sheldon Drzka – Translation and Adaptation
Deron Bennett – Lettering
Larry Berry – Design
Roland Mann & Jim Chadwick – Editors

ISBN: 978-1-4012-1436-4

All the pages in this book were created—and are printed here—in Japanese RIGHT-to-LEFT format. No artwork has been reversed or altered, so you can read the stories the way the creators meant for them to be read.

RIGHT TO LEFT?!

Traditional Japanese manga starts at the upper right-hand corner, and moves right-to-left as it goes down the page. Follow this guide for an easy understanding.

For more information and sneak previews, visit cmxmanga.com. Call 1-888-COMIC BOOK for the nearest comics shop or head to your local book store.

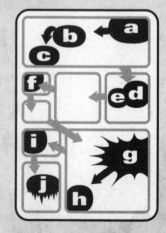